A Reasonable Doubt

By

Nancy Dane

NDB Publishing
Russellville, AR

Published by NDB Publishing
Russellville, AR
This novel is a work of fiction. Except for known historical events and people, the story and the characters are fictional.

Book design copyright © 2014 by NDB Publishing

Published in the United States of America

ISBN: 978-0-9912506-1-5
1.   Fiction: Historical
2.   Fiction: Romance: Historical

Other Books by Nancy Dane

Tattered Glory
Where the Road Begins
A Difference of Opinion
A Long Way to Go
An Enduring Union

Contact at:

nancydane.com
Facebook.com/nancydanebooks
Be sure to click the "like" button
for chances to win free autographed books!

DEDICATION

To Jackie Markham Guccione,
who once urged me to finish telling Billy's
story. She got to read a portion of this
manuscript before going home to be with her
Lord and Savior.

I miss you, dear friend.

A Word from the Author

This is Billy Tanner's story, or as he is called in this novel, Bill. If you have read my *Tattered Glory* series, he needs no introduction. If you have not, never fear; I try to write each novel as a stand-alone book with a minimum of backstory from previous books. Bill and Abigail are fictional characters, as are the Loring, the Tanner, and the Rawlings families. Many characters in this novel are real: Judge Meers, Jordan Cravens, Doc Ward, the Wallace family, Thomas Paine, and Governor Hadley, as well as a few other known historical characters.

In actual events, I tried to remain factual. Of course, I took literary license to portray real people's interactions with my fictional characters, and admittedly I portrayed my personal bent on those real events. I carefully researched before writing the novel and in the process completely changed the direction I had originally planned. Case in point: I had read many accounts of the Sidney Wallace story. If you've never heard of Sid, he was a colorful character who lived in Johnson County, Arkansas during the 1860s and 70s. In his lifetime some thought him an avenging angel, while others looked on him as a cold-blooded killer. I am skeptical of making heroes of such controversial characters, no matter how colorfully folklore has painted them. Yes, I had a preconceived prejudice against Sidney Wallace. Besides that, I thought enough had been written about him. I recall telling my husband that although Sid's story took place during the era of this novel, I had no intention of including him. That was before the source documents about the young man grabbed me by the throat and wouldn't let go. No matter what event I was researching, Sid's story kept cropping up. As you have no doubt gleaned by now, Sid Wallace is in this story. I don't ask you to take as fact my portrayal of Sid or of his guilt or innocence. Hopefully by the time this book is in print, the accompanying history book titled *Tarnished Justice* will be available on my web, so you may read the documents and decide for yourself. In order not to be a spoiler, I added more of Sid's real history at the end of this book.

While researching, I also gained a whole new understanding of the history of Arkansas politics. For those who hate politics, bear with me. I'll make this brief!

If you have ever wondered how a state whose people, for the most part, seem to embrace traditional conservative ideals but again and again vote for what we now call the liberal party, I think you may find some answers to your question in the pages of this novel. Suffice it to say that the hated carpetbaggers were of the Republican persuasion (which at that time was considered the liberal party), and the defeated Confederates were the Democrat Party (considered then to be the conservatives). It becomes a little clearer in the present day that, although the parties have flipped labels and drastically changed what they stand for, many people remain loyal to the way Great Grandpa and Great Grandma voted. At least in Arkansas, the taint of carpetbagger has been slow to fade.

The timber tax portrayed in my novel may or may not have been enacted in Johnson County at this time. It certainly was in other places, and the cotton tax is a matter of public record.

With regard to some of the real people I have portrayed, such as Ward, Meers, Thomas Paine, and Mr. Sarber, as well as other political entities, such as Governor Hadley, I mean no disrespect. As an author I have used quotes from actual newspaper columns, often from the *Gazette*, in my portrayal of these gentlemen. Please bear in mind that then, the same as now, newspapers had their own political agendas, and the views of the press may or may not have been accurate. Also please keep in mind, this is a work of fiction done by an author trying to impart a bit of history along with a lot of entertainment. I sincerely hope you will enjoy the read!

ACKNOWLEDGMENTS

There are so many people who have helped in the completion of this novel that I almost fear to name any lest I forget some.

As usual my husband has looked over my creation and given his valuable critique from the male perspective. I give him credit for my numerous male fans.

Special thanks to attorney Timothy Hutchinson for his legal expertise in helping me paint Bill's trial accurately. Any mistakes are completely mine, as Timothy certainly knows his stuff!

A big shout out to all my faithful editors! Thank you, Susan Brown, a dedicated editor, who read over the manuscript numerous times to correct more mistakes than I like to admit. Much thanks to Sheree Niece, Nancy Cook, and Les Howard, who always give great feedback and edits.

A big thank you to my husband for accompanying me on my fact finding mission to abandoned sawmill sites, as well as to some still in operation. The research trip to the Mountain Timber Sawmill was an educational delight. Thank you, Mr. Roy Chisum, for agreeing to my tour. Because of mill operator Fred Terry, I now have a better understanding of how things work in a modern mill, and I also gleaned a lot about how things used to be.

Chris Kennedy of Russellville always takes the perfect cover photo for each of my novels. This one is no exception.

A huge thank you to U. S. Senator Tim Hutchinson for taking the time to read the manuscript and to say such wonderful things in his endorsement. Also much thanks to Connie Zimmerman for her gracious endorsement.

A big thank you to you, my readers. Your emails and messages mean so much to me. Please keep them coming.

✖ Chapter 1

Tall pines swayed in wind sweeping up the hollow, bringing the first nip of autumn and stirring colored leaves that had already drifted onto graves in the small mountain cemetery. When Simon Mason requested the mourners to bow for prayer, the voice of Little Piney Creek filled the hush. Bill Tanner's head bowed, but no silent plea for comfort rose from his heart, and he didn't act the hypocrite by echoing the closing amen. He ought to feel sorrow. He was witnessing the frail remains of Viola Tanner ensconced in a pine box and lowered into a ragged hole that would be covered over with loamy soil and tamped down as soon as the mourners walked away. All he felt was relief. Perhaps that made him wicked.

Before putting on his hat and turning away, his eyes drifted over the crowd. The gathering was large, out of respect for the Tanner family, he figured, and not from any great liking for Ma. So far as he knew she had liked no one but herself and had no friends.

He liked and respected many here, and cared deeply for a few. Cousin Jenny and her big husband, Tap, and of course Uncle Ned and his family. And Cindy. He had given her the merest of glances, and yet her image was the one he would carry away. She grew more beautiful with each passing year. No one would guess by looking that she was the mother of those three boys, and if his glance was correct, soon to be the mother of a fourth. He hoped for her sake it would be a daughter. Granny had always lamented that every woman needed a daughter. He wanted Cindy to have the best—and with Elijah for a husband she did.

After accepting the sympathetic words and firm handshakes, Bill mounted the horse and left. Cindy's hand had been soft and her brief words kind, but he doubted he would ever return.

The low conversations in the dim saloon did little to disrupt Bill's thoughts. Seeing Cindy today had revived the sharp pain that had diminished with the passing years into a dull ache that he was able to ignore until something twisted the knife in his heart. He loathed himself afresh, loathed that he was Jared Rawlings' son, and loathed the Rawlings taint that had let him fall in love with a married woman. Then he gave a mental sigh. How could any flesh-and-blood man have kept from it, especially a loner such as himself, when they had been thrown together on the trail for all those weeks? Then, with a sliver of self-respect, he argued that at least he had more moral fiber than Jared. He hadn't even let Cindy know how he felt.

He moved an elbow to let the barkeep wipe the damp glass ring off the shiny counter. The whiskey might be raw, he mused, but Slim kept the bar as clean as Granny had kept her cabin. My! How he missed that old woman. He had loved her second only to Pa… He had never called Jared Rawlings Pa, not even in his thoughts. Except for a few who knew the truth, everyone thought Caleb Tanner was his pa, and he liked it that way.

He reckoned everyone along Piney missed Pa with his big-hearted kindness and Granny with her God-given knowledge of doctoring. The funeral today had him thinking of them more than ever. Thanks to a Yankee bullet, Pa's unmarked grave was a swamp in South Arkansas, but Granny's funeral a few years back had been the best ever attended in the hills.

Bill lifted the glass, took a sip, and then grimaced, wondering why he'd even ordered the rotgut. It was too early in the day to be drinking. He supposed he felt the need to wash away today's memories. He shoved back the glass. He wasn't overly fond of whiskey anyway, and this swill was a far cry from good moonshine, the smooth kind made by big Red Matthers. He wondered if any of the Matthers boys still had their pa's recipe. Crying shame if it had died along with Red.

"Another?"

As Slim lifted the bottle near his glass, Bill shook his head.

"No. One shot of that is more than plenty."

Slim gave a half smile. "Hey, Bill, I don't make it. I just pour it."

He was still Billy to his friends and family on Piney, but somewhere along the way he'd become Bill to the rest of the world. He pushed away from the bar with the idea of heading over to Cravens' office to show him the paper in his pocket. The deed signing over land to him had come as a complete shock. He had no idea Ma owned land. He wondered if Pa had known. He'd never mentioned it. It was strange how near the last Ma had rallied—seeming to regain her wits after years of near insanity—to tell him to be sure and look into the little humpbacked trunk that held her personal possessions. All his life she had forbidden him to even touch it.

He had no idea where the small hoard of money inside the trunk had come from. Pa had once mentioned that Ma's folks back East had plenty, but the ones who had come to Arkansas were as poor as church mice, or so Bill thought. Even though Ma's pa, Willard Kelly, had lived just beyond Hagarville, Bill had never met him. The old man had died when Bill was a small child. Long before that, Ma had had a falling out with her pa and hadn't spoken to him again. Apparently the old man had relented of his vow to disinherit her and had left the parcel of land to his only child after all. At least Bill figured that was the deed in his pocket.

He frowned deeply. Pa and Granny had struggled to make ends meet, and all that time Ma had money tucked away! One more reason to despise her. She had only used Pa as a convenience when she needed a father for her bastard. His mouth hardened. He let out a deep breath and tried to let the feelings go as well. Bitterness was poison. Hadn't Granny warned him about that often enough!

As he stepped outside, October sun lay warm on his arms where the shirtsleeves were rolled up, exposing tanned, muscled arms. He drew a deep, appreciative breath, hoping this business wouldn't take long. It was a lovely day and one he would rather spend in the woods. Orange and coral¬-draped maples grew near the board sidewalk in front of hotel and cafe where bright purple flowers spilled from window boxes. A few new buildings dotted Clarksville's main street, and some of the existing ones with tall false fronts, decrepit since the war, now wore fresh coats of paint. From where he stood he could see the blackened remains of the courthouse, half of which had already been a charred shell fired first by a Yankee torch almost ten years before. It had burned again only a few months ago. It would soon be torn down in preparation of building a new one. Bill had heard the new brick structure would be fine—and expensive, over

$30,000. He supposed just the thought that a railroad was coming had brought a small measure of prosperity to Clarksville.

Town was full of activity today. He supposed it was due to the newly mandated registration for the right to vote. It was the first time since the war that he and the other Rebel soldiers might be given back the franchise, or so he had heard. At least the Congress in Washington City had passed some legislation.

His strides lengthened as he faced south, bypassing the fence around the courthouse square, to head for the law office of Floyd and Cravens. Until finding the papers in the trunk, he hadn't known Ma retained Jordan Cravens. He figured Cravens was as good as any attorney in town, and besides that, Cravens had been a colonel in the CSA 21st Arkansas. Some of the other lawyers and many of the town officials were of the carpetbag stripe. Bill had no use for them.

As he stepped into the small office, Cravens nodded but immediately turned his attention back to the purple-faced man leaning over his desk. The angry man pounded a fist on the cluttered desk.

"I tell you, Cravens, they don't have more say-so than Congress! The Amnesty Act gives us back the right to vote, no matter what that carpetbag board and their cowardly president says!"

"I totally agree, Sam. But for now they're holding the reins."

Sam sneered. "So we just sit back and let them get away with it?"

"I never said that. Heaven knows I've tried. I even made a trip last week to see the governor—"

Sam scoffed loudly. "Aw! He's the biggest snake of all. Damned New York carpetbagger!"

"All the more reason to tread carefully. Law is on our side. We're making plans for ballots and side-boxes as allowed under the law. But we have to be careful to go exactly by the book, or the whole vote will get tossed out. Sam, please, impress that on your people. There are recourses—even all the way to the highest court in the land. If we want to be taken seriously, we have to behave as law-abiding citizens and not an unruly mob."

Sam slammed his hat onto his head. "All right, but folks are mighty worked up. We don't like taking off work to stand in the sun waiting while that bunch of baboons refuses to register us. Mark my word; we'll be lucky if there's not gunplay by the time this circus is over."

When Bill stepped aside to allow Sam egress, the disgruntled man stormed past without even a nod. Jordan Cravens stood and extended a hand. "Hello. What can I do for you?"

"Don't know if you remember me. I'm Bill Tanner, Caleb Tanner's son."

"Ah, yes, Tanner—didn't recognize you at first, but we've all changed a bit since the war."

Bill nodded agreement. Since the war the colonel had put on weight, especially around the middle. And yet, although he must be nearing forty, there were few lines in the wide face, and his hair, parted and combed to the side, as well as his mustache, was still dark and heavy.

Bill shook hands and tilted his head toward the door. "Election trouble?"

Cravens sighed, sat down, rocked back in the tilting seat, and pointed toward a chair drawn near the desk. Bill sat down.

"A veritable powder keg. The county board is refusing to register some of our townships. They've only registered a handful of men in others, and they've registered no one who was a Confederate soldier or who voted against the new constitution."

"No one who will vote against them," offered Bill.

"Exactly." Cravens raised an eyebrow. "The chicanery is going on all over the state. And Sam is right—it goes all the way to the governor."

Bill nodded. "I've heard that even if we are allowed to register and vote, it won't be counted fair and square."

"I figure that's the truth of the matter." Cravens reached for a cheroot from the box on his desk and offered it to Bill. When Bill shook his head, Cravens put the cigar into his own mouth and struck a match. "But I don't figure you're here to talk about the election."

"My ma recently passed away."

"Please accept my condolences."

"Thanks." Bill pulled the deed from his pocket.

Cravens gave the deed a quick look. "As you probably know by now, I've been tending to legal matters for Viola. She placed funds with me to be used for paying property tax. Let me get all the paperwork." He went into a small back room but returned shortly with a handful of papers. "Here are all the papers, including the tax receipts. I hope the receipts do you some good," he added. "Over in Pope County, I've heard they're auctioning off prime land for back taxes in spite of folks having legal receipts with proof of tax payment. Of course since the powers-that-be over there are the only ones with cash, they're buying all the best land, and buying it cheap."

Bill's eyebrows rose. "Are they doing that here?"

"County officials are buying up plenty of land, and they're getting it cheap. I haven't heard of falsifying tax records—yet." Cravens went on, "Here's an accounting of the money remaining in your fund." He glanced up through cigar smoke. "If you want the cash, I can have it for you by this afternoon."

Bill's eyebrows rose. It was a tidy sum, over four hundred dollars. "No, just keep it for now and keep paying the taxes until I notify you otherwise."

"Fine," said Cravens, moving the cheroot to the side of his mouth. "A farmer needs a nest egg. Too many in this county are living on credit."

"I don't hold with credit," said Bill.

"I wish more folks felt that way," said Cravens. "Merchants in town are shutting it off, anyway. McConnell just ran an ad in the newspaper that he's not selling anything else at the drugstore on credit, and all the grocery stores have followed suit. Swagerty told me the debt owed to Clarksville grocery stores alone is over fifty thousand dollars and most of it from farmers who ought to be raising what they eat instead of going into debt for groceries. Bad business. Times start getting better and credit gets easy. Folks get used to high living, until the bills come due. That much debt in a little town like this—well, the whole county could go bankrupt. We've overcome so much since the war; I'd sure hate to see bad times like that again.

Bill put in, "Can you tell me exactly where Ma's land is?"

"Of course. Here, I'll sketch you a map."

After Cravens had given him easy directions and clear landmarks, Bill left the office and got his horse. It was too late to go today, but he would go in the morning.

He slept late the next morning, something he rarely did. His mouth felt as if he'd eaten a rotten tomato. He blamed Slim's bad liquor. Under a cloudless sky, he crossed the covered bridge spanning Spadra Creek and headed toward Hagarville and the property that lay beyond. Soon farms grew farther apart. Mountains came into view in the blue-hazed distance, and alongside the trail the woods were a riot of color. He was barely conscious of the beauty. His thoughts were on the land he rode toward. Cravens had said it was good ground—not as prime as the bottomland near the river, but good, nonetheless, for cotton and corn and large meadows for hay and grazing. Bill thought he recalled the exact spot. There was a house set back from the road and surrounded by large oaks. He had no idea if the dwelling was livable or if he wanted to stay even if it was. He had a good job now, freighting timber for the railroad. He'd never really fancied farming Pa's mountain land, but farming good crop land was another matter.

Miles passed quickly beneath the tall black's hooves. Bill stopped at Minnow Creek to let the horse drink and graze while he sat on a rock near the small stream and ate a few bites from the lunch packed in his saddlebags. A breeze teased yellow leaves from a nearby elm and scattered them onto the creek, where minnows darted about like silver streaks in the lazy water. Trees and a rise of land beyond hid the view of farmland, land that had once belonged to Jared Rawlings. Now that Jared was dead, Bill had no idea who owned that land. His mouth hardened. He had no desire for it, or for anything that had belonged to Jared Rawlings. He despised even the thought of the man.

Keen to see his own property, he didn't tarry long and was soon on his way again. The land was flatter now with wide fields, some dotted with stubs of cornstalks and others holding yellowed stalks still heavy with drooping ears waiting to be gathered. Surrounding the wide valley rose low timber-covered hills, and to the north a distant mountain range, the blue peaks more flat topped than pointed. He passed the cluster of houses composing Hagarville, and staying on the right fork at a split in the wagon trail, he soon crossed Little Piney Creek, the blue water rushing over a stony bottom to hurry out of sight around a bend.

He sat up straighter in the saddle, surprised at the excitement in his breast. Ahead was the landmark Cravens had called Tater Hill. According to the map his land was farther on, two or three miles at the most.

Riding on, he passed a small frame house where numerous horses and wagons and a large group of men filled the yard. Angry voices reached the road. Bill drew the horse to a stop.

"Doc Ward ain't gonna register nobody! He's had us standing out here fer hours and who's he seen? Two men, maybe three?"

At that moment the door opened and a man stepped outside. Men gathered around the big man. "Sullivan, did ya get registered?"

"Hell, no! Damned bunch of liars—they don't aim for anyone in this township to register, and they sure don't aim for us to vote!"

One voice rose above the rest. "We have our rights! There's only four of them. We could teach them a lesson they'd—"

The door abruptly opened again. Bill recognized Doc Ward, the town constable at Clarksville. He had heard Ward was on the registration board. Ward wore a surly look as his eyes sought and found Sullivan.

"Sullivan, if you're determined to make trouble, I'll oblige. If you don't have a gun, I'll loan you one."

"I don't need a gun, Ward. I'm man enough to whip you with the two fists God gave me. If you're man enough to face me, come on out here. Like I told you inside, you're a lying coward. I came here in good faith to register and I signed the oath. But since you don't have any intention of doing this fair and square, you might as well ride back to Clarksville while you still can."

"Damn you," hurled Ward as his right hand dropped to his side.

Bill noticed several hands drop to pistol butts, but no one drew a weapon, for Ward quickly stepped back inside and shut the door. Without stopping longer, Bill nodded at a few men who looked his way and then rode on. He had no idea what township this was, but it wasn't where he should register anyway. Since the law required a new registration before anyone could vote, from the looks of things there wouldn't be many votes cast in Johnson County. And from what he had just seen, he figured the old man named Sam was right. It would be pure luck if there wasn't bloodshed before this election was over.

A couple of miles farther on, he stopped, eased his back in the saddle, and smiled. His heart quickened as he studied the terrain with keen eyes. In the distance a small frame house backed up against a north hillside with small fields to the south and rolling hills beyond. His land! It spread out before him, thickly timbered ridges and flats left too long untended, now overgrown with sprouts and bushes. In his mind's eye it grew fair and lush with deep grass, fat cattle, and acres of tall corn and white cotton. He wanted to see it all. He dismounted, tied the black off the road in the woods, and began walking.

It was a fair place. As he studied the land, the possibilities grew in his mind. He already felt the pull of the land and was surprised at his excitement. One hundred sixty acres, much of it flat, much covered with timber, and much of that hardwood with plenty of prime white oak, the butts perfect for stave bolts that netted

11

top dollar as tight cooperage whiskey barrels. The other timber would make lumber and crossties. There were a big demand for those and a ready market nearby.

Without a doubt, sumac, brush, and sprouts had gotten a firm grip on what had once been cleared fields, but hard work would put that right. There was work enough here to last a lifetime, and his hands itched to start. Nothing would suit him better just now than to put all his energy toward improvements, but he needed to use his money wisely. He had saved some and Ma's money would help, but he would need the money from the timber until the land began to produce. Timber was dependable income. He knew enough about row crop farming to realize one bad year could sink a fellow.

The sun was slanting low through the large oaks as he remounted and rode toward the house. Suddenly he stopped. A curl of smoke rose from the chimney. Just then a woman exited a shed and walked across the yard to disappear behind the house. Bill frowned and looked all around. Yes, this had to be the right place. It was exactly how Cravens had described it. But it should be vacant. He heard the blows of an ax on wood. Who was living here? Riding slowly forward he called out.

"Hello the house."

From behind the house, the woman stepped into sight again. Her calico dress was threadbare but neatly mended. Alongside came a young boy of about ten with coal black hair and eyes almost as black. He held an armful of stove wood, and the woman held an ax. Gripping it, she came forward. She kept the left side of her face averted. Bill wondered if she had sight in only one eye.

An old man, angular and bony, opened the front door and came onto the porch. Unkempt white hair stuck out like tufts on a fighting cock. His sullen mouth had the look of a perpetual frown. He held an ancient flintlock musket pointed at Bill's chest. "Scat!" he yelled. "Get on out of h'yar. You got no business h'yar."

Bill stared hard and unflinching. "I own this place. What are you doing here?"

The old man cursed. Although he lowered the gun, he remained belligerent. "I got naught to say to you," he said with his jaw stuck out. He turned and stomped into the house, slamming the door behind. His scowling face, however, immediately appeared at an open window.

The woman stepped closer. Bill dismounted and doffed his hat. "How do, ma'am."

She acknowledged the greeting with a nod as her troubled eyes darted worriedly to the old man.

"I'll get right to the point, ma'am," said Bill. "This is my land. Who are you and what are you doing here?"

The boy's scared eyes went to the woman.

Her face paled. As her legs seemed to buckle, she leaned the ax against the wall and placed a hand to the wall for support, a hand reddened and rough from work.

Then putting the hand over her left check, she faced him squarely. Extending above and below the hand was a long grayish-white scar. Her eyes dropped to the ground before slowly lifting to his face.

"I'm Abigail Anderson. This is my son, Jacob." She motioned toward the window. "And that is my father-in-law, Mr. Anderson—Mr. Talbert Anderson. Forgive us. We're squatting on your land." Her lips slightly trembled as she made the admission.

Bill looked around. The entire place had a run-down air with peeling paint, rickety porch, and missing fence rails, and yet the flowerbeds and garden were weed-free, the firewood nicely stacked, and the porch swept clean. There was a big washing draped over a sagging clothesline as well as some hanging on the garden fence. In the large garden most of the produce had been harvested. A few small tomatoes still dotted wilting plants. Curling, brown-tipped vines held orange pumpkins, and other vines clung to dark green, ribbed acorn squash. This was not an idle woman.

"It appears you've been here a while," he observed.

She stood straighter and drew a deep breath before answering. She was not young, about thirty, he judged. For just a moment her hand fell from shielding her cheek. In spite of the scar, and in spite of looking worn and tired, she was a handsome woman, full-busted and yet slender, with heavy, dark hair and large brown eyes. At the moment the eyes had a wary look. Bill noticed the worry lines between her eyebrows had deepened since his arrival.

"Yes. Three years." She looked past him toward the tall hill beyond. "I've been expecting this day. I knew someone would eventually come."

"Why—"

She anticipated his question. "We're originally from Missouri. During the war... well, things were very bad at home. While my husband was away fighting, we were ordered off our land by the army."

Bill nodded. He knew of the infamous General Order No. 11. The Union Army had ordered civilians from four Missouri counties off their property and at the same time had confiscated all grain, hay, and crops.

She went on, "My father-in-law and I loaded what we could into the wagon and kept going south. We ended up in Texas. Four years ago, word finally reached us that Frank—my husband—had been killed in the war." She met Bill's eyes. "After that Mr. Anderson insisted we go home. He said it was a lie. He became obsessed with the

14

idea that Frank was home, waiting for us. I argued but finally gave in. After months on the road, we got this far." She pointed to the road. "The old mule gave out right there, trying to climb that hill. That was three years ago. The house was vacant…" Her voice trailed away.

A riot of thoughts whirled in Bill's brain, most of all pity for the woman and the child.

"We'll be on our way," she said, but the words were hesitant.

Bill felt he could read her mind. "You have no horse or mule, do you?"

She shook her head. "But I've saved a bit of cash." She motioned to the drying laundry. "I do laundry and mending and a few odd jobs for neighbors, helping with chores and the harvest, and Jacob does odd jobs too. Hopefully I can find an animal someone is willing to sell cheap."

"There's no great rush," he said impulsively. "Winter is coming on, and it's a poor time to be on the road."

"But what about you?" she asked, as hope sprang into the troubled eyes. "Surely you need your house."

A loud string of oaths erupted from the house. "Abby, you harlot! Get on in h'yar and stop flaunting yerself at ever' strange man comes along!"

For an instant her angry eyes raked the old man. At the same time her face crimsoned. Bill stared toward the window. If the man weren't so old, he'd shut his mouth with a fist.

"Get on in h'yar, boy," called the old man, and although the boy's face had gone hard at the old man's words, he went.

Then Abigail looked Bill squarely in the eyes. "What he said—it's not true. I'm a moral woman, and a God-fearing one. I think that's why he hates me so." She tilted her head sideways again and rubbed both arms as if fighting a chill.

"I won't need the place until spring. You're welcome to stay until then."

Relief washed her face, and yet there was still a hint of wariness. "Oh, my—well, thank you, very much. I'll make sure we leave by then. Are you sure you don't need the house until then?"

"I'm sure."

"I certainly appreciate it." She glanced at the window before saying, "Would you join us for supper? There's a pot of black-eyed peas on the stove, and I can stir up some cornbread in no time. It's not much, but I'd like to thank you in some way for your generosity."

Bill figured the old man would rant even louder. Out of cussedness of his own, he decided to stay. "I'd be obliged, ma'am. I am hungry." His gray eyes twinkled. "But while you cook, I reckon I'll sit out here under the trees. I got a feeling I'd not be too welcome on the porch."

Her smile was wide and generous, showing perfect white teeth. "That might be a good idea. I won't be long. Make yourself at home." Then she gave a quick laugh. "Well, of course you will—after all it is your home."

Bill sat down on an old chair drawn near the back door and under a giant oak that was close by the chopping block. He leaned back, enjoying a cool breeze fluttering the brown and green leaves overhead, while wondering about the scar—what had caused such a long gash on the rounded cheek? It looked like a knife cut, healed now but leaving an enduring track. Maybe after longer acquaintance she would volunteer the information. He hoped it was not a tragic story. It sounded as if she'd had more than enough tragedy in her life.

Soon the smell of frying meat drifted from the door.

Along with peas, the woman must also have decided to cook bacon. The unmistakable smell was tantalizing.

Then he noticed only a small stack of stove wood alongside a few chunks remaining to be split. There was the ax, but no wedge that he could see. With lazy reluctance he stood. It was the least he could do for a home-cooked meal. She had leaned the ax against the block, rather than sticking it into the wood, as a man would have done. Bill eyed the blade. The edge was blunted and chipped. Since there wasn't a sharpening wheel in sight, he rubbed the blade against a big rock to get the rolled edges off. It wouldn't do a good job, but it would be better than nothing.

After a few minutes of working on the blade, he placed a chunk on end and swung with a powerful arch. The stick severed. He picked up a piece and swung again. Glancing up, he saw a curtain flutter. The woman watched from the window. She abruptly disappeared when he stared.

In a short while all the sticks were split and stacked. The woman stepped to the open back door. "Dinner is ready," she said and then added, "Thank you so much for splitting the wood. I'm a poor hand at it. And I've forbidden Jacob to touch the ax.

"There's a washstand,"—Abigail pointed to a shelf alongside the back door with a basin of water and a bowl of soft lye soap—"and here's a clean towel."

He washed, dried, and stepped inside to the aroma of baking bread mingled with the scent of fried pork. "That smells mighty good, ma'am." Then he nodded his head toward the backyard. "Who cuts wood for you?" he asked.

"I trade laundry services for wood from Mr. Peters down the road. He brings wood but doesn't split it."

Bill eyed the small pile. "He bringing more soon?"

She shook her head. "Not right away."

The old man spoke up, "Brought that just yesterdee. Supposed to last a week. Takes her hours ever' week to scrub clothes fer that louse and his brood of nits—ten of 'em. But the skinflint barely brings enough to keep cook fires fer three days. Wintertime we mostly go cold. He's a cheat. I told her but she don't listen. Ever' word I say is cast aside. If she goes cold, serves her right, I say."

Bill frowned. It was a small pile and of poor quality—especially considering the exchange of hours spent at a rub board. Although the old man was obnoxious, he did appear to be right about this. Mr. Peters was getting the better deal.

Jacob's jaw had jutted a fraction. "I could split wood. I'm old enough," he muttered.

Bill silently agreed with him.

"Shore ya could," agreed the old man. "Iffen yer ma had a lick of sense, she'd know it too."

When Bill sat down, Jacob and Talbert were already seated at the long plank table. The scowl on the old man's face deepened. "Waste of good hog meat on the likes of him. 'Taint right, I say, 'taint right," he grumbled.

Bill, ignoring him, looked around the room. It was sparsely furnished, the windows bare, but the table held the softening touch of a chipped vase with a bouquet of goldenrod, Queen Anne's lace, and a few other wildflowers. Bill didn't know their names.

The food looked as good as it smelled, the bacon fried crisp but not too brown, the cornbread golden, and alongside sat a large bowl of fresh black-eyed peas floating in enough juice to cover the cornbread if a body so chose to eat it. That was how Bill preferred his.

He sat and waited for her to sit. When she remained standing, he grew puzzled until Talbert spoke.

"Woman's place is to serve table—not sit with the men."

Bill's mouth drew into a tight line. He had known of the custom. It had never been practiced in his home. A meal never began until everyone was seated.

"Mrs. Anderson, would you like me to say grace?" Granny had insisted on grace before a bite was taken. It was a habit of years, one he had fallen out of in the army, but it seemed fitting here with the woman and child. Abigail looked pleased but surprised.

"Please do," she said. Jacob and Abigail bowed. Talbert, however, kept right on dishing up food and eating. When Bill said amen and looked up, Abigail raised her head. Her stare probed his face as if he puzzled her. As their eyes met, her gaze quickly dropped. She passed the plate of bacon. There were only three pieces left. At least five were piled on Talbert's plate. When Bill took only one, Abigail, after giving one piece to Jacob, forked another onto Bill's plate before ladling a generous amount of peas into a bowl and setting it before him.

Talbert's eyes drew into slits. "Oh, your ma named you well, Abigail," he said snidely. "Like Nabal's woman—yes, you are. Chasing after a man, enticing him with vittles. All just so's you can fling yerself at him."

Bill's spoon halted halfway to his mouth. His eyes were granite. "You might ought to pull in your horns, old man. You could find yourself in the same shape as Nabal. If I remember my Bible correctly, he didn't fare too well with his surly ways."

Abigail sucked in a surprised breath. Talbert chose to ignore the remark, but after a few seconds Abigail gave a tiny grin.

Bill rode across the bridge to find Clarksville's main street crowded. Near the courthouse square, a large group of men stood in front of a house, the location designated for the Spadra Township registration and where Bill should register. He dismounted, tied the black to a hitching rail, and edged his way through the crowd until he drew near the door. Frowns and loud voices were rampant.

"Hey, Bill—over here," called David Hadley. "Won't do any good to get close to the door. They're not letting anyone in."

Bill weaved his way to David. They had become good friends as well as partners in the freighting business.

Jordan Cravens stood nearby. He turned. "He's right," he said. "All day long they've let in fewer than a dozen and none in the last two hours."

David's bronzed arms were crossed over his chest. A grin that was half quirk reflected mischievously in his brown eyes. "And here I was looking forward to my first vote."

"I doubt it will happen this year, David—unless you're voting Republican."

David laughed. "No, sir. I won't be voting Republican. Me and Doc Ward and Judge Meers don't have much in common."

Jack Harris spoke up. "David, you and the seven or eight hundred of us waiting around out here. You can bet the few that do get inside won't be voting Democrat. And I'll wager they don't even have to stand in line to get registered. Someone said Republicans are being let in at the back door."

At Jack's remark angry mutters arose, punctuated with profanity.

"I doubt that," said Cravens. "I don't think they'd risk it. Not when they can slip the forms to them anytime, anywhere."

"You might be right, but I wouldn't put anything past

them. I wish there was something we could do—someone in Little Rock to appeal to about this nest of vipers on the board—"

Cravens shook his head. "I just got back from Little Rock. I saw Governor Hadley. For all the good it did I could have stayed home."

"What'd he say?" asked Bill.

Cravens lowered his voice so only the men close by could hear. "I don't want to start a riot and give the board an excuse to stop the election, so keep this to yourselves until things aren't so volatile." When the men nodded, he went on, "I pointed out Ward's incompetence and asked Governor Hadley to remove him as chairman. All I got was a laugh in the face and insults for my trouble. Hadley told me the Gazette newspaper had slandered Chief Justice McClure by printing that McClure claimed he would carry the state with only sixty men. The governor made a big joke out of it. He said in reality McClure could do it with twenty. McClure himself was in the room. They both had a big laugh."

Jack's face purpled. "Of all the damned—"

"We're not beaten yet," interrupted Cravens. "Not all the Republicans in Congress are crooked. If this turns out that Wilshire wins the congressional seat, Gunter has already talked to me about contesting it. I told him I'd represent him free of charge."

Bill figured the congressional seat being fought over by the Republican candidate Wilshire and the Reform Party candidate Gunter was bound to go to Wilshire, in spite of the fact that the Democrat Party had triple the amount of supporters. It was hard to win against a stacked deck.

"You may as well press your pants to go to court," said Jack. "With men like Ward and Meers in charge of the board, Gunter doesn't stand a chance in this county."

Albert Zachery overheard and added, "And Naylor and Sarber are just as bad."

"No argument on that," Jack agreed.

Bill didn't know Mr. Naylor, but he did know of John Sarber, the former Union general who had returned to Johnson County after the war and became prominent in politics. Sarber had been elected to the state senate. The legislature had even named a county after him. Bill had heard it was part of a bribe, along with a thousand dollars, paid to keep the county seat at Clarksville. Whether it was true or not, Sarber was now the new county across the river, carved out of Johnson, Scott, Yell, and Pope Counties. Some thought Sarber did a lot of good for the state, but most men of Bill's acquaintance looked on him as just another scheming carpetbagger.

Zachery went on, "The board says they registered so few the first day because they thought voting against the new constitution or opposing reconstruction disqualified a person. Plain as the nose on your face, they mean to sift out anyone who will vote Reform."

Just then the door opened and a man came out.

"That fellow is a Republican," said Cravens. "I'll bet he got registered." Then he called, "Hey, Halbert, did you get registered?"

The man weaved on his feet and his voice was slurred. "Course I did!" He took a flask from a vest pocket and raised it high. "And now I'm gonna register my mule."

Laughter erupted. "Everyone likes old Hal—even if he is a drunk and a Republican to boot," said Cravens with a chuckle.

"I like him too," admitted David, "but I figure his mule will get to vote before I do. See there—they shut the door again without letting anyone else inside. I make that only eight today, and they could have done a hundred."

Another man pushed his way through the crowd to join them. "Cravens, I just heard that Ward resigned."

"What?" exclaimed Cravens, incredulous.

"That's what I heard. They say there was some trouble out at Hickey Township."

Bill spoke up, "If that's on the far side of Hagarville, I was riding past and heard a fellow threaten to beat Ward, but nothing else. The whole thing fizzled out pretty fast."

Cravens frowned. "Whatever the case, I figure the board will make the incident out to be worse than it was. They're just looking for an excuse to stop the whole registration. I offered armed guards to make sure there was no violence, but they refused. I better see what I can find out." He started making his way through the crowd.

The door opened again and Judge Meers stepped outside. "Gentlemen, we're done for today. We'll resume again in the morning."

The announcement was met with disgust and loud remarks. "Judge," shouted one louder than the rest, "let's trade jobs. I doubt you're much good at plowing—but I know I can beat you hands down at registering."

Laughter sprinkled more derisive remarks. As the crowd dispersed, David's mouth drew down. "I got no use for Meers. He may be from around here, but he and Ward are as thick as thieves with all that damned carpetbagger crowd." Abruptly he changed the subject. "Did you find the land?"

"I did. It's a fair piece of property. Buildings and fences are run down, but the land has fine timber; with enough hard work it will make good farmland."

"That's good," said David; however, he looked glum. "Reckon you'll stop hauling now."

"No. At least not right away. I figure to pocket all the cash I can to fix things up."

23

"Good," said David, and this time he looked as if he meant it.

Bill tossed the cant hook into the empty wagon, removed work gloves, pulled out a kerchief, wiped his brow, and stuffed the rag into his back pocket. The sharp scent of freshly sawed oak timber hung pungent in the fall air. He leaned against the wagon bed and rested a boot on the wheel hub as he watched David approach, weaving his way through the logs and workmen in the mill yard. The once scrawny boy had grown into a fine-looking man with straight back and wide shoulders. Taking him on as partner had been a good move. He was honest and hard working.

David raised his voice to be heard over the whine of the blade and the sawmill steam engine. "Gilbert wants to cut back on your order—says he has a surplus of timber now." David quirked an eyebrow and his voice grew snide. "Of course then he went on to say that he hates to lose such a good contractor. And if you're interested, he'll try to keep you on, but it'll mean writing up a new contract."

Bill glanced at numerous log piles near heaps of sawdust. He'd been afraid of that. It seemed that every able-bodied man in the country had gone to work for the railroad, either cutting and hauling timber for crossties or driving teams hitched to scrapers to grade and cut the right-of-way. He had been one of the first locals to contract. His was a higher pay rate than the recent contracts. He'd figured Gilbert would weasel out on him before long.

"I won't cave to that bastard. Besides, with winter coming on we'll be shut down before long anyway. We'll have no trouble finding someone else to haul for in the spring." He pushed away from the wagon and stood. "For now let's ride into town and get a good meal for a change."

David agilely sprang into the wagon and settled his tall, lithe frame onto the wagon seat. "With pleasure. I ain't saying you're a bad cook, Bill. But last night that stray hound hanging around camp sniffed the leftover stew, and I'll swear after one bite he gave me a disgusted look before finally eating it."

Bill chuckled. "Next week is your turn to cook. And I doubt that hound will be one whit happier."

"No argument on that. I never was a hand in the kitchen. Grandpa wasn't much of a cook, either."

"I remember your grandpa used to make some tolerable shine, though."

"So I've heard. That was before I was born. By the time I came along, he bought his from the Matthers. He never let me touch it. He said my pa was a fine, kind man when he was sober but a mean drunk. I reckon Grandpa was afraid I'd take after him."

Bill recalled the bruises he'd seen on Bessie Hadley. Those bruises had turned the jury against Dub when Bessie was found dead in their cabin.

Aloud he said, "Reckon that was logical. Some men can't handle liquor. I can't see as how drink makes a better man out of anyone. Probably best to not even start it."

"I've never known you to drink, Bill."

"Oh, time to time I wet my whistle. But I've no great thirst for it."

David looked at the distant, purple-hued mountains and frowned. "Reckon, just in case, I'll leave it alone."

Bill supposed it was a great comfort to the boy to know they had hung the wrong man. David's pa had not killed his ma. And yet the memory of his folks' demise must be a sorrowful thing.

As if David read his thoughts, he spoke. "I been thinking a lot about my folks lately." He turned to face Bill. "I've never even seen their graves. Grandpa said they're both buried right near Little Piney Creek. Do you know where?"

"Nice little cemetery not far from where I grew up. Their home place is right near mine, too."

"I think I'd like to go see our old place—and the graves." David sat up straighter. "Hey, since we're between jobs, let's you and me sashay up there."

Bill quickly flipped the reins to urge the lagging mules. He was not about to stir up those painful memories again.

"Well, David, I got a few things to take care of, but I think it's a right fine idea for you to go. I'll give you directions how to get to Ned Loring's. He or Elijah will be glad to show you around."

David nodded. "I think I'll go."

✳ Chapter 2

Bill stopped on Main Street and looked toward
Spadra Creek. The water was low now, moving sluggishly
over the rocky bottom under a bright October sky that
had remained cloudless for two weeks. The mild weather
was perfect for hunting. He could envision a big whitetail
buck slipping through open woods in the mountains. He
hadn't tasted a juicy venison steak in ages. He let out a
deep breath. The weather was perfect for work too. And
he owned a farm now in need of a great deal of that.
His thoughts drifted to the woman. Lately he had been
thinking a lot about her. He found that surprising. Ever
since falling in love with Cindy, he had shied clear of
females.

"Stop it, Bill Tanner," he muttered. He wasn't fit
company for any woman, let alone a fine one like Abigail
Anderson. Besides, getting entangled with her would be
nothing but trouble. That old devil of a father-in-law
would see to that. No, he would stick to work and leave
both Abigail and the old man alone. With that resolve,
he went to David's old place where they stayed while in
town, got his horse, and was soon loping along the dusty
road toward Hagarville. Today he would make a list of all
that needed doing. Later he would load the wagon with
lumber and supplies and set to work in earnest.

He passed numerous horses and wagons heading into
Clarksville as well as wagons loaded with supplies heading

for the railroad camps. He answered greetings from those he knew and nodded to strangers. Gone was the tight-lipped suspicion of wartime travelers. But Bill supposed, along with a natural reticence, he would always retain a distrust of humans. He had seen too much in the war to do otherwise.

Midmorning he stopped in shade alongside the road to eat a biscuit stuffed with ham. When it came to breakfast, he wasn't a morning person and had rarely joined the family at Granny's pre-dawn table laden with meat, eggs, bread, gravy, fried potatoes, and a variety of preserves and jellies. He preferred a light meal later in the day after he had worked awhile.

In spite of the pleasant spot and refreshing breeze fluttering the golden hickory leaves overhead, he didn't tarry. He found himself anxious to be on the move. Soon the black was back on the trail. Bill's mind drifted to the woman and the habit she had of turning her face sideways to hide the scar. He wondered again what had done that to her. He doubted he'd ever find out, but he couldn't help being curious.

He stopped for a few minutes to chat with Sid and George Wallace. Sid, muscled, tall, and exceedingly handsome, spoke seldom. Bill understood the coldness in his fine eyes and the hardness in the full-lipped mouth. The look mirrored Bill's own soul. He supposed Sid's aloofness had grown from watching his pa, Vincent Wallace, a circuit-riding preacher, gunned down in his own front yard right before Sid's eyes when Sid was only twelve. It was never proven if the men in Union blue were regulars or deserters.

George carried the conversation with his typical happy-go-lucky charm. "We're heading to town to register. Sid here says they'll never let us vote, but we intend to try."

"From what I've seen," Bill put in, "they won't even let you register. Today is the last day, and they've registered less than two-dozen men so far. I stopped by again this morning and waited around for an hour. I never saw a single man come or go through the door."

"I told you so," said Sid, his eyes diamond hard. "If you expected otherwise, you're a fool, George."

"Oh, well,"—George's eyes twinkled—"I'd rather be riding into town to see Mattie instead of gathering corn anyway."

Bill grinned. He rode away while George continued to sing his fiancée's praises.

Bill purposefully avoided the house, unsaddled the horse at the barn lot and turned him loose, pulled on work gloves, and set to work on the pasture fences. Most of the rails were still there, just tumbled over. Someday he would replace them with the wire fencing he had heard about designed with barbs to keep cattle from pushing through, but he'd have to prosper some before he could afford such fencing. This was good ground for cattle as well as row crops. Other than grain for his stock, he would mostly raise cotton. There was a gin near Hagarville, so he wouldn't even have to transport the cotton far; and with the train soon to be running through Clarksville, there should be a good market for the crop.

For hours he worked his way along one edge of the field, stopping occasionally to drink in the landscape along with the pure pleasure of knowing it was his own land. A brown rabbit hopped from a thicket and then bolted at sight of him, zigzagging across open ground back toward brushy cover. From woods near the small creek meandering at the edge of the fence line came the drum of a woodpecker. Bill shaded his eyes and soon spotted the red head glistening in the sun. He had seen no sign of big game here, but the fields and woods were alive with small creatures and birds. He pursed his lips and whistled a bobwhite call and then grinned when a coyote stuck its nose from the brush.

He stooped, lifted another rail, and forced it into place. Suddenly he stood straighter. Across the field came Abigail. From one hand swung a bucket, and in the other was a small basket covered with a napkin. He removed his hat and wiped his sweaty face on a kerchief, which he stuffed into his pocket as she drew near.

Keeping the scarred side of her face turned slightly away, she said, "Mr. Tanner, I saw you working and thought you could use a drink and perhaps a bite of food."

"That's thoughtful, ma'am. I can use both." After taking the dipper from the bucket, he drank deeply. The water was cold and sweet. Then he reached into the basket she offered. He took a bite of the biscuit filled with honey and butter. It was good. Abigail made flaky biscuits. With a glove he dusted off a rock and gestured for her to sit.

"No, thank you," she declined. "I have to get back. I'm doing the washing." She ruefully glanced at red, water-wrinkled hands before rubbing the small of her back. "I needed a walk, a little break from stooping over the rub board. I left Jacob wringing the last tubful.

Bill remained standing but propped a foot on the rock and rested an arm on his leg. "I been working a little, but I have to admit, mostly I've been enjoying the view," he said, eyeing the valley and the far-off, color-bathed hills.

"This is wonderful land—tall timber and such big flats. I've often thought it was a shame for such good land to lie fallow." Her eyes traced the distance. "The woods are beautiful this fall. It is beautiful here in every season.

And peaceful," she said with a sigh. "That's what I love most."

He read much into the remark. He waited for her to continue. When she didn't, he finally said, "Reckon we've all seen some un-peaceful times."

She nodded. "Way too many—enough for a lifetime, I hope. I've loved living here." She gave a sad smile. "I've enjoyed pretending it was all mine. I've imagined the curtains I'd make and what color rugs I'd make for the floors." She suddenly flushed and turned to go.

"Thank you, ma'am. That hit the spot."

She looked back, nodded, and kept walking. He watched until she was almost out of sight. She had a graceful walk, straight back, and easy stride. It had been thoughtful of her to bring the food and water. She had taken the water bucket, but he would drop the basket off at the house when he left. There were two more biscuits to enjoy through the afternoon.

Late in the day, the boy ran across the field. He stopped nearby. "I finished my chores. Can I help?"

"Be glad to have a hand. Grab the other end of that rail and help lift it into place."

Jacob was a good, steady worker, and although he occasionally asked a question, he didn't chatter like most boys that age. Bill was surprised at how much faster the chore went with his help.

The light began fading. He had only finished one side of a field, but he was satisfied with the progress. He looked over the field choked with sassafras sprouts and blood red sumacs to envision rows of kingly cotton covered with plump white bolls. It would take a heap of work. Everything worth doing did. No doubt, it would take plenty of time and effort, but he figured he had both.

"Can I bridle your horse?"

"Sure," agreed Bill. "Watch out that he doesn't step on your feet."

Jacob ran to the small lot where the black grazed as Bill walked toward the house, flexing his shoulders to work the kinks out of his sore back. Abigail was nowhere in sight, but the clothesline sagged from the weight of a huge washing. Pant legs almost touched the ground. With a frown, he eyed leaning posts that needed stabilizers. He would tend to that upon his return. Obviously the old man wasn't much help. Bill doubted he did much except quarrel and make her life harder.

Before he rapped, Abigail stepped to the open door. He bared his head. "I sure enjoyed the biscuits, ma'am. You're a good cook."

She took the basket with a smile. "Thank you." She hesitated. "Won't you stay for supper?"

"Thank you, ma'am, but those biscuits filled me up just fine. I plan on coming back tomorrow. Do you need anything from town? I'll be going to the mercantile before I come back."

She considered for a moment, and then hesitantly said, "Thank you. Yes, yes, I do. Wait just a minute." She was back soon with a few coins in her hand. "If it wouldn't be too much trouble, I need a spool of white thread. Mr. Anderson went to Hagarville today with a neighbor, but he doesn't like to bother with such things."

Bill took the coins while doing a slow burn. *The old devil wouldn't even bring her a spool of thread!* "No trouble a-tall. And if there's anything else, I'll be glad to fetch it."

"That's all. Thank you so much." She paused and then added, "I'd rather he didn't know—"

Bill, shoving the coins into his pocket, interrupted. "If you're not around, I'll just leave it yonder on the stump by your washtub."

Her face softened. "Thank you." She spied Jacob with the horse at the edge of the yard and took two steps forward. *"Jacob Anderson! What in the world are you doing?"* She turned to Bill. "He knows nothing about horses. He might get hurt."

"The black is gentle." He bit his tongue to keep from saying more. He had no right to tell her how to raise her boy. "He's a good worker. I was glad for his help this evening."

She shot Jacob a look that brooded ill for the boy. "I didn't know he went out to the field."

"Just for a while, after his chores were done." When she still seemed disturbed, he said goodnight, put on his hat, and walked away. It was plain to see she was keeping the boy on too short a tether—why, he had seen boys younger than Jacob on the battlefield. There had been a ragged kid at Elkins Ferry who didn't look a day over ten, carrying a musket and shooting at Yankees. And Bill had read about a nine-year–old drummer boy from up North drawing a pension for being wounded. Still and all, it wasn't his business how Abigail raised her son. He'd do well to keep his nose out of it. Granny used to quote a verse about leading a quiet life, minding your own business, and working with your hands. So far he had practiced that as much as possible, and he figured he'd best stick to it.

Jacob handed him the reins. "He's a mighty nice horse. He let me catch him with no fuss a-tall."

Bill removed the blanket and saddle from the fence and threw them over the black's back. "If your ma agrees, I'll let you ride him sometime."

Jacob beamed. "I'd like that more than anything!" Then his face fell as he looked toward the house. "Ma won't let me. She won't let me do anything."

"Don't be too hard on her," Bill cautioned. "She's just trying to make sure you don't get hurt."

Abigail still stood on the steps as he mounted and gathered the reins into one hand. He lifted the hat and nodded before settling it onto his head. When she angled her face away again and raised a hand to wave, he started to ride on but abruptly changed his mind and rode close to the door. "Ma'am, I don't mean to be bold, but I figure you and me will be seeing a good bit of each other since I'll be working here. I wish you'd stop tilting your head sideways. I don't mind that scar. You're a handsome woman with or without it."

She blinked. Then she covered her cheeks with both hands and gave a nervous laugh. "Well, I don't know what to say." However, she turned her face completely forward and lowered her hands. "But, thank you. I seem to keep saying that to you," she said.

He fiddled with the reins and shrugged. "No more than I do you." With another nod, he rode out of the yard and onto the trail lacy with blue afternoon shadows. He had not gone far before a wagon passed, stirring dust from the rutted trail. Two men sat on the seat; one was old man Anderson wearing a scowl deeper than the wagon ruts. At sight of Bill, it deepened into hatred. The graybeard driving the wagon called howdy, but Anderson rode past without speaking. He turned to cut Bill with burning eyes. Bill figured Abigail would be in for a hard time. He rode toward town with a scowl on his own face.

Abigail watched Bill Tanner ride away. She touched the side of her face and ran a finger along the scar. Her heartbeat quickened. He had said she was a handsome woman...

"Stop being a fool!" she scolded herself in a whisper. Men often tried taking advantage of a widow. Hadn't a sweet-talking, handsome man fooled her once before? She wasn't about to blindly trust any man, not ever again.

Frank had had a veneer of goodness. It wasn't actually goodness at all, merely sugar coating to hide the poison inside. She had found that out too late. Bill seemed like a fine man, but Frank had seemed fine at first. Oh, he had been a charmer. He had even captivated Uncle Victor and Aunt Margaret. Of course, they were only too glad to get her off their hands, and she couldn't blame them. Seven children was a houseful. They had been more than kind to take her in with loving arms when Ma and Pa had died, and they had remained kind the ten years she had lived there and given her an education she could never have gotten any other way. It would have cut them to the quick to know how Frank treated her. She supposed that was one reason she had tolerated it and kept quiet—that and Frank being Jacob's pa. Besides, the Bible spoke against divorce, so she had stuck to her vow. In spite of that, she had hoped Frank wouldn't come back from the war, and she hadn't shed a tear when he didn't.

She looked down the road again. She needed to be careful. What if Bill Tanner was a wolf in sheep's clothing? She chewed her bottom lip and determined to guard Jacob from forming an attachment.

She called to him. He shut the barn lot gate and ran to her.

"Jacob, I don't want you going to the field anymore when Mr. Tanner is here."

"But Ma—"

"I mean it," she said. "No arguing. Now come help get the laundry in before supper."

He didn't say a word, but his eyes were angry as he jerked a shirt from the clothesline. With a discouraged sigh, she began gathering dry laundry and dropping it into a wicker basket. For the thousandth time she wondered how to protect without smothering. She had no idea. She had no idea how to raise a boy without a father. She was desperate to do it right, and yet she feared she was failing miserably. Lately Jacob seemed to resent her...well, not actually her. He resented the apron strings. If she didn't stop smothering him, she would lose him. He was already pushing her away. That was gut wrenching. Jacob was all she had.

Even if Frank had lived, she shuddered to imagine what sort of father he would have been—a drinking, card-playing, shiftless sort of man. Mr. Anderson was bad enough, and yet without him there would have been little male influence in Jacob's life; perhaps that good outweighed the bad. In his own selfish way, he did love the boy. And she knew he was right about her smothering Jacob. But she was so afraid. *What if something happened to him?*

The sun sank lower, stripping the yard with bands of gold. In the distance an owl hooted, and Abigail heard the jingle of harness and the squeak of a wagon. More than likely it was Old Able Cummins bringing Mr. Anderson home. Or it might be Mr. Peters coming for his laundry, which she had not yet folded. She picked up the basket and hurried inside, leaving Jacob to get the rest.

Her hands deftly sorted the mound of clothes and folded the ones not needing ironing. Through the window she watched Mr. Anderson climb stiffly from the wagon. He would be surly to find no supper on the table. That couldn't be helped. The washing had been extra large today. There was a little meat left from breakfast but no biscuits. Thoughts of Bill Tanner brought a crease to her brow as she once again questioned his motives. In spite of that she was glad he'd enjoyed the biscuits. She would fry cornpone for supper. That was quicker than baking bread. Thankfully, there were purple hull peas she had shelled earlier, and they didn't take long to boil tender. Not that she feared Mr. Anderson—he had not offered to strike her since she had raised the butcher knife to him years ago—but his black moods oppressed her. He had no light ones, but they did vary in shades of darkness; the blackest involved his comfort.

She watched him navigate the path, his face already a thundercloud. Sitting too long stiffened his joints and made him limp. Now he limped up the steps and through the door. His eyes, white hot in a pale face, raked her.

"Harlot!"

Abigail laid aside a shirt and straightened.

"I know," he railed, shaking a fist. "I seen him! I seen him riding off with a big smile like a cat that done swallered the cream!" His eyes narrowed into hateful slits. "Had it all made up betwixt ya, didn't ya?—me gone off to town so's you could be alone."

He was an old devil. He did nothing but rant and rave, all day long. Sometimes to keep from screaming she went into the bedroom and plugged her ears. It would do no good to point out that he had only decided to go into town that morning after old Able had stopped by. Reason held no sway with Talbert Anderson. She turned and began folding clothes. Although her back was turned, she felt his anger filling the room. It had been a long while since he had actually hit her, but now she glanced back. He grabbed a pot from the stove, took a step, and shaking with rage, raised it high.

Her voice was ice. "Hit me and you'll never lift a hand again."

Slowly the hand lowered, but hate oozed from every pore. *"You'll pay,"* he hissed. "Someday I'll make you both pay." He spun on his heels, limped into his bedroom, and slammed the door.

She raised her voice. *"You've got enough demons to drive a herd of hogs crazy!"*

She sank into a chair, propped her elbows on the table, and placed her face in her hands. She hated letting him goad her into shouting. How much longer must she tolerate him? She had gone over and over that question a million times, always without a good answer. Staying with him had seemed the only reasonable course during the war. A woman alone with an infant was easy prey, and those were desperate days. It was unthinkable to leave him to shift for himself in Texas when they arrived to find his kin gone. Then on the trip here his health had failed even more. She couldn't just leave him alongside the road. He was, after all, her father-in-law and Jacob's grandfather. She felt moral ties if not legal.

But with each passing year, he had grown meaner and—she faced the possibility—more dangerous. Often, when she angered him, he bared his teeth like an animal. She wasn't afraid. But she was cautious. Each night she slept with the butcher knife under her pillow. Some nights he paced the floor, and through the thin walls she could hear him ranting. It robbed her of sound sleep. She dreaded being caged up with him in the house when winter kept them indoors. Her only consolation was the old man didn't rail at Jacob. She slowly stood and began folding laundry.

"Damnation!" muttered Bill.

The black had thrown a shoe, and it was still miles

to Clarksville. Fortunately there was a blacksmith at Hagarville on the outskirts of the small settlement, and it was just ahead. He dismounted and led the horse.

Evening shadows were long and purple. Supper smoke rose from the rock chimney of the frame house beside the blacksmith shed. Bill noticed the sawmill behind the blacksmith shop alongside a pile of sawed stave bolts and near the creek. It took a special type mill to make stave bolts, and it was fortunate to have one so near. He planned to inquire the going rate the owner paid for bolts.

He tied the horse and walked down the rock walk to knock on the door. His eyebrows rose in shock. The man had a napkin tucked into his collar. He abruptly stopped chewing, and with wide eyes he studied Bill. Except for the deep cleft in the man's chin and his frame being stockier, Bill could have been looking into the mirror; there were the same black hair, steel gray eyes, and high cheekbones, and the same heavy black beard Bill possessed before he had shaved off his own.

Bill wiped surprise from his face and said, "My horse threw a shoe."

The man stepped back a little. "Care to come inside and have supper? Ma cooked plenty."

Such neighborliness had almost died during the war. Bill was glad to see it returning. "Thank you, kindly, but I'll just wait out here on the porch till you're finished."

The man pulled off the napkin and tossed it onto a sideboard near the door. "I was just done anyway."

A querulous voice came from deep inside the house, "Quinton, you ain't goin' back to work—not in them clothes! Iffen you light that forge, you're bound to get spark burns all over them good pants. Tell whoever 'tis to come back tomorrer! You'll get all smoky agin and have to wash, and we'll be late fer the pie supper."

"I'll be back in a bit, Ma." Quinton closed the door and began walking toward the shop. He shot Bill a sideways look. "You come far?" he asked.

"Not very." Bill knew Quinton was intrigued by the resemblance, so he offered the information. "I'm Bill Tanner from over on Little Piney." He waited for that to sink in and then added, "You rather I took my business elsewhere?"

Quinton shook his head. "No. Shoeing horses is my business. I know there's been bad blood between our families, but according to Pa it was Uncle Jared's fault. Sometimes I'm plumb ashamed of my kin."

Bill empathized. He knew a thing or two about that.

The forge had barely begun smoking when a bony woman with gray-streaked hair exited a house and crossed the road to enter the shop. "Thought you was done fer the day." Although she spoke to Quinton, she squinted into the dimness to study Bill with a shrewd look. "Horse throwed a shoe, did it?" Her shriveled skin encircled sharp, hawk-like eyes, thin lips, and a prominent beaked nose.

Bill did not answer the obvious. Although he usually got on well with the elderly, for some reason he felt an instant dislike for her. He knew the type. Forever circling her territory, she smelled gossip the way a buzzard smelled carrion and was just as fond of it.

"You riding through or visiting here abouts?"

"Riding through."

"Figure you must be Quinton's kin with you two being peas in a pod."

Bill's lips narrowed. "No."

Quinton pumped the bellows and began heating a horseshoe.

The old woman cocked her head. "Well, if you ain't a Rawlings, my name ain't Zetta Cowens."

"His name is Tanner," Quinton said.

"Ah!" Then she cackled as if that were a funny joke.

"Get on back across the road, Zetta, and leave us to our work."

She complied but not before pausing to look back and give another insulting cackle. Bill had lived for years with the bitter knowledge that Jared Rawlings was his real pa. And he figured Zetta Cowens knew it too, even if Quinton didn't.

Quinton shook his head. "That Zetta is the nosiest woman in the country, but she's a neighbor so I sort of put up with her."

The ring of hammer and the huff of bellows filled the silence.

Bill nodded to the sawmill sitting off the road down near the creek. "That your stave mill?"

"Yep."

"You interested in buying prime white oak?"

Quinton's eyes lit with interest. "Sure am. You have some for sale?"

"I plan to cut out a stand pretty soon."

"I'll take all you've got and pay top dollar if it's prime and split into stave lengths."

They discussed the timber market a bit more, and then Bill paid Quinton, mounted, and rode on through deepening twilight. Along with the disappearing light, brilliance faded from the timber and a whisper of chill slipped in on the night breeze. He ruminated on what had just happened. Much to his surprise, he liked Quinton. Granny had said there were some good Rawlings, but Bill had supposed she was being generous. Maybe she was right after all.

It was late when he arrived in Clarksville. Even the saloon was dark as he rode to the old Hadley shack situated alongside Spadra Creek. He unsaddled the black and turned him into the pasture to graze along with his team of mules and then made his way into the dark cabin. He and David sometimes used it on trips into town. Although it was a ramshackle mess, Bill preferred it to a hotel bill. He now had even more reason to conserve money. All evening he had been daydreaming of the fine improvements he would make to the farm and toying with the idea of buying his own small mill for sawing lumber and crossties. Stave mills were too expensive. But with Quinton's mill near at hand, he would haul and sell to him if he paid a reasonable price.

It was odd, he thought, how this land already meant more to him than the parcel inherited from Granny. He supposed it had something to do with the feeling that he had no real right to Granny's land. Lately he'd been contemplating deeding it to Elijah. Elijah was Granny's blood kin and had more right to it than he did. Besides, he never intended to live there again. It held too many bitter memories of Ma.

In spite of getting little sleep, Bill was up early. He hitched the mules to the wagon and headed for town to purchase chain, a new ax, and a couple of long, sharp-toothed crosscut saws. He wished he could afford to hire a four-man crew. For now he hoped David would agree to a low-paying job for the winter.

When the door opened, Bill was the first customer inside Swagerty's General Merchandise. He had known the major during the war, and now they spent a few minutes swapping war yarns—only the humorous ones. All the men Bill knew tried to keep the other kind buried deep under the sod of forgetfulness.

When the talk turned to politics, Swagerty came out from behind the counter. He folded arms on his chest and leaned back against the counter. "I suppose you tried to register?"

"Tried. Never even got close to the door. They weren't letting many through."

"I never saw a bigger farce. They filled out only a handful of applications and then closed down two days early. I heard that Meers and some of his bunch asked the governor to set the whole registration aside."

"Why," asked Bill, "since they only registered who they wanted anyway?"

Swagerty shrugged. "No idea, unless they're trying to cover up what a farce they've made of things."

Bill considered this. "If the governor sets it aside, there won't be time for another registration, but either way the election will be a hoax."

"That's for sure," agreed Swagerty. "And since this county is about ten to one Democrat, Meers and the board won't be popular no matter how it comes off. There's already been talk of tar and feathers. They'll be darn lucky if there's no gunplay." He pushed away from the counter. "Now, what you looking for today?"

Bill made his purchases, including Abigail's thread, and started out the door. After a moment's hesitation he walked back to the fabric counter and began fingering cloth. He had no idea what kind made good curtains. Swagerty stepped up.

"You needing some fabric, Bill?"

"What kind makes good curtains?"

Swagerty's eyebrows rose. "Curtains?" he echoed, then rubbed his chin. "Well, I reckon any of this calico would do, wouldn't it, Miss Lena?"

A pretty young woman with light brown hair and hazel eyes strode forward.

"Yes, it would. What color?"

Bill shrugged his shoulders. "Don't guess it matters too much—"

"Well of course it does," put in the lady clerk. "You'd better ask your wife before you buy the fabric."

When Swagerty's lips drew down, Bill recalled his conversation with Jordan Cravens. Considering the credit crisis facing Clarksville's merchants, he figured that Swagerty feared losing a cash sale.

"I have no wife," he said, "just a house."

"Oh, I see," she said, leaning near to critically eye more than two dozen bolts of cloth. "Then the only person we have to please is you. Do you like bright or dark colors?"

He thought of Abigail. "Bright I think."

"Any particular color you favor?"

He suddenly wished he could ask Abigail, and yet it would be unwise to let her think he was doing this just for her—even though he was. Hell would freeze before he'd buy curtains for himself. No window coverings at all, or at best an old blanket thrown over the window, would suit him fine.

She held up a bolt of plaid. "How about this one? It's cheerful without being gaudy. And plaid is so masculine."

It was varying shades of yellow, some almost the color of butter. The small intersecting green lines reminded him of spring. "That should do just fine," he said, hoping plaid wasn't too masculine for Abigail's taste.

"How many yards will you need?"

His brows drew together. "No idea."

"Perhaps you should ask whomever will be making the—"

Swagerty interrupted. "Just go ahead and take the whole bolt. It's brand new, none gone yet. Bring back what you don't use, and I'll refund your money."

"Fair enough," agreed Bill with relief.

The lady beamed. "And you'll be needing matching thread."

"I suppose so." Bill hesitated. "Does a body need anything else to sew curtains?"

She chuckled. "Nothing at all. This will fix you up just fine."

He saw a display of jackknives and on impulse bought one for the boy.

The yard was empty when Bill drove toward the barn. He unhitched the mules, untied the lead rope from the black, and turned them into the pasture behind the barn. The fence wasn't great, but it should hold them. After unloading his supplies, he picked up the parcel of fabric, thread, and the jackknife and started toward the house. He suddenly sidestepped as he almost stepped on a dark, speckled king snake sluggishly crossing the path in the deepening twilight. "Time you found a warm hole, old friend," muttered Bill. "Winter's coming."

"I know. And I dread it."

He whirled toward the voice. Abigail apologized, "Sorry, I didn't mean to startle you." She stepped away from the deep shadow of an elm tree. "I come out every evening to watch the sunset," she said.

Bill crossed the distance between them. She smelled of soap and a faint scent of lavender. He knew the scent because Granny used it in her clothes chests. "I must be losing my edge," he said. "Usually no one gets the drop on me like that."

"I saw you drive by. I figured it might be best if I got the thread now, without Mr. Anderson knowing."

Bill chewed his jaw. There was no way to keep the old devil from knowing about the fabric. "I got it," he said and then handed her the bundle wrapped in brown paper. "I got some stuff to make curtains for the house."

Abigail gasped. "Oh, my…you shouldn't have—I mean…" she stopped, flustered, before beginning again. "If you want curtains for the house, I'll be glad to make them, but I hope you didn't put yourself out for me."

He hedged, "A house needs curtains, I reckon. I'd be obliged if you'd make them." Then he waited as she unwrapped a corner of the parcel. "If that's not a good color, Swagerty—the store-keep—said I could bring it back and choose something else."

"I can't see it very well in this light," she said, "but it looks like a nice plaid."

He thought her voice sounded happy. "You can let me know tomorrow." He held out the packet containing the jackknife. "I got a little something for the boy—it's a jackknife."

Her eyebrows drew together with displeasure. "That's very nice of you, Mr. Tanner, but I don't think—"

"Ma'am, all the boys I know have a knife by the time they're his age; most are shooting guns. I was."

"It's not that," she said. "I don't mind him having a knife." She took her bottom lip in her teeth while searching for words. "Mr. Tanner, I'd rather you didn't buy him gifts." She glanced at the package in her arms. "I don't think you should be buying gifts for either of us," she said with serious eyes.

He drew back his hand but insisted, "You'd be doing me a favor by making the curtains. And Jacob helped me real good the other day. It's not really a gift. I figure he earned it."

He waited while she turned away to stare into the distance before finally facing him again. "I hope you'll understand. I think you are probably an excellent man.

But I don't know that for certain. I've been fooled before and lived to regret it. I don't want Jacob forming any attachments until I know for sure."

He nodded. "I can understand that."

She was quiet for a long moment and then she asked, "Have you had supper?"

"I'm fine. At noon I ate a big meal at the cafe."

"That was hours ago," she protested. "Besides, I baked an apple pie, and Jacob isn't here to eat it. A neighbor boy invited him to ride along with him and his pa while they took corn to the mill. They're a good family, so I let him go; he's spending the night. It would be a shame for that pie to go begging."

His teeth gleamed white in the dimness. "Don't see how I can turn that down."

He followed her across the yard, up the back steps, and into the house, expecting to be met with an angry outburst from Anderson. The room, however, was dark and quiet and smelled of baking. When Abigail lit the lamp on the table, to Bill's surprise and pleasure, Anderson sat slumped in the rocking chair in the corner, chin on chest, cradling an uncorked jug in his lap like a baby.

Abigail unwrapped the package. "Oh, this is perfect!" she exclaimed, running her hand over the fabric. She looked up, her face soft in lamplight.

He quickly said, "I don't mind one bit getting something different."

"No, really," she assured, "I would have picked this very material for your curtains."

He wondered if that meant she didn't like it for herself. He started to ask when a snore rose from the corner. They both looked at Anderson.

"He get drunk often?" Bill asked.

"He would if he could afford the liquor. He got that jug yesterday and drank half of it last night and finished it tonight."

Bill's eyes narrowed. "I'm guessing he used your money."

She shrugged. "To be perfectly honest, I was glad to give it to him. At least when he's drunk I don't have to listen to him." She turned away and began dishing food onto a plate.

Several times his eyes strayed from the plate to find her watching him, but she sat quietly while he ate the fried ham, collard greens, and cornbread. "That was delicious, ma'am."

"Would you like another helping, or are you ready for pie?"

A golden-crusted pie, with no wedges missing, sat on the table near the lamp. Pale slices of apple, glazed with sugary cinnamon, peeked through slits to hold the top crust high.

Bill sighed. "If I don't stop now, I'll have no room for pie. And that's about the best-looking pie I ever saw."

When he shoved back the plate after the third piece and declared it delicious, she smiled, stood, and began clearing the table and pouring steaming water from the teakettle into a large metal dishpan.

"I've been wondering," she said, "what you plan to do when the weather turns cold. I mean, you can't stay in the shed—you could throw a cat through the cracks."

"I aim to put up a stove and run the pipe out a hole in the wall. Then I'll add some batten to cover the cracks. I figure that will be as cozy as the shack in town where we've been staying the last two winters."

Her head swung around. "We?"

"David Hadley—the fellow that works for me. We

stay at his grandpa's old place in Clarksville when the weather shuts us down."

She sat down. "What work is that?"

"I've been hauling supplies for the railroad, mostly crossties."

"You'll give that up now to farm?"

"I aim to farm someday, but for now I'll be cutting and hauling this timber. Have to make some cash money first." He grinned. "Farming is expensive."

The smile erased lines around her full lips. Bill imagined how she had looked as a carefree, happy girl.

"I hope you'll eat with us. It's the least we can do since you're letting us live here."

"I'd like nothing better." He looked at Anderson. "But he won't like it. I don't want to make your life harder."

She let out a derisive breath. "He'll rant and rail no matter what."

"All right then—that is if you'll let me help out with food. I can kill game and maybe catch a few fish time to time, and pick up the other supplies you need in town."

"That would be a real blessing. And I insist on doing your laundry."

"I've got a feeling I'm going to get mighty spoiled not having to do my own cooking or laundry. Likely I'll get lazy and fat."

She chuckled. "More than likely you'll do enough farm work to prevent both."

"I never liked farming, but somehow owning this land has changed that."

Usually taciturn, Bill surprised himself by sharing in detail the improvements he envisioned. Her enthusiasm also surprised him. She was not on guard as she had been earlier, and actually seemed caught up in the vision as she made suggestions.

He listened with a growing appreciation of her keen mind. "Why, that's a fine idea. It wouldn't take much to run water down here from that spring. It sure would be handy to have plenty of water here and at the barn." He had seen a spring in the hillside behind the house. The water was clear and plentiful. He might be able to dam it up and maybe buy some cast iron pipe, or he could build troughs of logs sawed in half.

It was growing late by the time he pushed away from the table. "I sure do thank you for the fine meal and the conversation. Don't recall ever having a more pleasant evening." He walked to the door and then stopped. "Ma'am, I think you're wise to be cautious. But I want you to know I mean no harm to you and the boy. I was raised right near here on Little Piney Creek up in the mountains a ways, lived there all my life, and you can ask folks about me. I'm not saying I'm perfect, but there's no black marks against me."

She nodded. Then she stood and brushed imaginary crumbs from the table. As he removed his hat from the peg and put it on, she said, "I think Jacob would enjoy the knife." She kept her eyes averted as she added, "I had a nice time this evening too, Mr. Tanner."

"I'm glad." He paused with a hand on the doorknob. "It would be fine with me if you call me Bill."

She seemed to consider and then finally said, "You can call me Abigail."

"Goodnight, Abigail." He liked the way the name felt on his tongue.

✖ Chapter 3

Bill was surprised to see a large group of men gathered in morning sun beyond the fence near the charred walls of the courthouse. He dismounted, tied his horse to the hitching rail, and went to find out what was going on.

"The scoundrel, the dirty, rotten scoundrel! It's just like we figured. Now, what's to be done? That's what I want to know."

Bill didn't know the man who spoke or the half dozen who voiced loud agreement. "What's going on?" he asked in a low voice to a man he saw occasionally in the saloon.

The man spit a stream of tobacco juice before answering. "Notice posted on the door says we have to have a new registration. Of course since it's the fifth of November, there isn't time for that before election, and the governor knew that when he did it."

Bill knew this news would go down as raw as Slim's whiskey. The Unionist Republicans might put on a show of pretending the Southern man had his rights back, but it was only a show, at least in Johnson County. He walked away when an angry growl declared they ought to line up the Yankee-loving bastards and shoot them all. He didn't bother to argue that they had tried that before and failed miserably. He wanted his right to vote as badly as the next man, but he figured it was like Granny used to say—if you dance, you have to pay the fiddler. Well, they had fought and lost, and it seemed they would yet be a long time paying for it.

"I tell you they done it! I heared 'em with my own ears!"

Bill turned his attention to the heated discussion near the courthouse door. A gaunt man with an unkempt beard raised his voice again until every eye had turned his way. "Hit was Judge Meers hisself along with that bastard John Sarber who stopped him—stopped McCord from going on with the registration. He had rode into town to do it because Cravens had promised him a armed guard to stave off trouble. I heared McCord tell Meers and Saber so, right yonder at the head of the street. I tell ya, I heared hit with my own ears." The man turned to face the crowd. "But they told him if he knowed what was good fer 'em he'd do no such thang—'er words to that effect. I don't rightly recollect the exact words spoke, but I remember well enough what happened then. McCord turned his horse and headed right on out of town." Dark mutters met the news. "I tell ya," went on the gaunt man, "they ought to be lynched."

Bill had heard that more than once. So far it had only been talk, but he had no desire to get caught in the middle of a lynch mob.

He left the courthouse and dropped by the Hadley shack. There was no sign of David. Yellowed leaves had drifted across the porch and banked against the door, and from the cluttered look of things inside, no one had been there lately. Bill rubbed his chin and stared north, frowning. David must still be on Little Piney. Bill needed a crew, at the very least one man, to help fell the massive hardwoods. If David didn't return soon, he'd have to find someone else. But he liked David. They worked well together. David worked hard and spoke little, a combination that suited Bill's nature. After giving a hard pull to close the door that always stuck on the unleveled floor, he strode toward town and the saloon. If anyone was traveling to the mountain, he would send David a message.

Upon entering the dim room, he immediately grinned. "Slim ain't at all particular about letting any old riffraff in here, is he?" He slapped a wide-shouldered young man on the back. "Michael, you look like life's agreeing with you."

Michael Lane's white teeth flashed in a wide smile as he pushed away from the bar and shook Bill's hand. "It is. I'm footloose, fancy free, and lookin' for a good game. Can I deal you in?"

"Naw." Bill shook his head. "Never learned."

Michael's eyebrows rose. "Sure, you never."

Bill chuckled. "Well, no time for cards today. You wouldn't be heading to the mountain would you?"

"Just so happens I am. Why?"

"I need to get word to a friend of mine, David Hadley. He headed that way to visit Ned and Elijah. If he's still there, would you tell him I've got a big job waiting, exactly the kind he likes, backbreaking hard and not much pay?"

Michael laughed. "If he's there, I'll tell him. Where you living now?"

"Land I inherited from Ma, the old Kelly place, on the Dover road about five miles east of Hagarville."

Michael nodded. "I know the place. Camped there a couple of times, back during the war. Good graze for our horses. You farming?"

"I plan to timber and maybe farm some. You wouldn't be looking for a job?"

Michael hooted. "You know me better than that. I make enough at the card table to keep me happy. Had enough hard work when I was a tadpole. But I'll tell Hadley."

"Thanks."

Michael picked up a dusty hat from the bar, put it on, and strode from the saloon. Bill's eyes followed him. He recalled when Michael was a hard worker. Michael's pa had been about as footloose as they come. He hadn't worked enough to keep the family fed before he met his death from a Yankee bayonet at Wilson's Creek. Michael had taken up the slack back then, but now like his pa, he shied from manual labor like a wild horse from a lariat. Bill supposed the apple hadn't fallen far from the tree after-all.

Then he shook his head. He'd never given the expression much thought until learning his true lineage. Now it set his teeth on edge.

He spent the rest of the day shopping for a mill. He rode for miles to check on the leads he'd been given in town. Finally late in the day he found just what he wanted, a small mill complete with steam engine, and the owner was in the mood to sell. His sons had gone to work for the railroad and left him to run the operation alone. The price, however, was far more than Bill had intended to pay. When the owner refused to budge, he shrugged off a twinge of apprehension and agreed to the full price. He'd have to go careful and hope for no more unexpected expenses.

Bill returned to town, hitched his four-mule team to the freight wagon, and drove back to disassemble and load the mill. It would take several trips to haul it and the steam engine. He had a good spot selected to assemble the mill, a flat near the creek and handy to the timber.

Even though David arrived the third day, it took days of working every possible minute to build the shed and assemble the mill. David worked hard and steady, but he seemed subdued and quieter than usual. While they worked Bill did most of the talking.

"You ever cut timber?"

"I used to cut and sell firewood in town to make a little cash." David shrugged. "But not any big timber."

Bill frowned. "I helped Pa timber a big tract, and let me tell you, this kind of timbering is as dangerous as a cocked gun. There's about as much likelihood of getting killed timbering as there was in fighting in Van Dorn's army. You have to keep your wits about you every minute and not let your guard down for a second. A tree can fall wrong or kick back from the butt and smash you. Then there's the times a falling tree catches in the top of another tree or twists on the stump or a limb falls out and hits you in the head. Like I said, you got to keep your eyes open every minute." He suddenly stopped to give David a hard look.

"Did you hear a word I said?"

David blinked and looked up, still holding the hammer as still as it had been for the last several minutes.

"I thought not," muttered Bill and began the litany again. He figured David's trip to the cemetery had opened old wounds.

When the mill was finally assembled, Bill ran a critical eye over the operation.

"Without a doubt we need more men." He chewed his jaw. He had already spent too much to hire a full crew, but maybe he could find a man or two willing to take work for the wage he could afford to pay.

Just then Abigail arrived wearing a worn shawl against the frosty morning. She held steaming cups of coffee and she looked flustered.

"Breakfast is going to be a little late this morning. I'm sorry."

Bill took a cup. "No problem. We'll just work a bit first." When his eyes found hers, she dropped her gaze. "Something wrong?" he asked gently.

She let out a deep breath and looked toward the house and then back at him. "Mr. Anderson threw the biscuits into the fire."

"The old devil," muttered David.

Bill merely said, "Don't worry about cooking more. We'll be fine until dinnertime."

"I'm so sorry," she repeated before walking away.

"I figure that was out of spite for me," said Bill.

"The way that old sonofabitch hates you," said David, "he might just shoot you in the back someday."

"He might try," agreed Bill.

He glanced at the house where Abigail climbed the back steps and entered the kitchen. He suddenly realized it had been a while since he had thought of Cindy. Maybe time did heal all wounds. Whatever the case, he was beginning to feel alive again.

"Let's get the boiler filled and try out this steam engine. You know anything about engines?"

David shook his head.

"Me neither." Bill frowned again. "I helped in a mill a time or two, but I didn't learn much about the engine."

An hour later when they were no closer to getting the engine working, he stood from bending over and rubbed his jaw. After a bit he went to the barn, got his horse, and headed to Hagarville to do something he never thought he would do—ask a Rawlings for help.

Quinton removed a rag, already greasy, from his back pocket, wiped his hands, stuck it back into the pocket, and grinned as Bill offered his thanks.

"Nothing much to it. You'll catch on quick enough." With both men and Jacob leaning in to hear every word, Quinton pointed to the gearbox and gave a short lesson in the most common problems and how to fix them. Then he turned to the boiler. "I figure you know this, but you need to keep watch right here through the sight glass to see the water level—ya gotta make sure the water doesn't fall below this level here. You need one man to keep an eye on the engine and boiler, to always keep that tank filled and ready to pour here into this opening that feeds water to the boiler, someone dependable who'll watch careful and keep you up a good head of steam."

"I could do that," volunteered Jacob with excitement.

Bill smiled and ruffled Jacob's hair. The boy had been his shadow ever since receiving the jackknife. "I'm sure you'd do a great job, but who would help your ma with all the chores?" Jacob's face fell, but he nodded.

Quinton eyed the timber on the far hillside. "You do have prime white oak," he said, "best I've seen in a long while, just right for making whiskey barrel staves. Matter of fact, white oak is the only thing they use for liquor barrels. Like I said before, I'll pay top dollar for it."

Bill nodded. "I plan to have a load for you real soon."

"Glad to hear it." Quinton beamed. "And if you have any more trouble with the engine, just holler."

After Quinton rode away, Bill turned to David. "That seems simple enough. Maybe we can—"

David interrupted. "My mouth fell open when I saw that fellow. You two could almost be twins. He your kin?"

"Yes. You ready to cut some timber?"

David drew on gloves. "Might as well do some hard work and take my mind off my growling belly. I was looking forward to Miss Abigail's biscuits and gravy. How does she put up with that old man?"

Bill glanced at Jacob, who looked humiliated as he stared at the ground. Then he answered, "Don't reckon she has much choice."

On a flat near the mill, the two men pulled steadily back and forth. The long blade bit into a black oak tree, sending sawdust drifting from the cut and a pungent odor into the air. Conversation ceased. The pull and tug of the saw left little wind for talking.

When the cut was deep enough, Bill took a breather while David used a hammer to drive a steel wedge into the opening to keep the weight from binding the saw.

Bill's eyes lifted to the ridges. He wanted to cut the smaller timber near the mill before moving to the stands of giant white oaks growing tall and stately on the ridges. The flats had been timbered before. He suspected this area had originally been cleared for fields, the timber likely being used to build the first barns and cabin; perhaps even the lumber for the present house had come from here. Whatever the case, the trees were fair sized now, large enough for crossties and lumber. He reached for the saw handle again and began to pull.

Jacob had been watching the process, but staying far enough away to be safe. Now he stepped up. "Can I try?"

Bill relinquished the handle. David grinned, pulled hard, and then waited while Jacob, with gritted teeth, tugged. At first the saw barely moved. Slowly but surely the blade slid just a little, and then as he pulled with all his might, it moved toward him.

After three more cuts, back and forth, Jacob drew in a shaky breath. "This is harder than it looks."

"For a fact," agreed Bill. "I've got my wind back. Think I can take over now," he said with a twinkle in his eyes.

"That was fun, though," said Jacob. "Maybe I can help you some?"

"If you do what I tell you, and stay back unless I say otherwise."

"Yes, sir, I will!" His dark eyes glowed with a happy light Bill had not seen in them before.

As he stepped away, David said, "Hey Jake, you did real good."

Jacob flashed an even bigger smile.

When enough trees had been felled, trimmed, and cut into lengths ready to skid, they cinched each log with chains and hooked the chains to the doubletree behind the mules. The animals had pulled such loads before. Bill had trained them with voice commands, so when he spoke, they immediately began pulling. He had to be careful not to overload them, and yet it was still slow going. Bill frowned. Everything had been slow going today, especially with only two men. He determined to hunt for a crew right away. It was too late in the day to do much milling. Besides, there wasn't enough time to get up steam in the boiler. He'd have to get up way before daylight to do that.

David stretched, putting his arms up high to work kinks from his back. "I've been dreaming of Miss Abigail's biscuits all day. You think it's about time to go see if she has some ready?"

Bill grinned and began pulling off gloves.

David lowered his voice so Jacob wouldn't hear, "If that old devil threw them into the fire again, I just might kill him."

Talbert had not thrown the biscuits into the fire, for in the center of the table sat a plate mounded with them. Nearby sat a bowl of chicken and dumplings swimming in white gravy alongside another bowl full of plump yellow hominy, and on the small work table drawn near the stove sat an apple pie, browned and steaming, with five slits in the crust, just the way Granny had always made them.

The tantalizing aroma set Bill's mouth watering. "I'd call this a feast," he said, wondering if she had butchered one of the hens from her small flock that would have been better kept for laying but sacrificed because she was trying to make up for the lack of breakfast.

Abigail rose, laid down the fabric she was stitching, the plaid material he had brought from town, and hurried to fill two plates. She smiled. Evening sun slating through the kitchen window painted auburn highlights into her dark, heavy hair. "I hope it's to your liking."

Talbert solved the mystery. "Damn waste. That's what it is! Hussy traded a whole day's work for a chicken." He shot her a surly look. "You should a' took the cash."

"So you could spend it on liquor?" asked Bill in a tone with no evident malice, but the malice was there, under the surface and plain for Talbert to see before he stomped to his chair.

When both men were seated, Bill motioned for Abigail to sit. "Abigail, sit down."

"Oh, I'm not hungry—"

"I want to talk a little business with you."

Immediately she sat down, her eyebrows question marks.

"I need to hire at least a couple more hands. Would you be willing to cook for more?" He went on before she could answer. "I won't hear to it unless you'll take pay. That's only fair."

She slowly considered. "I wouldn't want Jacob exposed to the wrong sort of men," she said hesitantly.

"I don't want that sort working for me, either. Rest assured, if I hire them, they'll be the kind you won't mind the boy being around."

"Then I'll do it," she finally inserted over Talbert's loud protests, "and I can do their laundry too."

Bill shook his head. "Not unless they agree to pay you a fair wage. You can work that out with them if they choose to board here."

"Board here?" She looked perplexed. "Where would they stay?"

"When I fixed up the shack, I built a couple of extra bunks on the wall. I'll ask around here first to see if anyone is interested, and if not I'll ride into town and see if I can find any takers."

She poured him another cup of coffee. Conversation died as he worked to catch up with David devouring the delicious chicken and dumplings.

A few days later Bill drew the wagon to a stop. He had forgotten it was Election Day—or what should have been Election Day. According to the disgruntled crowd gathered in the saloon, there had been no polls open in Spadra Township or in most outlying townships, although the rumor was a few had been open.

Bill frowned. Today he was less interested in politics and more interested in hiring a few hands. His eyes scanned the street, but seeing no likely candidates, he headed for Swagerty's store but stopped just outside the saloon when he saw a lean young man with straight, sandy colored hair leaning against the building and petting the head of a mottled brown and black mountain cur. Bill had seen him sweeping up in the saloon. His name was Tobias McKennon, and his father, one of John Hill's men, had died at the Battle of Pea Ridge. Tobias was about twenty and had a misshapen hand and a decided limp.

The limp and the hand wouldn't interfere with him being the tender. He didn't need both hands to keep check on the gauges or to add wood, but he must be trustworthy. Quinton had warned the tender must be a cautious man.

Before offering the job, Bill would ask around about his character.

"Tobias, are you interested in a job?" Bill asked. The way the young man's face lit, Bill knew the answer even before Tobias spoke.

"Yes, sir! I surely am!"

As soon as Bill shared the details, Tobias quickly agreed to grab his gear and meet him at Swagerty's store in an hour.

Before Tobias limped away, he said, "I sure do thank you for the chance, sir. No one but Slim will hire me because of the hand and all. But I'm a hard worker and I'm smart. I'll do you a good and careful job. You can count on that." As he shook Bill's hand, he added, "By the way, Mr. Tanner, my friends call me Toby."

"And mine call me Bill."

Bill's remark was met with an ear-to-ear grin and a bright sparkle in the clear brown eyes.

Bill walked on. He had not stepped inside the store before noticing two of the Wallace boys, Sid's younger brothers, leaning against the hitching rail. Bill had known the family for years. They were good, salt-of-the-earth people.

"Howdy, boys."

"Mr. Tanner." They nodded respectfully.

Like Sid, they were fine looking, both with the bright blue eyes and dark hair characteristic of the Wallaces. They were young, still in their teens, but they looked strong. If they were anything like their brothers Sid and

George, they were hard workers.

"You fellows interested in a job?"

"What kind of job?" asked the tallest.

"Skidding timber and saw milling. Backbreaking labor, so don't take the job if you won't work. I'll board you and pay cash wages. I'll tell you up front the pay won't be high and the room is just a shed with bunks on the wall. But the lady who cooks does a fine job, so you'll eat good."

The tallest faced his brother. "You game?"

He shrugged. "It's not any harder than farming. And we never see a penny for that. Do you reckon Sid will let us?"

"He will if Ma says so. She just might since there's not much farm work just now." He faced Bill. "Yes, sir, we'll come if Ma and Sid say yes."

"Good!" said Bill.

"When do you want us?"

"Today."

The boys looked at each other, grinned broadly, pulled reins from the hitching rail, and mounted. "We'll be back real quick and let you know."

Through dust rising from the loping horses' hooves, Bill called after them, "If you're coming, bring your bedrolls."

While he waited, Bill strode into the store. Swagerty was nowhere in sight, but the lady clerk hurried forward.

"How did the curtains turn out?"

He blinked, racking his brain to recall if Abigail had hung them yet. She must not have finished making them. He thought he would have noticed—then again, his mind had been on other things.

"Don't think they're all sewed yet," he hedged.

With a twinkle in merry brown eyes, she persisted, "Well, did the seamstress like the plaid?"

"Yes, ma'am, she did. As I recall she said it was perfect."

"Wonderful. And what may I help you with today?"

He ordered a large bill of groceries. The Wallaces were only overgrown boys, but he figured they would eat like men; and David ate more than average. Just as the last of the groceries were boxed and ready to load into the wagon, the boys stepped through the door. Upon spying the lady clerk, both swept off hats. The older—Bill thought his name was Matt—grew red to the roots of his hair.

"How do, Miss Lena," he said, growing even redder.

"I'm very well, Mr. Wallace. And you?"

He managed to mumble a response.

Tom, not reticent at all, hurried toward Bill. "We can work for you, Mr. Tanner. We brought our bedrolls and gear."

"Good." Bill, his arms filled, nodded to the other boxes still sitting on the counter. "Grab that other stuff and let's head out. It's a long ride."

Matt followed Tom to the counter, but his eyes hardly left Lena's heart-shaped face. He hesitated at the door, stopped, turned, and finally managed to blurt out, "You going to the dance next Saturday?"

"I might," she said.

Matt's mouth opened and closed, but nothing came out. Finally, he fled outside.

"Ya dang fool!" scolded Tom. "Why didn't you ask her?" He turned to Bill and added with disgust, "We stood outside the store half the morning while he tried to get up nerve to ask her to the dance." He looked back at Matt. "You looked like a dang catfish—your mouth just opened and closed and opened and closed." He made the motions with his own mouth.

Matt groaned. Then without a word he climbed on his horse and hurried away. He was, however, waiting for them when they crossed the bridge, and he fell into line alongside Tom's horse and the wagon holding Bill and Toby and Toby's cur dog.

Bill was pleased to learn the Wallace boys had helped a little in their uncle's sawmill. It was comforting to know they had some experience.

It was dark before they arrived. Lamp glow shone through the windows and lay in patches on the yard where wood smoke and the appetizing scent of supper wafted on the chill air. David stepped from the shed and crossed the yard.

"You made good time," he observed, and then noticed the new crew dismounting. "Howdy, Tom. Matt." He shook their hands and then slapped Toby on the back. "Hey Toby, good to see you. Glad to have you boys. We need all the help we can get." Then he turned to Bill. "I got the fire going and banked in the boiler, so everything's ready to go in the morning. Miss Abigail has supper waiting. She's cooked enough for an army."

Jacob came outside and knelt in front of the dog. "What's his name?"

Toby shrugged. "I just call him dog. He ain't mine—he just sort of took up with me when I started giving him the scraps left over from the free lunch at the saloon."

"Care if I call him Little Bear?"

"Fine with me," said Toby. "Like I said, he ain't mine."

Jacob rubbed the dog's head. "Hello, Little Bear." While the dog wiggled all over, Jacob glanced up at Bill. "He's sort of colored up like the bear I saw a few days ago, except he's more striped."

"That's called brindle," said Bill. "You might want Little Bear along if you ever go hunting that bear. Mountain curs make great bear dogs—good hog dogs, too."

Bill was up by four thirty. The tender must be up early to get things ready, so he shook Toby's shoulder and was pleased that he came instantly awake and rose immediately without grumbling. The cur also rose from the floor alongside Toby's bunk, stretched, wagged his tail, and followed outside right on Toby's heels.

Toby proved to be a quick learner. He followed Bill's instructions perfectly. The withered left hand barely slowed him as he worked. Soon the water tank was filled to just the right level in the sight glass, the firebox filled with wood, the damper open allowing enough blaze to produce a good head of steam.

Although their breath was a white cloud in the cold, Bill was thankful to see the sun rise in a clear sky. That couldn't last forever. The fall rains had already held off longer than usual. When they came, he could keep felling trees and splitting stave bolts, but skidding logs would stop. The mules would bog down in the mud until the ground froze. Then they could skid logs to his mill and even haul staves to Quinton's.

After a huge breakfast of Abigail's biscuits, gravy, and fried ham, the men were ready to work. Bill lingered a moment after the others stepped outside.

"That was a fine meal, Abigail. I hope it's not too much work to cook for so many."

She stopped scraping a plate, smiled, and shook her head. "Not at all. I enjoy watching all of you eat." She glanced at the closed bedroom door. "Besides, he doesn't rant as much now that cash payment is involved."

Bill's mouth drew down. He had seen the empty jug alongside the chair where the old man had passed out the night before. He wondered how much of Abigail's hard-earned money would go for drink.

"Well, if it gets to be too much for you, let me know."

Her eyes grew soft. "Thank you, but I'm sure I can handle it." She followed him to the door, and after glancing at Jacob, who was finishing his breakfast, she lowered her voice. "I told Jacob to stay away from your work. I hope he's obeying."

Bill gave her a steady look. "It would do him good to learn by watching, and even helping a bit when he can. I'll make sure he doesn't do anything dangerous."

She looked at the boy and then dragged her eyes away. "He's all I have."

"All the more reason to let him learn to be a man."

Although doubt raked her face, she nodded. Before exiting the door, he glanced back once to see her frowning as she poured hot water from the teakettle into the dishpan. He wished she smiled more.

Frost lay silver on dead grass in the yard and iced the colored leaves strewn on the ground. The jacket felt good now but would likely come off as soon as he began working. Today they would work at the mill. He and David had skidded a fair amount of timber already. Besides, he was anxious to see the mill operate, and he would not leave that task to the young men without supervision. They were pulling on gloves when he arrived.

"Toby, the steam up?"

"Ready to go, sir."

"Think you can keep a close eye on the gauges and help carry off lumber too?"

"Sure."

"Can I help too?" asked Jacob, his eyes eager.

"As long as you don't neglect the chores your ma gives you, you can help Toby carry lumber to the stack."

"Yes, sir!" Jacob's face beamed.

"Matt, you roll. David, you run the edger, and Tom and Toby and Jacob can off-bear."

Jacob's face grew serious. "Sir, I'd like to be called Jake from now on—at least when Ma's not around."

Bill nodded. "Jake it is."

The boy flashed him a big smile.

Matt picked up a cant hook and rolled a log onto the carriage. Then he set the log-dogs, hooks that held the logs in place. The sawyer required the most skill. Bill didn't have much experience, but he had helped saw a time or two, enough to know how difficult it was. A good sawyer knew just how to get the most from every log, a skill that developed only with practice and a good eye.

With the throb of the engine and a deep sense of satisfaction, Bill stood on the ground alongside the carriage that was a system of sliding rails. He pulled the lever. The log moved forward. The whine of the blade intensified as it bit into wood and took the first slice from the log. The slab sliced off like soft butter. At the same time a sprocket chain carried the sawdust away to dump it outside to begin a sawdust pile. Toby, using his good hand, carried the slab away to start a slab pile. The carriage slid back. The process began again. This time David fed the board into another blade that sliced off the edge covered with bark. While Jacob carried it away, Tom took the finished board and began a lumber pile.

David spoke loud over the chug of the engine and whine of the saw. "Good as apple pie, ain't it?"

Bill grinned and glanced around. Mill noise prevented conversation, but all the men wore pleased expressions. The emotion gripping Bill surprised him. It was good, good to see his own timber from his own land running through his own mill. It was a heady thing, knowing with enough sweat and hard work he could take a tree from the land and turn it into lumber. He drew a deep breath, letting it out slowly with a sense of satisfaction. He knew there would be troubles and trials aplenty. Along with being the owner and boss, that was the way of business. For now he basked in pure exhilaration and the sense of accomplishment.

He called above the noise, "Jake, you're doing real good, but you best go help your ma now. She probably needs you." He didn't want to push the limits of Abigail's unenthusiastic permission to let the boy join them today.

Jacob left the shed, but he looked back with reluctance before running toward the house. Bill grinned to see the cur chasing at his heels. Clearly the dog had left off being Toby's shadow and now preferred the boy. It was small wonder. Jacob had loved the animal at first sight, and Bill suspected the added weight the animal now carried was mainly due to food gone missing from Jacob's plate.

As the lumber stack grew, Bill felt confident enough to attempt a crosstie. The first attempts did not turn out well; however, he finally had a perfect nine-by-seven tie, eight and a half feet long. Tom, with a broad grin, started a separate pile for ties.

Long before noon, Bill had shed the jacket and even worked up a sweat. Without returning to the house, they ate a cold dinner of biscuits and ham and washed it down with water. He didn't suppose the sawyer job looked very strenuous to the men wresting the logs, but by day's end he was exhausted and more than ready to stop milling for the day. Looking at the piles of lumber and ties, he was satisfied. They had done well...at least for a green crew. By week's end they were much more efficient and had a sizable pile of ties as well as a big stack of lumber. Bill looked ruefully at his work gloves. After all the crosscut sawing and milling, they were full of holes, and his hands were beginning to blister. He would have to buy more when he went to town.

❈❈❈

Bill had shut down the mill early this Saturday. Now he chuckled, watching Matt slick down his hair in the cracked mirror hanging on the shed wall. "I don't think a girl ever took any more pains getting ready for a dance," he teased.

Matt's face reddened. He was saved an answer when Tom put in, "Aw, with a ugly snout like Matt's, he has to try hard. I told him it won't do any good, though—Miss Lena isn't about to dance with the likes of him."

Matt's jaw jutted, and yet he still looked crestfallen. "She might," he said, sounding doubtful. "She for sure won't be dancing with the likes of you, Tom Wallace. You're hardly out of short britches."

Tom laughed good-naturedly. "Fine with me. I have my eye on Ida May Reed. She's pretty as a spotted pup, and I'm pretty sure she likes me, too."

Matt gave his hair one last pat and then both boys left, heading for town on their horses.

Bill, with sweaty hands and feeling as young and awkward as Matt Wallace, headed for the house. He had done a fair amount of primping himself. There was a nick on his freshly shaved jaw to prove it. He brushed a bit of lint from his best black pants and straightened the string tie around his neck.

Abigail answered the first soft rap on the door. In spite of trying not to show disappointment, his face fell. She still wore a work dress and a soiled apron.

"So you decided not to go," he said. He thought they had worked through all her objections, even the idea of where she and Jacob would spend the night. He had assured her that his cousin Carrie Hackett would be thrilled with their company. She was lonely since her husband Roy died and her boy had married and moved away. Bill planned to bed down in Carrie's barn.

Jacob sat at the table looking dejected. He had talked of little else except the trip to town ever since Bill had suggested the idea.

Abigail looked down. Then her head rose as she said, "I should have told you when you first asked. I knew we couldn't go."

"I know you said you don't believe in dancing. But I thought you might just like a trip to town."

"My clothing isn't fit for town," she admitted. Her cheeks crimsoned, making the scar on her cheek even starker. "But thank you so much for asking."

Bill felt like kicking himself. He should have known she had nothing fit to wear. He'd never seen her in anything that wasn't threadbare. Jacob's clothes were better. He figured Abigail had sacrificed to see to that. If only he'd bought her some dress goods along with the curtain material! Even with the thought came the knowing—she would never have accepted such a gift. He turned abruptly. A snore had risen from the corner of the room. Bill figured Anderson must have polished a jug off early.

Abigail smiled stiffly. In a failed attempt at lightheartedness, she added, "At least he'll sleep all evening. I'll have peace and quiet to read tonight. Matt loaned me a book about gold mining in California."

At a loss for words, he bid her good afternoon. He strode to the barn, where David was busy hitching mules to the wagon.

"I won't be going," he said. "But you and Toby go ahead."

David's brows rose. "Sure you won't come? You're all dressed up, and it'll be lots of fun. It's likely to be the last shindig of the season. Be too cold to travel soon."

"I'm sure."

"Then no need for us taking the wagon. We'll go faster horseback. Can Toby ride one of the mules?"

"Sure."

Bill had no intention of letting Abigail spend her evening reading about gold mining in California. He changed back into work clothes. There was no need to make her any more self-conscious about her ragged dress. While changing he puzzled over how to get her a new dress. He doubted old man Anderson would ever leave enough money to buy one—at least not until the two dresses she owned fell completely apart.

Later that evening he was no closer to a solution as he crossed the yard in a chill breeze to step around the cur lying on the steps. He knocked softly, taking no chances on waking the old man.

When Abigail answered, she held a book. She looked surprised.

"I thought you'd gone to the dance."

"I wasn't in the mood." He pointed at the book. "Hope you don't mind the interruption. It's not too late is it?"

"Oh, not at all. Please, come in. Jacob went to bed, but I've been reading. There's a fire in the stove. It feels good this evening."

He sat down at the pine table and laid down his hat. Then he took the cup of coffee she offered, and taking a sip, studied her over the rim. The lamplight put a soft sheen on her dark hair, reminding him of a well-brushed filly—although he doubted she'd be flattered if he said so. She caught him staring and began to look ill at ease. He'd not visited often after supper, so she must be wondering why he was here. He wasn't exactly sure himself.

"You like to read?" He dipped his head to indicate the book.

"I love to read." She sat down directly across the table.

Her look grew serious. "Did you know Toby can't read?"

"No, but that's not too unusual. Lots of folks around here have never been to school, even the young ones.

Suddenly her eyes lit. "I'm hoping to teach him. He'll have a much better chance finding a job after this one is over. He's smart, and I just know he'll catch on quickly. I want to give you the money to buy a first primer next time you go to town."

"Be glad to—on one condition."

She grew puzzled.

"Only if you ride along and pick out a dress or the dress goods to make one. A teacher needs to look nice."

For an instant, she glanced over at Talbert, hunched over and breathing deeply in the corner. "You have no idea how much I'd love to go, but I don't think I ought to buy—"

He cut her short. "I do. And if you don't buy one, I'm going to, and I'll keep on buying one every time I go to town until I run plumb out of money, so I reckon you better buy one before I go broke."

She shook her head.

"I mean every word," he vowed. "I'm not teasing."

"Please don't—" she said as it dawned how serious he was.

"Nope, my mind is made up. As a matter of fact, I'm riding in tomorrow. Unless you want a bright purple and red striped dress, you better ride along." He remembered Ma and Granny being scandalized when Lizzy Tate wore such a dress. "Besides, unless I'm mistaken, Jacob was mighty disappointed. He's been working hard and deserves a treat."

"I won't accept your gifts."

"I never paid you for making these curtains. I'll pay you so you can ride along and pick out your own dress goods." Then he looked straight into her eyes. "If it's because you don't really trust me, like I said, there's never been a word said against my character. I meant it when I said I will do you and the boy no harm."

She dropped her eyes to her hands clasped tightly together in her lap. "You've been nothing but good to us. Perhaps you can't understand," she began. She raised her eyes. "It isn't you, it's me. I have a hard time trusting."

"That's not necessarily a bad thing," he said slowly. "But all men aren't cut from the same bolt of cloth."

From the flush on her face he knew he had hit a sore spot.

"I'm beginning to see that," she admitted.

"Then come to town."

She propped elbows on the table, put her chin in her hands, and stared at him. "You're stubborn, aren't you?"

"Guilty," he agreed.

She glanced down at her worn cuffs and relented enough to say, "I'll think about it."

He had planned to stay longer, spend the evening getting to know her better, but he had an idea that he was keen to explore. With a last sip of coffee, he drained the cup and picked up his hat. "I'll let you get back to your book. Thanks for the coffee. I sure hope you and Jacob will go. We'll be leaving early, so don't bother cooking a big breakfast. Some of this leftover ham and biscuits will do fine to take along and eat on the way."

He walked toward the tumbledown barn, his shoulders squared with determination. A few days ago, when he had asked her to the dance, he'd been appalled to learn she'd never set foot off this place since the day she and Talbert had arrived from Texas and the broken-down mule had lain down between the traces and died. She deserved a day away, for certain. His mind spun with ideas to make tomorrow special. Although he would enjoy every second of sitting alongside her on a wagon seat, his idea would hopefully make the travel time shorter so she would have more time to shop and enjoy town. His fast-gaited walking horse made the trip in a couple of hours, but mules pulling the wagon would take twice as long. If he could repair the old buggy in the barn, the trip wouldn't take nearly as long as in the wagon. The black had pulled a buggy before. He had once belonged to a lady.

Chapter 4

Abigail watched until Bill's wide shoulders were no longer visible in moonlight. She liked it when he occasionally stopped by the house in the evenings after supper. He was a quiet man, saying little; nonetheless, she enjoyed his presence. She was beginning to believe he was truly a good man. She let out a deep breath and then shook her head. It was no use. She couldn't go. Mr. Anderson would be worse than the devil himself. Even if they left before he awakened, no telling what he'd do when he found out. Even so her mind rebelled as she looked down at the threadbare dress and caught her bottom lip in her teeth. She was almost naked. This dress wouldn't stand many more washings without turning to shreds, and the other one hanging on a nail in her bedroom was almost as bad. Her eyes lifted in the direction Bill had gone. *Would he actually buy a dress?*

"I wouldn't put it past him," she whispered. She smiled, softly closed the door, and instead of sitting down to read, she blew out the lamp and went to bed. Sometime during the night she heard Jacob's voice.

"Grandpa, it's cold in here. You ought to get in bed."

"You're a good boy," said Talbert as he stumbled off to bed. He would be extra surly in the morning for he had drunk his last jug, and undoubtedly he would want money to be off to town to get more.

76

It was still dark outside when she jerked awake and struck a match. In the flickering light, the clock hands read five o'clock. She had gone to sleep late and, after much tossing and turning, determined it would be too foolhardy to go. This morning she felt invigorated and, yes, brave. In the darkness she slipped out of the nightdress, felt her way into the clean dress, and tiptoed into the front room to light the lamp and call softly into the loft.

"Jacob, get up!"

After the second call, his tousled black hair appeared at the opening where he looked down with sleep-glazed eyes.

"Get dressed, sleepyhead. We're going to town."

His eyes widened, as did his quick smile.

She spoke low again while pulling on stockings and shoes. "Be quiet. We don't want to wake your grandpa."

While lacing the high-top shoes, she frowned at the worn stockings and scuffed toes of the boots. Perhaps with plenty of shoe blacking they wouldn't look too bad, and perhaps they would last another few months before the thin soles wore through. She set about polishing them and then on cat's paws went into her bedroom and retrieved the small stash of cash from the hiding place. Even though Mr. Anderson had torn the house apart more than once, he'd never found the money hidden in the tea canister.

Her heart raced at what she was about to do—she was going to town. And she was going with Bill Tanner. She felt certain he would be a gentleman. If not for that certainty, she wouldn't climb onto the wagon seat.

She had gathered a quick picnic of leftovers and put them into a basket when she heard a soft rap on the door. Without a backward look, she gathered the basket, her long cloak, and drawstring purse, and stepped outside right behind Jacob.

"Good morning." Bill's eyes twinkled in the early morning light. He reached for the basket. "I'll stow this behind the seat until we're ready to eat."

"It's just the leftovers. I didn't even make coffee," she said.

"We'll get some at the cafe in town," he said, "and it'll taste all the better for the wait."

"Where in the world?" she asked after spying the buggy.

He chuckled. "I found it under some junk in the barn and decided to fix it up last night. I couldn't do much with the ragged top, but I fixed the broken shaft. The seat cushion is a mess. I stuffed it with hay and threw a blanket over it. And I greased all the wheels and tightened up everything the best I could. It's no chariot, but I figure it'll get us to town and back."

"It's wonderful," she said and meant it. A buggy jolted some, but it didn't jolt like a wagon seat.

"Jake, you better put Little Bear in the shed or he'll follow us. He'll be fine in there till we get home."

Jacob hurried to shut the reluctant dog inside the shed while Abigail took Bill's hand and climbed onto the front seat. Jacob soon hopped onto the backseat just as a rooster crowed and the sun topped the far horizon to glimmer on morning mists rising from the brushy fields. Abigail eyed the sky with concern. Not a cloud marred the transparent blue. With a happy sigh she leaned back while Bill rounded the buggy to climb inside. She had little concern that Talbert would wake. He was a late sleeper; however, she didn't truly relax until the house disappeared from sight.

For a while she and Bill rode in companionable silence while Jacob, excited to actually be going, chatted away. When Bill yawned she said, "You must have worked on this buggy all night."

"I did get to bed a bit late," he admitted.

That had been a sacrifice for her comfort. The knowing made her smile. "It certainly rides better than a wagon seat," she said and was rewarded by a big smile before he grew serious.

"You deserve some comfort. You work too hard." He fiddled with the reins held loosely in his hands. "I feel real bad about saddling you with all the extra cooking and washing for me and my hands."

Before he could say more, she stopped him. "I thoroughly enjoy it. You don't realize what a blessing it is to have someone besides Talbert to talk to—people who are decent."

The furrows on his brow eased. "Well, I hope you'll enjoy this trip, too."

She gave a happy little laugh. "I'm already enjoying it."

"Good," he said and then flicked the reins. "Get up there, horse. There's a lady here who needs to do some shopping."

Abigail sat up straighter in the seat. She had forgotten there were so many people in the world. Clarksville was crowded with horses, wagons, and scores of people, a few ladies in dresses with puffed bustles behind and wide ruffles at the wrists. Some wore dresses with lines as simple as her own, but none were as threadbare as her bedraggled calico. She felt terribly self-conscious and reached for the cloak she had shed when the day had warmed to a pleasant temperature. At least the cloak wasn't quite as shiny thin as the dress. She put a hand to her cheek. If only there was some way to cover the scar. People always stared.

"What the—" Bill suddenly pulled the buggy to a stop, handed her the reins, and jumped down.

On the sidewalk Tom Wallace, fists tightened, faced a man who was years his senior and twice his size.

"Turner, that's not true. Sid never shot Dickey. Dub made up that dirty lie because he doesn't like Sid."

"You calling me a liar, boy?"

Tom swung. Turner's huge fists slashed, knocking Tom to the ground. The man stood over Tom, sneering. "I reckon you Wallaces is all alike. Can't fight without a gun and only then from behind a mask er a bush."

Tom came up swinging. Bill stepped up and caught his arms.

"Whoa, Tom." While holding back a struggling Tom, he glared at Turner, who stood with fists raised. "That's enough. He's just defending his family's honor."

The man snorted. "Wallaces got no honor. Dub Turner is my kin, and I say he ain't no liar."

Bill's jaws hardened. "No honor? Well, I say no honor is picking a fight with a boy."

The man's lips curled, but he dropped his fists, whirled, and began walking away. Just then Matt and Toby exited the store and with them a tall, young man, a handsome, older version of Matt. The young man pinned Turner with a cold stare. The look in his icy blue eyes sent a tremor down Abigail's spine. She had never seen such pure, unveiled hate.

Bill had seen the look, too. "Sid, he's not worth the powder it would take to blow him away. Don't let him get under your skin. No one listens to him."

Sid pulled his gaze back, handed Tom a handkerchief to hold on the bloodied nose, and said, "The boys tell me they love working for you."

Abigail blinked at the sudden shift in conversation. When Bill met Sid's remark with silence, she read meaning into the long, steady look they exchanged.

"I mean it, Sid. He's not worth it." Then Bill also changed the subject. "They're hard workers. I'm glad to have 'em."

Abruptly, Bill walked over, hitched the black to the rail in front of the store, and then reached a hand to help Abigail alight, leading her past the knot of men gathered around and talking low to Tom. It sounded as though the older brother was scolding him. Jacob, big-eyed, jumped down and followed them into the store.

Once inside, Bill led her toward the table piled with colorful bolts of cloth. A young woman joined them.

"Hello." She smiled brightly. "May I help you?" she asked while cutting pretty brown eyes at Bill. "I don't suppose you're after curtain fabric?"

Abigail joined in the good-natured laughter and then said, "I need dress fabric, and a McGuffey's First Reader," she said.

"We have a lovely selection. Look it over, and when you've chosen something, just call me and I'll cut it for you. And I'll go get that reader and have it waiting for you on the counter." She held out her hand. "By the way, my name is Lena."

Abigail shook hands, warmed by the friendly smile.

"I have a few other stops to make," said Bill, so take your time. I'll be back in a bit."

While Jacob headed for the section featuring guns and knives, Abigail turned her attention to the mountain of fabric. How could she ever choose? It was not all tasteful, but there were enough beautiful patterns to make the decision difficult. She gave a silent chuckle. *And not a red and purple stripe among them.*

Practicality won. She finally chose plain brown cotton. It would fade less and be more serviceable than the pretty brightly-colored patterns. It wouldn't do for a dance, but she wouldn't be going to dances anyway. With an inward sigh she placed the satiny navy blue with a tiny silver thread running throughout back onto the table, handed Lena the brown fabric as well as some white muslin for undergarments, and after giving instructions on yardage, wandered away to browse the dry goods: men's and women's ready-to-wear—dresses, trousers, shirts, cloaks, chaps, hats, and shoes and boots of all sizes. She lingered a moment to run a hand along the glossy toe of a particularly smart pair, women's dress boots with glass beads in the center of each button. If she saved hard, someday she might own such a pair.

She came upon Matt leaning against a shelf in the boot section, but his attention was not on boots. He looked past the shelves, toward the front of the store.

"Hello, Matt. Did you have fun at the dance?"

"It was wonderful, Miss Abigail." While his eyes sought the young woman who had shown her the yard goods, his face took on a rapturous look.

"Did you dance with anyone special?" she asked, and her eyes danced with mischief. She had heard Tom teasing him about a young woman who worked in town.

His face reddened, but after giving a wink, he admitted with manly aplomb, "I sure did. Miss Lena gave me five dances, more than she gave anyone else."

Abigail chuckled and walked on, leaving him to his daydreams as he stole another look through the shelves at Lena, who was helping another customer.

Then Abigail wandered into the housewares department to find washtubs, rub boards, pots, pans, shiny black stoves, and lengths of stovepipe. Nearer the front of the store, the shelves groaned with groceries, canned goods, and hoops of golden cheeses, and on the floor, barrels of vinegar, pickles, crackers, sugar, flour, and cornmeal. From hooks on the wall dangled varieties of saddles, harnesses, spurs, bits, and bridles. No wonder the store's odor was impossible to identify. It was a heady mixture of spice and leather and metal and cloth. She could hardly imagine such riches all in one place. The storeowner must be a prosperous man to stock such variety.

When she finally heard Bill's voice, she slowly made her way to the front where Bill's purchases were already stacked on the counter. The man behind the counter pointed to a newspaper in Bill's hand.

"I know for a fact the article is true, but it would look more valid if he'd signed his name."

Bill's eyebrows rose in agreement. "True, Major, but it wouldn't be healthy. These are serious allegations—serious enough to cause gunplay."

"They certainly are." The major's face hardened with indignation. "What they did was serious enough to land them in jail or at least get them thrown out of office if there's an investigation."

"Knowing who's in charge now, do you honestly think anyone will investigate an election in Arkansas, let alone one in Johnson County?"

The major grew crestfallen. "Probably not. But Cravens and a few others have some connections in Washington City. They're writing letters, hoping to shed light on this mess." He perked up a bit. "Since Baxter won the governorship by less than three thousand votes, they're saying Brooks is going to contest the election. Who knows, there might be an investigation."

Bill shrugged. "Far as I can tell it doesn't matter much if we end up with Minstrels or Brindletails—they're all either scalawags or carpetbaggers with their hands in our pockets."

"You're right about that," the major agreed. "If I recollect right, the tax rate before the war was never more than six mills, and now it's more than forty. Damn shame when a man has to decide if he'll eat or pay his taxes. I've got all this stock in my store and folks can't pay. Most of them want credit."

A new customer entered and the major hurried off. Abigail stepped up and looked at the paper. It was a copy of the Gazette, a Little Rock newspaper, dated three days earlier.

"Trouble?"

"Just an article reporting shenanigans in the last election," he said, folding the paper and putting it under his arm. "I doubt anything will come of it. Did you find what you wanted?" He frowned when he saw the brown cloth. "You sure that's what you want?"

"I'm sure," she said before turning back. "I'll be right back. I forgot thread and buttons."

When she was done, he carried the packages outside and helped her into the buggy. "Would you like to eat at the cafe before heading back?"

"I'd love to."

He placed the packages behind the seat and laid the newspaper on top. Before climbing in, he said, "Jacob, want to come with me? I forgot something."

While they were gone, she picked up the newspaper and scanned the front page. She was surprised to find an article titled *Johnson County*. It was a long one. As she read, her brow furrowed. Election officials in the new county of Sarber, just across the river, were accused of moving names of registered voters from Johnson to Sarber, and then voting them without the knowledge of said voters, casting all these votes for Mr. Sarber, the man the county was named after.

"This was done," read the article, "to pander to the corruptions of Sarber, who wants to be returned to the legislature at all hazards. And after dark at Anderson, the county seat of Sarber, three colored men voted—persons who were here in Clarksville, the whole of Tuesday and Tuesday night: yet Anderson is about twenty miles from here over the Arkansas River. We are informed that those who voted there were disguised and were supposed to be white men." Other angry citizens whose names had been thus manipulated were demanding to know how they could have voted in Sarber when they had never left Johnson. The article went on to state that the officials in the Johnson County clerk's office were complicit in the whole affair.

Abigail read on. Apparently, there were many such contested elections in Arkansas this year, including a hot dispute between Thomas Gunter, a former colonel in the Confederacy, and William Wilshire, the Republican candidate, both vying for a seat in Congress to represent the district that included Johnson County. Wilshire won, but according to many, it was by the same fraudulent means. Even the governor's race was called into question. The article said because of ballot tampering Elisha Baxter would sit in the governor's seat, but Joseph Brooks was the legitimate winner.

Abigail jumped when Bill spoke.

"You interested in politics?"

"Actually, I am," she said. "In school I loved studying about how the government works. I had a wonderful teacher who encouraged us to debate. We debated current affairs every Friday. It was my favorite part of the week."

He put more packages behind the seat, and while Jacob hopped in the back, he climbed up alongside her and gathered the reins. "I never went to school much," he admitted as he flicked the reins to start the black, "but Ma and Granny taught me at home. Ma was real good at arithmetic and Granny was high on the Bible, so I learned to read young."

Abigail smiled. She was quiet for a moment and then asked, "What was that all about—that fight between Tom and that man?"

"A few months back a couple of fellows got robbed. One named Dickey, the other named Dud Turner. Dickey got shot. Turner said the robber was Sid Wallace wearing a mask. The Turner I just had words with is Dud's kin. He has it in for Sid for running Dud out of the country."

"I assume Sid is Tom and Matt's brother?"

"Yes," said Bill. "Sid's no angel, but for darn sure he's no robber."

"He has cold eyes," she said, remembering.

Bill shrugged. "He saw too much back when he was a kid. He watched his pa gunned down by Yankee soldiers—or it could have been bushwhackers dressed like soldiers. Guess that might turn a fellow's eyes cold." He guided the horse into the street. "Enough sad stuff. You enjoying your trip so far?—aside from that little ruckus back there?"

She smiled. "Very much. And that store! I'd forgotten what a lot there is to choose from!"

"You need to come to town more often."

She gave a little laugh. She didn't argue, but she knew the price she would pay in Talbert's mood was not one she would want to pay often.

The meal at the cafe was a rare treat. It had been ages since she had eaten any cooking but her own. The steak was juicy and tender and the potatoes seasoned and fried just right; the biscuits were not as good as her recipe, but they were eatable. She was in no hurry to leave as they lingered over coffee and sugary cinnamon yeast bread.

Jacob was enjoying this as much as she was. His jaws were stuffed beyond good manners. She must remember to scold him later. For now she would just let him enjoy the meal.

"I hate to rush you," Bill said. "But I don't like those clouds rolling in, and from the looks of all those snowbirds feeding on the courthouse lawn, we might be in for some nasty weather."

She wiped her mouth on the napkin and stood immediately, a frown creasing her brow as she looked out the window at the sky. It was growing darker as gray clouds obscured the sun that had been shining brightly the last time she'd noticed. And by the time the buggy crossed the bridge and pulled the steep hill heading away from town, the wind nipping at the hood of her cloak had sharp teeth. Even Jacob ceased chattering about the marvels of the day as it grew colder a few miles farther on when the road turned and the horse faced into the wind. Abigail was glad he had worn his heavy coat. She could not control the shiver that persisted even though she ducked deeper into the cloak and pulled it tighter around her trembling shoulders. Bill glanced over with worried eyes.

He began pulling off his coat. "Here, take this."

"Certainly not," she said. "You'll freeze without your coat. I'm fine."

Nonetheless he stopped the buggy and held out the coat. "I'm not moving until you put this on, so you may as well do it."

"Please don't do this," she pleaded, and as the anguish in her eyes seemed to make him waver, she pushed her point. "You'll get sick and then I'll blame myself. Here," she said, pulling at the blanket that covered the ragged, straw-filled seat, "I'll wrap this around me."

He looked grim but complied by rising to pull the wool blanket from under them and bundling her in it like an Indian squaw. She smiled.

"Ah, that's much better. Honestly, I'm fine now." The blanket did feel wonderful, in spite of the musty smell.

He pulled the coat on again, but the pucker on his brow remained. "I could kick myself for not bringing more blankets," he muttered, studying the sky again. "Maybe we ought to turn back. Those clouds don't look promising. You could stay with my cousin until this weather passes. Like I said, Carrie would be glad to put you up."

"I'd rather go on. There's no telling how long it will be before this blows over, and we both have work waiting. I'm not so fragile that I can't take a little wet and cold. Besides, we'll be home in a couple of hours."

He finally relented and then urged the horse toward home at an even faster pace. At that pace, after a while, the wind penetrated even the woolen folds to chill her body. For fear he would insist she take the coat, she held shivers in check with steel determination until her teeth hurt from trying to bite down the chattering, while being thankful he didn't seem inclined to talk. She could not carry on a conversation.

The miles seemed to last forever, and yet by the horses' fast pace she knew they made good time. All she could think about was a warm stove and a cup of something hot. She preferred tea to coffee, but just now anything warm would be heaven. Bill interrupted her reverie.

"Hagarville is just ahead. We're going to stop at the blacksmith's shop for a bit to let you both warm up."

She nodded, grateful for a reprieve from the sharp gale. While holding the blanket, her hands had grown numb and blue. When he finally drew to a stop outside a small building and reached a hand to assist her, she could hardly step down, and when they stepped inside, the warmth actually felt painful to her throbbing face and hands.

XXX

Abigail gasped. Her eyes darted from Bill to Quinton and back again. As Bill made the introduction, her eyes asked a question although she didn't voice it.

"Ma'am, you look plumb froze," said Quinton. He quickly stoked up the fire in a potbellied stove in the rear of the shop and then pulled a chair near. "Sit here and you and the boy can warm them blue hands. Here's some coffee to help warm ya too."

He poured a generous amount into big mugs. She murmured her thanks and sipped it while Bill and Quinton talked.

"Thanks, Quinton. It was fair when we left this morning. Like an idiot, I forgot how fast Arkansas weather can change, especially in November."

Bill looked concerned at Abigail gripping the mug and shivering violently as warmth stole slowly into her body. Quinton also eyed her with concern.

"She's about done in, ain't she? I got some extra lap robes I'll loan you for the rest of the trip—they're fur, nothing warmer." Then he abruptly changed the subject. "What's the news in town?"

Bill related the squabble over the election. Abigail sensed he did so with caution as if he were testing hot water. Perhaps he didn't know this man's politics. But surely they knew each other well—at least they looked enough alike to be twins. "That election was a pure sham," said Quinton. "It was all rigged to begin with. I tried to register. Never even got close to the door."

Bill visibly relaxed "Me either," he said, and the two men began a friendly political discussion that Abigail feared would last too long. She dreaded returning to the cold; nevertheless, afternoon was ebbing quickly. Light faded early in November. Talbert's wrath would be horrible if she arrived home in daylight and unthinkable if she arrived after dark.

"Where you from?" Bill asked.

"Tennessee. Things are terrible back there. Carpetbaggers running roughshod over everyone, especially anyone who fought Rebel. That's why I loaded up my mill, lock, stock, and barrel. I put it all on the train and headed here. Pa was already here—came back in the late fifties, but he had left us two youngest to help Grandpa run the mill. Then the war come along and me and Joe joined up. By some miracle I lived through it. Joe didn't. Grandpa neither. He got shot in the head—not sure who done it. In his will he had left us both the land. He left Joe the house and me the mill, but I didn't want to stay. I thought I was getting away from them carpetbagging swine. Now in spite of having the franchise again, it looks like we'll have to put up with 'em another term."

"For a fact," agreed Bill. "And more's the pity." He set the cup down. "Thanks again for the coffee. We'd best get on the road. Abigail, you and Jake warmed up enough?"

Before she had time to answer, the door opened. The man in the doorway was an older, harsh version of Quinton and Bill. His eyes were granite. He eyed Bill and then shot Quinton a surly look.

"What the hell is he doing here? Don't you know who he is?"

"I know." Quinton stood and began gathering furry robes from pegs on the back wall. "Here, Bill, just drop these by next time you're passing."

Bill hesitated, but after a glance at Abigail, he took them and thanked Quinton. She hurried past the sullen stranger and climbed into the buggy. Before the door closed the angry voice reached them.

"That damned bastard's kin killed our kin—killed your own uncle. What you doin' helping the likes of him?"

The closing door muted Quinton's reply.

They drove in silence. Wrapped in one of the fur lap robes, Jacob was soon asleep. Bill knew that Abigail longed to ask what the incident at Quinton's was about, so he saved her the trouble.

Keeping his eyes on the trail, he broke the silence. "A few years back, my kin had a falling out with Quinton's kin. Quinton's Uncle Jared and some more of his kin tried to burn out my Cousin Elijah. They set his cabin on fire while he and his young wife were asleep, and then tried to shoot Elijah as he ran out the door. One of the horses knocked Cindy to the ground, and she lost their first baby."

"Oh…" Abigail gave a soft groan.

"They have three healthy boys now—in spite of Jared Rawlings." He paused for a moment as the memory of what had happened made him grimace. "Anyway," he went on, "Elijah killed a couple of them on the spot, tracked the rest into town and shot them in the mercantile."

"No wonder there's bad blood between your families," she said.

He surprised even himself by saying, "More bad blood between us than I care to admit." He faced her. "Jared Rawlings was my real pa."

Abigail gasped and then fell silent. Now he figured she really would mistrust him, mistrust the taint of bad blood. He had no idea why he had told her. Ever since Ma had revealed the truth of his lineage, he had admitted it to no one except Uncle Ned, and in a moment of weakness on the long trip to Shreveport, he had told Cindy, he supposed because he loved her.

Finally Abigail spoke. She leaned closer to be heard above the wind. "I know that has been very hard for you."

"About like eating poison," he confessed with honesty. "I despised Jared Rawlings when he was alive, and that hasn't changed since he died. I reckon most of the Rawlings are rattlesnake evil. I hate the idea of having a drop of their blood."

"But Quinton seems to be a fine man—at least from the little I saw of him—not at all like the others you described."

"He does seem different," admitted Bill. "My Granny knew them back in Tennessee. She always said there were a few good apples in the bunch and Calvin was the best of the lot. After Jared died, Quinton's pa, Calvin, sort of took the lead in the clan. He kept the feud from getting worse; at least he stopped the shooting." He faced her. "Only a few people on earth besides me know Jared was my pa. My ma was a pretty sorry excuse for a human, and I've already told you about Jared--but I was raised by the best folks in the world. The Tanners and the Lorings are God-fearing, honorable people, so hopefully some of that rubbed off on me."

She removed a hand from the furry robe to place it on his arm. She looked directly into his eyes. "A man doesn't have to be what his pa was. Otherwise Jacob would have no hope. His father was no good." Then she removed her hand.

"I've been wondering about your past. You don't talk much about it."

"It makes me unhappy, so I try not to think about it." She was quiet for a minute. Then, he listened intently while she described being orphaned at eight and married at eighteen. His hands holding the reins unconsciously drew into fists as she related her life with Frank Anderson. *In Frank's case, the apple didn't fall far from the tree*, fumed Bill with gritted teeth.

She faced him. "I know you've wanted to ask about this," she said tracing the scar. "Frank did it. He came home one afternoon, mean drunk. A neighbor man and his little boy had just left after bringing me a setting hen, a gift from his wife. Frank saw the wagon pulling away. He assumed the worst and went crazy. He said he'd fix me where no man would ever look at me again. I guess he'd have done worse, but I managed to grab the gun from his holster. I told him I'd kill him if he didn't drop the knife. When he sobered up he didn't remember any of it."

"Why the hell didn't you leave him?" demanded Bill.

She faced forward. "He was Jacob's father. And I made a vow—for better or for worse."

Bill seethed. At times he felt capable of great cruelty. He hoped it wasn't the taint of Jared Rawlings's blood. Nonetheless, he hoped a Yankee bullet or saber had not brought Frank a quick end—*he hoped it had been slow and painful.* He didn't think the Lord intended for a woman to stick around and let a man carve on her, but he didn't feel competent to argue scripture with Abigail. She probably knew ten times more verses than he did. Even so he knew he was right.

"Let's talk about something else," she suggested.

Suddenly trees bent low in wind ripping dead leaves from branches, stubborn and resistant to letting go. The sky opened. Rain, driven by wind that lashed the deluge into their faces and sent rivers gushing through rents in the buggy top, poured down on their heads.

"Aw, hell," Bill muttered, and slapped the reins, urging the black to a brisker pace. The animal sped up. "Wish it had held off a while longer."

"Jacob, are you all right?" called Abigail above the roar as the boy, roused from sleep, sat bolt upright.

"Where are we?" came the sleepy reply.

"Almost home," assured Bill. "Cover your head with the blanket. I'll get us there as quick as I can."

Abigail scooted away from the worst leak, pulled the fur robe over her head, and hunkered into it. Her voice rose loud enough to be heard. "Thank God for these robes. We'd be drowned without them."

Soon the road was a quagmire of ruts flowing with muddy water. Although Bill pushed the black as hard as he dared, they made slow progress on the slick, boggy mess. Dark overtook long before the house finally loomed ahead. Through the downpour, a dim light shone from the window.

"Just let us off at the porch while you go on to the barn," Abigail called. "I'll get my packages tomorrow."

"Ma, I need to turn Little Bear out."

"All right and then come right straight inside and change out of those damp clothes."

Instead of heading to the barn, Bill stopped the buggy and climbed out. He was not about to let her face Talbert's wrath alone. After helping her alight, he reached behind the seat and drew out a jug that he'd had enough forethought to buy. In spite of the wind, Talbert's curses came loud and clear through the open door as he snarled vile accusations. Without a word Bill set the jug onto the table and then helped Abigail remove the soggy lap robe and cloak. Then he took long steps until he was only inches from the purple-faced old man. His voice was deadly calm.

"Shut your vile mouth. And if you say one word to her about going to town today, I'll throw you out of this house so fast it'll make your head spin. You understand me?"

With bony fists balled tight, narrowed eyes glistening with rage, and yellowed teeth bared like a vicious animal, Talbert's body shook with fury. He raised a hand.

Bill spoke even softer. "You hit me, you'll wish you hadn't."

When the hand slowly lowered, Bill walked away. "Get on dry clothes while I stoke up the fire," he told Abigail, who had stood frozen in place, her eyes darting from Talbert to him before she hurried from the room and shut the bedroom door. Bill opened the damper, stoked the fire, draped the wet robes on the back of a chair, and turned to face Talbert.

"The jug is for you. I don't care how drunk you get, don't you say one nasty word to her. Not now. Not ever again. I mean it. I'll throw you out in a heartbeat."

Talbert glared and left the room. Bill knew he'd be back for the jug. And when he was drunk enough, it was unlikely the warning would still his vile tongue. Bill wondered what Abigail would do if he kicked the old man out.

December proved a wet, nasty month. Bill kept his crew cutting, hauling, and sawing, even though, except for the days the ground was frozen, the mud grew so deep they had to make new trails through the dripping woods to reach the mill, where the muddy bog almost buried their boots with each sucking step. The men worked without complaint, even Toby, whose limping gait made negotiating the quagmire extra difficult.

When the mill yard became a swamp, Bill left off cutting nearby and began again higher on the ridges to fell white oaks, saw them into lengths, and then split the logs into stave bolts. Only when the ground was frozen could they load the bolts and haul to Quinton's mill. True to his word, Quinton paid top dollar. Much to the delight of the crew, Bill was even able to raise wages. But Bill enjoyed most the days, like today, when they ran his own mill.

"Toby, how long you had that limp?" asked Matt while he unhooked the skid dogs from the logs and Tom rolled them closer to the pile with the cant hook.

Toby led the mules forward. "All my life. I was born with it. This, too." He held up the withered hand. "Ma said the doctor claimed there was nothing could be done—some kids was just born this way, no knowing why."

"Damn shame," said David as he rolled a log onto the carriage. "But you got a great way with mules, Toby. You can handle these ornery critters better than any of us."

Bill silently agreed. Each day his respect for Toby grew—for all of them. They might be young, but they were tough and getting tougher every day. Some days he felt old in comparison, especially when the old war wound acted up like today and the cold drizzle made him ache. He supposed it was a holdover from a bout with malaria in the army.

The loud whirr of the saw stopped conversation as the tangy aroma of cedar filled the air. He planned to build a chest with the wood because the tree had to be cut and the wood was too nice to waste. He wondered if Abigail would like the chest as a Christmas present. On second thought she would probably refuse such a nice gift. Bill drew in a deep, spicy breath. It smelled like Christmas. He decided he liked sawmilling as much as anything he'd ever done. Without a doubt it was hard, and yet he liked the rhythm, the flow of the process—making the judgment of how to fell a tree, watching it crash to the earth in just the right spot, the power of the throbbing steam engine, the feel of the lever in his hand as he sent the carriage forward to feed the log to the spinning blade—the challenge to make cuts that got the most lumber from each log. It was, without a doubt, satisfying. He wondered if he would find farming his own acres equally so. He would find out in the spring. He gave a brief grin. This morning when he had told the crew he would have to let them go in late February so he could begin getting the fields in shape for planting, he didn't know if the solemn faces were disappointment over no more work or over no more of Abigail's fine cooking. Abruptly the grin faded as he wondered if Abigail would remain in the spring or if she would let Talbert nag her into leaving.

A gust of wind shook the house. Near sundown Abigail had noticed a few flakes of snow. On the way to stir up the fire, she gave Jacob's bent head a loving caress as he sat at the table working on the arithmetic lesson she had assigned. After poking up the logs in the fireplace, she sat down with knitting in her lap while she kept an eye on the potato soup, thick and rich with onions and bacon, simmering on the stove. The cornbread was done and waiting under a cloth for the hungry men that should arrive any minute. She glanced outside at the growing darkness and wondered what was keeping them. Snow was falling thicker now, swirling in the wind.

As the needles clicked and the soft yarn ran through her fingers, she drew a deep breath and frowned. No matter how hard she tried pushing aside thoughts of Alice Bagley's letter, they kept cropping up like weeds in a flowerbed. Alice must have gotten her address from Cousin Joan; Joan was the only person Abigail had written to since she had been in Arkansas. Abigail tried convincing herself the news had no merit. Alice was a gossip, a busybody, always trying to stir up excitement, with no scruples about how she went about it. *Surely Alice was wrong!*

The needles stilled for a second as she glanced around. She had never expected to be this happy. The house was warm—thanks to the wood that Bill and the boys had cut. She gave a little chuckle recalling the look on Mr. Peters's face when she had told him she would no longer do his laundry in trade for firewood. She wondered who was washing for his huge brood now. It was hard to feel sorry for them. From what little she had seen of his children, they were as unlikable as their father. Even without the Peters' laundry, she had a heavy workload. Cooking and washing for Bill and the boys was enough to keep her falling into bed exhausted, and yet the work brought her so much pleasure.

Toby's lessons especially gave her a great sense of accomplishment. He was learning so fast she was hard-pressed to keep schoolbooks for him. He was already almost through the third reader and was beginning to copy words very legibly. It wouldn't surprise her to see him have a wonderful career someday. However, she silently admitted with a shake of her head, the biggest factor in her newfound contentment was the change in Talbert Anderson. Oh, he was still a devil—no doubt about that—hate still radiated from his bitter eyes. But he did his ranting and raving to himself. He'd barely shouted since the night she had come home late from town. She had no idea what Bill had told him. It must have been drastic to silence Talbert. Her conscience had given only a tiny twinge over not telling him of the letter. It was probably not true anyway, and he would have given her no rest night or day for insisting they return immediately to Missouri.

She began a new row on the scarf. The dark blue was perfect for Bill's black hair and gray eyes. Her cheeks grew warm as she wondered if the boys would notice all the scarves she knitted were brown except for this one.

When the mules passed by heading for the barn, she stood quickly, hid the scarf under balls of yarn in the basket, and began ladling soup into bowls and filling glasses with icy milk from a crock that had been chilling outside near the back door. She poured a generous glassful for each man and then put aside the rest for making gravy for breakfast. The cow was not giving as much as it had when Bill had first bought the Jersey a few weeks before. Abigail was thrilled to have milk and butter for cooking, and in the spring she planned to make cheese when there would be excess for such things.

Along with the men came cold air and snow through the back door. The sound of jolly banter put Abigail's mind to rest that anything had gone wrong.

"Fellows, we had a pretty productive day," said Bill, pulling off gloves. "We split enough stave bolts for a couple of loads."

"Yeah—in spite of Matt mooning over that girl until he could hardly work," said David with a grin.

"Me!" hooted Matt. "I seem to recall some fellow mentioning a girl named Deborah about a million times lately."

David lifted his head and sniffed. "Supper sure smells good."

Bill chuckled. He thought David had been moping since returning from the mountain. He figured it must be because of Cousin Deborah. He had seen her at Ma's funeral, and she had grown into a beauty.

He smiled at Abigail. "It does smell good. We're about starved. Sorry we're so late."

"That's all right," she said. "Soup keeps well."

Matt looked up after taking a few spoonfuls. "Miss Abigail, as a rule I'm not keen on potato soup, but this is delicious."

"I'm glad you like it." She began setting the glasses of cold milk alongside each plate. I've been meaning to ask how many of you to expect here for Christmas Dinner next Wednesday."

Matt answered quickly, "Ma will be looking for me and Tom home." He looked at Bill. "Are we working Christmas Eve?"

"No. We'll knock off Monday evening."

With the exception of Toby, everyone at the table smiled. Seeing his glum expression, Abigail quickly said, "Well, everyone is more than welcome to join us. Toby, you'll stay won't you? And you too, David?" She knew neither had family.

"I'd like that, ma'am." Toby's eyes didn't look as sad as they had just moments before.

David spoke up. "I appreciate the invite, but"—his face grew a little red as he faced Bill—"your Uncle Ned invited me. I'd like to see them all again."

Bill instantly knew Cousin Deborah was the reason David had been so distracted lately. He also suddenly realized thoughts of Cindy brought no keen desire to see her.

"Tell them all I said Merry Christmas."

"Sure will," said David as he fell to eating the steaming soup again.

Abigail asked, "Then you'll be joining us for dinner?"

"If it's not too much trouble," said Bill.

She hardly let him finish speaking before she assured it would be no trouble at all and then began planning the feast in her mind. If she had her way, it would be a delectable meal Bill Tanner would not soon forget. She studied his face, strong in the lamplight, the smile wide and handsome as he laughed and joked with the others, and she wondered, since he often spoke of his aunt, uncle, and cousins with fondness, why he didn't want to join them for the holiday. Whatever the reason, she was glad it was so. It was the first time she had looked forward to Christmas in a long, long while.

"Ma, can we have a tree?" asked Jacob.

"I don't see why not," she agreed.

He shot her a sunny smile. "I'll pick a good one."

"I know a good—"began Bill. Every mouth in the room instantly stopped chewing when Talbert interrupted.

"I'll help the boy get the tree." He scowled at Bill and then shuffled over to sit at the table. "Grandpas ought to help with such."

He took the bowl of soup from Abigail's hand where she stood wide-eyed from surprise. On second thought she supposed he only said it to spite Bill; and yet to be fair, he did care about Jacob. Jacob was the only thing he had left of Frank. And he had worshiped Frank. From the first day she met Mr. Anderson, she had reaped his resentment for—at least in his mind—taking Frank away from him. In reality, his cussedness had put the rift between him and his son, a rift that had persisted. They had not made up even on the day Frank went off to war. She supposed that was why he had such a hard time accepting that Frank was dead.

"But there ain't gonna be no candles on the tree, Jacob." Mr. Anderson went on, "Knowed of too many houses burned to the ground by that dang fool custom."

"We'll pop and string corn. I saw that once and it was really pretty," said Abigail.

Jacob nodded, willing to concede.

Cold wind rattled the windowpanes in the warm kitchen where steam rising from coffeepot and bubbling oatmeal fogged the windows. Abigail used a dishtowel to wipe a pane as she breathed in these hearty breakfast smells plus frying bacon and the aroma of cloves, cinnamon, and baking bread. She looked out at the clear Christmas morning. There had been snow flurries for days, but no accumulation. Jacob would be disappointed.

She stepped back to admire her handiwork. The curtains did look pretty and brightened the bare room considerably. She had hoped to get them all finished and hung before Christmas, but there had been no time, not with making presents and all her other chores. For the past two days she had been sewing every spare minute and finally had finished four pairs and only this morning had ironed and hung them.

Cooking for the men was a full-time job, even without the Christmas baking. The shelf near the stove was laden with pies, cookies, and two kinds of yeast bread, one with cinnamon and brown sugar, as near like the one at the cafe as she could make it. The potatoes were peeled and soaking in water, the hen plucked and waiting to go into the oven, the cornbread and biscuit dressing mixed and waiting until the hen was almost done before it would become a moist bed around it.

The tree stood near the front door draped with strings of popcorn and a few small packages hanging from the branches. The scarves for Bill, Toby, and Jacob and a sleeping cap for Mr. Anderson were under the tree, wrapped in the newspaper rife with Johnson County politics. Mr. Anderson had complained of his bedroom being cold at night. She had already given gifts to the ones who wouldn't be here.

She stirred the pancake batter and smiled. Bill had asked if Jacob had any musical instruments. She wondered what he planned to give him. She loved music and wished she had learned to play an instrument, but there had never been any money for lessons and no one in her family had been musically inclined.

After she had pushed her qualms aside, it pleased her that Bill had taken an interest in Jacob. Jacob was certainly enthralled with Bill. He followed closely at Bill's heels, and Bill didn't seem to mind. Her smile faded. Mr. Anderson was a different story. If possible he resented Bill more than ever. She knew he was jealous over Jacob's attentions. She hoped he behaved himself today and didn't spoil the fun for the rest of them. No matter how joyous the occasion, he constantly loomed like a gloomy, black storm cloud, keeping her and Jacob on edge dreading the thunder. Perhaps today would be different. At least breakfast would be pleasant. He rarely got up before midday.

"Come in," she called at the soft rap on the back door.

Bill entered first followed by Toby. Both men sniffed the air before pulling off coats and hats. "Smells like Christmas in here," said Bill.

"I hope you're both hungry," she said with a big smile, "or Little Bear will be in for a real treat."

"He'll be lucky to get any scraps," avowed Bill. He poured a cup of coffee and then cut his eyes sideways. "Would I get my hands smacked if I got one of these?" His hand hovered over the plate of sugary cinnamon breads.

"Probably not," she said, "but the oatmeal and bacon are ready so sit down and I'll dish it up."

Toby remained standing. His eyes went from the food to the tree and back again. "This is nice. We never celebrated Christmas at my house."

Jacob almost missed a rung while coming down the loft ladder. "No Christmas?" His eyes rounded. "Didn't y'all believe in Jesus?"

Toby shrugged. "Ma nor Pa ever talked religion."

Upon seeing Jacob's mouth drop, Abigail gave him a slight, warning shake of her head and quickly said, "Then we'll have to make your first celebration special. Sit down and have a warm piece of cinnamon bread before Bill eats it all."

Abigail sat down and took a sip of steaming coffee. "Tell us about Christmas at your house."

Before answering Bill thought for a moment. "We lived with my Granny Tanner. Some of the kin always came for dinner, so Granny would cook up a storm."

Jacob interrupted, "Did you get lots of presents?"

"No more than two or three, usually something Granny knit or wove on her loom. Pa was good at whittling, so he made my toys—whistles and tops and such. On Christmas mornings I'd be raring to get my presents, but

Granny insisted that we hear the Christmas Story first thing. She was right smart religious—so was Pa. I didn't much appreciate it at the time." He gave a sad smile. "Of course, now I'd love more than anything to see Pa with that old Bible in his hands."

Abigail noticed he made no mention of his mother. It was as if he had blotted her from his memory.

Bill went on, "Pa was a great fiddle player too, and so after the scriptures we'd sing a few hymns...I miss that too."

Abigail put in, "If you would read for us, I'd love to hear the Christmas Story this morning."

"I'd be glad to." Bill grinned and reached to tousle Jacob's hair as his face fell. "Aw, Jake, it's a short story and not at all boring like some of those who-begat-who chapters."

"I know," Jacob said. "It's about when Jesus was born. Ma reads it to me every Christmas. She already—"

He stopped mid-sentence when Abigail, along with a stern look, gave him another warning shake of her head.

She handed Bill her worn Bible and sat down to listen. Her mind, however, strayed from the sacred scene of starlit fields and angels announcing peace on earth and good will to men. She studied Bill's strong face and let the deep tones of his fine voice wash over her. He was a good man. She just knew it.

The second the Bible closed, Jacob talked around his last bite of bacon. "We gonna open the presents now?"

Abigail stood. "After the dishes are done. If you want to hurry things up, you can help."

"I'll help too." Bill stood and began stacking plates. "An old bachelor like me knows how to do dishes."

Jacob was gathering the dirty forks. "How come you never got married?"

Abigail paused from pouring hot water from the teakettle into the dishpan. Her cheeks reddened when Bill looked her way. She hadn't meant to be so obviously curious.

"Reckon I'm just too ornery for any woman to want."

"Aw," Jacob protested, "you aren't either."

Toby had gathered two coffee cup handles in his good hand and carried the cups to Abigail. "It's fellows like me that can't get a girl. A handsome feller like you could have your pick."

Bill shrugged. "The war came along, and after that I just got too busy to go courting, I guess."

"You could court Ma. She's—" began Jacob.

"Jacob Henry Anderson!" Her face flamed. "Of all the rude…!" she sputtered. "I've a good mind to send you right back to bed without opening your presents!"

Jacob blinked. "What'd I do wrong?" He looked beseechingly at Bill.

Toby couldn't stop the chuckle that escaped.

Bill gave Jacob a sympathetic wink. "I'll leave that to your ma to explain. For now let's get these dishes washed."

Abigail wanted to run to the bedroom, slam the door, and never come out. She had never been so humiliated! She had made matters worse by flying off the handle. Poor Jacob honestly had no idea what he had done wrong! And it wouldn't be easy explaining it either. She kept her face averted and scrubbed so hard, if possible, she would have scrubbed the faded rose pattern off the cracked china. She was actually glad when Mr. Anderson came into the kitchen.

"I saved your breakfast," she said and whisked it out of the warming oven that was inset in the stovepipe and set it on the table. She poured him a cup of coffee and set it alongside the plate while her mind raced. Could she possibly change the names she had written on the packages? *If only she hadn't made his scarf a different color from the others!* Now he would certainly think she had set her cap for him.

It couldn't be helped. Jacob was already sitting on the floor near the tree, and Toby and Bill stood nearby. She would just have to bear it and try not to look mortified when Bill opened the gift. After drying her hands on the dishtowel, she joined them, but she wished herself a thousand miles away.

Jacob thanked her for the scarf, but his eyes didn't light up until he unwrapped the gift from Bill, a silver-plated harmonica. "I always wanted one of these!" He looked up at Bill. "Do you know how to play this?"

"Yep. My pa taught me. He could play anything. We used to play for all the dances around."

"Will you teach me?"

"Be glad to."

Jacob blew a loud note and then stopped and grinned.

Bill added, "That mouth harp is G chord. If you learn how to play, I'll see about getting you some more in other chords."

When Jacob blew loudly again, Bill held up his hand, "Whoa. Loud isn't what you want." He took the harmonica, cupped his hands, and gently blew a few liquid notes and then handed it back to Jacob.

"That was lovely," Abigail said softly, for a moment forgetting all about her embarrassment. "Please, play some more."

"Be glad to, but I figure Jacob wants to see what's in those other packages. Might be one or two you're interested in too."

For the first time she noticed the packages in back, almost out of sight. Her eyebrows rose as Jacob bounced up and down.

"We fooled you!" He laughed. "I snuck 'em in here for Bill, and there's one from me, too!" He scrambled over the gifts close by to reach the hidden ones, grabbed the largest, and handed it to her. "Open it, Ma! This one's from me. You're gonna love it!"

She smiled and tore away the paper. Her eyes went wide and immediately shifted to Bill. It was the shoes she had admired in the mercantile. And they were just her size.

"How on earth did you know...?"

Jacob laughed even harder. "That's the best part! I drew around your old shoes and Bill took the paper in to Miss Lena. She got just the right size. She told Bill she saw you looking at that pair for a long time, so we knew you liked 'em."

"But Jacob, these cost way too much. I know you didn't have—"

"Jacob is a working man now. He's drawing a little wages right along for helping at the mill."

When she started to protest, Bill discreetly cut his eyes toward Jacob and then shook his head. She stopped. Perhaps it would be better to argue about this when Jacob wasn't around. She didn't want to spoil his pleasure. But the gift was too fine, too expensive. Bill should not have paid for it. She gave an inward groan at the glower on Mr. Anderson's face as he raked Bill with hostile eyes.

Jacob held out another gift. "Toby, here's one for you."

Toby took the gift but looked as if he wished the floor would open and swallow him. "I never bought nobody nothing," he mumbled.

"Gracious, that's all right Toby," reassured Abigail. "Last Christmas I couldn't buy a single present. If it weren't for the money you men have paid me there would be no presents this year either, so in a way, you helped buy much of what is under the tree."

"Thank you, ma'am." Slightly mollified, he opened the package. He took out the scarf and looked at it. Then he swallowed. "This is real nice, Miss Abigail—I never seen a finer one." He looked at her. "This is the first present anyone ever give me, and I sure do thank ya."

Tears sprang to her eyes. *The poor boy!* She was glad he was here. He needed a family.

She sat up straighter, feeling her cheeks warm, as Bill began opening his present. He took out the scarf and stroked the soft wool.

"It's mighty fine." His eyes found hers. "Thank you."

Her gaze dropped but not before her heartbeat had quickened.

Jacob got another package. "Grandpa, this one's yours."

He opened the knitted cap and gave her a cursory thank you, but his brow stayed furrowed. She fervently hoped again that he wouldn't spoil the day.

"Ma, this one is from Bill."

"Just what I needed," she said and meant it. She was thankful the gift was nothing personal, merely a set of plates to replace the mismatched, chipped ones.

Soon afterwards Bill and Toby left to tend to the animals, and Jacob tagged along. Abigail bent and began picking up the strewn paper.

"Ain't decent!"

Abigail stood with a sigh. She knew what was coming. It would be easier to stop the sun from rising than to stop Talbert Anderson from venting his spleen.

"Decent woman don't take personal gifts from no man what ain't her husband. And don't you forget fer one minute, Abigail Anderson, that you got a husband."

"Frank is dead," she said, knowing it would only add fuel to the flame and yet unable to stop herself.

"You want to think that, don't ya? He ain't and you know it—deep in yer bones you know it."

She would have felt better if he had yelled. The quiet, certain tone was what chilled her. She turned away, rubbing goose-fleshed arms. The old devil had voiced her worst nightmare and he knew it.

Somehow she lived through the rest of the day with a smile pasted on her face. She wanted to keep the day special for Jacob, but even the beautiful music Bill played on the harmonica did not dispel the black cloud hovering.

�֎ Chapter 5

In the last light of day, Bill hunkered deeper into his coat and glanced back at the house. He had no idea what had upset Abigail…he didn't think it was Jacob's remark. Without a doubt she had been embarrassed, but not withdrawn and morose. It was a good thing he had decided not to give her the pretty fabric he had bought for a dress. Otherwise he would have thought she was offended. He shook his head. No, something else had happened. She had been different when he had returned from the barn and sat down for dinner. He shook his head and walked on.

Toby sat inside the bunkhouse shed. With the stove door open, he poked at blazing sticks in the stove. He looked up and smiled as Bill came inside.

"That was nice, wasn't it—having Christmas like that. Course I reckon you're used to such, but this was just about the nicest day I ever had. Miss Abigail is a mighty nice lady, and she sure can cook, can't she?"

Apparently Toby hadn't noticed the strain that had developed during the afternoon, and now Bill didn't mention it.

"Yes, she can, and it was a nice day."

Abruptly, Toby's face fell. "I'm dumb as a goat. After all that time she spent knitting my scarf and teaching me to read, and I never once thought of buying her a present."

"Well, you can get her something next time you're in town."

Gloom disappeared as he gave a wide smile. "I'll do that. Yes, sir, that's exactly what I'll do."

Bill sat on the bunk and began pulling off his boots. "You'd better bank that fire and turn in. I told the boys to be back early. I want to run the mill tomorrow, so you'll need to roll out in time to get the boiler going."

"Yes, sir," he said, but kept sitting awhile longer, staring into the blaze.

Bill had almost dozed off when Toby's voice came through the darkness, "What do ya reckon Miss Abigail would want?"

Bill rolled over, punched up the pillow, and said, "Go to sleep, Toby."

He roused when David returned, and roused again in the wee hours when the Wallaces arrived and tiptoed inside to climb into bunks. He caught the whiff of liquor and figured the boys would not feel too spry in the morning.

✕✕✕

Just as Bill had expected, the Wallace boys moved slowly the next day, and even David seemed lost in a fog. Bill himself was quieter than usual as he ruminated about the change in Abigail's demeanor. She had been subdued again at breakfast and it worried him. Only Toby had abundant energy, and when the mill noise allowed, he chattered nonstop about his Christmas.

"Damn!" yelled Tom as he took two running steps alongside the carriage and waved his hand. Bill immediately ceased pulling the lever. "Sorry," called Tom, "got my jacket sleeve hung."

After Tom had disentangled his sleeve from the metal

frame bracing the log dogs, Bill signaled for everyone to gather around. He raised his voice above the whine of the engine. "No one appears too pert today, and I sure don't want any accidents, so after this log, we'll stop for dinner and—"

He looked around as Toby pointed toward the road. A buggy carrying two well-dressed men in heavy coats and hats drove past the house, left the main road, and bumped down the rough trail to stop near the mill. One man climbed down and gingerly stepped around frozen puddles and piles of logs. Bill put the engine out of gear and nodded at Toby to power down the steam. "Y'all go on and eat. I'll be there shortly."

The barrel-chested man with a long handlebar mustache stuck out his hand while the other thinner man lolled near the buggy. "Mr. Tanner, I presume? I'm Emory Ellis and this is my associate Mr. Harvey."

He nodded toward a man with a marled eye, plainly sightless and bordered by a gray scar protruding down his cheek. Bill had seen saber cuts before. He figured Harvey for an ex-soldier.

Bill shook hands with Ellis and nodded to Harvey. "What can I do for you?"

Ellis slowly looked around. "You certainly have a prosperous operation here. I daresay, with a nice mill like this and all that fine white oak timber yonder, you're making money hand over fist." He gave an insincere smile.

Bill felt his hackles rise. This time his tone was blunt. "What do you want?"

"Ah, yes, I know you're busy, so let's get right to business." He motioned to the other man. "Harvey, bring the tally book, please. Mr. Tanner, I'm here to notify you of a special levy that was placed on all timber operations and wood harvested in the county. And you are in arrears." He opened the black cover and ran a finger down the page. "Yes, here you are. It appears your rate is twenty percent." He shut the book with a brisk snap and smiled again. "The fee is due and collected at the first of every quarter. I'll need to see all past invoices for goods you've sold or bartered in the past six months. Until you catch up the back payments, we can work out an extra percentage, say three percent more until the total is caught up."

Bill rocked back on his heels with arms crossed over his chest. His eyes had turned to steel. "You're saying I owe twenty percent of all the wood I've sold or ever will sell?"

"That's right. And there's an operating fee for the mill. All businesses are required to pay—"

"Jordan Cravens never mentioned any such levy. Who authorized this?"

The men exchanged quick looks. "Mr. Tanner, everyone has to do their fair share to keep the county running—"

"Was this voted on in that bogus election?"

"I told you he was a damned Reb," muttered Harvey.

Ellis went on, "It wasn't precisely on the ballot, but the consensus of the county board—"

Bill's face purpled. "So you thieving carpetbaggers thought you'd waltz in here and rob me with your sharp pencils. Well, I got news for you—you damn well won't!" He took two steps forward.

"See here, Tanner,"—the oily façade vanished as the man stuck out a belligerent chin— "you have to pay or we'll shut you down. And if you resist you'll land in jail."

"Watch him, Ellis," said Harvey, eyeing Bill with mistrust. "He's a dead ringer for that last fellow at Hagarville who pulled a gun on me."

"Get out," Bill ordered, "and don't ever set foot back on this land."

"Oh, we'll be back," snarled Ellis, "and next time the sheriff will be with us. We can take your mill and your place and anything else we want, and there's not a damn thing you can do to stop us."

Bill stooped to pick up a piece of stove wood lying near the boiler. As Ellis backed up, Harvey pulled a derringer from his coat pocket.

Bill hurled the stick, knocking him backwards into the sawdust pile, but Harvey hung onto the derringer until Bill kicked his hand and the gun went flying. Bill grabbed him and slammed his head into a post supporting the mill roof. Bill darted a glance at Ellis. He still held the book, not seeming inclined to join the fray, so Bill turned back to slam Harvey's head into the post again. While Harvey clung weakly to the post, Bill pounded his face, finally knocking him down. Then Bill aimed a vicious kick at his head, and he sagged unconscious.

Bill heard the high-pitched whine as a bullet knocked bark from the post near his head. He whirled just as the second shot echoed. Although Ellis held the derringer, he was pale and his eyes were terrified. The sharp pain searing Bill's forearm barely slowed him as he charged forward.

Ellis stood frozen as Bill's iron grip twisted the gun away and used it to smash his mouth before hurling him into the side of the buggy. The horses shied and pranced as Ellis, blood spurting from his busted mouth, slid to the ground and covered his head with his arms. While he cried out in pain, Bill stomped his arms and head and then lashed a vicious kick into his midsection. Bill heard yells and the thud of running boots as the boys sprinted across the yard, but he didn't slow from lashing out with the toe of his heavy boot.

David arrived first, panting. "What the hell?" He took Bill's arm. "Hey, you're about to kill him. Sure you want to?"

"Yeah, I want to," he snarled. "The bastard shot me." He aimed another savage kick and then stopped. Although he wanted to kill him, he didn't want all the trouble that would ensue if he did.

Both Wallace boys had arrived out of breath. Toby brought up the rear running with an awkward gait.

Bill stooped and grabbed Ellis by the collar and began dragging him toward the boiler, oblivious to the man's whimpering cries. Tom's eyes widened as he noticed the bullet hole in Bill's sleeve and blood dripping onto the ground.

Just then Harvey groaned and rose on an elbow. Tom aimed a swift kick, knocking him back down. "Lay still, you sonofabitch!"

Bill dropped Ellis, reached to open the boiler door, and rammed the poker deep into the red-hot coals. He used a boot to shove Ellis back down as he struggled to get away. "I invited you to leave a while ago. Now you'll not leave until I'm finished with you."

Ellis, wide-eyed with horror, watched Bill shove the poker deeper into the coals. "What are you going to do… Please don't, I beg you. I'll do anything you say."

"When I'm done with you, I suggest you get into that buggy and leave the country. If you go to the law, or try to get back at me in any way, I'll kill you and it won't be quick." He looked down with glassy eyes. "You understand?"

"Let me go right now. I swear I won't tell anyone. And I'll leave today and never come back."

Bill made a scoffing noise. "I know your kind. You'll agree to anything to save your hide, but quick as you get the upper hand again, the promises are all forgotten. So I'm gonna give you something to remember this one by." Bill turned the poker in the coals. "When I was in the army, I watched a fellow branded with a big C on his chest for cowardice. Never forgot it. A thief is no better than a coward, so I figure you ought to have a big T. David, rip his shirt open."

With only slight hesitation, David hunkered and jerked open the coat and pulled on the shirt, sending buttons flying.

Ellis tried desperately to crawl away, but David held him.

"Let me go. Oh God, please!"

He began screaming even before the red poker seared his white, quivering flesh. Bill turned his head against the smell of singed skin as he burned a deep red welt and then lifted the poker and brought it back down to burn a T.

Ellis screamed and screamed again and then began to whimper. As Bill pushed the poker back into the hot coals, Matt swore under his breath and then gagged.

Bill pointed at Harvey. "Throw a bucket of water on him."

Tom complied. And when Harvey tried to stand, Matt held him.

"Bring him here," Bill ordered.

Although Tom and Matt exchanged stricken looks, they dragged the struggling man forward. Harvey gave a loud cry, but not until the iron had blistered his skin. Then he penned Bill with hate-filled eyes. Bill instinctively knew this one would be trouble.

"I ought to kill you right now," he said. "I'll tell you the same thing I told your partner—you cause me even a speck of trouble and I'll kill you in a way you'll beg to die. You're not taking what belongs to me." He gestured to the boys. "Throw them both into the buggy."

117

After the men had been dumped into the buggy and it had driven away, Bill's eyes followed them. Then as the blood pounding in his ears lessened, he sagged against the post, and wincing, eased off the coat. His arm hurt like the devil, but the wound was only a deep graze.

"That was awful," muttered Toby. "What did them men do to make you do that to 'em?"

Bill looked up. The Wallace boys were as pasty-faced as Toby. Although their eyes asked the same question, they stayed mute.

Bill explained in few words, and then he added, "I know what I did seemed cruel, maybe even evil, but short of killing them, something like this is all that will stop them. I don't aim to stand by and let a damn bunch of carpetbaggers steal what is mine, what I've worked hard for."

David spoke up, "I think you did exactly the right thing—except maybe you ought to have killed 'em. After all, they shot first."

Bill let out a deep breath. "I thought about it. But a fair trial would be hard to get with their kind running things."

David looked down the road. "Maybe so, but that second fellow didn't look near scared enough to suit me.

"Me either," agreed Bill.

"You'll have to watch your back."

Toby, looking dazed, shut the boiler door. He shook his head and muttered. "I never saw anything like that." He stooped to pick up the black book Ellis had dropped in the scuffle.

"I've seen worse," said David. "When I was Jacob's age I saw two men blown to hell at point-blank range with a shotgun. Believe me, this was nothing compared to that." David pointed at the arm. "You need to get to the house and get that arm cleaned up. Think you need a doctor?"

Bill shook his head. "No. It's just a flesh wound and it bled out good."

Abigail ladled soup into Toby's bowl and then glanced out the window, wondering how long those men would keep Bill talking. She would wait before dipping his soup. She finished filling all the other bowls and then stepped to the window. Suddenly her grip on the curtain tightened. She gasped.

"What's wrong?"

When she didn't answer, David stood, took two long strides to the window, and then he swore.

A shot rang out, halting his words. He spun on his heels and headed out the door. The other men quickly followed.

Abigail, her face gray, quickly turned toward the back door. "Jacob, don't you dare go outside." Her lips pressed together as her eyes swung back to the mill.

She watched dismayed as Bill beat a man and kicked him senseless. *What had made him so angry?* Then with her heart in her throat, she watched in stunned disbelief as he dragged the man toward the boiler and reached for the poker. Warm bile rose in her throat. She went cold to the marrow of her bones. *Surely he wouldn't do it!*

At the first blood-curdling scream, she groaned. She jumped when Talbert spoke at her elbow.

"There's yer fine man. What do ya think of him now?" he asked, his voice thick with sarcasm and his eyes gleaming with triumph. "Good example for the boy, now ain't he?" He gave a coarse laugh before getting his jug and going to his room.

As more agonized screams rent the air, she fled to the bedroom and slammed the door. She fell onto the bed and pressed the pillow to her lips to keep herself from screaming. *She thought she knew him, but she didn't! Not at all! Even Frank had not been so cruel—at least he had been drunk when he hurt her. Bill was stone-cold sober!*

She drew a sobbing breath. Tears squeezed from her tightly closed eyes. Suddenly she realized that Jacob was still in the kitchen. She didn't want him looking out the window and seeing Bill torture a man! She wanted to stay in the room and never come out; nevertheless, she rose from the bed, wiped her eyes, and opened the door. Jacob turned from the window, his wide-eyed stare reflecting shock.

"Ma, why did Bill burn those fellows—what did they do?"

"I don't know, son." She didn't want Jacob marred by this, but she could think of no reassuring words.

"Maybe they did something terrible," began Jacob, "like killed his family or something…"

Abigail glanced toward the mill. *Perhaps they had—perhaps Bill had a valid reason.* She had seen terrible atrocities in the war, a few things she would have avenged herself if it had been in her power to do so. She felt a flicker of hope.

Just then the back door opened. Toby limped inside and collapsed into a chair at the table. He wiped a hand over his gray face.

"Toby, why—" began Jacob.

Toby's voice was shaky as he interrupted the question.

"All I know is that was the worst thing I've ever seen."

The door opened again and Bill stepped inside. His eyes flickered from Abigail to Jacob and back. They stayed fixed on Abigail's stiff face. She saw the questioning look and the bloody arm and yet she could not say a word.

"Miss Abigail," said David, "do you have some carbolic

acid or something to clean up his arm?"

"No."

David's brow knit at the curt answer. "Well, then we'll make do with soap and water and a bandage of some kind. You got anything?"

She turned, went into the bedroom, and for a long moment leaned her head on the door facing. She had read the question in Bill's eyes. Perhaps he did have a good explanation, but she would have to hear it before letting down her guard. With lips pressed tight, she tore off a portion of a ragged sheet that she used for bandages and dust cloths and returned to the kitchen. All the men sat at the table, shaken but silent, while David filled a pan with soapy water and washed the wound. Bill looked up as she entered. David dropped the wet rag back into the soapy water, took the bandage, tore it into strips, wrapped the wound, and tied the bandage snug.

Bill pulled his sleeve down and buttoned the cuff. "Thanks, David." He glanced around. "I want all of you to finish sawing those trees and then we'll call it a day. David, you run the saw."

He nodded. "All right. Come on, fellows, you heard the boss."

Bill waited until they left before saying, "Jacob, I'd like to talk to your ma alone."

Jacob headed for the ladder but Abigail stopped him. It would be too easy to eavesdrop, so she sent him outside and remained a statue until he left.

"I hate that you and the boy saw that," began Bill.

She turned to stare out the window. She heard him let out a deep breath.

"What did they do?"

"They're carpetbaggers, threatening to shut me down or jail me if I don't pay them a big percentage of everything I make selling timber."

She turned back. "You tortured them for that?"

He studied her a moment. "They'll live." He waited a bit before adding, "Now they'll think twice before they try robbing me or anybody else." He went on, "Abigail, mortal fear is all that will stop men like that. They're rotten to the bone, crooked northerners who came down here to rob us blind. I won't stand by and let them."

When she remained silent, he finally stood and left the room.

David stepped near and motioned for Bill to look behind him. He left off pulling the lever and frowned. Then he motioned for Toby to slow the engine. As the noise lessened, he walked toward three men who had dismounted their horses. The tallest wore a badge, and he spoke first.

"Bill Tanner?"

Bill nodded.

"I'm Sheriff Crampton and I have a warrant for your arrest." The men accompanying him kept their hands near pistol butts while they warily eyed David and the boys, who watched from the mill shed.

"What's the charge?" asked Bill, although he already knew.

"Assault and battery." He glanced at Bill's crew, who were scowling as they gathered in a knot. "You coming along peaceful or does this have to be difficult?"

Bill drew off his gloves. "I'll come peaceful." He looked back at the boys. "David, you take over—"

The sheriff interrupted. "There'll be no more milling. I've got orders to shut you down until you pay the county what you owe on your timber business."

Bill swore. "You know that levy is robbery, plain and simple."

The sheriff shrugged. "I'm just doing my duty, Tanner. I leave the rest of it up to the judge."

"Can I get a few things from the bunkhouse?" Bill asked while pulling on his jacket.

Sheriff Crampton, pulling at his heavy gray mustache, looked around at all the men now facing off like mad roosters at a cockfight and shook his head. "Naw, let's just head out. If need be someone can bring your stuff later." He took handcuffs from his deputy. "Now, stretch out your wrists."

"Those aren't necessary. I told you I'd come peaceful and I will."

"I'm a cautious man, Tanner." As the clasps shut, he nodded toward the boys. "I hope they don't aim to do something stupid like follow us to cause trouble."

Bill raised his voice. "Keep out of this, boys. Cravens will handle it."

Abigail stood on the porch, shading her eyes to watch them pass. In spite of his agitation, Bill noticed how pretty she looked in the morning sun. His frown deepened as he realized this would probably deepen the rift that had developed between them. He wondered how much the fine would be—probably stiff. Because the men he assaulted were officials, they would make an example of him. However, he was relieved there had been no warrants for the boys.

Jacob rounded the corner of the house with Little Bear at his heels. He spied the horsemen and stopped. In a flash he darted toward Bill. "Where they taking you?" Before Bill could answer he had sprinted forward to head off the sheriff. When the sheriff didn't slow, he trotted alongside. "Don't take Bill!"

Talbert's voice was harsh, *"Come back h'yar, boy!"*

But Jacob only stopped running when the sheriff spurred his horse forward. By the time Bill's horse came abreast, tears streamed down the boy's face. He reached to touch Bill's leg and ran alongside for a few steps.

"It's all right, boy. I'll be back. You take good care of your mama."

Jacob swallowed and then nodded. "Yes, sir, I will."

The sun soon retreated behind the clouds. The bleak, gray landscape matched Bill's mood, and by the time Hagarville came into view he wished for a heavier coat. Bill caught a whiff of wood smoke coming from nearby chimneys.

Zetta Cowens, coming out of the blacksmith shop, saw them approach. She turned around to call back inside to Quinton. In a few seconds he also stood on the roadside. "What's going on, Bill?" he called.

"The sheriff wants the pleasure of my company."

Zetta's cackling laugh rang out, but Quinton, crossing big arms across his chest, glowered. "Branding varmints ought not be against the law, Sheriff." Crampton rode on without answering.

Bill was half frozen when they reached town. They climbed down in front of the three-story red brick building facing the town square and currently housing the jail. It probably wouldn't be needed much longer. Even now he could see workmen across the way working on the new courthouse.

He welcomed the heat of the pot-bellied stove, even though it warmed a jail cell. Sheriff Crampton ushered him into the cell, closed the door, and locked it. Bill had been tied up before when Lieutenant Bo Morrison was conscripting for the army, but he had never been locked in a room against his will. When the lock clicked, he was surprised at the feeling, not exactly panic, but not pleasant. He looked around at the bare, windowless walls and wondered how any man could stand confinement.

"I want to see Lawyer Cravens."

"Time enough for that tomorrow," said Crampton. "For now I'm going home for a late supper and a good night's sleep." He inclined his head toward the big-bellied deputy. "Wilber, here, will take good care of you if you don't give him any trouble."

No one mentioned feeding him, so Bill supposed he would go without. It was not the first time; he had often gone without food for days at a time in the ill-supplied Confederate Army. He kept on his boots and stretched out on the hard cot, but his eyes stayed wide open. Glancing around at the dim cell, he had to stifle a groan.

He wasn't merely worried about himself. He worried about Abigail. Of course she had managed before he came along, but her troubles had lessened considerably after his arrival. Things had been different between them lately. She was upset that he had branded those vermin, but he figured she would get over it in time—that is unless he ended up going to prison. He didn't figure their relationship had deepened to the point that she would hang around, waiting.

He drew a deep breath and wondered how this could possibly end well. Granny had always claimed that everything happened for a reason, and in God's good time it all turned out for the good. He wasn't sure he believed that. His eyes traced the darkening room. He would get through this somehow, but his skin already crawled with wanting to be away. He wondered how long the sentence would be if he was found guilty.

"Tanner, here's your supper."

The overweight jailer Wilber unlocked the cell just long enough to set a tray inside the cell. It was a bowl of thin soup and a slab of cold, dry cornbread that must have been cooked for a week. Bill took only a few bites before setting the tray down near the cell door.

Wilber gave a mirthless chuckle. "If you're in here long enough you'll not be so picky. Might even get so you look forward to meals—ain't much else to look forward to in there."

Bill didn't comment, but he doubted he'd ever look forward to eating slop that would choke a pig. He lay down again, wondering what Abigail had cooked for supper. Then his mind turned to all the events that had led to his arrest. He still had no regret for what he had done to Ellis and Harvey. They deserved it. Nonetheless, he wasn't looking forward to the price he might have to pay. However, all through the long, sleepless night, his thoughts were of Abigail more than of anything else.

Jordan Cravens sat in a straight-backed chair drawn near the cell, the only concession made by the jailer, who had refused a chair for Bill, so now Bill stood looking through the bars while he and Cravens kept their voices low. The Sheriff had not come in yet, but the jailer sat nearby, sipping coffee, with his feet propped on a desk.

"I won't sugarcoat it. It is serious," said Cravens. "You're right. I figure they will try making an example of you." He paused and then added, "But I'll see Judge Meers later today to see about bail."

"From what I know of Meers, I'm out of luck. He's in tight with all the carpetbaggers."

Cravens shrugged. "Not completely. I'm at odds with the judge politically, but he's not a bad judge. In most things I've found him fair-minded. He pulls all the strings he can to legally get what he wants, but unlike most of them, I haven't known of him stepping across the line."

"Good. Then what's the worst I'm looking at?"

"A big fine. And three to five years."

Bill stared at the floor a moment. Then he gave a low whistle. "That's worse than I thought."

"You'll have a jury trial, and I'll do everything in my power to get the right sort on the panel. But a lot will depend on the judge."

Bill let out a deep breath. "Then I sure hope you're right about him."

Cravens had not been gone long when the sheriff entered. He took the mug of coffee the deputy poured and then approached Bill's cell before taking a sip. "You look like hell, Tanner. Not conducive to sleep, being in jail, huh?" When Bill didn't answer, the sheriff chuckled. He motioned Bill closer. When Bill stepped to the bars, the sheriff lowered his voice. "I had a few visitors last night. They asked me to deliver a message. If you'll turn over your timber rights and your mill and leave the country, all the charges against you will be dropped. Otherwise you're looking at hard time at Little Rock. It's a deal you ought to consider." He took another sip of coffee and studied Bill over the mug rim as Bill's eyes narrowed into slits. He swallowed, lowered the cup, and said, "Goes against the grain, I know, but sometimes a fellow has to take the lesser of two evils."

"You tell those thieving bastards I said no."

The sheriff shrugged. "Suit yourself. But believe me, that penitentiary ain't no place a man wants to be."

Bill turned his back and sat down on the cot. He hated the thought of prison. But no one was running him out of the country and taking what was his without a fight! Caleb and Granny had molded him indelibly in that mold. He gave a wry grin. *Even Jared Rawlings would never have caved to the sonsofbitches!*

It was late afternoon before Cravens returned. Bill stood quickly when he entered. He let out a relieved breath when Cravens nodded and handed a piece of paper to the jailer. Bill retrieved his hat and coat from the bunk and followed Cravens outside.

"I paid your bail out of the cash you left in my keeping."

"Was it enough?" Bill asked while getting into his coat.

"Yes, but there's only a couple of dollars left."

"I appreciate it, Colonel." Then Bill frowned. He only had a few dollars in the tin can at home. He'd spent way too much on the mill, and along with paying the boys and the bad weather, he hadn't recouped it yet. "I'll get your fee paid as soon as I can."

Cravens grinned, took the cigar from his mouth, and blew a cloud of smoke. "Been a while since anyone called me colonel. I'm not worried about the fee, Tanner. I know you'll pay when you can. For now, let's just hope I can keep you out of jail. It will be a few weeks until your trial. I'll hold it off as long as I can. As soon as I know, I'll let you know the date."

Bill headed for the livery stable. The deputy had said the black was stabled there.

On the ride home, as Bill passed the scattered farms and rode through little settlements, he ran things over and over in his mind. As one problem collided into another, he finally pulled the black to a halt and stared at the gray sky. "Sufficient unto the day," he quoted. Granny had been a great one to quote scripture. She had urged taking one day at a time, and right now he figured that was the best he could do. With resolve he pushed aside the specter of prison to concentrate on his need for money.

"If the bastards want my mill and timber bad enough,"

he muttered, *"no telling what they'll try."* He rode on, rejecting first one plan and then another. He needed money and needed it quick. Finally, he decided to hide his mill deep in the woods. He would keep milling on the sly and pray they didn't find out. It was late afternoon before Bill finally reached home. His mood lightened as he saw Abigail's supper smoke. It felt as if he'd been gone much longer than a night and a day.

When he knocked, Abigail called, "Come in." She looked up from bending over the stove. He thought there was a flicker of relief on her face before she quickly turned back to the stove. She didn't turn back until the firebox was refilled, the door shut, and the damper adjusted. She began ladling pinto beans laced with chunks of ham from the kettle into a big bowl. A large platter of fried potatoes sat in the warming oven alongside a plate piled high with slices of steaming yellow cornbread.

Hat in hand, he waited for her to speak. Finally, after she sat the beans onto the table, she said, "I'm glad the sheriff let you go. I was afraid he would put you in jail."

"He did. I'm just out on bail. I'll have to stand trial."

She turned quickly to face him. "Oh, no!"

Then she seemed to take herself in hand and tried to wipe away emotion. "Have you eaten? I just sent Jacob to get the men."

"What are they doing?" he asked surprised they were all still here.

"They've been clearing ground all day. David said if you couldn't mill you'd need to grow cotton or you'd lose the place."

"He's right." Bill sat down and studied her face. "I figure you're sort of worried about what will happen if I go to prison. I've been studying on that on the way home. I hope you'll stay on here, watch the place, and take care of things until I get out."

She drew a quick, scared breath. "Do you think you'll go to prison?"

"I hope not, but it's a possibility. Lawyer Cravens will do all he can. With Ellis and Harvey and their bunch running things it doesn't look good. They want my mill and they want my place. Putting me in jail is a good way to get both, if I can't pay the taxes. But I'm not giving up without a fight. I'm going to try to lay by enough to pay the taxes, and you living here would keep them from just taking over." He gave a wan smile. "If my granny was alive, she'd be praying." He met Abigail's serious, brown eyes. "I'd sure appreciate yours."

Her voice was no more than a frightened whisper. "Oh, yes, I'll pray!"

"And will you stay come spring?"

She hedged, "I'll think about it."

Just then the boys came tramping inside. Wide smiles lit their faces as they saw Bill sitting at the table.

"Hey, you're back!" David slapped him on the back before straddling a chair. "What happened?"

Bill gave a quick report and then thanked them for staying on to clear the fields. He planned to apprise David and Toby of his plan to move the mill and sell timber on the sly. He would need their help. Matt and Tom were both fine boys, but Bill wasn't certain how close-mouthed they would be. He couldn't afford the risk and he couldn't afford their wages, but most of all he didn't want them involved in any legal trouble if he were caught selling timber. It would be hard having only a three-man crew to work the timber, and one of them crippled, and yet Bill could think of no better options. Besides, Toby had surprised him. What Toby lacked in physical ability, he made up for in determination.

"I've decided we'll finish clearing that field, and then since I can't afford your wages, I'll have to let you boys go," he said. "You've been good hard workers. No man could ask for better."

All faces fell, but Toby's most of all. Bill quickly added, "Toby, if you'll work for room and board and a little pay along as I can afford it, I'd be glad to have you stay."

Toby's face brightened. "That'd be fine with me. I sure want to keep on with my lessons with Miz Abigail."

Bill would talk to David in private and then fill Toby in as well about his plans for the mill. He thought they would both be willing to take the risk.

✖ Chapter 6

Bill paused a minute to get his breath, take a drink of water from the canteen, and then pass it to Matt and Tom, who took long draws before passing it back. He decided that grubbing sprouts was hot work even in late January when the winter sun shone brightly like today and a fellow had been hard at it since sunup. As was his habit lately, when his eyes sought the house, his mouth drew down. He hated the strain that had developed between him and Abigail. If things didn't change, he figured she would pack up and leave in the spring. A door had slammed shut between them, and he wasn't sure how to pry it open. He missed the relationship, the bond that had been growing between them before the carpetbaggers came. He wasn't altogether sure what she was thinking. He had tried talking to her when he returned home from jail, but she refused to discuss it. For the life of him, he couldn't understand why she would be so sympathetic to the carpet-bagging vermin.

His frown deepened. If he had a chance, he'd give them worse than a T on the chest. It galled him to the bone when the sheriff had shut down his mill—at least stopped his ability to sell anything. Bill was waiting impatiently while Cravens worked on the legality of the issue. He figured the attorney was right. Cravens held out little hope of any solution except to pay the bastards. As he said, it was hard to beat a stacked deck. Bill was fortunate to be out on bail.

It might be the Rawlings blood in his veins, but he wanted to hunt down Ellis and Harvey and make good his threat. Both men had left the country, or at least no one had seen them since the day of the branding. They had disappeared soon after filing a complaint and reporting to their superiors.

"That was a waste of time, Matt, and you know it," said Tom.

"Maybe so, but Ma had to try," argued Matt. "They dang near robbed us into the poor house and they ought to pay."

Bill's attention snapped back to the present. "What?"

"Aw, they're taking depositions in town to repay folks for what the Yankees took. We had to testify for Ma's claim last week. Tom says it's a waste of time."

"They're not gonna pay but a third of what they took," avowed Tom, "And they won't give Ma a dime—even though she swore to being loyal Union. That sticks in my craw."

Matt shrugged. "Maybe she was loyal. Her brother was. Besides, she only said what Judge Meers told her to, and he's the one who swore she was loyal."

"I know," said Tom, "and I appreciate him trying to help but still—"

"Someone coming fast," interrupted Matt.

While Bill corked the canteen, he frowned at the rider pounding down the road at a breakneck pace. As the man drew near, he left the trail and headed across the field straight for them. By the time he halted the lathered horse, David and Toby, still holding grubbing hoes, hurried to join them.

"Matt, Tom," panted the fellow as if he had been running, "I've got some mighty bad news. Sid sent me to tell you."

Matt stepped closer. His grip on the hoe had tightened until his knuckles were white. "What is it, Hank? Spit it out."

The man hesitated just a second before blurting out, "It's your brother—George. He's been shot. He's dead."

Matt's grip on the grubbing hoe tightened. "Dead?" he echoed while turning to Tom.

Tom's face went white. "Who did it, Hank?"

Hank avoided answering. "Sid says for y'all to come right straight home and not to talk to no one you might see along the road."

The brothers exchanged stricken looks. Without a word they started for the barn at a lope.

Bill stepped up. "I'm Bill Tanner. The boys work for me, and I'm a good friend of the family. What happened?"

Hank nodded. "Sid said I should tell you. He doesn't want the boys to know until he tells them himself for fear they'll go off half-cocked. It was Dud Turner shot George—shot him from an alley off Main Street."

Bill's lips thinned.

"A while ago Dud came back from hiding out in the nation—reckon he thought Sid had plumb forgot that he accused him of being a highwayman, but Sid hadn't forgot, not by a long shot. Last week he found Dud laughing and drinking in Pat Flood's Saloon and give him the what-fer. Sid would have killed him if I hadn't stepped in and drug him off." Hank's lips narrowed. "Wish I'd let him beat the life out of him. Then George would still be alive."

Bill's eyes sought the road where the boys had just ridden away. His frown deepened.

Bill removed his hat and wiped muddy snow from his boots onto the scraper before stepping inside. He didn't see Sid or the boys, only the casket with a view of George's handsome face, cold and pallid, and the parlor filled with people. He made his way through the throng after nodding to Miss Mattie Blackard, George's fiancée, who with red-rimmed eyes stood near the door. He stopped every so often to speak quietly to someone he knew until he reached Mrs. Wallace, who sat on the settee holding a crumpled, lace-edged handkerchief in one work-worn hand. She raised a drawn, colorless face to acknowledge his greeting.

"Ma'am, I'm mighty sorry for your loss." He hated the hollow-sounding words. But what was a body to say? There were no adequate words. He supposed those were as good as any.

"Thank you, Billy." She gave a weak smile and put out her hand. "And I want to thank you for taking such good care of Tom and Matt. They love working for you."

He took her hand. "They're fine boys, ma'am, and hard workers. I'm glad to have 'em." He shuffled his feet. "If there's anything I can do—anything at all, just say the word."

She glanced around and then gave a slight pull on his hand. She lowered her voice as he bent near. "Speak to Sid. He respects you. Tell him to let the law handle this." For a moment she held the handkerchief to trembling lips. "I don't want to lose another son."

"I'll speak to him, ma'am. I surely will." He patted her hand and then gave it a tiny squeeze. He stepped back as the next comforter arrived. Like an echo, the words repeated, "...so sorry for your loss."

Bill made his way outside to stand in weak winter sunshine in the Wallace yard. Ruth Wallace loved flowers, and in summer her yard was filled with fragrant blossoms, a rainbow of colored bushes and climbing vines. Now, everything was dead, the bushes and tree limbs naked and bleak except for a few leaves clinging stubbornly to the giant oaks surrounding the yard.

Men gathered in small groups, debating the day's event. Even though he listened, Bill kept quiet.

"Dud should have stayed in jail. Self-defense—in a pig's eye! It was murder, and Sid isn't going to let this slide by, even if the law does."

"He's out of jail?" asked Bill.

"Yeah. Judge Meers released him on a writ of habeas corpus."

Bill chewed his jaw. He didn't like the sound of that. He began making his way through the crowd looking for Sid. The man was probably right. Sid wouldn't let this slide. He had not gone far, however, when Cade James stopped him. He hadn't seen Cade since he had stopped selling him ties for the railroad.

"Howdy, Tanner."

"Cade." Bill shook Cade's wide, calloused hand.

"Tickled me when I heard what you did to Harvey and Ellis. They sure had it coming. They've just about shut my business down in Johnson County. No one can make money hauling ties anymore, so my supply has about dried up—and not just here. Damned carpetbaggers have instigated taxes and fees all over the state."

Bill nodded. "I won't pay, so I stopped milling. Guess I'll give cotton farming a try."

Cade scoffed. "There's a bigger tax on cotton than on timber."

"Honest?"

"Gospel."

Bill swore under his breath.

Cade went on, "If you do decide to start hauling again, I can sure use the ties. In the mean time, you'd better watch your back. Harvey is a mean one, and Ellis is a coward, the kind to be a back-shooter like Dud Turner."

"I'll go careful," Bill assured, and then he told Cade a hurried goodbye when Sid and his brother William crossed the yard. Tom and Matt trailed a few steps behind. In long strides Bill caught them before they entered the front door. Sid's face was drawn, and he looked years older than the last time Bill had seen him.

"I can't tell you how sorry I am about George." Bill nodded toward the side yard. "Sid, can we talk?"

"Sure. Boys, go on inside and see if Ma needs anything."

Sid followed Bill to the edge of the yard, their boots leaving tracks in the thin blanket of undisturbed snow. They stopped under a tall tree out of earshot of the crowd. While Bill talked, Sid pulled a piece of loose bark from the elm and rolled it between his fingers. He listened until Bill finished.

His lips curled. "Hell, Bill, so, you want me to let the law handle this—the same law that put you in jail a while back? Nothing legal and right about how this town is being run now."

Bill gave a dry laugh. "I agree." He looked squarely into Sid's eyes. "I told your ma I'd talk to you. She's afraid for you."

"I won't be stupid," he said.

"Fair enough." Bill briefly gripped Sid's shoulder. "Let me know if I can help. I mean it, Sid."

"I appreciate it."

Deep in thought, Bill mounted the black and rode away. On the dirt road, where the snow had been churned into muddy water, he passed more horses and buggies and wagons heading for the Wallace house, but he barely nodded as they passed. Sid was right. Legal didn't hold the same meaning it had before. Men were now in charge who hated Southerners and who made laws and regulations merely to line their own pockets. Cravens had urged restraint and abiding by the law, but Cravens made his living practicing law. Bill made his with his hands. His scowl deepened. The little money he had before was gone. Without cash he would lose his land. Cravens said property taxes had tripled, and they were due in the fall. He still hadn't paid Cravens' fee, and there would be more fees when the trial came. He needed to work the mill or make a crop, and he damn sure didn't intend letting someone who hadn't sweated a drop take his profits.

By the time he reached Hagarville, he had revised his plan. It wasn't solid yet and by no means foolproof; however, he did see a glimmer of hope. Quinton might not go along with it, but it was worth a try. He could make far more money selling staves than cross ties. He halted the black in front of the blacksmith shop, where gray smoke rose from the stovepipe.

Quinton, smiling broadly, shook his hand. After hearing of George's murder, Quinton shook his head. "Damned shame. From what I know of Sid, this won't go down easy, not with his brother shot in the back and the murderer set free. I was afraid you'd land in jail for a good stretch yourself."

"I'm just out on bail," Bill explained. "Cravens is trying to get the trial put off as long as possible."

Quinton swore loudly. "We got no law now except when it comes to stopping a man from making an honest living."

"That's about right," Bill agreed, "and that's the main reason I stopped by. Do you have any plans to reopen your mill?"

Quinton snorted. "Hell, no! Not with those buzzards sitting on the fence just waiting to swoop in and pick my carcass clean to the bone."

"Why don't you sell in Pope County instead of Clarksville?"

"Aw, they'd just watch and stop me at the county line."

"What if we hide your mill?"

Quinton scratched his jaw through the thick beard. "You might be onto something there. I've knowed plenty to hide out liquor stills to avoid the tax. Don't know why a feller couldn't hide out a lumber operation if he was a mind to. We'd have to go real careful, hide it way back in the woods..."

Bill nodded. "I have a place on my land that would work, and we'd not have to haul the staves far at all. And we can haul directly to the railhead in Russellville. It's farther than Clarksville, but we can't risk hauling in this county anymore."

Quinton's eyes lighted. "Maybe we can pull this off without paying the bloodsuckers." He sobered. "I reckon Pope County is about as rotten as Johnson...or worse. My Uncle Ambrose says there's a big bunch of thieves running things. He says they've had three crooked Yankee sheriffs since the war. All of them ended up shot. The latest killing happened just last week, so I don't know about the new feller. We'll have to go careful. This will only work if we play our cards real close to our chest. I got kin spread all over Pope County. They'll help every way they can."

"You sure you can trust this kin of yours?"

"Not a doubt about it. We're clannish to the death."

Bill's eyebrows rose. "I know that, but what will they say about you working with me? They might not like that. I don't see how we can keep it secret."

Quinton grinned. "Like I said, we're clannish. They'll help if I ask 'em." Quinton went on, "I have a good, high-paying market for my tight cooperage staves. They've been right upset at Little Rock since I shut down. Not many in the country does better quality work than me."

Bill knew it was no idle brag. He had heard many say the same thing. Quinton had learned his craft well in Tennessee, where whiskey barrel-making was a fine art. It was a dangerous task that took a steady hand and a good eye, and many men had been maimed doing it. Quinton milled the staves to perfection and then put the barrels together. For shipping, he took them apart again to be reassembled by the buyers, who swore that Quinton's barrels never leaked a drop.

"With your prime white oak timber, we should both make good money—enough to risk the headache."

Bill stuck out his hand. As they shook hands, Bill asked, "Do you need help moving your mill?"

"I do. But I'm thinking you need to lay low in this—not be seen with me at all. After I get things all squared away, I'll get Pa and we'll move it. I figure the county collectors will come around asking for proof I sold out. I'll cuss them out good for forcing me to sell the mill, and then I'll show them a bill of sale made out to someone in Pope County. I figure the biggest problem we'll have is keeping them from finding out when we start hauling again."

They made plans, finally deciding Quinton would claim that after he had sold the mill, he had freighted it to the buyer. If the ruse worked, Bill would hide his mill, too. Then he could saw and haul railroad ties as well.

"Ma! Come quick! It's Grandpa!"

Abigail laid down the half-peeled potato and hurriedly wiped her hands on the kitchen towel as she rushed to the front door. "What's wrong?"

Jacob had already sprinted across the porch and was trying to lift the crumpled body lying at the bottom of the steps where Little Bear ran around in circles barking. Jacob's voice was shrill with panic. "He just fell over and couldn't get back up."

She hurried down the steps and touched the old man's arm. "Jacob, run get Toby." But before Jacob had turned around, Bill came riding into the yard. He slid quickly from the horse's back and bent over Talbert.

"What happened? Did he hit his head on the ice?"

"No, sir," said Jacob. "He was talking and then his words didn't make sense. His eyes sort of rolled back in his head. The next thing I knew he was on the ground."

"Get the door open," Bill ordered. He lifted Talbert, carried him inside, and laid him on the bed where Abigail had hurriedly turned back the quilts.

"He needs a doctor," she said.

Bill glanced up. "David make it back?" When Abigail shook her head, he said, "Jacob, run fetch Toby."

In a few minutes, Toby arrived in a limping run.

"Take my horse. He's already saddled. Ride to Hagarville and ask Quinton where's the nearest doctor. I know one lives around there somewhere, but I'm not exactly sure where."

Toby nodded and quickly turned away.

"Don't try running the black on that road. It's freezing over again. Just keep him to a fast walk."

Abigail stared at the drooping mouth and the open eyes. Unless she was mistaken, he had suffered an apoplexy of the brain. When she felt the draft of frigid air, she stepped into the other room to close the front door, which Toby had left open in his haste. In the fading light she saw Bill bending over the bed to wipe muddy water from Mr. Anderson's face. Tears sprang into her eyes.

"Oh, Bill, if only…" she whispered. She felt so alone. But she could not ever trust him again. She had seen a fiend, and there was no denying it. Her heart had been bleeding ever since. When she reentered the bedroom, Bill straightened up from bending over the bed. He glanced at Jacob.

"Jacob, it's cold in here. Stoke up that fire in the kitchen." After the boy had left he lowered his voice. "My granny was a doctor of sorts, and I've seen such before. I reckon you know that most folks don't recover from a spell like this?"

"I know," she said. She rubbed her arms and let out a deep breath. Her brain was foggy and her feet felt wooden. She should be doing something, and yet she couldn't think what, so she sank into the rocking chair that Bill had just brought into the room for her. She nodded and mumbled, "Thank you." Then she remembered his trip to town and added, "I've been praying all day for the Wallace family. We never know what a day will hold, do we?" She glanced at the old man as she spoke. He had no idea when he had yelled at her before heading outdoors that he would have to be carried back inside. She had the swift thought—was that the last time she would have to put up with Talbert Anderson's abuse?

She looked up at Bill standing in the doorway. "How is Mrs. Wallace holding up?"

"It's hit her hard, of course. They're a close family, so the rest of the boys are helping her get through it. She'll be fine given enough time."

"Will the boys be coming back to work for you?"

"Not for a while. Sid says he needs them on the farm. Mostly I figure he knows their ma would like them close for now."

"I stirred up the fire," said Jacob. "Is Grandpa going to be alright?"

Abigail took his small hand in hers. "I don't know, son. We'll have to see what the doctor says."

Bill patted his shoulder. "Jacob, let's go feed the mules. Run on to the barn. I'll be there in a minute."

Abigail studied Talbert's prone form again. "This will go hard on Jacob."

"I figure it will," Bill agreed. "I'll help any way I can—I want to. And I don't want you worrying about a thing."

It was all she could do to keep from scoffing. Not worry! That was all she could do. Things had been impossible before, and now this! She felt no love for Talbert Anderson. *Perhaps it's a sin,* she thought, *that I've let his harsh ways harden my heart. I don't even feel pity.* How long would the old man linger? How long would she be forced to be near Bill Tanner when it was tearing her heart out?

This could require numerous visits by a physician. She had no idea how much a doctor would charge. It would be another drain on her hoarded cash, but it couldn't be helped. She was always frugal, and yet it seemed ever since she had decided to leave Bill's farm the minute the weather faired, her coins had diminished at a shocking rate. Jacob had outgrown his clothes and shoes, and her old cloak had become so threadbare it wouldn't turn the wind. She had only purchased another knowing that if they traveled early in the spring a heavier one would be a necessity. She could only hope Mr. Anderson's illness would not be a long one. But as she studied the waxy sheen on the shrunken cheeks and bony forehead, her shoulders sagged.

When a gust of wind hit the house, Abigail jerked awake, surprised to find she had been dozing. Pushing aside the quilt draped around her, she wondered how long she'd been asleep. She had worked hard all day and been exhausted even before Mr. Anderson's spell. A soft glow of lantern light shone from the other room, enough to show that he had not moved, although now his eyes were closed.

The smell of cooking lingered, tempting her with hunger. Bill stood when she entered the kitchen. He kept his voice low. "I fixed supper. Jacob ate and I sent him to bed a good while ago. You looked worn out so I let you sleep, but I saved you a plate."

"Toby's not back yet?"

"No. I figure he had to go on to Clarksville to find a doctor."

She sat down at the table and thanked him for the food he placed in front of her. "This looks delicious. Fried potatoes, ham, and cornbread. I had no idea you were such a cook."

"A bachelor has to learn or go hungry. My cooking's not nearly as good as yours, though."

She took a few bites. The cornbread wasn't as good as hers, but certainly edible. The potatoes were crispy and done to perfection as was the ham. "It tastes wonderful."

He filled her cup with steaming coffee, poured another for himself, sat down across the table, and took a sip. "Talbert got a little restless. When I touched him, his skin felt cold so I put another quilt on him. He hasn't stirred since."

"Thank you for the quilt you put on me too." The fork paused halfway to her mouth. A patter of ice struck the window, driven along by wind rattling the panes. "Oh dear, that's sleet! I hope Toby and the doctor aren't riding through that gale."

"Abigail," Bill paused.

She waited, wishing he would say something, and yet the way his serious eyes probed her face, she dreaded what it might be. She laid the fork down. "What is it?"

"This may not be the time," he said, "but I don't know when we'll get a chance to be alone, so I'm going to speak my mind. I hope you'll do the same. I've grown to care for you and at one time I thought you might have felt the same about me. I want to know what's wrong between us. I know you didn't like what happened with the carpetbaggers. But it started even before that—near as I can tell, it started Christmas Day. You've been different towards me ever since. In my mind I've gone over and over what I might have done." He shrugged. "I may be thick-headed, but I can't recollect one thing."

"You didn't do anything wrong at Christmas," she hedged, dropping her eyes and smoothing her skirt.

"Then what's wrong?"

She drew a shaky breath. It might be a relief to voice her fears, at least some of them. It wouldn't mean she trusted Bill, because she didn't, but for the kindness he had shown he did deserve some explanation. She looked up. "I received a letter from a neighbor in Missouri. Her son thinks he saw Frank alive in a prison camp hospital. The man he saw had his face bandaged so he couldn't be sure, but it might have been. My husband might still be alive. On Christmas Day, Mr. Anderson reminded me of that in no uncertain terms."

Bill swore under his breath. For a few seconds he stared out the window at the black night. "Even if he is alive," he said, "a man that could do that to a woman"—he pointed at her scar—"doesn't deserve you. I know you feel duty bound because of your vows, and because he's Jacob's pa. But do you really want Jacob raised by such a man?"

Her brow puckered. She bit her lip to keep from saying more. Bill seemed blind to his own violence.

It was almost dawn when Toby arrived with the bleary-eyed, middle-aged doctor. With only a curt hello, the doctor stepped to Talbert's bedside and began an examination.

"Sorry it took so long," Toby apologized under his breath. "He was gone up toward Fort Douglas delivering a baby. We come as quick as he got back."

Abigail took his cold hand. "Thank you, Toby. You're frozen. There's ice all over your hat. Come warm by the fire, and I'll get you and the doctor some hot coffee and breakfast."

The doctor sat down and gratefully accepted the steaming cup. "I'm not sure how the medical profession survived during the war when we had no coffee. I never drink a cup now without thanking God." He took a sip. Then his face grew serious. "Ma'am, your father-in-law has suffered a stroke. He may regain some abilities, but at his age it's highly unlikely."

"Do you think he'll die?" Bill asked.

"That's hard to say. If he doesn't have another stroke, he could live for a long while. I've known of people living for years—then again, he could die today. There's just no way of knowing. He will require a lot of care. He's paralyzed on his left side."

Abigail nodded. On the inside she shuddered. She loathed the thought of touching him, bathing him, changing his soiled bedding. She drew a long, shaky breath. She wasn't sure if she could bring herself to, and yet she knew she must. She wondered if it would be wicked to pray he died tonight. She did not know how much longer her strained nerves could endure being here, seeing Bill each day and falling more in love. Staying was torture. Her mind skittered away from the suffering leaving would cause.

✕✕✕

In the glow of lantern light, Bill pulled the last piece of pipe from the wagon. Suddenly he held up his hand for quiet. Keeping his voice low, he said, "I heard something."

The other men stood stone still, ears straining. Finally, Quinton whispered, "What did it sound like?"

Bill stayed quiet a bit longer. "I reckon it was just wind rattling a limb."

"Bet it was," Quinton agreed. "Not likely anyone would be slipping around spying on us out here in the woods tonight." He blew on his wide hands to warm them. "Hit's cold as a well-digger's butt out here. I'm heading home. I'll see you fellers in the morning."

"I figure Abigail has plenty cooked if you'd like to eat a bite first."

"Thanks," said Quinton, but Ma will have supper waiting. I'll be back bright and early. If we're lucky we'll have the mill back in operation in a couple of days."

"Sounds good," said Bill. "Hope we can get to hauling right away."

After Quinton had guided the team of mules out of sight, David gave a big sigh. "I'm glad we finally finished up. This night work ain't to my liking. Abigail probably threw our supper to the hogs."

Toby chuckled. "Except we got no hogs, and Miz Abigail would never do such a thing. She'll have it warming on the stove as usual."

"Sorry we had to work so late the last few days," said Bill, "but I want to get this done before those thieves come back. This frozen ground will hide our tracks."

It was a good spot, a secluded hollow near a small spring with enough water to keep the boiler filled. He blew out the lantern and looked up at the cold, star-filled sky. The sight never failed to stir him, to set his mind wondering what might be beyond the stars. Granny used to tease that stars were tiny holes in the sky that let the glory of God peep through. He hoped Granny's prayers still held sway with God; he would need them!

While he walked past dark tree trunks, he breathed a quick prayer that the Almighty would give him favor and keep the authorities from catching him. He desperately needed money. Providing for Abigail and Jacob was his responsibility now. She would have her hands full nursing the old man.

He planned to begin cutting timber just as soon as they got the mill reassembled. His meeting with Cade a few days before had gone well. Cade had been glad to accept delivery of the staves and ties at Russellville. Bill and Quinton planned to travel at night hauling the loads in hopes no one would see them before they crossed the county line.

When Bill crossed the yard, Jacob ran from the house through the dark to meet them. "Can I turn Little Bear loose now?" he asked. "He sure doesn't like being tied up."

"Yeah, you can let him loose. We're through."

The dog had barked incessantly the night before, following them into the woods. Bill supposed there had been a coon rambling. Whatever the case, he didn't want the dog drawing attention to their venture.

The minute they walked through the door, Abigail began setting platters of bacon and cornbread along with a large bowl of pinto beans onto the table. She waited until Jacob had gone to bed before asking how things had gone.

"We got the mill unloaded. It will take us a few days to get it set up again, and then we can start cutting. We'll just mill staves for a while until we can get my mill moved too."

"I hope the weather warms," she said, setting a steaming cup next to Bill.

As she drew back, her arm brushed his shoulder. He looked up. Their eyes met and held for a split second, long enough for him to know that she had reacted to the touch as well.

"How long do you think it'll take us to haul the loads to Russellville?" asked Toby.

"Russellville?" asked Abigail in surprise.

"Yes, we're hauling through Pope County because they've got no claims against us. It's a little farther than hauling to Clarksville, but going the back roads, we're just a couple of miles from the county line. We can't risk hauling across Johnson. If they catch us, they'll take everything Quinton and I have and probably put us in jail to boot. Since I'm already under indictment, it would go extra hard on me."

"How long will it take to make the trip?"

"Two days going and one coming back—that is if the weather holds. The roads aren't great, not to mention all the creeks to ford. Big Piney can be a booger if it rains."

Abigail's lips drew down. "I wish you didn't have to haul so far."

Bill blew on the coffee and took a sip. "Me too, but it seems the best way to make enough cash money to pay taxes and keep us from starving."

Bill remained seated after he had finished eating and David and Toby had headed for the bunkhouse. Abigail had begun clearing the table. "What's wrong?" he asked. "You got mighty quiet there all of a sudden."

She made a scoffing noise and paused from pouring steaming water from the kettle into the metal dishpan. She turned to meet his eyes. "What's wrong? A better question might be what isn't."

"Abigail, sit down for a minute."

She slowly dried her hands on a dishtowel and then sat down across the table from him.

"I've been wanting to talk to you." He hesitated, unsure how best to proceed. Finally he said, "I know things haven't turned out the way you'd hoped. Things are extra hard on you just now—having to care for the old man, taking care of the boy, cooking for us, and all the other chores you have to do. I know it's too much. I just don't know what to do to make things easier…I thought about asking Toby to give you a hand, but the truth is I need his help too much myself. Even with only one good arm, he's a worker. If I could afford it, I'd hire someone to help you."

Her back straightened. "That isn't your responsibility. I wouldn't allow it even if you could."

Taken aback by her tone, he stared. For a minute, he looked down to fiddle with the cup handle. "It may not be my legal responsibility," he said, looking up to meet her wary eyes, "but I feel responsible for you and Jacob—and glad of it."

She sucked in a sharp breath. "Well, you're not responsible for us." Then she stood and began scraping and stacking plates as if her life depended on it.

"Is this about Frank? About you being afraid he's still alive?"

The scraping fork stilled. "Even if he's dead, we're not your responsibility. I know how much you've done for us and will always appreciate it, but please, don't believe for a second that you owe me anything."

He stood and crossed the space between them. He ignored that she stiffened. "Abigail, I've not actually spoke the words, but I reckon you know I love you. I think I have since I first saw you standing in the yard with that ax, turning your face away so I couldn't see this." He traced the scar with his finger. His lips opened to say more, but abruptly he turned on his heels and strode out the door and shut it behind him. With a groan he looked up at the sky and swore at himself under this breath, *"Bill Tanner, you're a fool!"*

Why did everything in his life have to be so damned complicated? He knew she had feelings for him. He could feel it—could see it in her eyes. He wanted to ask her to marry him, but he couldn't! He might be going to prison for a long time. And even if he asked, she would never say yes as long as she thought Frank was alive.

Abigail turned to stone. She stood rigid until the door closed, all except her heart. It almost jumped out of her chest. Then she collapsed into a chair and buried her face in her hands. He loved her. She didn't doubt it. And she loved him. But that didn't change the facts. She must not let him know. She must not encourage him. She must not be beholden to him...not any more than she already was. And that was plenty!

She might risk herself, but never Jacob. He was already too fond of Bill. He had been overjoyed when Bill returned from jail. She needed to get him away from here!

She lifted her head when Mr. Anderson made a racket. *Could she not have even a moment to herself?* When the guttural noises continued, she finally rose wearily from the chair, picked up the lamp, and with dragging steps, entered the bedroom. His rheumy eyes were open and accusing and, as usual, filled with hate. The gray hair and beard that she had combed earlier in the day were now awry, sticking out from his head and chin like a wild creature. In agitation, he thrashed about his good arm

151

while the crippled arm lay limp and useless at his side. He was wet again. She had made large diapers of quilted material, but the second they were wet, he raised a fuss of unintelligible noises and grunts. Normally she ignored his outbursts and woodenly did her duty to feed and clean him. Tonight she felt resentful and waspish.

"You know, if I was a mind to, I could just leave you here all night in your own filth." Her eyes narrowed. "And if I decided not to feed you, no one would know. You'd just wither up and die."

Instantly his anger turned to panic, and as he gripped the quilt like a frightened child and tried to speak, she grew ashamed.

"But I'm not going to do that," she said in a matter-of fact tone. "I'm going to feed you and keep you clean. But you might occasionally act the least bit grateful."

He grew still. When he slowly reached to pat her arm, her eyes widened in shock. It might only be fear that prompted his action; even so, it certainly made her feel more charitable.

When he was dry and tucked in with an extra quilt against the cold biting through the walls and glazing the windows with ice, she blew out the lamp and went to her room.

Even though she was exhausted to the point of feeling sick, she tossed and turned, reliving each word Bill had spoken. Standing stiff had been one of the hardest things she had ever done when in reality she had longed to walk into his arms, to feel loved and protected. Now that he had openly declared his love, it seemed to complicate things a thousandfold. She lay awake far into the night worrying what to do. And yet she seemed to have no choice.

She was up by four o'clock and had breakfast sitting on the table when the men came through the door. She avoided eye contact with Bill. He gave no evidence of their last encounter. Just like Toby and David, he gulped down the hot food, thanked her, and then hurried away. She stepped to the window and looked until his broad back was out of sight in the pool of lantern light. With a deep sigh she turned away. As her gaze fell on the table, her shoulders sagged. Another set of dishes...and today was washday. She wondered if she'd ever feel rested again.

"Jacob, get up," she called into the loft. "Come eat breakfast. As soon as the sun is up you need to start hauling water to fill the washtubs."

By the time the sun had crested the ridge above the tree line, the kitchen was steamy, filled with the clean scent of soap, and the first tub of bedding was scrubbed, ready to hang on the line. Abigail stepped outside into the frosty air. She squinted against the bright day. Then a faint smile hovered as she looked at the new, taut clothesline Bill had hung. He was forever doing thoughtful things to make her chores easier. She bit her lip and then shook her head as she set down the basket of heavy, wet laundry. It was dangerous to let her mind go wandering down that path. And yet the more she determined to put him out of her thoughts, the more determined he seemed to stay. Uppermost was the fear that he would go to prison. Sometimes she broke into a cold sweat as that dread flooded her.

The washing was extra large today. She had skipped doing laundry the week before because of bitter weather. By the time the last wet pair of pants dangled from the clothesline, Abigail realized it had been a while since she had checked on Mr. Anderson. Taking long steps, she hurried inside, hung her coat on a peg near the door, and went into his room. Her eyes suddenly widened. "How in the world...?"

Somehow he had dragged himself off the bed and onto the chair. He sat slumped in the chair, a sure sign he was improving. That thought did not make her happy.

"Jacob," she called, "come help me get your grandpa back to bed."

※※※

Tall oaks on the ridge were dark blotches against the dim glow of the morning sky as the men made their way through the woods, the only sound their boots crunching frozen ground, their breath white clouds of vapor that soon disappeared into frosty air. Bill glanced up at the lightening sky, relieved to see few clouds. They could cut frozen timber, but sleet or snow slowed progress and ice made the task next to impossible. He hoped the weather stayed clear and cold. A thaw would make the ground soup and stop them dead in their tracks.

He stopped, set the canteen on the ground, and leaned the ax against a tree. When David yawned loudly, he turned and grinned. "What's the matter? Didn't get your nap out?"

David snorted. "Not hardly. You don't look so chipper yourself. I heard you tossing and turning in your bunk too."

Bill's eyebrows rose. "I've got plenty to keep me awake, but I didn't figure a young, footloose fellow like you had a care in the world."

"Oh, I got plenty," he grumbled. After a pause he added, "Just maybe I ain't so keen on staying footloose."

Surprised, Bill halted. "You serious?"

"For all the good it does me." David shrugged. He leaned against a tree trunk while staring at the crosscut he had just un-slung from his shoulder. "Your cousin Deborah doesn't appear to feel the same—at least not about me." He looked up with troubled eyes. "What do you know about Michael Lane?"

"Michael? I like him fine, but he's not husband material. Is Deborah interested in him?" Bill asked with a frown.

"I'm afraid so. She lights up like a lamp when he comes into the room."

Bill didn't like the sound of that. Michael was a good friend, but Deborah was kin. She was special. He had watched her grow from the cradle into a lovely young woman. She could do far worse than David, but he feared Michael would only break her heart. Ned would never sanction the match. He finally said, "I reckon you can put your mind to rest if that's what's eating you. Uncle Ned would never agree to a match between those two."

"Problem is," said David, "the pa doesn't always get his way in matters of the heart."

"Too true," agreed Bill. He wondered if Deborah would listen to a cousin. It was worth a try.

The conversation abruptly halted as Toby arrived, breathing deeply. Bill and David chuckled when Toby said, "You two going to jaw all day or are we gonna cut stave bolts?"

Soon the saw was biting into a giant white oak, and by noon there was a fair-sized pile of split staves. They alternated the tasks of sawing and splitting. In spite of the crippled hand, Toby was using the maul with astonishing strength and skill. By the time they took a short break to eat the lunch Abigail had packed, they had shed jackets and sweat glistened on each brow.

Bill looked around at all the treetops lying on the ground. It was a shame to waste so much good timber. It couldn't be helped. He didn't have time to move his mill, even if he dared. Besides, there was more money in staves, and he desperately needed cash. His small hoard had dwindled astonishingly fast, and there was still Cravens to pay.

"At this rate, we should have a couple of wagonloads ready in no time," said David. "Do you reckon Quinton can mill them fast enough that we can haul a few loads before the roads thaw?"

"He thinks he can."

"You got a plan to keep us from getting caught while we're hauling?"

"We'll take the back roads and leave here in plenty of time to be out of the county by daylight. The roads will be rougher, but we can't risk being seen. I'll drive one wagon and Quinton the other so either you or Toby can scout ahead. The other can keep an eye on our back trail. If anyone decides to come after us, at least we'll have a little warning."

"Sounds good," said David as he stood and stretched. "Tobe, I reckon I got enough kinks out of my back to take my turn splitting," he said with a grin at Toby, who was rubbing his lower back. "We'll all be glad for a break from splitting while we help Quinton in the mill."

The next week they worked from the wee hours of the morning until late evening, always needing a lantern to see the way home from the mill. Abigail kept supper warming on the stove. Bill hated that their schedule kept her working far into the night. Although she swore it was no problem, he noticed she had bags under her eyes now and was losing weight.

After supper, he stood and began clearing his plate from the table.

"I'll do that," Abigail insisted. "You all need to get some sleep before your trip."

He walked over to the counter and plunged his plate into the soapy water and began washing it. "From now on, when we're this late, we'll all help wash up. No need for you to be washing dishes until midnight. You have too much to do as it is, taking care of Talbert and all."

Toby and David stood, and carrying their dishes they headed toward the dishpan.

"He's right, Miz Abigail," said Toby. "You just sit right down and rest yourself a bit. We'll have this kitchen clean in no time."

When she protested again and remained standing, David gently took her shoulders and pushed her into a chair. "Now, ma'am, it ain't advantageous to argue with the boss. Besides, if you ain't already figured it out, let me tell you, Bill is one ornery cuss who won't take no for an answer. Save your breath and just sit a spell."

She shook her head, gave a tiny laugh, and accepted defeat graciously by saying, "Well, thank you." Bill looked over as he wiped a plate and handed it to David to put into the cupboard.

When the chore was done, she thanked them all again. Bill was the last man out the back door. He lingered a moment. "While we're gone, I hope you'll get some rest."

For a moment her eyes had a tender shine. It quickly vanished as if a shutter had closed. "That's very kind," she said primly. "God bless you all on the trip. I'll be praying for safe travels."

"I appreciate that," he said, wondering again why she had changed so drastically.

The eerie glow of swirling fog in lantern light seemed fitting, thought Bill as they started on the clandestine journey. He flipped the reins to start the two broad-hipped mules straining into collars, their heavy steps in perfect time to the creak of wheels on the frost-covered trail. Black woods looming on both sides of the wagon swallowed the dim glow, but there was still enough light to see the rise and fall of the rutted trail and the outline of the wagon ahead and Quinton's wide back. No one else was in sight. David scouted ahead while Toby kept an eye on the back trail. With any luck they would be well out of the county by daylight, even with the wagons heavily loaded.

There weren't many dwellings along this trail, but enough to make Bill nervous. He feared someone might go to a window to see what the dogs were barking at. He hoped they didn't get too curious, not enough to mention in town that wagons heavily loaded with staves had passed their way in the wee hours of the morning. It wouldn't take the sheriff long to get curious too.

They did pass a few dark farmhouses with barking dogs, but Bill saw no lights. By the time the sun had turned the sky a light gray, he figured they were well into Pope County. He figured their biggest worry now would be heading home with cash money. There were always plenty of riffraff wanting to lighten a man's pockets, not to mention crooked officials looking for bribes.

As the sun rose higher and Bill jostled on the wagon seat, he muttered, "This road is rough as a cob." But he thought the terrain was pretty. Near the trail, on the left, jutting shelves of rock fell away into a steep gully that bordered a small creek snaking along the bottom of the rugged hollow. On the right the timber-covered hill towered over the trail. He squinted into the sun, glad for the slight warmth in the winter rays. His hands were cold, even inside the gloves.

The trip progressed with only a few delays to cut trees and attach them to the backs of the wagons before going down the steepest inclines where the brakes weren't sufficient. And they made a few stops to let the mules breathe after pulling the steepest hills. After a few rugged miles the trail grew smoother as the land began gradually to level into grassy pastures dotted with grazing cattle and then opened into wide fields, barren now, holding only traces of stubble from last year's crops. They stopped for a short break at noon to eat biscuits that Abigail had filled with fried ham, and then they washed them down with water from canteens.

In late afternoon, through the trees, Bill saw the glimmer of Big Piney Creek. It was wide, and the water was ice-crusted near the shady edges but neither too deep nor too swift just now. The mules crossed with little urging and then climbed the far bank, the black mud still frozen enough to allow the wheels to roll without slowing. When the ground thawed, Bill knew it would be a different story. Then the roads would be greasy and slick; the black mud in the bottoms and the red clay in the hills would cling to hooves and wheels and bog them down with every difficult inch. For now he was thankful for the ease.

They made camp soon after crossing Piney, but far enough away from the stream to avoid the mist that hugged a creek at night and soaked everything it touched. While Bill and Quinton unhitched and fed the mules, Toby and David began setting up camp and building a fire started with dry kindling that had been stashed under the wagon seat. Soon a cheery blaze lit the gloom, and after a while the crackling sticks began to settle into a bed of coals. Before Toby added more wood, David raked some of the coals aside, and then hunkering near the blazing campfire, he took a pocketknife from his trousers and slit an x in the top of a large can of beans.

"These beans are froze hard as rocks," he grumbled and began breaking them loose from the can with his knife. He hunkered and poured them into a cast-iron skillet and set it on the coals. "I reckon the cornbread is froze, too," he added while reaching into the tin bucket that Abigail had packed the night before. He laid the frozen chunks of bread onto a tin plate and then set the plate over the pan of beans, using it as a lid.

After a few minutes, Toby sniffed the air and his nostrils flared. "Don't burn them beans. I'm hungry."

Bill and Quinton walked up in time to see David snatch the smoking pan from the coals. He swore as he burned his fingers, and then as he grabbed the plate off the pan, he swore again.

"Didn't anyone ever teach you that a pan set over coals gets hot?" said Quinton with a laugh.

"And no one ever taught him to cook, neither," said Toby as he looked at the smoking beans.

David scowled. "If you think you can do better, Toby McKennon, I'll be glad to let you do the cooking." Then his lips drew down and he sighed. "I ain't scorched a pot of beans since I was a shirttail kid and Grandpa took a strap to me for wasting food."

Toby quickly tried to make amends. "Likely they ain't burned beyond eating…and the cornbread looks fine."

But the beans were beyond eating. When Bill spit out the first bite and washed his mouth out with coffee, Quinton raked his into the fire un-tasted and then sat down and leaned back against the wagon wheel. He dipped a piece of cornbread into his coffee cup.

"Don't look so glum," he told David. "I've seen the time in the army when cornbread and coffee was a feast."

Bill looked up from sipping his coffee. "Who'd you serve under?"

"General Polk."

Bill nodded. "I was a courier for Hardee and later on got moved to Bragg's command. You and me might have crossed paths at Chattanooga."

Quinton's brows rose. "Could be. I was there. I've heard tales about Bragg."

"And none of them good, I'll wager," said Bill. "He was a mean sonofabitch."

Quinton dusted cornbread crumbs from his hand before reaching into a pocket and pulling out a pipe and a sack of tobacco. He packed the pipe and then leaned to get a smoldering stick from the fire, held it to the tobacco, and began puffing.

"Yeah, that's what I heard," he said. "Bad business when men speak worse of their officer than of the enemy. Can't say much good about Polk's general-ing…but he was God-fearing. Reckon before the war, he was high up in his church. Folks called him the fighting bishop. Treated us good. Even so, it was no picnic." He glanced over at Toby and David. "You boys can be glad you were too young to fight in that war. I pray to God there's not another one."

Toby nodded. "Pa got killed at Pea Ridge."

David frowned. "Like you said, I was too young to fight; even so, I had to dodge lead a few times. And I darn sure know what you mean about going hungry. I'm a veteran at that."

"Reckon most everyone in Arkansas is," agreed Bill, stretching. Then he yawned. "It's been a long day. I'm turning in. I'll see you fellows in the morning."

Cade James was not at the shipping yard, but the clerk had an empty car ready. Quinton stood ready to board the train. He stuck out his hand to shake Bill's. "You boys go careful. If everything goes good, I'll be back in a few days." He was going to Little Rock, along with the barrel staves, to negotiate a price for this and future loads.

Bill and the boys started back home with the empty wagons after leaving Quinton one of the saddle horses at the livery stable for the return trip. Since the wagons were now empty, Bill decided to risk going home on the good roads.

"We'll go back through Dover," he said. Upon seeing the boys' faces brighten, he quickly dashed their good spirits. "We're going that way, but we won't be stopping to see the sights. I'm hoping to have enough staves split for another load to mill by the time Quinton gets back. We'll be lucky to haul two more loads before spring thaw turns these roads to mush. I'd rather avoid towns altogether, but the good road will save us hours."

Russellville had grown since becoming the railhead; however, it was still just a small settlement with only a few stores and scattered dwellings. With the coming of the railroad, if things progressed true to form, Bill figured it would soon catch up with Dover, a few miles to the north, which was the county seat and the largest town around.

They made few stops and with the wagons empty made it home in a day. Bill gave a soft smile to see lantern light making yellow squares of the windowpanes like the yellow blocks on one of Granny's quilts. It was nice to have lamplight to welcome a man. He'd come home too many times to a dark, cold cabin. He dusted off the worst trail dust while silently admitting the best part of coming home was Abigail waiting inside.

XXX

Quinton arrived before the week was out. "They paid even more than I'd figured," he said with a big smile as he held out a roll of cash to Bill.

Bill took the money and then whistled low before putting it into the pocket of his heavy coat. He did quick calculations. At this rate, he should soon have enough to pay property taxes and Cravens' fee, and maybe even make a few improvements on the farm. "We have enough split for another load," he said.

"Good," said Quinton. "I'll be over early. Maybe we can be ready for another haul before long."

Bill turned back to the house, his steps light. Maybe his luck had turned; maybe things actually would work out and he wouldn't have to go to prison.

The house was growing dusky, but Abigail, busy in the kitchen, had not lighted the lamps. Old man Anderson was seated near the stove where he spent most of his time now, head lowered, dozing, a quilt draped around thin shoulders. Still unable to speak or walk, he nonetheless seemed more contented to sit near the stove.

In the last light of the winter sun, Bill saw Abigail pouring sliced potatoes into a cast iron skillet of hot lard. As the grease popped and crackled, she pulled back just a bit to avoid getting splattered and then finished adding the last of the potatoes. She put a lid on the pan and turned, surprised to see him standing and watching.

"I didn't hear you come in," she said.

"Didn't mean to startle you." He nodded toward the front door. "I came in the front." He stepped to the washbasin, washed and dried his hands. "Want me to get him back into bed?" he asked.

"Yes, please. He already ate a bowl of soup."

"You still have to feed him?"

"No, he can manage pretty well now. Oh, he spills a lot, but I think it's good for him to do what he can."

Bill touched the bony shoulder. "I'm taking you back to bed." The dark eyes opened and instantly filled with venom. The old man tried to pull back. Bill chuckled. "Old devil ain't lost his spunk, has he? Still hates me like poison." He gently lifted the skeletal frame like a baby.

Abigail frowned. "I've told him he ought to appreciate what you've done for him—for us. But hate is so fixed inside him; I don't suppose he'll ever change."

"Maybe the hate keeps him going—gives him a reason to live."

Abigail shuddered. "I'd rather be dead if that was all I had to live for."

Bill nodded. "Me too." He paused long enough to meet her eyes. "Love is a better reason." He walked on, grinning at her rosy cheeks. As he put Anderson into the bed, he couldn't resist the temptation to lean over and mutter, "Someday, I'm gonna marry that woman, and there's not a damn thing you can do about it, old man."

Abigail glanced up when he returned. "Supper's about ready."

He drew in an appreciative breath. "Smells good. Nothing I like better than fried potatoes."

She replaced the lid after pushing the potatoes around with a long-handled spoon and then opened the oven for a quick peek at the browning cornbread. As the aroma of baking bread drifted out, she asked, "Where are the boys?"

"Finishing up at the mill. We want to get an early start."

"I guess you'll be heading out again with another load soon?"

"Probably near the end of the week." He pulled out a

chair, sat down, leaned the chair back, and propped one boot heel on the bottom rung. "Jacob's been learning a lot about milling staves. Quinton says not everybody can learn the art, but he thinks maybe Jacob can. He's bright and quick with his hands." When she stayed silent, he finally asked, "You don't think that's a good idea?"

"It's a fine idea for a boy to learn any good skill, and I'm sure Mr. Quinton is excellent at what he does. But don't go filling Jacob's head with ideas that will only disappoint him. The way Mr. Anderson is improving, I figure we'll be able to travel soon."

"That's a fool idea!" exploded Bill, the front legs of the chair hitting the floor with a bang. She flinched as if he'd struck her; even so, he didn't soften his voice. "Why are you so all-fired determined to leave? You got a roof over your head and food in your stomach. And no one is mean to you here. You said you've got no place to go—no kin who would have you and the old man. Besides, you'd probably not last a week on the trail before someone robbed you and left you afoot." His eyes narrowed. "Are you still in love with Frank? Is that what this is about? You want to go looking for him?" He huffed an aggravated breath as she stared, hard-eyed and silent. "Well, there's no need to go looking! I asked Cravens to do some digging. If Frank's still alive he'll find him, and then I'll buy you a train ticket to go back to the sonofabitch." He stormed outside, slamming the door.

He stood shaking in the cool air. He'd left his coat and hat inside, but it was anger that had him trembling. Most of all he was mad at himself. *Hell! She didn't love Frank.* She'd made that plain. And yet he couldn't understand why she kept straining to leave like a wild filly tied with a rope. He was good to her, good to Jacob—she said so herself all the time. It made no sense to him. And that made him mad. He wasn't prone to temper, but when he did get angry, he was mad to the bone and not quick to cool off. He owed her an apology, but he wasn't going back inside tonight. He'd better stop the fool daydreaming. His luck hadn't changed one damn bit.

They managed to make two uneventful trips before the weather finally caught them. The first day had started out well enough. Even though by midmorning the weather had warmed a bit, the roads were still hard and dry. By noon, as the temperature rose, Bill knew they were in for trouble.

Quinton, on the wagon seat ahead, affirmed his worries by calling back over his shoulder, "We better not stop to eat. The bottom is going to fall out of this trail as soon as we get out of this red clay land and head down into the bottoms."

Even though they pressed on, soon the mules were laboring through thawed, soft, creek bottom mud. The soil was sandy here, so it didn't cling to hooves and wheels like black glue; but it still slowed them to a crawl. Bill groaned aloud as he saw Quinton's wagon suddenly lurch and tilt as one front wheel sank to the axle. His own mules stopped before he had to pull the reins.

As Toby and David rode horses near, Quinton, scowling, stood alongside the wagon, staring at the wheel and tugging at his dark beard. "Reckon if we hook your team with mine, they can pull it out?"

Bill shook his head. "I doubt it, but we can try. If not we'll have to unload some. Come on, fellows. Climb down. Looks like we're gonna get our boots muddy."

After double hitching the teams, the men put shoulders to wheels and strained as Quinton yelled at the mules, urging them forward. The mules strained into collars, and the men pushed with necks bulging. The wheel didn't immediately climb out of the hole. They managed to scoot the wagon forward until, finally, the wheel hit more solid ground and climbed out. With gloves and boots and pants mud-covered, they started on again, Bill being careful to stay out of Quinton's ruts. However, they had only traveled a quarter mile before both front wheels on the lead wagon sank.

Quinton, swearing, climbed down, and they began the process again until Bill yelled, "Whoa! This ain't working."

Panting, the others stopped pushing. David, drawing in deep breaths, suggested, "Maybe if we cut brush and put under the wheels—give 'em something to catch on."

"It's worth a try," Bill agreed.

Although they cut armfuls of brush and finally even small trees, the mud sucked them under without giving the wheels a toehold.

"Nothing to do but unload," said Bill. Amid the loud groans, he added, "May as well get used to it. I doubt this is the last time."

By nightfall they had unloaded and reloaded seven times and had not yet made it across Big Piney. Exhausted they ate cold beans from the can and slept near the campfire in muddy clothes and boots. It was the first time in weeks that Bill had not tossed and turned before falling asleep. This night held no thoughts of Abigail and the strained silence that had fallen between them.

The pale, gray sky was streaked with low clouds when Bill sat up and groaned, rubbing his sore shoulders. Someone was already awake for he smelled coffee. He started to rise but groaned again.

"Toby, I might just live if I get a cup of that, but I ain't really sure I want to," called Quinton.

Bill, gritting his teeth, stood. "What's the matter, Quinton? Ain't you feeling chipper this morning?" He bent to take the coffee pot from the fire and poured a cup. "I'm raring to go."

Quinton gave a derisive laugh. "Sure you are. I see you limping like my grandpa."

Just then David came riding into camp. He piled off the horse and took the steaming cup Toby handed him. "Good news. I been scouting up and down the creek, and I found us a good rocky crossing. The near bank is a little steep, but the far bank is good. We'll have to cut a trail to get to it, but it's the most solid ground for miles. I don't figure cutting a trail will take as long as loading and unloading, and it'll be a damn sight easier."

After a hurried breakfast, Bill and Quinton rode the horses. First they rode to their regular crossing, and then following the trail David had blazed, they reached the place he described. It was a beautiful spot, just above a pool where water cascaded into a small fall before hurrying down the creek. The bed was a rock bottom, plainly visible through the clear water, and the far bank a gradual, rocky incline where the mules would have perfect footing, but Bill rubbed his jaw and frowned while studying the near bank.

"What do you think?" asked Quinton.

"It's mighty steep. We'll have to use a good drag, but I think it's our best bet. What do you say?"

"Unless we want to stay here till kingdom-come, I say we better try it. That place we been crossing is so soupy the bank ain't likely to dry out for weeks."

"Then let's ride back and get the axes and start cutting trail."

The extra work cost them half a day, but Quinton was right; as the ground thawed more and more, the regular trail became almost impassible, even for an empty wagon. It was after noon before they finally guided the lead mules to the bank.

Toby let out a long, low whistle. "Hope them mules and wagons don't go ass-over-teakettle getting down that bank. We better cut a dang good drag—like that huge oak tree yonder."

At first the mules hesitated to step off the lip of the ridge, but with a little prodding from Quinton they stepped out and were soon taking running, sliding steps down the steep incline, the wagon right on their heels. Quinton ran along beside, hanging onto the lines and calling encouragement. He followed them into the water, where they ran a short way and then slowed as the loaded wagon ceased pushing them.

"Cut the drag loose, boys," called Quinton. "I'll take 'em on across and then come back to help."

By the time he returned riding one of the mules, they had finished attaching the drag to Bill's wagon. Bill urged the mules over the lip, but as they ran forward, the drag suddenly hung and cocked the wagon sideways. Bill jumped clear as the load dumped and staves clattered onto the ground and into the water. In spite of the heavy drag, the mules kept running, splashing water high into the air and yanking both wagon and drag halfway across the creek before finally stopping.

"You hurt?" yelled Toby.

Bill floundered to stand, but his boots slipped on the slick rocks and he sat down again, hard, in the chest-deep, icy water. He swore a loud oath and then caught sight of David's red, contorted face. "You think this is funny! How about I whip you when I get up from here?"

Toby and Quinton laughed as well, while David gave a loud haw-haw before wiping his eyes and saying, "Aw, Bill, cheer up. We got both wagons down the bank."

Bill carefully stood, teetering with arms outstretched, and this time managed to stay on his feet. "Since you're so damned cheerful, I don't suppose you'll mind reloading the wagon while I quiet the mules and pour the water out of my boots."

"Be glad to," called David, and he, Toby, and Quinton began gathering up bundles of barrel staves and wading out to the wagon.

"It appears this will be our last load for a while, and I can't say I'm sorry," declared Quinton. "I'll be glad to stay home and do some smithy work for a change."

Bill, shivering from the icy water, threw a bundle of staves onto the wagon. "A red-hot forge sounds mighty good to me just now, or even the hot sun beating down while I plow—which is what I plan to be doing come next week. For now let's hurry up and get done so we can build a fire and dry these wet clothes."

Chapter 7

"Actually, it's a good time to have your trial," said Cravens as he tilted back in his office chair. "Congress is holding hearings on that sham of an election Arkansas had last fall, mostly the congressional contest between Gunter and Wilshire. There'll be depositions taken right here at my office for the next couple of weeks, and I don't figure the powers-that-be will do anything too egregious with all that scrutiny. We should have a better chance getting a fair jury seated."

In spite of the reassurance, Bill's mouth drew down. "It's a lot sooner than I expected. I'm not looking forward to this one damn bit."

Cravens went on, "All I can promise is I'll do my best."

"That's all any man can do," said Bill as they shook hands. "What time do I have to be here Monday?"

"Eight o'clock."

Bill stepped out into the May sunshine. He had been too busy plowing and planting to enjoy the season, but as his eyes lifted from the green grass of the square, to the scaffolds of workmen laying brick on the new courthouse, to the stately oaks shading Main Street, on up to the blue, cloudless dome above, he paused to take a deep breath of the mild, fresh air. The more he thought about going to prison, the more his skin crawled. He had seen Uncle Ned come home a skeleton of a man after his stay in Ship Island Prison; of course, that was a prisoner-of-war camp.

Surely the Little Rock Penitentiary was better than that, and yet he had heard horror stories. He mounted the black and headed home with a tight fist squeezing his heart, knowing the next few days would decide his fate.

As a parched man thirsting for water, he rode homeward, his eyes drinking in wild flowers and grassy pastures that were nurseries to long-legged colts and frolicking calves, and fields thick with sprouts of corn and leaves of cotton. As usual his thoughts lingered on Abigail and the strain that had fallen between them. He had given up trying to understand. Nevertheless, it was spring and she was still here—of course that was only because Talbert couldn't travel. Bill had kept his distance. She seemed determined to keep him at arm's length, and yet at unguarded moments he saw her watching him. Unless he was absolutely crazy, her sad eyes were filled with longing. He suddenly shook his head. Maybe he was crazy.

When he stopped at Minnow Creek to let the black drink, he lingered longer than necessary, hunkering under one of the trees, leafed with spring green, bending low to shade the small stream. On the bank nearby grew a small clump of yellow-blossoming wood sorrel; he picked one of the clover-like leaves and held it in his work-hardened palm. He smiled sadly. The plant made him think of Granny. She had used it in making her fever tonic, and he'd often seen wild turkey feeding on the seeds in the fall. When he was a boy, she had held up one of the leaves, pointed at the three heart-shaped leaflets, and said, "Billy, looky h'yar—Hit's jest like God—Father, Son, and Holy Ghost—the three of 'em separate but all one." He had never forgotten. He sat down and leaned back against the tree trunk to watch lazy water tease the bushes and ripple over smooth, gray pebbles while he wondered how many autumns and springs he would pass behind prison bars.

"Reckon I'll know soon enough." He lowered his head and groaned. "Oh Granny, I wish you was here praying for me." He dropped the leaf into the water and watched it float away, swirling a little as it hit a small eddy before drifting from sight. When it disappeared, he let out a deep breath, remounted, and started on his way.

He was about to bypass Quinton's blacksmith shop until he happened to see the big man through the open doors. He abruptly halted to dismount. He almost turned back as he neared the shop and heard voices, but Quinton saw him.

"Howdy, Tanner. Haven't seen you in a coon's age." Quinton's eyes danced as he gave a sly wink. He and Bill had hauled a load of stave bolts just the day before. "Where you been keeping yourself?"

"Staying busy." Bill looked around to see an older man who resembled Quinton. Muscled arms and sharp-eyed vigor belied the silver hair and craggy lines on the weathered face.

"This here is my pa, Calvin Rawlings. Don't reckon you've met?"

Bill shook the hard calloused hand, keenly aware of scrutiny from steel-gray eyes that matched his own. Zetta Cowen's voice broke the silence. She looked as sly as a cat playing with a mouse.

"Calvin, ain't no use denying—he's a Rawlings and there ain't no two ways about it." She glared when Quinton tried to interrupt. "I knowed Viola Kelly years ago when she run after Jared something shameful."

Calvin turned a steely look that quelled the acid tongue. "And I remember a gal named Zetta who tried the same and never got the job done."

Zetta sputtered, but no words came. Then she turned on her heels and left in a jerking half-walk, half-run.

Bill met Calvin's eyes. "What she says is true. Ma told me. I've no liking for the fact that Jared was my pa—to be honest I hate it."

There was no animosity on Calvin's face as he nodded. "I can understand that. Jared had his faults. I admit he brought shame on our name, but he wasn't all bad. I want you to know, back where we come from in Tennessee, Rawlings is a name to be proud of. I'm still proud of hit." He gave Bill a long, sober look. "No matter what, blood is thicker than water, and that bears rememberin'."

Quinton stared at him for a bit before saying, "Reckon that makes us cousins."

Bill gave a slight grin. "I don't mind that. You've been a good friend."

When Calvin gave a puzzled look, Quinton explained, "Pa, we're sort of in business together. They shut Bill down, the same as me. It was his idea I move the mill to his place. He's cutting the staves, and we're milling 'em and hauling on the sly. We're both trying to stay a jump ahead of the law."

"Appears I didn't stay far enough ahead," said Bill. "I stopped by to tell you that my trial is Monday."

"Damn!" Quinton huffed an aggravated breath, and after crossing big arms over his chest, he explained Bill's predicament to Calvin.

After Calvin pondered for a minute, he asked, "Cravens think he can get you off?"

"No way of knowing. I made some bad enemies." He looked at Quinton. "I need to ask a favor."

"Glad to do anything I can, Bill."

"If I don't get off, will you look in on Abigail and the boy? The old man still can't walk. If I go to jail, she won't have the income from cooking and washing for my crew. I'm worried how she'll manage her winter wood and such. If you'd stop in as you pass by and check on her, maybe bring her stuff from town when she needs it, I sure would appreciate it. This won't last long, but here's a little cash to buy what she needs."

As Bill reached into his pocket and pulled out some bills, Quinton held up a restraining hand. "Hey, you ain't in jail yet! Besides, I'm glad to help."

With a nod, Bill pocketed the money. Then, after a slight hesitation, he added, "She's a good, moral woman. I know folks probably say otherwise, with me and my men living there, but it's not so. She's as circumspect as they come."

Quinton nodded. "She'll be treated like a lady."

"Thank you." Bill turned to go.

"Do you think David and Toby want to keep hauling stave bolts?"

Bill stopped. "I never considered that possibility. I'll ask them."

The more he thought about it on the way home, the more it seemed a perfect solution if they could manage alone. It was a huge job with three men cutting; two would be extra hard. He would be glad for them to cut the timber if they would pay the taxes and look after Abigail. He doubted he'd be returning home Monday. Ellis had skipped the country months ago, but Harvey had stayed and lately had been making his brag in the saloon that Bill Tanner was going away for a long, long time.

Abigail gathered Talbert's dirty sheets into a pile. She looked out the window and saw Bill riding slowly across the yard. Even at a distance, he looked solemn. Something bad must have happened. Taking her bottom lip into her teeth, she began to worry. The constant dread of his trial weighed heavy on her.

She turned toward the chair near the bed. Still unable to say a word, Talbert made garbled noises. Seeing his sullen look, she realized she had not propped a pillow behind his back. He seemed to prefer sitting that way. She put down the laundry, stuffed a pillow behind his back, and turned to go. He made another noise. She had no idea what he was trying to say, although from the murderous look it certainly wasn't thank you.

"You're welcome," she said with spite, gathered the laundry, and on her way out shut the door. She drew a deep breath. "I've done it again," she whispered, vexed with herself. She had to ask forgiveness several times a day. Each morning, no matter how determined she was to do right by the old man, the good intentions seemed to evaporate along with the morning mists. "It's a good thing the Lord never runs out of mercy," she muttered.

"What happened today?" she asked Bill as she poured a cup of coffee and set it on the table in front of him.

He took a drink before answering. "My trial is Monday."

She sucked in a quick breath. She had known it was coming but not this soon.

"Abigail, more than likely I'll go to prison for at least a couple of years. I've asked David and Toby to stay on and keep selling timber and to give you a share of the profits. They've agreed. That should keep you going or at least help."

"Oh! If only you hadn't branded—"

His eyes hardened. "I wish I'd done worse." As her

mouth drew into a thin line, he said, "I reckon that's hard for you to understand, but now Harvey may try to take this place after I'm in prison."

Suddenly she sat down, her eyes wide. "You think he can?"

"Cravens says Harvey and that group have already taken property illegally, and no one has stopped them. The only thing stopping Harvey now is fear of me."

She felt panic tighten her throat. "Then what will I do?" She hadn't meant to speak out loud. Her face flushed. "I mean it would be hard to move with Mr. Anderson the way he is and all."

"Don't go unless they throw you out. I hope it doesn't come to that, but if it does, give 'em hell." He gave a tiny grin. "Don't look so startled. I've heard you give it to Talbert a time or two." Then he sobered. "I've told David and Toby, if there's trouble, to go straight to Cravens. If I go to prison, I'll make arrangements with him to deed the land to you and hope that will keep them from getting it."

"Deed the land to me?" she echoed with surprise.

He gave her a long look. "No one I'd rather have it."

Shock washed over her. Her cheeks grew warm under his direct gaze. She could not believe he was serious.

"But perhaps David?"

"No. There's nothing to stop Harvey from bringing charges against him too, if he's a mind to—remember David was in on it."

"But surely you have kin with greater claim to the land?" She quickly dropped her eyes to keep from looking into his. "I've no claim at all. And I wouldn't feel right about it."

"It might be the only way to stop them from stealing it. Harvey wants revenge, but the rest just want this place.

They tried to make a deal with me to sign over everything. They said if I would they would see to it that Harvey dropped the charges."

Without thinking she quickly reached to cover his hand with her own before quickly taking it back when he looked up with surprised eyes. She stammered a bit but finally got the words out. "Wouldn't giving up the place be better than going to jail? It's just land. You can save and buy more. If you're thinking of Jacob and me, we'll manage. We can move to town and I can work—" She abruptly halted when he made a scoffing sound.

"I'll not give the bastards one square foot of what's mine."

"Not even to stay out of prison?" she persisted.

"Nope—not even then."

She stood and turned away. Here it was again—that unyielding hardness—a harshness that made him able to torture another human without blinking an eye. It was a harshness she feared, and as he said, a thing she could not understand. And yet her heart ached to think he might go to prison. Harvey and Ellis and their kind should be the ones going to prison for cheating people. Of course that wasn't going to happen, not when they were the ones running things.

She heard the door open and shut, and she looked around to find him gone. With sagging shoulders she sat back down, groaned, and put her face in her hands. *How heartbreaking it all was!* Then she slowly shook her head. It was unthinkable that he might deed the place to her. With all her heart she prayed that wouldn't be necessary.

With a sigh she stood, got the laundry basket, and went out the back door. She had taken two sheets from the line when her nose wrinkled. At the same instant Little Bear rounded the corner of the house, the acrid scent of skunk filled Abigail's nostrils.

"Jacob Anderson, don't you dare touch that dog! He's tangled with a skunk, and I won't have that smell on you. I already have a hard enough time scrubbing your clothes clean." Abigail scolded from routine—the same way she folded laundry and dropped it into the basket sitting underneath the clothesline—but her mind was hardly on what she said. Her eyes swept over the flat fields and far ridges. It was unthinkable that Bill wanted to deed this to her!

Chapter 8

Not much of a courtroom, thought Bill as his eyes traced the dusty interior of what used to be Emmitt Gossett's mercantile and was now the temporary courtroom while the new courthouse was being built. Slat-backed benches sat in rows where shelves had been, the only exceptions being two chairs for the prosecution, two for the defense, one each for judge and witness, and three small wooden tables, the one for the judge only slightly larger. It didn't appear the floor had been scrubbed since Emmitt died, and even before that he wasn't much of a housekeeper. The room was filling with people. Some were friends, but Bill hadn't sent word to the mountain so he doubted his kin had heard about the trial yet.

He nodded to David, who sat alongside a clearly nervous Toby, Tom, and Matt. Bill tried to look calm. He didn't want anyone to know how his heart raced and his mouth was as dry as cotton. Cravens appeared composed—of course he wasn't the one facing prison if things didn't turn out well!

While Cravens whispered in his ear, Bill leaned near with his hands gripped between his legs and his head bowed forward. A spider crawled across the bare, dusty floor near his boot. Out of habit he stepped on it.

"I don't know all of these men," muttered Cravens, "but I was able to cull the ones I know were Ellis' cronies."

Bill glanced up. He knew several of the men, but none were close acquaintances.

Cravens went on, "One thing I know for sure is, it doesn't hurt that those gentlemen are here." He inclined his head toward two men sitting near the back in neat, tailored suits, one with a bowler hat perched on a knee. "They're in town to oversee the depositions ordered by Congress. There will be no depositions today, so I invited them to the trial. I figure the prosecution is more interested in not looking crooked to them than they are in getting you convicted. And you can bet Meers will be on his toes to do things exactly by the—"

"All rise!"

Bill stood, along with everyone else, as Judge Meers entered and took a seat. He had just sat down when all eyes turned toward the door at the back of the room. Bill's eyebrows rose. Calvin Rawlings and Quinton, followed by a score of broad-shouldered men, walked down the center aisle until reaching the first row of spectator benches. They all bore the Rawlings stamp, the same wide shoulders and the same piercing gray eyes.

For a split second, Calvin looked toward the store's old counter. His jaw twitched slightly, and then his face grew impassive. Bill sucked in a quick breath. Until now he had forgotten that the counter was the exact spot where, years ago, Cousin Elijah had shot and killed Jared and Jonas Rawlings.

"Can we please have these seats?" Calvin whispered loudly. He and his men had surrendered weapons at the door, and yet even unarmed, there was unmistakable power and menace in the group. The few men sitting on the front benches willingly stood and found other seats while Calvin and his men sat down. The Rawlings clan turned inflexible, unblinking eyes on the jury, with the exception of Calvin, who locked eyes with the judge.

Judge Meers' lips drew down. He waited for the whispers to cease. With a stern look, he finally spoke.

"I won't tolerate trouble. And I won't tolerate any intimidation in my courtroom. Calvin Rawlings, is that clear?"

Calvin, crossing arms over his chest, returned a look, equally stern. "Yes, Judge, clear as day. We're just here to see justice done for our kin, yonder."

A loud murmur filled the room. The judge's eyes swung to Bill and back to Calvin. Then he scowled and pounded the gavel for order and the proceedings began.

Bill didn't know the prosecutor, a slender young man with a narrow face, ginger-colored mustache, and bushy sideburns of the same reddish hue. He stood to his feet to call Radcliff Harvey to the stand. Bill kept emotion from his face as Harvey was sworn in and began answering the prosecutor's questions.

"I work for the county as Mr. Ellis' assistant. We collect fees owed to the county."

"Do you accompany Mr. Ellis every time he makes a collection?"

"No, not every time. He asked me to go along to Tanner's because he knew Tanner would be trouble."

"Objection, Your Honor. That's hearsay."

"Sustained."

"Mr. Harvey, let me rephrase the question. Did you understand why you were accompanying Mr. Ellis to Tanner's?"

"Sure. Tanner was way behind on his levy fees despite attempts to collect, and we expected trouble. Mr. Ellis had heard that Tanner and his kin were known to be violent." Harvey gave Bill a hard stare with his one good eye. "Why, his kin murdered two men right in this very room—shot them point blank with a shotgun."

"Objection! Mr. Tanner's kin are not on trial here."

"Sustained. Mr. Prosecutor, please instruct your witness to stick to the facts of this case. It will save us all a lot of time."

The prosecutor bowed slightly to the judge. "Yes, Your Honor. Now, Mr. Harvey, please relate what happened after your associate, Mr. Ellis, asked you to accompany him to the Tanner place."

"Tanner was working at his mill. Ellis was nice and businesslike, trying to convince Tanner that he needed to pay what he owed, but immediately Tanner got violent. He grabbed a stick of wood and came at us. I pulled my derringer, but he knocked it out of my hand and began to beat me. Tanner was a fiend, a madman, completely out of control. Ellis managed to get the gun and fire a shot. But he only nicked him. Then Tanner used the gun to pistol whip Ellis. I couldn't stand up—he had busted my ribs. About then his men came running." He leveled the hate-filled eye on Tom and pointed at him. "That sonofabitch there kicked me while I was down. The whole bunch of them ought to go to jail."

"Objection."

"Sustained. No one is on trial here but Mr. Tanner. You will keep your remarks attuned to that."

Harvey shot a sullen look at a group sitting on the right side of the room and muttered, "I wanted to bring charges against all the bastards, but—" When the gavel fell, he didn't finish the remark.

Bill supposed Harvey had been advised to come after only him. He wasn't sure why; whatever the reason, he was thankful the boys had not been arrested.

Harvey went on, talking louder. "After Tanner beat the hell out of Ellis, he dragged him over to the boiler. Ellis screamed and begged and cried for mercy, but Tanner,"—he leaned forward, pointing a long finger—*"branded him like he was no better than a hog or a cow!* And after he finished with Ellis, he ordered David Hadley, who's sitting right there, to drag me over."

Harvey tore open his shirt, popping off buttons in his rush to expose the mark on his chest. *"Then he did this to me!"*

The brand was no longer an angry-red, but it was still puffy and harsh enough to draw gasps from the women and frowns from the men. Bill did not like the expressions on the faces of the jury.

Harvey was panting as he sank back farther into the seat. He waited a bit before going on.

"Tanner threatened us. He swore he'd kill us if we told. Ellis was so scared he ran off. But me, I don't scare so easy." The eye he turned on Bill was both calculating and mean.

When the prosecutor sat down, Cravens stood and faced Harvey.

"Mr. Harvey, how long have you lived in our fair town?"

"Four years come August."

"Where did you reside before that?"

"Objection. This has no bearing on the case."

"I believe it does, Your Honor. I would like to establish some facts that are pertinent to the case, and Mr. Harvey's background is one of them."

The judge thought for a second. "All right, Mr. Cravens, we'll see. Overruled."

"Where?" he repeated.

"Maryland."

"How long did you live there?"

"All my life, until the war. But I don't see what that has to do—?"

"Do you have relatives in Arkansas?"

He shook his head ever so slightly.

"Speak up, please, Mr. Harvey."

"No."

"What prompted you to take up roots and move half a continent away to a place where you have no family?"

"I had a friend here."

"Ah, so your friend urged you to come?"

"Yes."

"Would I be correct in assuming that friend is Emory Ellis?"

Harvey glanced at the judge. "Well, yes, Emory is the one who invited me."

"Would you please tell the jury how you and Mr. Ellis met and how long he had lived in Arkansas before sending for you?"

"We worked together back east. He'd lived here a couple of years before I came."

"What kind of work did you and Mr. Ellis do back East?"

"Government work."

"Specifics, if you please."

He waited a bit before answering. "Tax collecting."

"Was Mr. Ellis in the army—perhaps saw the South during the war and fell in love with the land?"

"No, he wasn't in the army."

"Does he have relatives here?"

He shook his head. "None that I know of."

"Your Honor, this is getting us nowhere," objected the prosecutor.

"Prosecutor Sewell, I tend to agree. Cravens, make your point quickly, or I won't allow this line of questioning to proceed."

"Yes, Your Honor." He faced Harvey. "I know you can't speak for Mr. Ellis, but did you come here for business opportunities?"

"Well…yes, in a manner of speaking."

"Was it a permanent move—I mean did you move furniture—household plunder? Or did you perhaps just pack a carpetbag of belongings?"

As chuckles swept the room, the prosecutor thundered, "Objection!"

"I withdraw the question, Your Honor." Then, as the laughter died down, Cravens asked, "What kinds of work have you engaged in since moving here?"

"Like I said, I work for the county as Ellis' assistant."

"Aren't you more than just his assistant?"

Harvey raised an eyebrow. "Not sure what you mean."

"Aren't you and Mr. Ellis partners in land speculation?"

Harvey's mouth became a thin line. Cravens stepped to the table where Bill sat and picked up a handful of papers.

"Here are deeds to more than three dozen properties in this county in either your name or Mr. Ellis's name."

Harvey's face grew surly. "There's nothing illegal about owning land."

"No," agreed Cravens, "definitely not, but how one obtains it is another matter. According to these records, each parcel deeded to you or Ellis was purchased for back taxes or fees owed, and each was purchased for only a fraction of the worth. Is that correct?"

"Objection!" The prosecutor turned stormy eyes on the judge. "May I remind the court that this witness is not the one on trial?"

"Your Honor, Mr. Harvey's character as a reliable witness is pertinent."

Judge Meers took off spectacles and pinched the bridge of his nose. "Overruled."

Bill thought Meers looked as if the word had tasted as bitter as green persimmons.

"Mr. Harvey?"

"We bought the land for taxes owing."

"Were you and Mr. Ellis attempting to collect back taxes from Mr. Tanner?"

"No, just his timber levy."

"And how is that fee determined?"

"It's a percentage of the operation."

"And what percentage is that?"

For a split second, Harvey's eyes darted to someone seated among the spectators. He licked his lips before answering, "Seven percent."

"Seven?" Cravens laid down the papers. He picked up a black book and opened it. "Do you recognize this book?"

Harvey shrugged. "I'm not sure."

"Well, it has Ellis' name inside the front cover and an accounting of transactions conducted with various men in the county, including Mr. Tanner. Let's see..." He flipped a few pages and stopped. "Yes, here it is. Bill Tanner. There's an estimate of his timber operation, the value of his mill and sawed logs, as well as standing timber. And there is an assessment of twenty percent. As a matter of fact, that is the assessment of every name in the entire journal." He snapped the book shut. "Mr. Harvey, isn't it true that you and Mr. Ellis were padding the assessments and pocketing the extra thirteen percent?"

"Objection!"

Before the judge could rule, Harvey pointed at the book. "That's Emory's book. I can't be held to account for what he did."

"Overruled. I want to hear where this is going."

"There's also another set of entries in this ledger." Cravens flipped open the book again and thumbed through until he found the right spot. "It says here, 'Paid to R. T. H.' And the amount is exactly five percent of each transaction. R.T.H.—aren't those your initials?"

Harvey's eyes narrowed into slits. "It's no crime to make wages, and those were my wages."

"Doesn't the county pay your wage for collecting fees?"

Harvey's jaw tightened. "Yes. But I contracted with Ellis to do other work besides fee collecting."

Cravens studied the book again. His eyebrows rose. "Then, you contracted for five percent of each transaction above and beyond what the county paid?"

Harvey grew more sullen. "Yes."

"Did you threaten Mr. Tanner by saying you intended to take his property and that there was nothing he could do about it?"

"I never said that."

"Did Mr. Ellis make that threat?"

"Not that I recall."

Cravens walked over to pick up several sheets of paper from the desk. He handed it to Harvey. "This is a copy of official county records of land purchases. Is your name on this list?"

Harvey's eyes went over the paper.

"Objection. This has no bearing on the case."

"Your Honor, it does have bearing. If you will permit me to go on."

Meers lowered his chin to stare at Cravens over the top of his glasses.

"Overruled. But proceed with caution, Counselor."

"Is your name on the papers?"

"Yes."

"How many times?"

He did a quick count, touching the paper each time he counted under his breath.

"Looks like thirteen times."

"So you've bought thirteen parcels of land in the county. How many acres do you own?"

"Objection! Irrelevant and—"

"Judge, this is very relevant," interrupted Cravens. "All of these farms went for back taxes and fees, purchased for a fraction of actual value—the same land-grab scheme I intend to prove was being worked on my client."

"Objection!"

The judge's eyes swept the room, but lingered for a moment on the gentlemen from Washington. He focused sternly on Cravens.

"Counselor, I will allow you to go a bit further with this, but let me warn you, no more theatrical statements. Restrict your theories to your summation."

"Thank you, Your Honor." Cravens locked his hands together behind his back and took a few steps before turning back to the witness. "Mr. Harvey, do you own thirteen large tracts of land in this county bought for back taxes and fees at a fraction of the assessed value?"

"I bought and paid for them, legal and binding."

"Please look at the papers in your hand and then tell the court—are any of the buyers not county officials?"

"Objection! Your Honor, the county officials are not on trial here. This has no bearing on this case!"

"Sustained."

"Exception, Your Honor. A man has a right to protect his property from thieves, and I am trying to show that Mr. Harvey is a thief," said Cravens.

"Exception noted," said the judge, trying unsuccessfully to hide a scowl.

Talk rippled across the room. *"The damned bunch of thieves running this county are the ones who ought to be on trial!"*

Bill thought the loud remark had come from one of the Rawlings. Over the mutters of agreement, Judge Meers pounded for order.

When things quieted, Cravens went on. "Do you personally know every man on the list?"

The prosecutor stood. "Objection!"

"Sustained! Mr. Cravens, if you insist on going on with this, I'll hold you in contempt."

"Then, I have no further questions for Mr. Harvey."

Cravens turned on his heels and sat down. He leaned his head back when someone tapped his shoulder. Bill glanced around to see Quinton hunkered down, talking low into Cravens' ear. Cravens nodded. Before moving away, Quinton clasped Bill's shoulder.

The prosecutor stood. "Your Honor, I call Nathan Alexander."

Meers' brow slightly furrowed. "Nathan, keep your seat a minute. Mr. Sewell, would you and Mr. Cravens please approach the bench?"

Bill could tell there was an argument going on between the prosecutor and the judge. When Cravens sat down, Bill leaned to ask, "What was that all about?"

Cravens shielded his mouth before giving a lopsided grin. "Meers said it wouldn't be fair to call Alexander because he isn't on the prosecution's list of witnesses, but I told him I have no objection. Since Harvey lost all credibility, Sewell is trying to redeem the case, but he's about to open a big can of worms. Meers know it, but Sewell isn't smart enough to see it yet. He will when I'm done with him."

The prosecutor took a white handkerchief from an

inside pocket of his black suit jacket and wiped his brow. "Mr. Alexander, please state your occupation."

"I am a county employee."

"To be more specific, aren't you a fee collector?"

"Yes, sir."

"Does your job require you to travel around the county in an official capacity to visit citizens at home on their own land?"

"Yes."

"So you have dealt with numerous people who were required to pay monies to the county?"

"Yes."

"Has any one of those citizens ever branded your bare flesh with *a red-hot poker*?"

"No, sir, they've not."

When the prosecutor finished, Cravens approached Nathan.

"Mr. Alexander, how long have you lived in the county?"

"About six years."

"And before that?"

"I lived in Illinois."

The judge shot a look at Cravens. Bill thought it was a silent warning to not even mention a carpetbag.

"Mr. Alexander, do you collect timber fees?"

"No, that was only Ellis and Harvey."

"Then what fees are you responsible for?"

He licked his lips. "Mostly the levy on cotton."

"What is that percentage?"

He hesitated. "Last year, ten. It's going up this year, but I'm not sure how much yet."

"Have you ever collected more than the specified amount?"

"No, never." He sat up taller. "I only collect what's legal."

"I see," said Cravens. "Do you own land in the county?"

Sewell's face reddened. "Objection! Your Honor!"

Nathan's eyes had darted nervously to rest on someone seated behind Bill.

Cravens took a few steps closer to the bench. "Your Honor, I agreed to let the prosecutor call this witness, even though Mr. Alexander is not on the witness list. And I can see no relevance his previous testimony has to this case; therefore, I ask lenience to ask him a few questions—certainly more relevant than Mr. Sewell's questions were."

Meers expelled a deep breath. "Overruled. Proceed."

"According to these records, you've purchased eight cotton farms for back taxes. Is that correct?"

"Yes."

"Are you a cotton farmer, Mr. Alexander?"

"Well, no."

"You mean you've never grown a crop of cotton?"

"No."

"Do you perhaps intend to raise some other crop?"

He barely mumbled, "I'm not a farmer."

"I'm curious, sir--why would a man purchase eight farms if he doesn't farm?"

"It's an investment."

Cravens nodded. "Ah, I see—you're a land speculator. No further questions."

An angry ripple swept the room. When the prosecutor had no cross-examination, Cravens glanced at his notes and then looked up. "I call Horace Platt to the stand."

Meers's brows beetled and his frown became a scowl. "Counsel, please approach the bench."

Bill frowned as well. Judge Meers was getting angry, and Bill didn't want to be tried before a hostile judge. Obviously Meers didn't want county officials questioned about unjust fees and corrupt practices. Bill had no idea if

Meers was corrupt, but as circuit judge he would appear guilty by association.

After a few words with the judge, Cravens turned. "I call Horace Platt."

Although Meers tried to appear calm, his face had flushed and the veins in his neck were bulging. He looked daggers at Cravens.

"Please state your name and occupation."

"Horace Platt. I'm the county assessor."

"So, Mr. Ellis and indirectly Mr. Harvey worked out of your office?"

"Yes."

"Your office keeps track of all fees and taxes paid into the county and the disbursements of such fees after collected?"

"Yes."

Cravens nodded. "And who decides the rate of such fees, and after the monies are collected, how they are spent?"

Platt fidgeted with the brim of the hat held in his lap. "Sometimes assessments are put on the ballot."

"Am I correct in stating that neither the cotton nor the timber assessments were ever on a ballot?"

"No," he muttered.

"Sir, please, speak up—no, they were, or no, they were not?"

"No, they were not."

"Then who decided the percentage?"

"It was agreed on by a county board of officials."

"Am I correct in assuming these same officials decide the disbursements?"

Another angry ripple swept the room.

"Objection! This testimony is totally irrelevant. Your Honor, it appears counsel has forgotten what this trial is about."

"Sustained! Mr. Cravens, you have been warned. Do not persist with these deviations."

Cravens gave a slight nod before facing Platt again. "Was Mr. Ellis on the board that voted the timber assessment?"

Platt looked imploringly at the judge. Then he swallowed. "I can't say exactly. I wasn't there when the vote was taken."

"I see. No further questions."

When Cravens sat down, Bill spoke low, "It seems crazy to rile the judge."

Cravens leaned closer. "Everyone knows you're guilty. Your only hope is getting that jury madder at Harvey and the officials than at you. Don't worry; Meers won't do anything too egregious—not with those Washington men looking on."

As the morning progressed, although the doors and windows were open, men began mopping sweat from damp brows, and the few women present began fanning with anything at hand.

Cravens stood. "I call Eugene Bates."

Judge Meers' eyes narrowed ever so slightly.

Bates was a middle-aged man, stoop-shouldered and lean, his face furrowed and darkened by hours in the sun. He raised his hand, swore on the Bible, and then sat down.

"Mr. Bates, what is your occupation?"

"Before the county took it, I owned and operated a saw mill. Right now, to keep the wolf away from the door, I'm farming a few acres that belong to my wife's father."

"Just out of curiosity, sir, what would you say was the profit margin on your milling operation?"

He squinted his eyes a bit. "Can't say for certain, but a far cry less than all the fees and taxes. That's why I couldn't pay both."

"You say the county took your mill?"

"Yes, sir. It was Ellis and Harvey who shut me down when I couldn't pay."

"Please relate the details of your business dealings with Mr. Ellis and Mr. Harvey."

"About eighteen months ago, they come out to my mill one day." Bates pointed toward the book on Cravens' table. "Ellis had that very book. He flipped it open and said I owed might nigh three hundred dollars in fees and taxes. I ain't seen that much money but few times in my life, and I shore didn't have it at the time. Times has been hard since the war, and cash money tight. At first Ellis was polite-like, but when I told him I didn't think I owed no such fees, he got mean. Pretty quick I saw how the land lay—he aimed to take my property."

"Objection. Supposition."

Bates, eyes flashing, quickly shot out, "Well it ain't supposition that someone else ended up with what was mine!"

Meers pounded the gavel. "Sustained. Not another outburst, Mr. Bates!"

Cravens continued, "When Mr. Ellis and Mr. Harvey came to your mill to collect the fees, how did you react?"

"Picked up my double barrel and run 'em off my place."

"Then what happened?"

"A few days later, the sheriff come and served me papers. I told him how they was a' trying to cheat me by chagrin' terrible high fees. He said he didn't have no say-so over the rates, and he said I had to get off my land. I argued my cause to just about ever' official that'd talk to me. Hit done no good a-tall. A month or so back I heard it all sold at auction, bought fer just the taxes and fees owed."

"Mr. Bates, was it Mr. Ellis or Mr. Harvey who purchased your land?"

"No."

"Who bought it?"

"Objection. Irrelevant!"

"Overruled." Meers, looking miserable, actually squirmed in his chair.

"Hit was Horace Platt."

Cravens' voice rose to be heard over the sudden mutterings by the crowd. *The County Assessor bought your land?"*

"Well, not exactly Platt hisself. I was told hit's his mother's name on the deed, but she lives way off somewheres and I don't calculate she wanted the mill and the land herself."

"No further questions."

The prosecutor remained seated. "No questions."

Bill drew a deep breath as Cravens called David to the stand.

David placed his hand on the Bible and repeated the oath. "Yes, sir," he answered Cravens' question. "I've known Bill for most of my life and worked with him and for him for the last five years." David looked at the jury to make sure they were paying attention. "He's always been honest and fair with me and with everyone else.

"Yes, sir," he went on, "I was there when Ellis and Harvey drove up. Since it was dinner time, Bill sent me and the other fellows there"—he pointed toward Toby, Tom, and Matt—"on to the house to eat, so I didn't hear what was said. But I did hear the   gunshot when that bastard Ellis shot Bill."

The prosecutor leaned forward. "Objection, your honor—speculation. He didn't see who fired the shot."

Meers gave the prosecutor a scathing look. "Sustained. The jury will disregard the statement—even though Mr. Harvey has already testified that Mr. Ellis fired the shot."

The prosecutor, looking chagrined, leaned back. He began straightening papers on his desk while Cravens instructed David to go on with what he saw.

David related the event truthfully and in detail. The prosecutor had no questions.

Tom first and then Matt gave passionate versions of the incident, neither one lying, and yet their disdain for Ellis and Harvey was obvious. As Matt finished and Toby took the stand, Bill's palms grew sweaty. He knew the trial had almost concluded, and he still wasn't sure how to read the jury. Some had smiled when Cravens made the allusion to carpetbags, and a few had openly frowned when Harvey's land speculation came to light. Yet Bill could not discount the grim expressions when Harvey had bared his chest. He figured a lot would depend on the closing arguments.

Toby lowered his right hand, took a seat, and began answering Cravens' questions. "Tobias McKennon. Yes, sir, I've lived here all my life, always in town until Mr. Tanner hired me, and then I moved out to his place. Oh, he's a fine man, and a good boss—treats me more like kin than a workman."

Toby painted a vivid picture of the day and concluded by adding, "I reckon it was pretty strong...what Mr. Bill done to those men. But I've worked alongside him all these months—watched him slog through mud and snow to cut timber—pullin' on that crosscut till his hands blistered and bled. I've seed him work late into the night and get up long before first light, day in and day out, and work till he 'most dropped. Ain't right for men with soft, clean hands to come along and take what they ain't sweated a drop for. Any man worth his salt would have done the same as Bill if he had the nerve Mr. Bill does."

Cravens wore a soft smile when he sat down. "I think Toby did a better job with closing remarks than I can," he leaned to whisper.

The wind seemed to have gone out of the prosecutor; at least Bill hoped it had when he failed to cross-examine any of the boys. However, when he stood to give his summation, Bill's palms grew sweaty again.

"Gentlemen," the prosecutor addressed the jury, "you've heard some moving sentiments today about Mr. Tanner—how hardworking he is, how he was wronged by what some perceive to be evil men—but I remind you, members of the jury, the American system of law and justice must not be winked at. If you, the jury, turn blind eyes to the violent acts of Mr. Tanner, it would set a terrifying precedent and send the message that any man bold enough to take the law into his own hands will not have to answer for it. He is free to become judge, jury, and executioner. Is that the kind of government, the kind of justice you want for your children and grandchildren? The kind of place that allows rules to be made by the meanest and the strongest? And carried out by any means and without restraint? *I think not!* Therefore I urge you to do the right thing. This man clearly perpetrated the crime. Did he plead his cause to those in authority? Did he go to the law, the courts, to settle his grievance in a civilized manner? *No!* What were his actions?" The prosecutor pointed a finger at Bill. *"Maliciously and with great cruelty, he tortured men—singeing their flesh—branding them as if they were cattle!"*

Sewell stopped to draw in a shaky breath. Sweat glistened on his smooth, high brow.

"Gentlemen of the jury, it is your duty to your families,

to society, to find him guilty and to recommend he be punished with the strictest letter of the law. That, sirs, is the only answer to such barbarism, such disregard for law, if we are to retain the sanctity and peace of a civilized society." He mopped sweat from his brow once again and then he sat down.

Bill's heart raced. There was a look of solemn agreement on the faces of the jury. Sewell's argument sounded too convincing. Bill looked askance at Cravens. When the attorney didn't meet his eye, he felt as if he'd been kicked in the stomach.

Slowly Cravens stood and approached the jury. "Gentlemen, the prosecutor would have you believe that the American system of law and justice is at stake here." He walked slowly, back and forth. "And perhaps it is." He paused a moment. "American justice requires a jury to hear all evidence and then to pass judgment. It is for a jury to decide innocence or guilt. It is for a judge to decree a fair and just punishment for a defendant found guilty. Our forefathers established trial by jury as the best possible way to see justice done and not merely to have a set of rules applied.

"Before you begin this deliberation, I wish to remind you, the *meanest* and *strongest*—using the prosecutor's very words—are not always the physically powerful. The meanest and strongest can be the politically powerful. Against such power the common man has always been disadvantaged—much like a squirrel caught in the jaws of a coyote. And who can blame the squirrel for struggling to free itself?

"It will be your determination, gentlemen, and yours alone, whether Bill Tanner stands condemned for defending his right to make *an honest* living. It will be your determination alone whether he is locked behind prison bars…or whether he goes home today, a man free once again to make his living by the *sweat of his brow.*

"I urge you to look beyond the action for which Mr. Tanner is on trial. Yes, look beyond that to see the cause. When the miscreant—the evil man—is endowed with power and allowed to act with impunity, the innocent suffer. Gentlemen, you can send a strong message today—the message that the common citizens in this county shall truly have the right to life, liberty, and the pursuit of happiness; that they will be allowed this pursuit unhindered by the graft of the privileged few."

Bill hardly heard Meers's final remarks to the jury about weighing the evidence and not being swayed by emotion. As they filed out, he studied each face. He prayed Cravens had swayed them, but the solemn expressions remained fixed, unreadable.

"What do we do now?" he asked.

"Wait," said Cravens, "and that's the hardest part."

People began to file out, but others stayed seated, talking. Bill figured, like him, they were wondering aloud about the verdict.

"Your opinion?" asked Bill.

Cravens shook his head. "I honestly don't know, Bill. This is one of those times it truly depends on their mood. As I said before, you are guilty—we didn't even try to dispute that. My sole strategy was to gain sympathy for you and outrage at the way things are being done in this county. Sewell made some strong points—I'll give him that. But it galls honest men to see graft triumph. Like I said, we'll just have to wait and see."

Bill let out a deep breath, looked down, and nervously rubbed his hands together. "Scary thing to have your fate in the hands of twelve strangers."

"For a fact," agreed Cravens. "But it's far better than

no jury at all."

Bill glanced up. "Yeah, I reckon Meers would have locked me up and thrown away the key."

"Perhaps. The governing fear rebellion from the governed. And what you did certainly signifies rebellion to the carpetbaggers in power here."

When Calvin and Quinton approached, Bill stood and shook hands. "I sure appreciated you fellows coming and speaking up for me."

Calvin gave a nod. "Hit don't hurt fer them to know that you got kin, and kin that ain't afraid of 'em."

Cravens stood and shook hands with both men. "Quinton, I certainly appreciated the suggestion. Alexander made a first rate witness."

Bill had wondered what Quinton told Cravens, but he had forgotten to ask. "So that was what you whispered in his ear."

Quinton grinned. "I said I'd take the stand and tell how Ellis and Harvey done me, but I figured Nathan would be better since he ain't kin."

Bill swallowed. It would take some getting used to—this having the Rawlings take him into the bosom of the family. He had spent years hating even the sound of the name.

"I appreciate it too," he said, and meant it.

※※※

Minutes dragged. Bill kept looking at Cravens' pocket watch each time the attorney removed it from his vest.

"They've been gone a long time. Is that good or bad?" he finally asked.

"Good, I think. It means there's some argument, and that means they don't all agree on a conviction."

Bill fidgeted, rubbing the soles of his boots over the rough floorboards. "Then I reckon I can stand the wait." But he felt as if he would jump out of his skin if they didn't return soon. He tried to think about something else and for a few seconds managed to turn his thoughts to Abigail. That morning, right before he climbed into the saddle, she had started to say something. He wished she had. Her lips had closed and her hand had gone to her throat in a nervous gesture as if she were afraid of the words lodged there, while her eyes devoured his face. What kept her mute? He had no idea. She was not indifferent. He knew it. And yet she had stood in the front yard, sunshine glinting off her glossy dark hair, and watched him ride away. When he looked back, just before rounding the curve, she still stood watching.

Suddenly Cravens stiffened. Bill looked up to see the jury filing in, each solemn face still unreadable. It was the longest two minutes in his life while Judge Meers returned and took his seat.

"Have you reached a decision?"

One juror stood. He was a rail-thin older man with a deeply lined face and faded brown eyes. "We have, Your Honor."

As sweat poured down Bill's sides, he held his breath. He could hear his heart beat in his ears while he waited for words that could change his life forever.

"The jury finds the defendant not guilty."

Bill bowed, gripping hands together in his lap, as Cravens pounded his back. Vaguely he heard the commotion, mostly cheers and whistles amid a few disgruntled mutters. He looked up.

Harvey approached, piercing him with hate-filled eyes. As he passed by, he bent low and hissed, *"This isn't over, Tanner—not by a long shot!"*

The black had almost reached the covered bridge spanning Spadra Creek when a boy came running and calling, "Mr. Tanner, hold up! Mr. Cravens needs to speak to you."

With a frown, Bill turned the horse around. He had only come to town for supplies and was anxious to get home and finish plowing, but Cravens must have something important to discuss. Surely there had been no sort of hitch about the trial. That had been over and done two weeks ago.

He stepped into Cravens' office. Then he took a seat on the bench against the wall. Apparently he had come at a bad time. The office was packed. The room was stuffy from so many bodies and the close air strong with the odor of sweat.

Bill was anxious to head home, so he hoped he wouldn't have to wait long. His business with Cravens shouldn't take long; at least that is what the boy had said.

Bill cocked his head to listen. The men from Washington also listened while a man Bill didn't know interrogated Judge Meers. Bill noticed that Meers was sweating heavily. "Do you, or not, know of any fraud having been committed by the board of registration in October, 1872?"

"No, sir." Meers spoke with a solemn, precise voice.

"Do you not know of many persons in Johnson County whom the Republicans claimed and counted in their estimate who would have voted the Democrat ticket if there had been a regular election held in all the precincts of Johnson County?

"That's a thing a person couldn't know unless he had seen it tried. Yet my opinion is that, to some extent, such would have been the case."

"That will be all for now, Judge Meers, but I may call on you again."

Bill's ears perked up when R.W. Ward—or Doc as he knew him—was sworn in. Bill recalled the last time he had seen Ward. Doc had almost drawn his gun at the registration. Bill figured there might be questions about that. And there were. Ward answered in detail, and mostly told the truth as Bill remembered the incident—although Bill had seen no one pick up rocks to stone Ward as he was testifying.

Bill knew the registration had been a farce, but he doubted Congress would do a thing about it. One thing he knew for certain—there were plenty of hard feelings in the county because of the sham. He listened to more of Ward's deposition, hoping there would be a break soon so he could talk to Cravens and be on his way. However it was another hour before a halt was called and Bill got to speak to the attorney.

"Hello, Tanner. Let's step outside. Quite a show isn't it?" Cravens nodded to the men still inside and huddled around his desk.

"You think this congressional investigation will do any good?"

Cravens flipped an ash from his cigar. "I think it already has. There's still a lot of bitterness over the election—talk of retaliation. Over in Pope County they had the same shenanigans pulled at their registration and election. Not long ago both Sheriff Dodson and Frank Hickox, the county clerk, were shot dead. There's been a pretty strong claim made in the depositions taken over there that both men tampered with the ballot boxes so that Dodson and the other Republicans would win. Looks like that—and maybe some more high-handedness—cost them their lives." He took a puff of the cigar and blew a fragrant cloud of smoke. "At least the talk here about lynching or shooting the board has cooled off some.

People seem willing to wait and see if Congress actually does something."

"What did you need to talk to me about?" Bill asked. "I just got a letter answering my inquiry about Frank Anderson."

❀ Chapter 9

Abigail looked out over the gently sloping field plush with corn growing green and fresh beneath the mild June sun. The sight somehow eased the tension between her shoulders. She smiled, took a deep breath of the fresh morning, and thought once again how thankful she was the mule had given out at the bottom of that very hill. She wondered what their lot would have been if it hadn't. Then again, she was glad she didn't know. Likely their story would not have had a happy ending—not that the story had ended yet, and not that there weren't still plenty of problems. But the good Lord had heard her prayers and spared Bill the fate of prison, and for now she and Jacob had plenty to eat and a good roof over their heads. Bill had kept his distance, given her no cause to fret. Even Mr. Anderson was not the fiend he had once been. Most days he simply sat on the porch in the sun and left her in peace.

Peace. What a wonderful thing! And one she would never again take for granted.

She walked on to the vegetable garden and began hoeing around tomato and bean plants. From the nice rain two days before, the soil was not dusty and yet not too moist to work, which was a good thing, because weeds were springing up quickly in spite of the fact that she had hoed the entire garden clean a few days before. She loved working the garden, the rows of beans, squash, tomatoes, green onions, and lettuce, curly leafed and tender, as pretty to her as any flower. And yet her eyes kept drifting to the road. It was probably too early for Bill to return from the trip to Clarksville. Since he had gotten a late start the day before and had to spend the night, he might have left early this morning.

It seemed her eyes always searched for him. She paused a minute, leaning on the hoe. It had been hard the last few months, keeping the cold distance, especially the morning he had left for trial. She had almost yielded and gone into his arms. That long day had been pure torture, wondering, waiting, not knowing if he would come home. Late in the day, the soft knock on the back door had been Toby. She had made him promise to come straight home the second he heard the verdict. She had wept in front of him. By the time Bill arrived she had regained her composure enough to keep from flying into his arms. He had no idea how much she wanted to, and it must stay that way. She loved Bill, but violent men made poor fathers. Jacob was more important than her own heart. Nonetheless her eyes strayed again to the road.

"Abigail, stop it!" she scolded, already knowing it would do no good.

She finished hoeing and then noticed there were enough slender green beans hanging from the plants for a nice dinner, so she propped the hoe against the fence, went inside for a basket, and was soon back in the garden, forcing her eyes to stay on the plants and away from the wide wagon road that ran in front of the house before finally curving from sight.

"Ma, what's that song you're humming?" asked Jacob.

She glanced up. "I didn't realize I was humming."

He flashed her a wide grin. "I like it when you hum. That means you're happy."

"I suppose I am," she said with a smile, studying him. He was such a beautiful child, perfectly proportioned features, teeth even and white, his black hair reflecting blue-black like a bird's wings in the sun. Of course she would soon have to stop thinking of him as a child. He had shot up three inches in the last year. His sun-browned feet were bare now, but she could see they had grown too big to fit in his old boots.

"I finished cleaning out the chicken coop and I'm ready to start on the barn. After I'm finished, can I go fishing?"

"I suppose so. Fried fish would taste good with fresh green beans."

"Thanks, Ma," he called back over his shoulder as he ran away with Little Bear right at his bare heels that flashed in the sun.

She smiled again and returned to plucking long pods and dropping them into the basket. Then her head cocked toward the road. In spite of her earlier scolding, her heart skipped a beat. She forced herself not to look up until Bill halted the horse nearby. Because of the coolness that had developed between them, it surprised her how swiftly he crossed the yard and hurried toward her. His face was wreathed in a big smile. She stood and then wiped her hands on her apron.

He rushed forward and took her hand. "Abigail, I have wonderful news." He hesitated for a moment and the smile faded. "'Course, I don't reckon it'll be so wonderful to Talbert."

She left her hand in his tight grasp. "What is it?"

"Frank is dead and I have proof."

Her eyes widened. "How—"

"I've had Cravens checking on it for months. He just now heard back from the authorities at St. Louis. Frank was never in that hospital. He was killed in battle, and Cravens has a sworn statement from his commanding officer. He was with Frank when he died. He lived only a few hours after a bad saber wound."

Abigail sucked in a quick breath. *Her worst fear would never come true!* Frank would never appear at the door again to make life a nightmare. She suddenly went limp with relief.

Bill gathered her against his chest. "This means you're free, and we can get married."

In a daze, she smelled the clean, sweaty scent of him and felt his lips on her hair before suddenly coming to her senses. She pushed back.

"What—?"

She couldn't think what to say—how to tell him. His puzzled look cut her to the quick. She turned away to stare at the distant hills rising beyond the field.

"Abigail, tell me," he said. "Isn't that what's been wrong all this time? Weren't you just worried Frank was still alive?"

She looked back to see his fists clenched tightly by his sides, his eyes pain-filled and wounded. Her heart twisted, and yet she had to hurt him more. Her eyes filled with tears even as her spine straightened. She longed to reach out, to hold him again, and wipe the pain from his face. Instead she crossed her arms across her chest and gripped them tightly.

"Bill, I can't marry you."

He studied her face for a long moment. "I'm not blind. I know you care. I figured all this time it was because of Frank. Since that's not it, I think I deserve a reason."

Her eyes dropped. "Yes, you do." It was hard to lift her eyes, but she faced him. "You're right. I do love you. But I have Jacob to think of."

"But I—"

She shook her head. "I know you care for Jacob, but Bill, I saw what you did to those men. I can't risk Jacob being hurt. Frank was a violent man. And so are you."

He exhaled as if the wind had been kicked from his lungs. He stared at her for a long moment, the hurt plain in his gray eyes, and then slowly he said, "You're right—I can be violent. Sometimes a man has to be to stay alive. I'm not cruel without reason, though, never have been. I do what has to be done, but I've never harmed a woman or a child, and I've never hurt a man that wasn't trying to do me harm. Abigail, that's the difference between me and Frank." He paused to look down at the ground and then back at her. "But I don't reckon all the talk in the world will convince you, if you can't tell the difference already."

When he turned and walked away, she sank to the ground, her skirt billowing over the bean vines, as she covered her face with her hands and cried.

For the next few days, Abigail did the chores by habit, hardly thinking about the tasks. Over and over again, she measured and sifted Bill's words, weighing them with every argument her mind could devise. There was sense in what he had said. Without a doubt, there were different types of cruelty, and yet could she completely trust a man who was capable of what Bill had done—could she trust him not to cross the line in a fit of temper? In reality there was no way of knowing. Only time would tell. Was she willing to risk Jacob's life on it? The indecision was driving her crazy. Bill would be home soon from another trip to Russellville. She needed to make up her mind, and yet her head ached from thinking, so she tried pushing the worries to the back of her mind while she fixed a small breakfast, fed Mr. Anderson, and headed for the garden to work before the sun grew hot.

She frowned. The evening before the Irish potato plants were covered with thick green leaves. Now they were riddled, some leaves completely gone down to the stem. She bent for a closer look to see fat, striped bugs eating away.

She stood, calling to Jacob where he sat on the porch talking to his grandpa. He quickly ran down the steps and across the yard.

"Jacob, there's potato bugs on the plants—put some coal oil in a tin can to drop the bugs in."

"Why?"

"To kill them."

"Why can't I just squish 'em?" he asked.

"Just do what I said!" she snapped. Then she sighed, rubbed her forehead, and using a softer tone, added, "Be sure to check each leaf, top and bottom. Those bugs can destroy an entire crop in no time."

While he ran to get coal oil, she took strips of cotton rags from her apron pocket and began tying the new growth of tomato plant onto wooden stakes that she had driven into the ground earlier in the spring. Thanks to ample rain, the plants had grown tall and were covered with small green tomatoes.

"Work is a blessing," she muttered. "It keeps a person from going completely crazy from thinking." She paused, glancing over at the riddled potato plants. This indecision was eating away at her like a destructive bug. It was time to make up her mind, once and for all. She stood up straight, squared her shoulders, gave a deep sigh, and stared unseeing into the blue distance. "I just can't risk it," she said aloud. "It would be totally selfish. I can't do that to Jacob."

211

The hot summer passed, week-by-week, with Abigail praying Mr. Anderson would improve enough so they could be on their way before bad weather. Bill remained kind but aloof, like a stranger steering clear of her. It tore her heart out to see Jacob go from puzzlement to hurt over Bill's coldness toward her.

Now fall was almost upon them, and although Mr. Anderson had improved a bit, there was no way he could travel. Lately, more often than not, Abigail's head ached, she supposed from the worry. She rubbed her temples and then cut a long okra pod and dropped it into a basket already holding a few late summer squash lying atop half a basket of red, ripe tomatoes. She put a finger to her mouth to moisten the tingling skin that had been pricked by the sharp, hairy spines. Then she waved back at Jacob as he passed the garden on his way to the woods.

"Be careful," she cautioned. "While you're walking, make sure to keep the gun pointed up at the sky or down at the ground."

He flashed a grin. "Yeah, Ma, and make sure I know what I'm shooting at before I pull the trigger. You've said that about a million times already."

She gave a wan smile and watched with concern as he strode from sight with the old shotgun, in the crook of his arm, pointed at the sky. She wished she had forbidden the squirrel hunt, and yet she knew she must fight against being overprotective more than ever now that Jacob would have no man to guide him.

Suddenly her head jerked up at a sound near the fence.

"He's a right fine-looking lad."

A man stepped from the shadow of the large elm growing at the edge of the garden. He had a marled eye in a wide face with a prominent flat nose.

Abigail stiffened. She didn't know him, but he was up to no good. No honest man came up on a woman in such a sneaky fashion. Her eyes darted, searching for a weapon. The hoe, a few steps away, wasn't much of a weapon, but the ax was beyond the fence and buried deeply in the chopping block where Bill had stuck it.

The man gave a shrewd look. "You just stay put," he said.

"What do you want?" she asked, her voice sounding bolder than she felt.

"You might say I'm collecting sums owed me. Name is Harvey." He gave a cold chuckle. "I see you know the name. Then you know your man owes me plenty. And if you don't want a heap of trouble, just go get his money—all that money Tanner's been getting from selling staves over in Pope County. Yeah, I know all about that. I've been biding my time until he made plenty of hauls. "

"I have no idea where Mr. Tanner keeps his money. He's not my man, and he doesn't share his business affairs with me."

"Well, you better find it quick." He drew a long knife from a sheath at his belt. "Like I said, that's a fine-looking boy. Be a shame for something to happen to his face—maybe a nice long scar to make him look more like his ma."

Abigail sucked in a quick breath. "I'll give you all the money I have. But I'm telling you the truth. I have no idea where Mr. Tanner keeps his money—or if he even has any."

"Oh, he has some all right, and you know it."

"I don't know. He should be back any minute. You can ask him."

He struck her across the mouth. Her head jerked back and she could taste her own blood."

"Quit lying. I know he left early this morning with a big load of stave bolts. Now you better tell me quick—where's the money?"

She grew desperate. "Honestly, I don't."

He worked his jaw back and forth as he eyed her carefully. "Maybe you're telling the truth. Then again maybe you ain't, but I'm not leaving here until I have his stash. He burned a brand on me, and his fancy-pants lawyer cost me my job with all his butting into my business at that farce of a trial. Now I gotta leave the country, and I'm not leaving empty handed. You find me that money or I'll take it out in blood and I don't much care whose—yours or the boy's." He gave an evil grin. "I figure Tanner would squirm more if it was yours."

"I'd give it to you right now if I knew where—"

"Then we'll search." He grabbed her arm and started toward the house. "Don't try anything foolish like getting a gun. I've no aversion to shooting a woman—you wouldn't be the first." His hard eyes revealed it was no idle threat.

Her mind raced, thinking what to do—where she might find a weapon. Jacob had the only gun, but there was the butcher knife under her pillow.

Harvey paused for a moment on the porch to look in the front window before opening the door. "Where's the old man?"

"In bed." She pulled back as he tugged her arm.

"Get in there," he snarled and then shoved her inside. The steel grip hurt her arm. His eyes darted all around. He let go of her arm, gripped her chin, squeezed her cheeks, and forced her face toward him. "I'll give you one more chance before I tear up your house."

She talked through squeezed jaws. "I told you, I don't know where it is."

"Then we'll start in here," he said and stepped into the front bedroom where Mr. Anderson lay staring, big-eyed, at the doorway. "Old man, where does Tanner hide his money? Tell me and maybe I'll let you live."

As Talbert, clutching the quilt, made guttural noises, Abigail said, "He can't speak."

"What's wrong with him?" Harvey was already pawing through drawers and dumping the contents onto the floor.

"He had a stroke." While she spoke, Abigail began inching toward the door.

"Stay put or you'll be sorry."

Harvey's tone stopped her in her tracks. He pulled out scraps of the curtain fabric from her sewing drawer. When the wooden spool of thread fell onto the floor, he stepped over it and pointed, ordering her to sit in the chair. "Put your arms back." He started a tear in the fabric with his teeth and then finished ripping by pulling it apart. Then he wrapped and knotted the strip until it bit tightly into the flesh of her wrists.

Talbert, struggling wildly, waved his right arm while the left remained limp at his side. His desperate attempts to speak were growls that left spittle on his thin lips.

Harvey strode toward the bed. "My ma used to hide money in the bed." He grabbed the edge of the mattress, and with a jerk, dumped Talbert, along with the bedding, onto the floor.

"Don't!" protested Abigail, all the while knowing it would do no good. She had to sit and watch as Talbert thrashed around, trying unsuccessfully to get up, while Harvey drew the knife from his belt again and made a long slash in the mattress, sending feathers spilling out and scattering into the air. He plunged his arm deep inside to feel all through the feathers before finally giving a disgusted snort and drawing out a feather-covered arm. He brushed at them, sending more feathers into the air to float among dust motes in the beam of morning sunlight streaming in the window.

Harvey stalked from the room. Abigail looked all around, searching for something to help free her. Her scissors were in the sewing drawer, so she stood, bending over to accommodate the chair, and made her way awkwardly across the room, thankful that he had not tied her feet.

"Lie still, Mr. Anderson," she cautioned. "I'll get you up as soon as I can. If you keep thrashing around so, you'll hurt yourself."

She saw the shining metal tip of the shears almost covered by a piece of the plaid fabric, and turning her back to the drawer tried to reach them, but the chair kept her too far away. She turned back and used her teeth to move the fabric and then to lift the scissors from the drawer. The cumbersome weight hurt her lip, but she dared not put them down again until she made it across the room to the dresser and laid them down. It was low enough she could reach the scissors in spite of the chair. Finally her numb fingers closed around them. For fear Harvey would return, she staggered back and sat down in the same spot. Drawers banged and pots and pans clattered to the floor, and then she heard boots overhead as Harvey riffled the attic. She had no idea where Bill hid his money, but she was fairly certain it was not in the house. Apparently Harvey came to the same conclusion; the back door creaked as he stomped outside.

While she struggled trying to cut the fabric, she prayed he found the money. Her heart was in her throat fearing Jacob would return. Then she suddenly realized if Harvey found the money, more than likely, he would not leave her alive. He would probably kill her and Mr. Anderson as well to make certain no one ever told the tale. With renewed effort she fought the restraint. Her wrists burned where the flesh was rubbed raw, but she could not get a proper grip on the scissors. The fabric held tight.

Finally Harvey stood in the doorway, breathing hard. Sweat glistened on his brow and ran down the side of his broad nose. He used a sleeve to swipe it away. Abigail shoved the scissors onto the seat and squirmed enough to cover them with her skirt.

"I never found a damn thing. That means you'll have to find out where it is before I come back." His eyes narrowed. "And I will be back. If you don't want me to carve on your boy, you better have it by then. I ain't fooling around—if you don't have it, I'll cut the boy." He pointed the knife blade to his marled eye. "I'll start with his eyeballs."

While ignoring Talbert's fresh outburst of desperate mutters, Harvey cut the cloth holding Abigail's wrists. "Now, you can tell Tanner and he will come after me… and he might get me. But one thing you can know for certain, if he doesn't, I'll come here, middle of the night or broad light of day, and I'll find the boy. What's left of him won't be worth burying." He stared hard into her face while she rubbed the feeling back into her wrists. "You understand?"

"I understand perfectly."

"Good. Now you find that money quick. I won't wait long."

As soon as he was gone she hurried to help Talbert to the chair. "Are you hurt?" she asked, feeling of his bony shoulder that had taken the brunt of the fall.

He shook his head, grabbed her arm, and pressed so tightly it throbbed. She patted his hand and then brushed away wispy feathers clinging to his hair and beard. "I know you're scared for Jacob. I am too." She glanced toward the door and added, "I'm not sure what to do." She drew in a deep breath and for the first time wished Mr. Anderson could talk. He was trying so hard to tell her something. Her mind whirled. Her first instinct was to grab Jacob and leave here as fast as she could. But how would they survive on her small hoard of cash, and what about Mr. Anderson? What would he do without her? Finally she asked, "Should I tell Bill?" His vigorous nod left her with no doubt. Mr. Anderson thought Bill should know. And yet she could not forget Harvey's threats.

"Ma! What in the world happened?"

She turned to see Jacob standing in the doorway holding the gun and two dead squirrels by the tail. His eyes widened when she rushed to gather him close—squirrels, gun and all—into a fierce hug.

"What happened?" he repeated. "Are you and Grandpa all right? Your faces look like you saw a ghost."

"A man tried to rob us."

"Did he find our money?"

"I don't know," said Abigail, walking swiftly into the kitchen. A tornado would not have done more damage, she thought, seeing every drawer open and everything possible dumped–sugar, flour, cornmeal, and coffee in intermingling heaps. The tea canister lay on its side, and the small roll of bills was gone. "Yes," she said with bitterness, "yes, he did." It wasn't much money, but she had worked hard for it and it was all she had. Now there was no way she and Jacob could run, and she'd be even more dependent on Bill.

"He sure made a mess," said Jacob in awe as his eyes went over everything. "It's all right, Ma. We'll be fine," he assured with a tremor in his voice. "I'll make us some money." He held up the squirrels proudly. "See, I can hunt now. I can sell meat, and David is teaching me how to fix the hides so I can sell them to the fur trader when he comes through."

She gave a trembling smile. "You're growing up so fast I know you'll take care of us someday soon, but for now I don't want you to worry about making money. I'll take care of that."

"Ma," he asked abruptly, "did he find Bill's money?"

"No."

"I didn't think he could. Bill hid it real good."

Her eyes widened. "Bill told you where he hides his money?"

"No. He just said he hid it where no one could ever find it."

Abigail chewed her lip. She needed time to sort things out, to come up with a plan to keep Jacob safe. Mr. Anderson thought she should tell Bill. And she wanted to. Bill could deal with Harvey. But what if he failed? What if Harvey made good his threat? Her blood ran cold at the mere thought. And what if Bill killed Harvey and they sent him to prison, or worse yet, hanged him? There was no easy answer to the dilemma. For now she could only pray.

Frowning, she looked all around. "We'll clean the squirrels and then come back inside and clean up this mess."

"I can clean 'em."

"Jacob, I don't want you going outside without me."

Upon seeing his perplexed look, she added, "That man might come back. We need to keep the gun close and watch carefully."

It took two days to clean up what Harvey had wrecked in a few minutes, the longest task re-stuffing feather ticks with stray feathers that covered bedrooms and loft. The bunkhouse had straw ticks, so they were easier to repair, but it was still an arduous task, stuffing the straw and mending the long rents made by Harvey's wicked knife. While she worked, Abigail worried. She wasted no time searching for Bill's money. She had no intention of giving it to Harvey even if she found it. She figured that he would still kill them, so she diligently kept watch with the shotgun near at hand while she rejected first one plan and then another.

When Bill's wagon drove past the window the next day, heading for the barn, she headed outside. She didn't want Jacob overhearing.

Bill patted the mules. "You both did a good job," he said, breathing in the good, sweaty, animal scent as he pulled the collar from one mule and hung it on the barn wall. He glanced up surprised to see Abigail entering the barn because she stayed as far from him as possible these days and vice-versa—even though he still watched with a heavy heart when she wasn't looking. Now, he kept right on removing the collar from the other mule while he waited for her to speak.

"I need to talk to you," she began.

He noticed her pale, drawn face and stopped to give her undivided attention. As her story unfolded, his jaws tightened.

He studied the packed dirt of the barn floor and rubbed his jaw while murder rushed through his veins. If only he had killed the sonofabitch when he had the chance. He knew he should have. Now Abigail and Jacob were paying because he hadn't.

She held her arms tightly across her chest as though she were cold even though it was a warm August evening and crickets sang in the twilight. "I've kept the shotgun close, but who knows when he might show up. And poor Jacob—I won't even let him go to the outhouse alone. He's getting sick of that."

Bill nodded.

"I don't know what to do...." her voice trailed away.

"I do," he said coldly. "But for now we need to get you and Jacob away from here as quick as we can."

Her eyes widened. Then her face flushed. She turned to stare out the barn door. "I'd have left already if I had any money. He stole all I had hidden in the tea canister. And then there's Mr. Anderson."

Bill began removing the harness again. "He'll have to go with you," he said, matter-of-factly. "The mules need rest, but we'll leave first thing in the morning. Don't worry—tonight the boys and I will keep watch."

"Where would you take us?" she asked with round eyes.

"You'll be safe on the mountain. Granny's cabin is empty. It was a little dusty last time I was there, but still set up for housekeeping. Uncle Ned and Aunt Becky and my cousin Elijah will help you anyway they can. You'll like them fine." He didn't mention Cindy, but he knew she'd be good to Abigail too. Somehow he still found it hard to say her name aloud.

Abigail stood on the porch until Bill's wagon disappeared over the lip of a ridge covered with tall pines that swayed in the moaning wind. She never remembered feeling so desolate, not even when her parents had died. At least she had had other family to lean on then. Now there was no one. She felt abandoned, and oh, so very alone!

The daylong trip had been painful enough—sitting alongside Bill, her shoulder occasionally brushing his. He had flinched each time it happened. The contact had been unavoidable on the narrow seat with Bill, her, and Jacob perched side-by-side while Mr. Anderson lay on a mattress in the wagon bed along with their meager belongings. Bill had left with hardly a word. She understood that she had grievously hurt him. Her own heart felt shattered into a million pieces. She still refused to put her own happiness ahead of what was best for Jacob.

While she silently groaned, she rested her forehead on her hand where it gripped a rough post holding up the shake-covered porch roof. Somehow she had to make a home for Jacob in this small cabin tucked deep in the mountains in the middle of nowhere. Somehow she had to keep her fear hidden. Somehow she had to be strong enough, wise enough, to be both mother and father to her son.

"Oh, Lord," she groaned, *"help!"*

When her face lifted, she sucked in a startled breath. In those few seconds, the sunset had tinted the horizon with splendor; pink, coral, and crimson had washed across the evening sky as if painted with a heavenly brush. It probably wasn't a sign. God most likely hadn't sent the glorious sunset just for her. In spite of that, she felt a tiny bit better.

Without a doubt the scenery had been beautiful on the way to this place—overlapping mountains, clear rushing streams, and deep, rugged hollows. In spite of that she felt a stranger in a foreign land, but perhaps, like Abraham in the Bible, God would bless her even here.

"Coming," she answered when Jacob called. With one last glance at the brilliant sunset, she went inside.

The kerosene lamp Bill had lit cast yellow light on log walls and handmade furniture. Her eyes fell on a loom pushed into one corner. It was of unusual construction, plainly handmade and sturdy. She ran a hand over wood, dusty, but as smooth as satin from years of use. The loom must have belonged to Bill's granny. He had mentioned she was a great weaver. There was an unfinished piece of yellow cloth still attached and yellow yarn on the spindle.

"You never got to finish the piece, did you?" she whispered to the unknown woman who had lived and loved and worked within the log walls.

"Ma, this is great!" called Jacob, poking his head from the loft opening. "Can I sleep up here? There's a bed and all kinds of neat things, some tools and a big chest, and even a bunch of funny smelling little bags full of stuff hanging from the rafters—"

Abigail interrupted. "Don't bother any of that. It doesn't belong to us. Remember we're just guests."

"I won't," he assured. "But would it be all right for this to be my room while we're here?"

"I suppose," she agreed, already turning her mind to what to make for supper. Mr. Anderson's appetite was poor lately and she tried to make things he liked, but tonight she was bone weary. Although he wasn't fond of eggs, they would be quick and easy to fix. She had carefully wrapped and packed three-dozen in the water bucket. It sat on the floor alongside all the boxes and bundles Bill had placed near the door. He had laid a fire in the fireplace and lit it before leaving. Abigail had found that odd on such a mild evening. Suddenly she sucked in a breath and her eyes widened. *There was no stove!*

She stared in dismay. There was a spit rack with swinging arms for holding kettles in the fireplace and a large spider with lid for baking, and numerous pots, pans,

223

and kettles on the hearth and on the shelf nearby, but she had never cooked like that. Her shoulders drooped even more. Even cooking eggs would be a challenge tonight. At least she did have leftover biscuits in the basket that had held their lunch.

Abigail twisted her hair into a knot, pinned it at the nape of her neck, and stepped outside. While sipping a cup of bitter coffee, she watched the sun peep over the horizon to lighten dark shadows that became barn, shed, and chicken house. As it rose higher above the trees, it bathed morning light over rolling fields of tall corn, the leaves beginning to brown and curl, the mature ears full and hanging down, and she saw pastures that had been grazed, although she saw no cattle now. Clearly someone still worked this land. Since it wasn't Bill, she wondered who...possibly his Uncle Ned or his cousin Elijah. They had passed both dwellings on the way here, but no one appeared to be home. She wondered how long it would be before someone came calling.

With that thought, she tossed the rest of the bitter coffee onto the ground while at the same time making a face at the empty cup. There was a lot of scrubbing and dusting to be done before she would welcome company; equally important was mastering good coffee over a fireplace flame.

She had no chance to do either. Breakfast dishes were barely washed and put away before Jacob, with the dog at his heels, ran from the yard into the pool of sunlight streaming in at the open front door. "Ma, a wagon's coming."

Abigail's eyes darted around the room. "Keep that dog out of here," she ordered while she quickly straightened

224

the fabric curtain hanging over the cupboard, hung the dishtowel to dry on a hook, and looked down at her apron. It was still neat so she kept it on and stepped to the door, shading her eyes against the brightness. Two women sat in the wagon, and a boy about Jacob's age rode in the back. The women smiled as they climbed down and approached the porch. Each lady carried a basket. As they drew closer, Abigail saw one was about her own age and the other was older, although still well preserved. Both were attractive but totally different in build and coloring; the younger, tall, full-figured with shining brown hair and eyes; the other petite with blonde hair done into a neat matronly knot while the front fell into a soft wave across her forehead. Her lovely eyes were a rare shade of emerald green.

"I'm Becky Loring," she said, "and this is my daughter-in-law, Cindy."

So, thought Abigail, *this is the young woman who lost her baby when Bill's real father set her house on fire.*

"That's Cindy's eldest, Ben, over by the wagon." She paused to ask, "I assume Billy told you about us, that we're his kin?"

Abigail smiled. "Yes, yes he did." She'd have to get used to hearing him called Billy. "This is my son, Jacob, and my father-in-law, Mr. Anderson, is inside in bed. He's an invalid. Please come inside, but excuse the mess. I haven't had a chance to straighten anything."

Becky set her basket on the table. "Gracious, of course you haven't! We came to help—that is if you don't mind?"

Actually Abigail did. She gave a nervous smile. The women were nice and she had no reason to be nervous, and yet she felt ill at ease and gawky, and found herself turning her face aside to hide the scar. These were Bill's loved ones and she wanted to make a good impression, so she merely said, "Thank you."

Cindy had returned Abigail's smile but remained quiet while Becky added, "I hate that we weren't home when you passed by yesterday. I'd have cooked supper for all of you. Nothing is harder than moving and trying to get meals ready in the chaos." She removed a bonnet and hung it on a hook near the door. "Billy stopped by on his way down the mountain and told us you'd moved in. We'd all gone to a funeral of a neighbor."

"Oh, I'm sorry. Was it a friend of Bill's...Billy's?"

Becky chuckled and exchanged quick looks and smiles with Cindy. Abigail sensed a deep friendship here and she envied it. It had been years since she'd shared a close friendship with a woman.

"Actually," said Becky, "Tom Sorrels was more the kind of neighbor everyone sort of put up with and tried to like—not a bad person, just sort of difficult in some ways...like most of us, I suppose. 'There's none good, no not one,'" she finished with the scripture quote and a smile. "Now what can we do to help?"

With a shrug, Abigail held out both hands. "Heavens...I don't know..."

Cindy set the large basket on the table and then drew a rag from it. "I reckon I could dust the cupboard shelves? Granny kept curtains over 'em, but dust still has a way of creepin' in, don't it?"

For the first time, Abigail gave a genuine smile. Cindy's grammar was faulty, but her smile was warm and sincere and Abigail warmed to her instantly. Becky, on the other hand, still made her nervous.

"That's a good idea," said Becky, immediately taking charge. "But let's sweep first so the dust won't just settle on everything again. I brought an extra broom in the wagon and some scrub buckets."

Abigail wasn't offended. She had worked alone far too long to be good at delegating.

Becky turned to smile at the boys. "Ben, would you and Jacob please bring in the other things from the wagon and then unhitch and put the team in the barnyard? And don't you boys stray too far today. We'll be needing plenty of water."

"Sure, Grandma," said Ben.

"Yes, ma'am," assured Jacob. "When you need a bucketful just holler." Then, after carefully eyeing each other in silence, both boys headed for the wagon.

As though reading Abigail's mind, Becky added, "Ben's a good boy. You need not worry about your boy being with him. All Cindy's boys are well behaved. She has two more at home and a three-month-old baby girl, Rebecca Pauline—we call her Polly after her other grandma. That baby is the apple of our eye. My daughter Deborah stayed home to take care of her. She'd rather take care of that baby than eat! Now, I'll hush up bragging on my grandchildren so we can get to work," she added with a chuckle.

While Abigail unpacked the barrel holding her cleaning rags and scrub brush, Becky swept the kitchen and moved toward a bedroom. After she had rapped on the door, her voice drifted into the kitchen. "Hello, Mr. Anderson. I'm Becky Loring, your neighbor. Here, let me fluff your pillow. There. That's better. I'm going to sweep, but I'll try not to choke you with dust."

"She's got a good way with sick folks," said Cindy with a soft smile, not slowing work while she talked. "So did Elijah's granny."

"Bill told me his granny was a doctor of sorts."

"She never claimed to be no doctor, but truth be told, I reckon she knowed more than some of 'em. She had the healing gift. She used yarbs—herbs, that is—to make medicine, and she knew every healing plant in the mountains. She delivered hundreds of babies...."

Abruptly, Cindy's face grew still and solemn before she added, "And she lost but a few."

Abigail discerned the reason for the painful pause. Cindy's own baby was one of the few lost. "I'd love to learn how to use herbs," said Abigail quickly. "I found bags of them hanging from the rafters."

Cindy's face brightened. "I'll be glad to teach you. I don't know as much as Granny did, but she taught me some. She even said I had the gift too." She blushed a little. "But I don't know if that's so."

"I suppose the loom was hers?"

"Oh, my yes! Granny loved to weave! And she loved that loom, too. Her husband—Elijah's Great Grandpappy Tanner—made it for her. She'd always tell folks how it was the first thing he made when they moved here from Tennessee, even before he made a table or a bed. They slept on the floor because she wanted the loom first." Cindy gave a sad smile. "Becky and I love to weave, but we just couldn't bear to take that loom out of here when Granny passed on. Besides, we sort of figure Billy might want it for his wife someday." She cut her eyes sideways just a bit as though judging Abigail's reaction to the remark. Then she added, "So Ned and Elijah just flew in and made us another one."

Abigail kept her face expressionless. Of course the women were curious about her. Bill was family and they cared about him, and more than likely he hadn't told them any details. One thing she had already gleaned about Bill Tanner—except on rare occasions, he liked to keep quiet more than he liked to speak. She wasn't sure how to answer the friendly prying, so she stayed quiet as well.

While they cleaned and then unpacked the few barrels and boxes and put things to place, Cindy kept a friendly conversation going. Finally she said, "Things is beginning to look good and homey again—like it used to." Her smile had a wistful sadness. "Well, I need to go home for a bit to nurse the baby, but I won't be gone long. It's just a short piece if I take the shortcut."

True to her word, Cindy wasn't gone long, just long enough for Abigail to reflect on the pleasant conversation and to digest the new things she had learned about Bill. He had always been quiet. He was wounded in the war and almost died. His family loved and respected him.

Almost, she began to hope…. Abruptly she jerked back her thoughts like the bit on a runaway horse. Bill himself had shared that these were not his blood relatives, just kind people who had taken him into their hearts. Caleb Tanner was not his real father. She must not lose sight of that. Judging from Bill's own words, Jared Rawlings had been cut from a different bolt of cloth, a violent man and quick tempered. Even Bill feared the blood that flowed in his veins. She'd do well to remember that.

By the time they paused for a bite to eat at midday, she was actually enjoying the company, even Becky's. Both women were so friendly, so forthcoming, that it was impossible to remain aloof. Abigail found herself sharing the barest details of her past and how she had met Bill and why she had to leave his farm, although she waited until the boys had gone back outside before sharing that detail. The women exchanged glances.

"We know. Bill told us. By now every man on the mountain is keeping an eye peeled," assured Becky. "You can put your mind at rest. You're safe here."

"I haven't felt safe since it happened," Abigail admitted.

"Oh my," said Cindy, "I'd be scared out of my wits if anyone was to threaten my babies! I don't know what I'd do."

"Yes, you do," said Becky with conviction. "The same thing you did when that marauder tried to shoot Elijah—the same thing Ned and Elijah would do," said Becky. "And if I know Billy Tanner, he won't rest until this is settled." She patted Abigail's hand lying on the table. "Rest assured, you're among friends. Like I said, you're safe here."

"Thank you." Abigail hoped it was true. For the first time in ages, the knot of fear deep inside began to relax, replaced by the warm glow of friendship and acceptance. "Maybe I can finally get a decent night's sleep."

Then, to her satisfaction, the conversation drifted to Bill again. As both women shared tales from Bill's past—Becky's going back as far as his childhood—Abigail gained a deeper appreciation of who he was, of these his people, and her heart warmed with the telling. She drew her mind back to Becky's story.

"So Bill found out from a fellow soldier that Caleb had been shot and that Cindy was stranded, half dead, and without a wagon. He found her, and together they went on to Shreveport and fetched Ned home from the army hospital." Becky's eyes misted with the telling. "After his time in that awful Union prison, Ned was more dead than alive. Cindy nursed him night and day and brought him back to me. I've never been more grateful for anything in my life!"

Cindy put in, "Billy helped with the nursin'. And on that trip he saved both our lives more than once."

Abigail noticed Cindy's cheeks had reddened a bit. She must be uncomfortable with praise.

"Ned sings both of your praises," said Becky with a soft smile. Then, seeming for the moment to forget Abigail's presence, she said, "I worry about Billy, though. I always have. Even as a boy he was so withdrawn inside himself.

And after the war, it got worse. Of course it's no wonder, having to care for Viola like he did and her mind gone the way it was. He just holed up here at this cabin. He spent too much time alone."

Cindy spoke softly, "I've prayed and prayed he'd find a good woman."

Abigail mulled over all they said. Cindy thought Bill a valiant, honorable man of sterling character, and one she owed her life to. It would take some careful thought to consider all she'd heard today. Abruptly, Abigail stood to offer more coffee from the pot sitting near the coals.

"No, thank you. I've had plenty," said Becky as she stood. "We'd better get back to work. It won't be long before we have to go."

While Abigail and Cindy washed the curtains, hung them to dry in the sun, and then shined the windows to a gleam, they chatted, mostly about their children. Abigail was drawn more and more to this unpretentious woman of the hills.

"Your mother-in-law mentioned marauders. What happened?"

"It was bad times here during the war. Most of the men were off fighting in the army—except for a bunch of riffraff that rode around preying on women and takin' food right out of the younguns' mouths."

Abigail nodded. "It was the same in Missouri. But Elijah was here?"

"He got conscripted and fought for a good while before he came home. After that, one day some bushwhackers come." Cindy's face went still as did her hand holding the polishing cloth. "They killed my little brother Pete and 'most killed Ma. I ran for Elijah. He killed some of them, but just as I got here one of 'em had him in his gun sights. My heart stopped beatin'. If he'd killed Elijah,

I don't think hit would have ever started beatin' again." She started rubbing the window again in slow, deliberate circles. "I had Granny's shotgun so I did what had to be done."

Cindy gave no more details, but Abigail needed none. Cindy had killed the bushwhacker. Abigail had never killed a human. But with Jacob's life in danger, she wondered if she would be capable of it.

Chapter 10

Evening shadows dappled Spadra Creek and made long, dark shade of false-fronted buildings and houses along the street. When Bill rode into Clarksville there were few people on the streets. He figured most were home enjoying supper as he headed straight for Cravens' office, although he had little hope of finding the lawyer there. He tied the horse to the hitching rail, and although the interior was dusky, he tried the door. It was locked. For a moment Bill stood, indecisive. He could go to the saloon, always a fount of information, but he figured Cravens would have more accurate information than the hangers-on at the bar, so he remounted and rode on.

A pleasant-faced woman answered his knock and graciously led him toward a closed door. She rapped and stuck her head inside. "Jordan, a gentleman to see you."

Cravens sat at his desk. He stood when Bill entered.

"Tanner, good to see you," he said as they shook hands. "It's stuffy in here. Let's sit outside on the portico," he suggested. Bill followed him outside onto the wide porch before Cravens asked, "What brings you to town? From the looks of you, it's nothing good."

Bill laid his hat on the porch and sat down in the chair Cravens indicated with a nod of the head. "It's not. What can you tell me about Harvey since the trial—any idea where he's staying?"

"I saw him earlier this evening in town, but I have no idea where he's staying. Why?"

Bill didn't want to confide too much. He certainly didn't want Cravens finding out about his illegal timber operation, so he played his cards close to his chest. "Abigail thinks she saw him out at my place. I figure he's up to no good."

Cravens frowned. "He strikes me as the kind to carry out that threat he—"

Bill cocked his head. Shots weren't uncommon in town, usually a drunk getting crazy and firing off a pistol, but the shotgun blasts were close and not from the direction of the saloon. Cravens, staring into the gathering darkness, cocked his head to listen. Bill followed him off the porch when a man shouted for help. Just then, right beyond Cravens' yard, a horse thundered past, racing down the road. Bill didn't get a look at the horse or the rider. It was too dark and trees blocked his view.

By the time they arrived downtown, a crowd had gathered on the street in front of Dr. Maffit's office. Judging by the excited voices and snatches of conversation, Bill figured someone had been shot.

"What happened?" asked Cravens.

Several answered at the same time. "Doc Ward's been shot."

Bill soon gleaned that no one saw the shooter—he just blasted away with a shotgun and then took off on a horse. Doc was inside, badly wounded but alive, and Dr. Maffit was with him now.

He turned to Cravens. "That was probably the shooter we heard ride past your place in such a hurry."

Cravens glanced back down the road. "He's long gone by now. Be hard to track him in the dark, but I figure the sheriff will get a posse together. I'll tell him what we heard."

To Bill's surprise, the sheriff seemed in no hurry to raise a posse. He did, however, question several people, asking what they saw and heard.

Bill spoke low to Cravens. "Think this has to do with the election?"

The tip of Cravens' cigar glowed red in the darkness where they stood outside of the lamplight spilling from the doctor's windows. "Could very well be. Or it could be something totally unrelated. Ward's the constable. He probably has enemies."

Suddenly Bill's ears perked up. He stepped around a man with broad shoulders to see who had just spoken. He couldn't make out the speaker; nevertheless, he certainly didn't like what he heard.

"What makes you think it was Wallace?" Bill asked. There was no answer.

He scowled. The man who had made the accusation seemed to have melted into the night. But the damage had been done—proven by low mutters of speculation about Sid. Bill stayed around for a while longer before heading to the Hadley shack. He'd do a little more asking around tomorrow to see if anyone had seen Harvey. And before heading home, he'd stop by the Wallace farm and check on the boys and have a private word with Sid.

✕✕✕

Tom, beaming, shook Bill's hand. "Good to see you! Me and Matt were just talking about you yesterday—wondering how you were getting along."

"Fine." Bill started to say more but Tom interrupted.

"And how's Miz Abigail and Jake?"

"They're both fine. But keep your eyes and ears peeled for Harvey. He threatened both of them, trying to get to me."

Tom's eyes shot lightning. "That bastard!"

"Don't worry," assured Bill. "He won't find them now. I took them someplace safe. Have you seen Harvey lately?"

Tom shook his head. "And he better hope I don't," he growled.

"Is Sid around?" Bill asked.

Tom glanced toward the barn. "You just missed him. He rode out a few minutes ago, but he wouldn't be good company anyway. He's surly as bear today."

"Why's that?" asked Bill, heart quickening.

"Oh, he was up all night with fever and those chills he gets." Tom grinned. "And to top that off he had the trots bad—spent most of the night sitting on the chamber pot." He studied Bill's serious face. "Why? Something wrong?"

"Doc Ward got shot last night."

Tom gave a low whistle. "He dead?"

"Not the last I heard, but he's in bad shape. Doc Maffit doesn't think he'll make it."

"Who did it?"

"No one knows. Someone blasted him with a shotgun and then rode off."

Tom's brows drew together with suspicion. "And you came here to talk to Sid...are folks saying he did it?"

For a second, Bill chewed his jaw. "Some are," he admitted.

"Well, they can all go to hell," swore Tom. "He was right here all night." He drew an angry breath. "And there's more than me can swear to it. The Blackards were visiting—even spent the night. Miz Rachel and Mattie and William." Tom kicked angrily at a rock, puffing up dust. "Ever since that damn lie about Sid robbing and shooting Dub Turner, folks have gotten it in for him. You'd think George gettin' killed would be enough for 'em. Matt said he heard some fellows at Flood's Saloon the other day spinning a yarn about what a mean one Sid is—how he went all the way to Kansas and killed one of those fellers that shot Pa." He grimaced. "Hell! Sid ain't never been to Kansas in his life."

Bill nodded sympathetically. "I reckon some folks like a good story better than the truth." He gave Tom a friendly slap. "Don't fret. Likely nothing more will come of this—it's just idle talk. Tell Sid I dropped by. You and Matt don't be strangers. Come out to the place and visit."

"We'll do that," said Tom, but the scowl remained as Bill mounted and rode away.

Bill left town with no news of Harvey. No one at the saloon had seen him in weeks. What he did hear was more suspicious talk of Sid shooting Doc Ward. He was beginning to think the gossip was orchestrated. Someone was setting Sid up. He wasn't worried about Sid, though. Sid had a good alibi and plenty of witnesses. What he was worried about was finding Harvey. Abigail and the boy were out of danger now, but no man could threaten what Bill loved. He aimed to hunt Harvey down and kill him like the dog he was.

※※※

Bill pulled back the lever, stopping the saw. He stepped away from the shed just as David piled off his horse.

"Was there any sign of Harvey in town?"

David shook his head. "No, none a-tall. But there was a big stir going on. You aren't gonna believe this—someone shot and killed the judge."

"Judge Meers?"

Quinton laid down a hammer and stepped out into the sunlight too. "Judge Meers?" he echoed Bill's question.

"Yep," said David. Shotgunned him from ambush up on East Hill while he was walking home. He lived a few hours. They carried him into Littlebury Robinson's house—he's the one that found him."

"Was Meers able to talk—did he see who did it?"

"He told Robinson he saw the shooter but didn't recognize him."

"I'm glad of that," muttered Bill. "They can't lay this at Sid's door. Meers knew Sid for darn sure."

David gave his head a slight shake. "You'd think not—still and all—Sheriff Crampton sworn out a warrant and Sid's been arrested."

Bill's brow furrowed. "*What!* I thought Meers said he didn't recognize—."

David shrugged. "That's not holding much sway. Tom Paine is saying how Sid told him he was going to kill Ward, and then after Ward was shot, Paine said that Sid bragged he'd done it. And there's others saying Sid threatened the judge for letting Turner go after he killed George. Paine says he figured the judge was just trying to protect Sid because he felt sorry for him."

Bill exploded. "*That's the damnedest fool thing I ever heard!*"

"I agree. But they're still going to try to pin it on Sid."

Bill's fists clenched. "Those damn, lying, thieving sonsofbitches."

Quinton spoke up, "Well, if it goes to trial, there's not a jury on earth would heed that kind of evidence—a fellow who didn't speak up for days to say a man told him he was going to kill a man. And who would believe that a near-dead man would try to protect his own killer? Ah, no one will buy that hogwash!" He turned, reentered the shed, and said, "Come on, boys. We got to finish this load."

Bill stayed where he was. "Anyone talk to Tom and Matt?"

"I rode out and talked to them. They're madder than hell."

"I can imagine," said Bill and then swore again under his breath as he stared into the distance. "Surely Quinton's right. A jury will never convict him." And yet nerves crawled in Bill's stomach. He hoped Quinton was right, and yet lately it seemed reason was at a premium. He feared for Sid.

Bill returned to the shed, operated the saw, and then helped load the wagon in preparation for the early morning trip to Russellville; all the while his mind turned over the news. He wondered who had killed Meers and Ward. He'd be willing to bet it was the same man, and he'd be willing to bet there was more than one man in on it. It had the reek of crooked politics. He wasn't privy to the inner workings of Clarksville's politics, but he'd bet a thousand dollars if you followed the power and money far enough, you'd find the killer at the end of the trail. When he returned from the trip he intended to go see Cravens and find out what he knew.

XXX

Cravens leaned back in his chair and made a tent of his fingers under his chin. "There's no way I can be Sid's attorney. I've been summonsed to testify about the night Ward was killed, about hearing the shots and the horse running away."

"Isn't there any way we can get the trial moved to Dover or Ozark or even Lewisburg?"

Cravens shook his head. "Withers, the judge they appointed, has denied Barrow's request for a change of venue."

Bill scowled. "You know as well as I do that Sid can't get a fair trial here. This is some kind of trumped up deal.

Even the Gazette article said Meers told Robinson he saw his killer but didn't recognize him. It's crazy Sid was even arrested." Bill huffed an aggravated breath. "So tell me about this Barrow—is he a good lawyer?"

"He was Wilshire's attorney—the one I went toe to toe with when I represented Tom Gunter during the congressional hearings."

Bill sat up straighter. "Barrow was the lawyer for that carpetbagger? How in the world was he appointed as Sid's attorney?"

Cravens shrugged. "A good attorney doesn't stand on politics; he gives any client the best defense he can. I can't say how Barrow will perform in a murder trial. I've only dealt with him on civil matters."

As Bill stood to leave, Cravens added, "Bill, watch your own back. I heard some talk the other day. Word is the sheriff was told to keep an eye on you. Talk is you may have some kind of illegal business going on."

Bill opened his mouth.

"Please," Cravens stopped him when he began to interrupt, "I don't want to know any details. I'm just telling you to watch your back."

"Thanks for the warning," he said. "I sure will."

Bill was less than pleased with Cravens' evasive answer. He left the office with more questions than when he came, and there was a sinking feeling in the pit of his stomach when he thought of a carpetbagger's attorney defending Sid.

On the way to the Hadley shack, he considered Cravens' warning. He would tell Quinton and the boys, they needed to be extra careful.

He stopped to watch workmen covering the red bricks on the second story of the new courthouse with a sparkling coat of white paint. Although the trial had been the topic of conversation everywhere else Bill had been today, here the mutterings were about the higher taxes the new courthouse would require.

"I reckon we do need a new building," admitted one graybeard, "but hit don't in no wise have to cost sech a fortune. Meers got up all these-here new taxes, and now he ain't around to help pay."

"At least we'll have a courthouse to show for it," said another man whom Bill had seen in the crowd the night Ward was killed. "But did you read in the newspaper what this murder trial is going to cost? Too bad someone doesn't just get a rope and save us a bunch of tax dollars."

Before Bill could speak, the old graybeard interjected, "Here now! I'll hear no sech talk! Sid Wallace is innocent until proved guilty in a court o' law. And I'll thank you to keep yore mouth shut from sayin' otherwise."

Upon hearing voices of agreement, the man gave a sullen laugh. "All right, all right, old fellow. Keep your shirt on. I was just thinking of the taxpayers."

Bill walked on, relieved that Sid had supporters. But would any of them be on the jury tomorrow?

Bill arrived at the courtroom early; even so, there were few empty seats. Folks must have come from miles around. He doubted Emmitt's store had ever held so many people. Most were men, although a fair amount of women, all dressed in Sunday best including fancy hats or bonnets, sat on the straight-backed benches. Someone had gone to the trouble of sweeping and dusting the place, and the large front windows gleamed.

Near the back of the room, he found a place on the end of a bench with just enough room to squeeze in alongside a broad-shouldered man wearing a wool jacket that smelled of wood smoke. Bill craned his neck. Mrs. Wallace and her sons were seated near the front, all except for Sid, that is. He was nowhere in sight. Bill spied David across the room, sitting alongside Toby and Quinton. He caught David's eye and nodded. Just then he felt a hand on his shoulder. He looked up to see Ned Loring's kind eyes in a lined face that was unusually solemn. Behind stood Cousin Elijah, who nodded while giving a brief smile.

Bill stood and motioned Ned to sit.

Ned thanked him and sat down. "Bad business, this. From what I'm hearing this won't be pretty. I doubt Vince's boy will get a fair shake."

Bill nodded, recalling that Uncle Ned and Pa had been close friends with Vincent Wallace. "I'm afraid you're right."

There was a stir as Sheriff Crampton and Deputy Kline entered along with Sid, in manacles, walking between. As Bill and Elijah stepped from the aisle to let them pass, Bill gave Sid an encouraging nod. Although Sid's jaws remained tight, he returned the nod. Bill and Elijah joined the dozens of men lining the back wall of the mercantile.

Elijah crossed arms over his chest, bent near, and spoke low in Bill's ear. "I stopped by this morning and saw Abigail and Mr. Anderson. She said to tell you they're doing fine. Jake went hunting with my boy. They're getting thick as thieves. Both of them want to live out in the woods just like a couple of Injuns."

Bill grinned. "Good. That boy has been too much alone with only grownups."

The crowd quieted as Judge Withers entered and sat down.

"State of Arkansas against Sidney Wallace." The

statement went on with legal terms, and then a list of jurors was named. Bill knew few of the men listed.

Finally Sid's attorney, Mr. Barrow, stood. "The defendant moves the Court for leave to challenge the regular panel of jurors now in court and all jurors summoned in the cause for irregularity and partiality in selecting the same." Barrow went on to enter a sworn statement that Sheriff Crampton and Deputy Kline had entered into a conspiracy not to give the defendant a fair and impartial trial by selecting jurors prejudiced against him. To support the statement, Barrow then introduced two witnesses that swore Kline had made remarks in their hearing that a jury could be obtained to convict the defendant if he could be arrested.

Kline took the stand. "Yes. I remember the conversation, and I did say that if the defendant was arrested that I thought a jury could be obtained in Johnson County; but I didn't say they would convict him—the defendant—without law and testimony." He gave a half smile. "Besides, I didn't summon any of this panel."

Bill was not surprised when Judge Withers refused to sustain the challenge to the panel of jurors. Then testimony began in earnest. The first three witnesses testified about the night Ward was killed, about hearing the shots but not seeing the shooter. Dr. Maffit testified about the extent of the wounds. Then a man named Thomas Paine was sworn in. Bill didn't know the man, but he had seen him around town a few times.

"On the Monday night before Ward was shot, I had gone to the courthouse square when I saw Sidney Wallace, yonder, crouched down behind the courthouse fence on the inside, nearly opposite Ward's office. He had a double barrel gun and some pistols. I spoke up and said,

'Hello, who's there?' Sid said, 'Is that you, Tom?' and I said, 'Yes.' Then we went outside the fence and talked together. Sid asked me where Ward sat at, and he told me he was watching for Ward. I told him where Ward usually sat, and then Sid told me that he intended to bust old Ward's hide for him."

A loud murmur erupted in the courtroom. Judge Withers pounded the gavel.

When the talk died down, Paine continued, "Then Sid said, 'Just let Ward sit there and I'll shoot him in two.'"

The courtroom erupted again. Bill heard outrage, but most people scoffed at Paine's statement. Matt Wallace's voice carried over all. "Sid's not even friends with you, Tom Paine. He'd never tell you a thing like that!"

Judge Withers's gavel pounded. He pierced Matt with a steely look. "Any more such outburst, young man, and you'll have to leave this court." He looked around the room. "And that goes for the rest of you," he threatened. He faced Paine. "Continue."

Paine's brows knit, as though he was trying to remember. "Sid told me he intended to shoot or kill until he was killed. After that he said if I ever told what he'd said that he'd shoot me in two. Then after Judge Meers was shot, I was at Sid's house and he said, 'Tom, don't tell that I killed Doc Ward. If you do, I'll shoot you.'"

There was another stir in the room, but this time Matt kept silent, even though he violently shook his head. Elijah leaned close to whisper, "Talk about a loose load of hay—*who would ever believe this?*"

"I sure don't," agreed Bill.

Paine went on, "After Sid was arrested I went to see him in jail, and he said, 'Tom, if you should be brought before the Ward jury, I don't want you to remember anything, for if they find out I killed Ward, it'll take two or three hundred dollars to prove out of it.'" Paine paused and then added, "Sid told me that just a few days ago—right before this term of Court."

Bill hoped Barrow would tear Paine's story to shreds, but he was disappointed. When the attorney stepped up to cross-examine Paine, there were a lot of questions about when and to whom Paine had given testimony to an examining court about his conversations with Sid, but no real hard-hitting questions about not going to law with the matter. However, Barrow did attempt to extract an admission from him about changing his testimony.

"Mr. Paine, did you not testify to the Grand Jury an entirely different statement purported to be said by Mr. Wallace—did you not say in that testimony that Mr. Wallace said 'before he would be taken, he would kill some of them, and that he did not intend to be taken?'"

The prosecutor stood. "Your Honor, I object to the introduction of such testimony."

"Sustained."

Barrow spoke up, "Exception, Your Honor."

"Noted. Counselor, you may take time to prepare a Bill of Exceptions."

During the pause, Bill's eyes wandered the room. Suddenly he tensed. Harvey stood near the door. At the same moment Harvey glanced his way and then bolted outside. Bill charged from the room, not even taking time to explain to Elijah. It was the first glimpse he'd gotten in months of the villain, and he didn't want him getting away. The sidewalk, crowded with the people unable to get inside the building, had a carnival atmosphere. People laughed and joked, and one man was even taking bets on the possibility of Sid hanging. None too gently, Bill shoved him out of the way to search the street. Harvey had disappeared, and no one had seen which way he went. In a lope Bill ran down the sidewalk, looking into alleys. There was no trace. With a frown he studied the streets and then headed for the livery stable. It was a long shot; horses lined the hitching rails. But maybe Harvey had stabled his mount.

Just then a horse shot past the far end of the alley, heading west. It was Harvey riding a tall, muscled bay. Bill raced toward the Hadley shack where he had stabled the black. Harvey's horse was larger, but the black could run like the wind. The only problem was that Bill still had to bridle and saddle him.

Hours later, Bill pulled the black to a halt, turned up his collar, and blew on his hands. The chill, early November wind pressing through his jacket made his hands cold on the reins. He hated to admit defeat. Harvey simply had too much of a head start. The huge bay had made deep tracks, and wide, the few places it had walked in the dust, but somewhere along the way, it left the trail without a trace. Harvey had been canny about hiding his tracks.

Exhaling a deep breath, Bill turned the black around and headed back to town, even then studying the road with keen eyes. It was late afternoon by the time he arrived on Main Street to find the sidewalks almost empty.

"Trial must be over," he muttered, and then headed for the Hadley shack. He hoped the news was good, but he wouldn't place any bets on it.

He turned the black loose to find what graze it could along with Toby's mule and David's horse in the pasture rife with yellow weed blossoms and tall, yellowed grass. The sun was disappearing below the brilliant autumn treetops bordering the fence when he walked toward the cabin. David met him on the porch. Bill's heart fell when David shook his head.

"He's gonna hang."

Bill groaned "How in the—"

David bit out, "It was the damnedest mess of chicanery I ever heard. The only evidence they had was Tom Paine's testimony." He nodded vigorously. "Yep, that pack of lies was the only speck of evidence…oh, there was a couple of fellows who swore Sid had made some threats to them in private, but not one of them had anything to back up their accusations. The only physical evidence they claimed to have was the big horse tracks Cravens found near his yard the morning after Ward was killed." David grew sarcastic. "*Sid rides a big horse, so of course it had to be him.*" Then his voice shook from anger. "I'm telling the truth, Bill, *every time* Sid's lawyer tried to question a witness, the prosecutor objected, and the judge sustained the objection—*every stinking time!*

"Even though Barrow had men lined up to witness for Sid, they never even got heard. He called McMurry and Connelly and Joe Stuart, but the prosecutor objected and they never even got to testify. Barrow wanted to call John Foley and Will Hutchenson—he told the judge that both of them would swear that Tom Paine had told them he didn't have any idea who killed Ward. The judge wouldn't let them testify, and he wouldn't let Barrow call Paine back to the stand so he could question him about that either."

"*What?!*" exploded Bill.

David nodded. "And that ain't even the worst of it. There was a fellow there to testify that just a few days before Ward died, Ward said his enemies had all been trying to kill him for a while but hadn't got the job done yet. And Mrs. Highland was in court and willing to testify that a few years back, when Ward boarded with her, he had been shot and almost died. After the prosecutor objected,

Judge Withers wouldn't let either of them testify." David put his hand in his pockets and huffed a loud breath. "I'll swear half the day was spent in Barrow writing down exceptions after the judge had sustained the prosecutor's objections. Barrow must have a list a mile long. But every darn time Barrow objected, the judge overruled."

"Did anyone get to testify for Sid?"

"His ma and Will and Tom and Matt. And the two Blackard ladies who had spent the night at the Wallace's—they all said the night Ward was shot that Sid was home with chills and a fever—"

Bill interrupted. "I was over there the next morning. Tom told me Sid had been bad sick the night before. I even offered to testify."

"Wouldn't have done any good. I forgot to say, even a guard at the jail testified that he had to get quinine for Sid because he's had chills since he got arrested. Jury heard all of that, and yet it never made a speck of difference." David changed the subject, "Elijah said you took off after a fellow. Was it Harvey?"

"Yeah. I looked around and saw him standing by the door. He took off horseback. I tracked him a ways out of town, but he had too much of a head start. I lost him out near Lone Pine."

"Wonder why he was at the trial," said David.

"I've been wondering the same thing," admitted Bill. He found it odd that Harvey would risk it. Harvey must know he was looking for him."

Just then Toby limped across the yard, returning from town. "So you made it back. Guess David told you the bad news. Everybody at Slim's is mad. Charlie Clark is even saying he's gonna kill Paine, and everybody is saying the trial was the biggest joke ever was...of course over at Flood's, they're celebrating."

"Figures," muttered David. "That saloon caters to the carpetbaggers."

Bill wondered if the sheriff would let him see Sid. He doubted it, but tomorrow he'd try.

The shack floor was hard and the cracks drafty. The blanket was not much padding, so Bill's sleep was restless. There was, however, a thought that made him sit bolt upright during the night. Something had nibbled at the edge of his mind all evening like a rabbit in a lettuce patch. Suddenly it came clear. *The horse tracks he'd been following all day!* Sid wasn't the only one to ride an oversized horse. Harvey did. And Harvey had an ax to grind with the town officials. He had lost his job and been rejected by them—at least publicly. Bill's mind raced. *Or it could be that Harvey had used his gun for hire.* If he needed money, he seemed the type to do it.

Bill ran the possibilities through his mind. Harvey might not have done it, but it seemed to fit. Cravens had seen Harvey in town the evening Ward was killed. For political reasons if someone with power wanted the constable and the judge out of the way, more than likely they'd hire the job done...or it could be that someone was hostile over the carpetbaggers and their election fraud. Plenty of blood had been spilled in Pope County over that. Just a week ago he had read an article in the Little Rock Gazette about murders committed by Pope County officials and the revenge killings committed in return, done by Dover citizens. No reason to think it couldn't happen here. Bill was fairly certain of one thing—if Sid Wallace wanted to kill Judge Meers for letting Dub Turner go free, he wouldn't have waited two years to shoot him. Furthermore, no one had come up with a plausible reason why Sid would want to kill Ward.

Bill wished he'd figured all this out before the trial. It might not have changed the verdict, but it might have given Sid's attorney some fodder for the mill. It might not be too late. David said Sid's attorney was filing an appeal. Bill decided to go see Cravens. Maybe Cravens would know how to proceed.

"Interesting theories, Tanner." Cravens stared into space for a while before saying, "Harvey was pretty bitter over losing his job, and I heard a rumor that he lost his landholdings in a business deal gone wrong. I can't see him killing the judge and Ward over it, though. But he would be a likely candidate to hire if someone wanted murder done. If Sid didn't do it, I would tend to think the murders were political—anger over that sham of an election. Some of the voters were highly incensed. Perhaps some furious Democrat did do it. No Republicans wanted Meers and Ward out of the way. They were all in it together." He stopped, frowned, and thought a bit before adding, "Unless someone has something to hide and was afraid they'd talk. I have been thinking what a coincidence it is that Ward and Meers sat right here in this office less than a month ago giving depositions to Congress, and now they're both dead. Whoever wanted murder done, Democrat or Republican—or someone else altogether—like I said, Harvey would be a likely candidate. He has no scruples and he's cold-blooded to boot, and from what you say, he needs money." He paused abruptly. "But remember, the judge said he saw his killer but didn't recognize him. Meers knew Harvey."

"Yeah, I thought about that too," said Bill with down-turned mouth.

After pondering a moment longer, Cravens slowly added, "Of course, Meers might have meant he saw the killer's back but couldn't see his face enough to recognize him." Suddenly Cravens leaned forward to look Bill squarely in the eye. "You might have something, all right. Although it would be mighty unhealthy to talk about this around town."

Bill's eyebrows rose. "So I figured," he said. "That's why I came to you. Any idea how to go about proving any of this?"

Cravens pursed his lips before finally answering. "It would do no good to go to the sheriff since you have no proof. Besides, as you said, we're not sure whom to trust. I suggest you keep trying to find Harvey, and I'll start asking some discreet questions. No need for me to tell you, if it was a paid assassination it'll be hard to prove—and dangerous too. We need Harvey, and we need to make him talk. And we don't have much time. Sid's execution is just a few weeks away."

Bill put in, "David Hadley said the trial was a farce."

Cravens appeared to choose his words carefully. "It was lopsided to say the least. Barrow has almost fifty exceptions to appeal to the State Supreme Court."

"Surely they'll overturn the verdict."

Cravens gave a wry laugh. "I wouldn't count on it—not with Poker Jack as Chief Justice."

"Poker Jack?"

"John McClure. He was a Yankee lieutenant colonel with too much fondness for cards—got him dismissed from the army. Didn't stop him from rising high in Arkansas politics, though."

"So what you're saying is our supreme court is run by carpetbaggers too?"

"Precisely."

Bill groaned. He wondered if they could keep Sid from hanging even if they found the proof. He paused with his hand on the doorknob when Cravens called his name.

"Bill, there's one thing you need to keep in mind."

"What's that?"

"Even though the trial was a farce, Sid is an angry young man. He might actually be guilty."

Bill nodded. It was a remote possibility, but he wouldn't bet a plug nickel on it.

He stepped out into a mild, cloudless morning. The oaks and maples near the town square were a blend of coral, orange, yellow, gold, and brown. It was a perfect day. It hurt him to think of Sid behind bars.

※※※

Bill paused in front of the tall, red brick building. The last time he had been here he had been the one behind bars. He didn't even relish the idea of visiting as he went inside. He followed the deputy up two flights of stairs and waited while the jailer unlocked a door.

"Another visitor to see the prisoners," he called to a guard in the hallway.

"Johnny, wait a minute," called the guard. "Miss Lena says she's ready to go back down."

"Sure," said the deputy. He and Bill stepped back to let her pass. She wore a bonnet and a much nicer dress than she usually wore while tending store. Her rosy cheeks looked rosier than ever as she nodded to Bill before proceeding down the steps.

When Bill entered, Sid approached the bars. "Howdy, Bill."

They shook hands the best they could with Sid's hands in manacles.

"Rotten deal you got," said Bill and then halted in surprise. "*Tom? Matt?* What are you doing in here?"

Sid's eyes were granite. "Damned bastards arrested them, too. Claimed they might be a menace to the public or some such rot. Truth is, they're afraid the boys will go for them,"— Sid nodded toward another man—"like Charlie there went for Paine on Main Street yesterday."

Bill saw two more prisoners in cells farther down the way who also wore manacles. The only prisoners not chained were Tom and Matt. Apparently, the jailers didn't consider them too dangerous.

"I heard Paine got shot yesterday," said Bill.

"Paine fired too, but as you can see, only Charlie is in jail. How is Paine?" Sid asked.

"Heard it was only a flesh wound," said Bill.

Sid scowled. "That's too bad," he said. "I want to see him in hell before I swing."

"I'm sure hoping that will never happen, Sid." Bill didn't want to give Sid false hope and yet he wanted to encourage him. "I'm following up on a few leads, and I hope to have some proof that you're innocent before Barrow goes for the appeal."

"I thank you, kindly, but I'll swing no matter what you prove. Someone needs a scapegoat and I'm it." Sid, gripping the bars, looked down at the floor for a minute before looking back to meet Bill's eyes. "I don't suppose I have anyone but myself to blame. I let resentment over Pa's death eat at me—and it showed. Pa used to quote Proverbs all the time about a man's good name being more valuable than gold. You remember he was a preacher?"

"Yes," said Bill. "Pa and Granny loved to hear him preach, and we went to some of his brush arbor meetings when I was a kid."

"That's good to know." Sid gave a sad smile. "Years ago I made threats about killing folks—about getting even. I sort of liked the idea that people were afraid of me. Guess that made me a likely villain when people started dying around Clarksville."

Tom spoke up, "Everybody says stuff when they're mad."

"But not everybody stays mad for years," said Sid and then let out a deep breath. "I hate this most of all for Ma."

"I'm glad Sheriff Crampton didn't arrest Will," observed Bill. "At least your ma has one son to be with her during all this."

"Yeah," said Sid bitterly. "The newspapers are saying what desperate characters the Wallace boys are—all except for Will. They're high on him. I reckon he said stuff they wanted to hear."

Bill didn't pursue this, and Sid said no more on the subject.

"One good thing," interjected Tom, "Matt's gal came to visit. I figure he's glad to be in jail if Miss Lena will come every day like she promised."

"Then why's he looking so glum?" asked Bill, glad to change the subject. "Matt, you look like you just swallowed a dose of Granny's sulphur and molasses."

"Aw, it's Sid she's sweet on," Matt grumbled. "That's the only reason she ever gave me the time of day. She was wanting to get close to him."

Sid scowled. "That's not—"

"Yes it is so," burst out Matt. "She hardly even looked at me the whole time she was here. Her eyes kept eating you alive."

Tom chuckled.

"Well, don't worry, little brother," said Sid. "I won't be around much longer to get in your way."

"Aw, hell, Sid! I'd ten times rather have you around than any old girl I know," avowed Matt. "You heard Bill; he might have proof to get you off."

"Even if by some miracle Bill can prove I didn't kill Meers and Ward, don't forget, at my first trial the other day they gave me four years penitentiary time for shooting Dickey, so I'll not walk away from this a free man."

"It beats hanging!" Matt turned anguished eyes on Bill. "Do all you can to get that proof."

"I will." He shook Sid's manacled hands again and nodded to Matt and Tom before looking back at Sid. "I'll come back every chance. It may be a while, but don't think I've forgotten. I'll be doing everything I can for you."

Sid's eyes were sad. "I appreciate it, Bill. I don't hold out much hope, but it means a lot to have real friends."

Bill descended the stairs with a heavy heart. Sid was right. It would take a miracle, even though he intended doing everything in his power to get proof. For the hundredth time he wondered if Harvey had killed the men. And if it wasn't Harvey, who would profit most from having Meers and Ward out of the way? For the hundredth time he drew a blank. He had no idea. And he simply wasn't in the right political circles to find out. That wouldn't stop him from asking questions. Bill nodded to Deputy Sheriff Kline, who was sitting at his desk sipping a cup of steaming coffee, and then he headed out the door.

Bill glanced at the sun dropping low, just above the treetops. It was too late to start this evening, but first thing in the morning he intended heading to the mountain. Lately he'd spent every spare minute looking for Harvey. He hadn't seen Abigail in a month, but she was never far from his thoughts.

He decided to go to the store to ask Major Swagerty a few questions. The major might know something helpful.

Miss Lena was at the counter. "I'm sorry, but Mr. Swagerty is out of town on business. He should be back—" She stopped in mid-sentence to exclaim, *"What in the world!"*

Bill's head had already swung toward the door and the commotion outside. Men were yelling and shots were firing. "Get down behind the counter, Miss Lena," he ordered and then stepped closer to the windowsill, staying back far enough to avoid a possible stray shot.

"What is it?" called Lena from behind the counter.

"Some kind of commotion near the courthouse." Bill gave an inward groan. The trouble was at the jail. He saw a man step from the building and fire toward the third story window, the floor that housed the jail. People ran down the street and sidewalk. Most ran in the opposite direction; however, some ran toward the jail, firing pistols.

Bill recognized one shooter. It was Tom Paine, the man whose testimony had convicted Sid. Tom raised a pistol just as the barrel of a shotgun poked from the upstairs window. Tom suddenly spun around, hitting the ground. Almost simultaneously another man fell near Tom. Bill groaned aloud. He figured Sid's chances of surviving this were slim. And Matt's and Tom's, too.

"Swagerty!" came the booming voice of Deputy Kline as he poked his head in at the door.

"He's not here," Bill answered.

Kline stepped inside and ducked behind the doorframe. "Who's running the store?"

Miss Lena's head poked up. "I am."

"I'm taking some barrels of gunpowder from the back storeroom. Tell Swagerty the county will pay for them later."

"What's happening?" asked Lena with wide, scared eyes.

"Those damned Wallaces have taken the jail and started shooting people. If they don't surrender I aim to blow them sky-high."

Lena's face went white. *"Oh, you can't do that!"*

"The hell I can't," swore Kline, shoving more shells into the cylinder of his pistol. "Sheriff Crampton left me in charge, and I'll do whatever it takes to stop Sid Wallace from escaping—even if it means blowing up the building."

Suddenly Kline's eyes narrowed with suspicion. "Tanner, you were just at the jail visiting, weren't you?"

"I was," Bill admitted. "I'm a friend of the Wallaces, but I had nothing to do with this. If you'd let me, I'd like to try and talk Sid out of this."

"You can try while I get the powder ready, but I doubt it'll do any good."

Bill stepped into the street and quickly approached the building. Gunfire was sporadic now and all coming from the street. "Hey Sid," he called.

"I hear you," Sid answered with a shout.

Kline and a group of men hurried down the sidewalk, ducked below the awning, and entered the door. They each carried a keg of gunpowder.

"This is no good," yelled Bill. "You're only going to get yourself and the boys killed. Throw the guns out and come on down."

"I can't do it, Bill. You know they'll shoot me."

"If you don't, Kline is going to blow the building with gunpowder. He's rigging it now." He paused, wiped his face with one hand, and drew a deep breath. "Sid, you can't let the boys get killed. Think of your ma."

Silence greeted his remark. Then, after a few minutes, Sid called through the busted window.

"Kline, if I throw out the guns, you gotta promise you won't hurt the boys."

"Throw them out, Sid," yelled Kline. "I ain't promising you anything except to blow you all to kingdom-come if you don't. I got a trail of powder leading to five kegs on

257

the bottom floor, and I got a match ready to strike. Your call."

After a short pause there was a clatter of broken glass as shotguns hurled through the window and hit the ground. With a loud boom, one discharged on impact, sending shot toward the onlookers. Bill flinched. The crowd scattered, but no one was wounded.

Kline ran outside. "That all the guns?" Kline asked a guard standing close by.

"Yep, that's all of 'em."

Kline wasted no time reentering the building and loping up the stairs. Bill stayed outside looking up at the broken window.

"Paine's still alive," he heard someone say, "but he's hit mortal. Don't know if David Winters is gonna live or not. He's hit in the arm and back."

Bill stood like a stone and felt just as heavy-hearted. He figured Ruth Wallace had had just about all the misery one woman should bear, and yet there was more to come. He wished he could spare her this.

It wasn't long before someone tapped his shoulder.

"Kline wants you inside."

Bill headed into the building, stepping past the kegs and the trail of gunpowder snaking across the floor. "You ought to do something with those," he said to one of the guards. "Be bad if someone lights a smoke."

"Hell, yes," barked Kline coming down the stairs, "get those kegs out of here and back over to Swagerty's." Then he motioned Bill into a chair. "I questioned the guards. They say you didn't have anything to do with this. It seems when Lawrence went downstairs for water, Tom and Matt grabbed John, got his gun, and forced him to open the cell, but I figure this might not be the last escape attempt. I'm putting the word out right now to all of Sid's friends—starting with you—that I'll shotgun any man-jack of you that comes close to this building before Sid swings. Is that understood?"

Bill nodded. He understood perfectly.

Chapter 11

Abigail lit the lamp and drew it near the edge of the table in order to better see her sewing. *That boy is outgrowing everything*, she thought. *There's not much hem left in these pants to let out.*

It was only a whisper of sound a little louder than the sleet drumming on the roof shakes, and yet with heart pounding, she froze. Something or someone was on the porch. In spite of Becky's assurance that she was safe here, she often felt as if prying eyes watched. Just that morning while doing laundry in the yard, she had turned quickly to see a man disappearing into the woods. It could have been anyone, a lone hunter or a neighbor taking a shortcut; nonetheless, her breath caught and a chill traced her spine. He was just the right height and build for Harvey, and this was not the first glimpse of him. There had been two other times. Although she had never gotten a good look, each time her heart had filled her throat. And for days afterward she had made Jacob stick close to home.

Now she stabbed the needle into the garment, rose up, grabbed the shotgun from hooks above the fireplace, and pointed it at the door. A knock echoed.

"Abigail, it's me, Bill."

She exhaled, and with knees still weak, she put back the gun and opened the door. Black night surrounded the shadow that was Bill, barely visible in the dim glow

260

of lamplight. Sleet streamed from the wide hat brim and slicker before he stepped inside and removed both.

"Hope I didn't startle you. I planned to be here a lot earlier, but the roads are slick. I had the devil's own time getting here." He hung the hat and slicker on pegs near the door and then took off the gloves and stuffed them into the slicker pocket.

"Why in the world did you come in this weather? Is something wrong—are Toby and David all right?"

"They're fine." He stepped near the fireplace to warm his hands. He blew on them, rubbed them briskly together, and held them toward the blaze again. "The bad weather didn't start until I was halfway here. You know Arkansas weather," he said while quirking an eyebrow.

The day before had been warm, almost balmy. Even the morning had been pleasant before heavy clouds rolled in. She had put out an early washing that now hung draped around the room on chair-backs and an improvised clothesline tied to pegs in the wall. She had snatched the clothes and hurried inside right before the sky opened first to pour icy rain that changed to sleet in late afternoon.

"Glad to see you have plenty of firewood. I was afraid you might be running low."

"Elijah and Ned keep me well supplied." She gave a warm smile. "Oh, Bill, I love your family. They're the kindest, nicest people I ever met."

A pleased smile lit his gray eyes. "I knew you'd get along with them just fine." Then his eyes wandered the room and his smile faded. "What's all this?" he asked. "You're not taking in laundry again, are you?"

The clothes were men's work clothes.

"Yes, I am and doing mending for two gentlemen, Mr. Lawrence Tate and Mr. Galantine Walker." She felt miffed seeing his displeasure. "You didn't expect me to just sit here doing nothing, did you?"

"Walker is all right, but Lawrence is a bad apple-- believe me, you don't want him hanging around." Bill, looking sullen, turned back toward the fire.

Abigail drew a deep breath. She had longed to see him, and now he was finally here. She didn't want to argue. "Bill, I need to make a living."

He didn't look around. "Yeah, I know—so you can leave."

She began hesitantly. "I've been giving that lots of thought." She reached to idly smooth the piece of mending lying on the table. "I'm in no hurry to leave."

He turned to search her face. "Do you mean that?"

When she nodded, he still looked uncertain.

She said, "I don't want to leave, not ever."

She expected him to rush forward to gather her close; instead, he stood still, looking serious rather than joyful. She wanted to tell him that the more she learned from Cindy, the more she knew she'd been wrong. She could trust him, even with Jacob's future. But his reticence suddenly made her ill at ease.

"What made you change your mind?"

"I suppose Cindy had as much to do with it as anything. We've had lots of long talks. She certainly thinks highly of you."

He didn't move, and his expression remained solemn, making her heart sink.

She drew a shaky breath. "I thought you'd be pleased…."

"I am—if you really mean it. I reckon I've grown leery of getting my hopes up."

"I suppose I have been extremely double-minded," she admitted, "but I mean it, Bill. I want to stay…that is if you still want me."

Suddenly his long strides rapidly closed the distance, and his kiss was firm and long. When she finally pulled away her cheeks were warm. "Gracious, there for a minute you had me worried. I was afraid you didn't want me anymore."

He reached to touch her cheek. "That'll never happen." He kissed her again, this time slow and searching, and she returned the kiss with all the love and desire in her own heart.

This time when they drew apart, she traced his cheek with a loving caress. In the light of the fireplace he looked younger than he had in ages, the tension lines eased from his face, replaced by happy smile lines.

"Abigail Anderson, you look mighty pretty in firelight. By the way, I don't like the sound of that Anderson part—reckon we could change it right away?"

"I reckon we could," she answered with a big smile.

"Good," he said. "I'll get Simon to do the ceremony—"

"Bill," she interrupted, "don't you think we ought to wait until spring? You already said you didn't think it would be best for us to leave the mountain until then, until you had a chance to make certain Harvey was gone for good. And you have to stay in the valley and work…"

He frowned, but after a bit he slowly nodded. "I don't like it one bit, but that's probably best. Don't reckon a few more months of waiting will kill me," he said with a dry smile, "but it might."

She snuggled close, loving the feel and smell of him, a mixture of cold outdoors and a faint hint of his horse and the rough woolen shirt holding the manly scent that was exclusively him. "Just so you'll know," she whispered, "I hate waiting too." She kissed him then with all the yearning in her heart. When they finally parted her heart raced so fast she knew he must have felt it through his shirt. She turned upon hearing a noise coming from Mr. Anderson's room. "I better go see what he wants," she said. "Build up the fire in the stove while I go check on him, and then I'll fix you something to eat. By the way, thank you so much for the cookstove you sent."

She returned shortly. "I think he wanted to know who was here." Her eyes twinkled mischievously. "Or maybe he wanted us to know he was awake."

Bill chuckled. "The old devil. How is he?"

"Much better. He still can't talk, but he can walk a little now with a cane. And, believe it or not, he's gotten nicer."

Bill's eyebrows quirked.

"No, it's true. He isn't as surly as he used to be, or as demanding. He loves spending time with Jacob. And he seems to really like Becky's company. She spoils him by bringing special treats—he loves her dried apple fritters—and she sits and talks to him. I suppose he is lonely…" She sighed. "I don't think I've been a very good daughter-in-law. It seems all I have time for is work."

He drew her into his arms again and kissed the top of her head. "You've been a darn fine daughter-in-law. Most women would have left him alongside the road years ago. And about all that work you're doing—I don't want you taking in washing or mending any more. I can provide for all of us just fine."

"How is your work going?" she asked, motioning him to sit and then pouring a cup of coffee warming on the stove. "I never did master cooking on the fireplace. I don't know how your granny did it. Cindy says she was a great cook."

He took a sip of steaming coffee. "She really was. I don't know how she did it either. I'm not much of a cook, even with a stove."

"And your job?" she asked again.

"Going fine. Of course this weather will make things harder, but we've made several good hauls lately with no trouble." He paused. "I do have some bad news, though."

She dropped into the seat across the table with dread seeping into her. "What?"

"They're going to hang Sid Wallace, and Tom and Matt are both in jail."

"Oh, no!" she whispered. "That's terrible. What did the boys do?"

"Nothing, at first. The sheriff locked them up to keep down trouble after Sid's hanging verdict. But Matt and Tom tried to help him escape, and then it really got ugly." He went on to tell about the trial, the escape attempt, and the shooting of Thomas Paine. "They sent Sid to the penitentiary at Little Rock until time for the hanging. I reckon they were afraid he'd try to escape again."

Abigail sorrowfully shook her head. "That's tragic. What was Sid thinking to be so foolish?"

Bill shrugged. "When a fellow is facing hanging, I don't suppose he thinks too straight. Folks in town had gotten up a petition to free him. There were already hundreds of signatures, but it won't help now. Lots that were for him because of that joke of a trial have turned against him now. Barring a miracle, he'll swing for sure. If he hadn't killed Paine, he might have gotten a fair hearing at the appeal, but not now."

She wondered if Sid really had killed the judge. She had seen a merciless look deep in his cold blue eyes, the same look as Harvey's. With enough provocation, she felt certain he was capable of murder, and the judge had turned loose his brother's killer. That might be enough provocation.

"Poor Tom and Matt." She sadly shook her head. "And their poor mother! I feel plumb sinful being so happy myself. I can hardly imagine what she must be going through."

After they had talked awhile Abigail suddenly jumped up. "You're probably starving! I'll warm the stew we had for supper. It's venison." She gave a huge smile. "From Jacob's first deer. Elijah took him and Ben hunting, and he let Jacob take the shot. I've never seen a boy so happy in my life. He and Ben are inseparable now." She paused. "I've let the apron strings loose and given him much more freedom, and I can tell it's been good for him."

Bill put in, "Seems like being here has been good for you, too. Your eyes are shining, and I never saw you looking so happy."

She gave a little laugh while putting stew in the pan and setting it onto a stove eye. "Bill Tanner, did it ever occur to you that might just be because of you? It isn't every day a woman finds out she's getting married to the man she loves."

He gave a slow smile. "Whatever it is, it's good to see you happy. I hope you're never sorrowful again."

"Well, that's not realistic, but for now I am happier than I've ever been."

"I do believe I am, too," he said. "And I like it. Let's keep it that way."

She turned to give a wide, generous smile. "Let's," she agreed, "for as long as possible." The warm glow in her heart was a joyous thing, but even as she spoke, deep inside she felt another shiver of dread. Nothing this perfect could last for long. She wondered if she should mention seeing that man. More than likely she was just being notional. Besides, she didn't want to spoil the happy evening.

Bill ate two large bowlfuls of stew and a generous serving of cornbread. "Tell Jacob that's just about the best venison I ever tasted."

"Can't you tell him yourself—in the morning?" she asked. "I figured you'd sleep up in the loft with him."

"Naw, I better get on over to Uncle Ned's. They're expecting me." He placed the spoon back into the bowl and wiped his mouth on the napkin. "Folks talk here the same as everywhere, Abigail. I don't want to bring any shame on you."

"All right," she said, "You'll come back in the morning?"

"For a few minutes, but I can't stay long. Quinton wants to make another haul by the end of the week. It probably wasn't the smartest thing—me coming on such a quick trip. But I couldn't stand not seeing you."

"I'm certainly glad you came. I do wish you could stay, at least another day, but I understand." Although her smile was brave, some of the pleasure had gone from the evening.

⚜

It was Christmas again. Abigail had no idea where the last year had flown, and yet it had gone in a flash. Here she was once again in a different house and surrounded by new people; however, she could no longer call them strangers for they had quickly taken her in as one of them, and she was as happy as she had ever been. Jacob, too, was radiant. He loved living here, and he and Benjamin Loring were already inseparable friends.

Abigail had racked her brain trying to think of Christmas gifts to take along when they went to the Loring cabin for Christmas dinner. Finally she had decided to make a deep dish rabbit pie in Granny's big iron spider kettle. Aunt Margaret had been famous for quail pie made of breaded quail breast that were fried crispy and then placed in a baking pot and covered with just enough water, salt, and pepper to make a thick gravy and topped with biscuit dough and baked until the birds were tender and the biscuit crust golden brown. Abigail's mouth watered just thinking about it. She had no quail, but Jacob kept her supplied with rabbits from the snares he and Benjamin set each day. She doubted rabbit would be as tasty as quail breast, but it was worth a try.

The steaming pie now sitting on the table did look delicious. She had made a smaller one to taste—just in case it was a flop she would leave the big pie at home and go empty handed as Becky had urged her to do in the first place.

With a quick prayer, she dipped a small helping onto a plate and took a tentative nibble. A slow smile spread her face. It wasn't quite as good as Aunt Margaret's bird pie, but it was nonetheless delicious. She was relieved to have a suitable offering for the dinner.

When Ned came to get them in the wagon, Mr. Anderson surprised everyone by walking outside with only a cane for assistance. While Jacob clamored into the back of the wagon to ride with Benjamin, Abigail set the rabbit pie under the wagon seat. She was taking no chances with two rowdy boys in the back.

Cold air stung the insides of her nose and pinched her cheeks, and yet she felt wonderful to be outdoors in bright sunshine, heading to a festive gathering. She found a ready laugh for every silly thing the boys said along the way.

A lone horseman passed. Enveloped in a heavy coat and hat wrapped with a muffler, his size was barely discernable and much of his face was obscured. He nodded to Ned and then his eyes met Abigail's.

Suddenly she sat up stiff. Blood drained from her face and the smile fled, replaced by wide eyes.

Ned glanced over. "That him?" he asked, speaking low.

"Yes, I think so." she whispered. "All I could see was eyes, but I think so."

Ned pulled a shotgun closer to his leg and then urged the horses along. "Don't worry. We'll soon be at the cabin, and then Elijah and I will check him out."

✕✕✕

It was late afternoon before Ned and Elijah returned. They held cold hands toward a blazing fire in the big fireplace and then gratefully took the coffee Becky offered. With voice low to keep conversation from children's ears, Ned said, "We tracked the fellow off the mountain. Albert Walker said he saw him when he passed by his place. He said it was the fur and hide buyer from over Dover way."

Abigail was relieved, and yet she felt terrible. "Oh, I'm so sorry I've ruined your Christmas—and all for nothing!" Throughout the day, she had tried bringing the man's features to mind. The hard eyes had been the same color as Harvey's and had seemed cold and evil. And yet she couldn't be sure. In retrospect she realized, upon seeing her, the eyes had held no flicker of recognition.

"Christmas isn't ruined," insisted Becky. "Everyone is here safe and sound and dinner is ready on the stove."

"If anything it'll taste better for the wait," said Ned with a smile. "We're hungry as bears, and that food smells mighty fine."

But the day was ruined for Abigail. She felt totally guilt-ridden for being paranoid enough to send two men away from hearth and home on Christmas Day. She determined to keep her eyes open and her mouth shut.

If Harvey came around, she would make certain before sounding an alarm.

Abigail stopped humming and hurried to peek through the curtain to see why Little Bear was barking. She tensed when she saw David Hadley. It was the middle of the week, and he should be working with Bill instead of coming to the mountain. His horse looked lathered and muddy as if it had been ridden hard. Heart pounding, she drew back from the window. She held the door open even before he climbed from the saddle.

"What's wrong, David?" Her hand went to her throat when he climbed the porch steps without answering.

He stepped onto the porch. "It's Bill, Miz Abigail. He's been hurt."

"How badly?" she asked, going pale. Knees buckling, she gripped the doorframe, ignoring the icy blast of air chilling the cabin. "What happened?"

David drew a deep breath and stepped inside. "Bad enough." He drew off his hat and fidgeted with the brim. "He got swept off into the creek when the wagon turned over. He hit his head and it knocked him out. Before we could fish him out, he almost drowned in that fast water. It was terrible cold—had chunks of ice floating in it. He has a big lump on his head, and he got a lot of water in his lungs. We packed him back to the house as fast as we could. Now he's got a high fever and is awake, but he's out of his head. The doctor was still with him when I left. Toby and Quinton thought I should come right on and get you."

Feeling frantic, Abigail looked toward the bedroom. *What should she do about Mr. Anderson and Jacob? She couldn't just leave them! And yet she must go to Bill! He might be dying!* She sucked in a terrified breath. It had taken David hours to get here, even if he ran the horse. Bill might already be dead. With gritty determination, she pushed that idea aside to concentrate on what to do. Nonetheless, no ready answer presented itself.

"Ma'am," said David, "I took the liberty of stopping by and asking Miz Becky if she could help out. She and Deborah said to tell you they would be here in a few minutes and for you to get packed up and ready to go. Miz Becky is going to stay with Talbert and the boy."

"Thank God!" exclaimed Abigail, hurrying toward the bedroom. She paused when David spoke again.

"Ned is loaning a saddle horse or a wagon." He met her scared eyes. "Saddle horse is faster, but it'll be hard on you if you're not used to riding. Just tell me which."

"I'll ride," she said. She entered the bedroom, grabbed her satchel, and began stuffing warm clothes inside. She had barely finished when a wagon entered the yard, and shortly Becky entered the cabin with a heavy coat and hat on her arm.

"Abigail, here's a good wool coat and hat that Granny made for Ned. They will be big on you but will turn this bitter wind, and here's pair of my heavy gloves that will fit you. Don't you worry about a thing around here. Deborah and I will take good care of Mr. Anderson and Jacob. You just concentrate on getting Billy well. Oh, and Deborah is packing some food for the trail."

Abigail bit her bottom lip to stop the trembling. "Thank you so much," she whispered as tears pooled her eyes. She struggled into the hat and coat and quickly followed David out the door. Ned sat on the wagon seat and his eyes were full of worry.

"She's going to ride," said David, stashing her satchel in the wagon before climbing into the saddle.

"All right," said Ned. "We'll take the wagon to the house and get the horse. I told Benjamin to saddle it just in case.

Abigail sat stiffly on the seat, willing the team to fly. Although Ned hurried them along the trail, they seemed to creep. Finally Ned's cabin came into view, across the brim-full creek and nestled among tall pines swaying in the cold wind. Already Abigail was thankful for the heavy coat. Although she was clumsy from the poor fit, it did—as Becky had said—turn the bitter February wind. Ned slowed to cross the creek; even so, water splashed high onto the wheels and wagon bed. Recent rain had the creek running high but not yet flooding.

"When this stream floods, there's no getting across until the water goes down," said Ned. "Hope it won't rain any more."

Since there were other creeks to ford on the trip, Abigail imagined that at best she was in for wet feet. But nothing mattered now except getting to Bill. She was out of the wagon before Ned had completely stopped.

David was already leading a long-legged mare through the barnyard gate with Benjamin walking along beside. Ned climbed down, got the satchel from the wagon, and after he helped Abigail mount, tied it to the back of the saddle. When Deborah hurried from the house with a parcel, she handed it to David.

"Here's a little food for the trip. I hope Billy is better when you get back. Please tell him we're all praying."

David took the food, staring at Deborah with his heart in his eyes. "I'll tell him." He looked as if he wanted to say more but he didn't.

She added, "Take care of yourself too."

His face beamed. "I sure will." Then he mounted and looked around at Abigail, who was trying to stuff the extra bulk of coat over her knees. "All set?" he asked. "I'll keep a fast pace, but if you need to slow down, just sing out."

Abigail nodded. But she had no intention of asking him to slow down, no matter how miserable she became. The trip was pure misery. Under cloudy skies without a hint of sunshine, they followed the trail for miles through the woods, up hill and down, across icy streams wide and small, and all the while a sharp wind blew either at their backs or in their faces. Ice crystals formed on her muffler, her wet boots, and even on her eyebrows. She became so cold she could hardly feel her feet until she tried dismounting, and then pain shot through both frozen lumps, making her barely able to stand. David didn't stop often. Occasionally, he insisted they get off for a bit and walk to warm themselves and to rest the horses; otherwise, he kept a fast pace, and Abigail somehow managed to follow, although at times tears streamed from her eyes over her misery and especially the burning pain in her side, the result of not having ridden in years. Night fell and still they rode. Everything became surreal, a dark, painful blur. Abigail almost lost the urgency of reaching Bill. All she could think of was her own wretchedness, and yet something deep inside drove her on and kept her from calling out to stop. Finally, when she had given up hope of being able to stick in the saddle for one minute longer, David turned to call back, "The house is just ahead."

With his help she fell from the saddle and climbed the porch. A bit of lantern light spilled onto the porch when he opened the front door and removed his muffler long enough to say, "I'll take the horses to the barn and be right back."

She stumbled inside and staggered into the front bedroom where the lantern light glowed. Toby jumped up from a chair drawn near the bed. Bill's eyes stayed closed in a face as flushed as a winter sunset.

"Miz Abigail! You look like a lump of ice! Here, sit down and let me get them wet boots off yer poor feet!"

Instead she limped to the bed and removed the glove to feel Bill's forehead. It burned under her cold hand. Her voice was a raspy croak. "Where's the doctor?"

"He had to go check on another patient, but he'll be back quick as he can."

"What did he say about Bill?"

"He says hit's too soon to know." Toby swallowed before going on, "I won't lie, ma'am; he says Bill's took bad." He tried to sound hopeful but his voice faltered, "He's a strong man with a mighty big will to live—that counts for a lot."

He led her to the chair. "We got to get you warmed up before you catch your death…" His words abruptly stopped. "Before you get sick," he quickly altered the statement.

✖✖✖

For days Bill hovered between life and death. Abigail barely left his side. During his fevered thrashing he often muttered and sometimes even yelled. It was then she got a glimmering of the hell he had endured in the war. And she got a more intimate glimpse into his private hell. Cindy's name was too often on his tongue.

Abigail touched his fevered brow with pity. "My poor darling," she whispered, "so that is why you never wanted to go home."

After knowing Cindy, she understood how Bill could love her. Of course that was over and done; at least she knew there was nothing improper between them now. She had no doubt of that, and yet the knife in her own heart hurt no less. She wished he had told her. She would have understood. She had loved before. Perhaps he would tell her in due time, but for now, his past silence made her insecure.

Finally the fever subsided. Abigail was so very thankful when the doctor said the worst was over. She returned to her room that night for the first time to sleep the night through. Before climbing into bed, she caught sight of her wan reflection in the mirror. She compared her scarred face to Cindy's perfect, gentle beauty.

Abigail knew Bill loved her. But how much? Was he always comparing her with Cindy? If so she felt he would be forever disappointed. She blew out the lamp and climbed into bed. In spite of exhaustion, she had a good cry before falling asleep.

Abigail heard voices. She peeped through the front room curtains to see a man stepping onto the porch where Bill, still too weak to work, spent long hours sitting in Mr. Anderson's rocking chair placed in the cold sunshine. She didn't recognize the fellow. She returned to the kitchen where she was making bread, and just in case Bill brought the man inside for coffee, she put the coffee pot onto the stove and then added water to the teakettle as well. A cup of tea sounded good. Suddenly the stranger's voice rose to an angry pitch. Abigail cocked her head a minute and then headed into the front room and leaned close to the window to listen.

"He'll for damn sure hang if we don't do something. This is our last chance. We couldn't get near him while they kept him at the penitentiary. Will you help us or not?"

Abigail grimaced. She wanted to hear more, but just then the teakettle began to whistle loudly. Tiptoeing away from the window she hurried to set the kettle off the stove. By the time she returned the man was leaving.

Before long Bill came inside. Abigail looked up from kneading bread dough. With the back of a flour-covered hand, she used her wrist to push back a wisp of hair that had fallen over her forehead. "You had company?"

Bill stepped to the stove and poured a cup of coffee from the large pot and took a sip before answering. "Yes."

Abigail waited for him to go on; however, he took his time. Finally after letting out a deep breath all he said was, "That was Sid's cousin. He said the state supreme court has refused a new trial. They've brought Sid back from Little Rock."

"He rode out here just to tell you that?"

He avoided the question. "Ruth Wallace has gone to see the governor to ask him for a stay of execution. Tom and Matt are both locked up in the Crawford County jail. I'm going to town tomorrow to see Sid one more time."

Her eyes widened. "You're in no shape to go. You're barely out of your sick bed."

"Well, I'm going," he said.

She had hoped he would confide his plans to her so she could talk him out of helping Sid escape, but that wasn't happening. She punched the dough down, laid a dishtowel over it, wiped hands on her apron, and sat down. "Are you one hundred percent positive Sid is innocent?"

Bill chewed his jaw, giving it serious thought. "Ninety-eight percent. There's always that remote possibility, I reckon."

"He just might be guilty, and if he is he ought to hang."

"Sometimes it's awful hard to judge between right and wrong," he said slowly.

Her eyebrows rose. "Usually the right and wrong of a thing are pretty obvious."

He made a scoffing sound. "I've not found life that

simple. There are things spelled out black and white in the Good Book, and those a fellow can't argue with; but there's plenty more that's not. A man has to do what he thinks is right, knowing he'll someday face his maker."

Abigail knew there was little use trying to talk him out of it, and yet she must try. "Please don't do anything foolish," she pleaded. "I hate to see Sid hang—but as you just said, we can't be certain, and somewhere we have to draw the line between choosing law or vigilante chaos."

Bill shrugged. "That would be a good argument if things weren't being run by a bunch of crooks who are making their own brand of chaos."

Abigail drew a deep breath. She hated the turmoil roiling inside. She had thought all of this behind her, all of this distrust of Bill. Instead, like a re-injured wound, it opened again raw and bleeding. What was this attitude in Bill that made him think he could mete out his own brand of justice? Perhaps Sid was innocent of killing Meers and Ward. She didn't know. Nonetheless, he had most certainly killed the man who testified against him. That didn't seem to faze Bill.

He looked at her now with something akin to pity in his eyes. "You don't understand, do you? The law that we knew and respected is as dead as the Confederacy."

The day was cold but clear, the sky vividly blue, a good day for doing laundry decided Abigail. Bill had left with hardly a word. She knew he felt the rift between them, and yet he had made no move to make things right. That hurt her, puzzled her, and made her angry all at the same time. Now she viewed Bill through different eyes. Each silence seemed fraught with some hidden, unspoken reality. She almost wished she'd never found out about Cindy. Try as she might she couldn't get it out of her mind. She often wondered just exactly what had happened between them, and she couldn't help wondering if Bill loved her now as much as he had loved Cindy then.

She needed time to sit down and sort it all out, but for now she simply did not want to face the issue. It was too painful. So, hoping he would not do anything foolish enough to land in jail again or worse still get himself shot, she had given a deep sigh and watched him leave. As soon as his horse was out of sight, she began filling the water reservoir on the stove, and then she set up the tubs outside. While the water heated, she separated the colors from the whites, mixed bluing for the whites and starch for the items that needed it. All the while her thoughts were on Bill and what might be happening in town.

Abigail's hands stilled on the wooden paddle stirring slivers of lye soap into the steaming water in the wash pot. Her eyes went over the empty fields and woods, the trees on the far ridge naked of leaves now and stark against the horizon. Would she still be here this time next year? Two days ago it was a question that would not have entered her mind. With a deep sigh she began stirring again.

"What's the matter Abigail?"

Even before she turned, she knew the voice. Her hand tightened on the oak paddle.

"That sigh sounded mournful." Harvey gave a sadistic chuckle. "Tanner not making you happy?"

"What do you want?" she asked, already measuring the distance to the house and the shotgun propped behind the front door.

He was not holding a gun, but his jacket hung open and she could see the pistol shoved into his belt as well as a knife scabbard with a long handle protruding.

"You already know what I want—at least part of it. You'll know more soon enough," he said and his eyes glittered with hate. "I need money bad to get away from here. I'm sick of hiding in holes like a varmint."

She hoped to distract him long enough to get a running start. Pretending indifference she began stirring the pot again. "I thought you owned plenty of land. Why would you have to hide in a hole?"

He ignored the question. "I'm all out of patience, so I'm only going to ask this once—where's the money? And before you say you don't know, let me show you something."

He reached into his pocket and pulled out something. All the blood drained from her face. It was a wooden whistle. Cindy's pa, Simon Mason, had carved some for his grandsons, and he had made Jacob one as well. Abigail had no doubt this one belonged to Jacob.

"Knew you'd recognize it," he said with a wicked smile. "I'm through messing around. I took the boy so you'll know I mean business. When you give me the money I'll tell you where he is."

"Have you hurt—"

"Get me the money."

"Have you hurt Jacob?" she asked again.

Her heart almost beat out of her chest as he considered the question a long moment. Finally he said, "No. But I can if I take a notion." He paused a second and then gave an evil grin. "Better yet, since Tanner is so partial to branding, I think I'll do a little burn job on you like I did back in the war. I've put more than one woman's feet in the fire to find out where she hid her valuables."

Abigail hardly heard the threat. Did he have Jacob tied up somewhere—perhaps scared, cold, and hungry?

She tried to keep her voice calm. "I won't get the money unless I know Jacob is safe," she said.

He pulled the knife from the scabbard and grabbed her arm. "Look, bitch, I'm through fooling around."

She swung the oak paddle with all her might. It struck him in the temple. He staggered backwards, but not before she felt the sting of the knife that had pierced her hand. Hesitating only a split second, she darted toward the back door. It was closer than the front. However, she had only taken a few running steps when he quickly closed the gap. She toppled the washstand between them, leapt across a clothesbasket, and began running faster than she had ever run in her life, expecting at any moment to feel a bullet. At first she simply ran, giving no thought to where. As she sped past the barn she risked a glance back. She had managed to put a whisper of distance between them, but he was coming fast. He would catch her before she could make it across the fence. She rounded the building and darted into the barn's back door. It opened into a wide aisle with stalls opening off both sides. She had planned to run right through and out the front again. Harvey had anticipated this. He was already pulling open the front door.

Her breath came in ragged gasps while she frantically searched for a weapon and a hiding place. She grabbed Bill's cant hook from the wall. The long, curved hook wasn't much of a weapon, but there was nothing else in sight. She darted into the tack room and hunkered down behind a barrel. With supreme effort, she tried slowing her breathing so Harvey wouldn't hear.

"I know you're in here," he said.

He walked cautiously down the aisle, looking left and right and then out the back door. She felt a flicker of hope. He wasn't sure that she was in the barn after all.

If she could stay hidden, he might leave. She held her breath, not even daring to wipe the blood dripping down her hand as she kept her eye glued to the crack between the boards.

Harvey pulled a tarp from the wagon and looked into the empty bed. Then he kicked at a pile of hay, scattering it, before entering the next stall. He paused, indecisive, and then went to the back door again to look out. He stared hard at the chicken house and the shed sitting just beyond the barn.

"Your boy's tied up and hidden nearby. If you don't come out, I'll cut him," he threatened. "Think he'll look good with a scar to match his mama's?"

Abigail's heart skipped a beat, and yet she kept still as a stone. He might be lying about having Jacob. Something about the way he spoke didn't ring true. Harvey changed tactics.

"If you come on out I'll let you live. I could have shot you already, if I wanted you dead, but I want that money. If you don't come out, when I find you I'll burn you first and then I'll slit your throat, and that's a promise. That's not quite as good as getting Tanner's money, but it'll do. Like I said, Tanner is gonna pay for what he did to me, one way or another. *How is up to you*, Abigail. Either way, if you don't come out right now, I'm going to kill your boy."

While she crouched, trying not to breathe or shake, he entered each stall, shoving aside anything that might be a hiding place. Her heart pounded even harder when she heard his boots in the next stall.

"I'm gonna burn that bitch and her brat and enjoy doing it," he muttered, and then finally his heavy footfalls entered the tack room where she huddled. He made a quick look around the room and then grabbed the barrel.

She leaped up. She swung the hook, aiming for his eyes. He gave a piercing scream of pain and rage. It might not have been sufficient to stop him, but the impact had jarred her arm enough that she knew it had done some damage. She did not wait to see how much. With a bound, she rushed past where he bent, holding his face, and flew out of the barn on toward the house and the shotgun.

Her worst nightmare came true as she heard his heavy boots. She glanced back. Harvey was right behind her with the knife raised. He panted, out of breath, and his good eye was white hot with rage. Froth foamed on his lips. The hook had gouged deep beside his marled eye. Blood flowed from the wound, making him look like a crazed madman. She would not make it to the porch. He was too close. With a final burst of speed she made it to the chopping block barely in time to grab the ax. She whirled, wielding the ax. It caught him in the thigh, right above the knee. The knife fell as he staggered and grabbed the chopping block to keep from falling. For an instant he stared at the blood pouring from the gaping wound, and then he cursed and drew the pistol.

She brought the ax down again. It knocked the gun to the ground and sent blood spurting from his hand. She raised the ax and swung again. It struck only a glancing blow to his left shoulder, but as he raised his arm to ward off the blow, he lost balance and fell. Her heart was exploding and her breath came in loud, ragged jerks. Without pause, she lifted the blade and swung again, this time hacking into the arm he raised as protection.

"Stop, you crazy bitch," he screamed, "before you kill me! Then you'll never find the boy."

She raised the ax. "Tell me where he is, right now."

"All right!" he screeched. "Like I said I never hurt him. I didn't want to wrestle him all the way down the mountain. He's tied up in a deserted cabin close to Ned

Loring's. Bind up these wounds and I'll take you to him."

She paused only a moment. *Jacob would never be safe as long as this fiend lived!* With superhuman strength she raised the weapon higher.

Harvey's eye widened in horror. "No!"

The blow jarred Abigail's entire body. The ax sank deep, severing the top of his skull.

She sagged, hardly able to comprehend what she had done. She stared at the gore, turned away, and vomited. Then her eyes fell on the whistle. Harvey was dead, and he could never hurt Jacob now…but what if they couldn't find the place he had tied him? Or what if he had already hurt Jacob? As doubt assailed, she averted her eyes from looking at Harvey's body. She had committed murder. She supposed they would hang her as they were hanging Sid Wallace this morning, but she would worry about that later. For now she must find Jacob! She tore a piece from the bottom of her ragged skirt and wrapped it around her bleeding hand and rushed to the pasture to catch a mule.

Chapter 12

Tight jawed, Bill looked at the wooden scaffold in front of the new courthouse. People stood in groups watching the workmen make final touches. He supposed Sid's hanging was only a circus to most onlookers. Town was certainly bulging, a record crowd. There was barely room to navigate between the horses, wagons, and buggies clogging Main Street.

A chill March wind tugged at his hat brim and scuttled low, gray clouds holding a promise of rain. He pulled the black to a stop and dismounted a short way from the jail. Armed guards surrounding the building eyed Bill warily as he approached. One held out a rifle barring his way.

"No one allowed past here except by special order of the deputy."

"Tell him Bill Tanner wants to see the prisoner."

The guard called over his shoulder, "Hey, Bob, tell Kline that a fellow named Tanner wants to see Sid."

Bob returned shortly. "Kline says Wallace's kin and some other folks are already with him now."

Bill wasn't surprised. He had doubted he would get to see Sid, and even if he had, he wasn't sure what he would say. What did a man say at such a time?

"Is Sid's mother with him—did she make it back from Little Rock?" he asked.

The guard nodded. "Yep, she's been with him all morning—her and Will and some of his other kin.

284

Preacher just went up a bit ago, and there's a reporter from Little Rock up there too."

"Thanks," said Bill, starting to turn away. He turned back. "Lots of folks in town. Have things been peaceful?"

"So far," said the guard. "The sheriff is sick, so Kline is in charge. He got wind of an escape plot and arrested a few suspicious fellows, but since then everything has been quiet. But I'll be all-fired glad when this whole thing is over. The hair is standing up on the back of my neck."

Bill thanked him again and started to walk away. He supposed Sid's cousin would always feel hard at him for not helping with the escape plan, but he had known it was futile. Just then the guard called him back.

"The deputy says you can go up. Sid wants to see you. You'll have to hand over your pistol, and I'll have to search you first."

Bill nodded, looked up at the upper story window, drew a deep breath, and after the guard had patted him down, headed inside. His tread was slow and deliberate on the wooden stairs. Dread gripped like a tight fist. After passing several more armed guards, he stepped through the doorway.

William and Mrs. Wallace stood in the aisle as close to the bars as possible where Sid sat inside a cell. He wore a black broadcloth suit and a crisp white shirt. His hands were shackled and his manacled feet chained to the floor. It seemed Deputy Kline was taking no chances on another escape attempt. Miss Lena stood nearby crying softly into a handkerchief, as well as white-faced Mattie Blackard, George Wallace's brokenhearted sweetheart. Bill nodded to the minister and to a well-dressed man he didn't know—probably the reporter from Little Rock.

Sid saw him and gave a brief, tight smile. "Tanner, good of you to come."

Bill stepped near and said, "Sid." He waited for words that wouldn't pass the lump in his throat. Finally he managed. "Sure hate to see you in this fix."

Sid gave a mirthless chuckle. "Me too. But it is what it is, and there's no use crying over spilt milk, I reckon." He went on, "I was hoping you'd come. I have a favor to ask."

"Anything I can do," said Bill and he meant it. He had the awful realization that he might have prevented this hanging. *If Harvey was guilty, he might have found him and made him confess.* Although Bill had looked for days, he had found no trace. Finally he had gone back to work, cutting and hauling timber, telling himself he had to make a living. And he supposed that was true. But now seeing Sid and knowing he would be dead in a few minutes, he thought if only he had looked a little longer...

"See what you can do about getting the boys out of jail. They're only kids and they didn't hurt anyone."

"I'll do everything in my power to see they go free," assured Bill. "I'll go see Cravens this very day," he said and then shuffled his feet in embarrassment as he realized what today held for Sid.

"Thanks. And keep an eye on 'em. They're good boys, but they can be a handful," said Sid with a sad smile, looking at his mother.

She returned the smile even though tears dripped down her cheeks. Bill pressed her arm in sympathy. "I'll look out for them, and I'll give them a job anytime they're ready," he said. He stepped back to let Mrs. Wallace and William continue their visit.

Bill wanted away from there, away from the pain, away from the sorrow; however, he stayed a bit longer to make certain Sid had no more need of him. After a bit of low conversation, Sid asked the preacher to say a prayer. Bill bowed his head, and soon after the solemn amen he slipped out the door and down the stairs, totally sick at heart. Bill pulled his hat on and stepped onto the sidewalk.

A hack, surrounded by an army of armed men, sat in the street bearing a coffin. Bill had witnessed soldiers condemned to death having to ride to their executions in such a fashion. He detested the gruesome practice.

Bill waited in the crowd until Sid was escorted down the stairs, surrounded by law officers. Sid's chains had been removed. His face showed more agitation than it had a few minutes before, and yet he retained his composure without words or tears. He climbed into the hack and sat down alongside the coffin. Then his family was escorted outside. Bill fervently hoped they would not go to the hanging, and yet he knew they would. He joined them, walking just behind William and Mrs. Wallace and Miss Mattie as they made their way down the street toward the gallows.

The crowd of men, a small number of women, and even a few children grew eerily quiet. Bill could hear boards squeak as Kline and Sid climbed the stairs leading to the gallows. The minister, reporter, and several more men followed and stood quietly on the platform. A tall wooden fence of sorts surrounded the structure but stopped short of hiding the people on the platform and the ridgepole holding a knotted, dangling noose.

William's face, drawn and taut, had gone white. After one glance upward, Mrs. Wallace moaned and covered her eyes with her handkerchief. Bill's teeth clenched so tightly his jaws began to hurt. There was a slight stir when someone fainted. Bill looked over to see two men pick up Miss Lena and carry her away.

After a brief word with Kline, the preacher stepped forward, bared his head, and addressed the crowd. "Let us pray."

Bill, along with all the men, drew off his hat and bowed. Although the prayer was heartfelt and sincere, it was long. Bill wanted the ordeal over and done. For Sid's sake and his family, Bill wished the minister would finish. Mrs. Wallace was trembling, so he wasn't sure how much longer she could stand. Finally the preacher ended the petition and said, "Amen."

Kline leaned to speak to Sid, who nodded and then stepped forward. No one seemed to breathe as Sid opened his mouth.

"Gentlemen, I suppose you came here today expecting to hear me make a long talk. I have no confessions to make to men. I make my confessions to God. I die in defense of myself and friends, and my only regret is that I have not half a dozen more lives to lose in the same way." Then Sid stepped back.

A murmur of talk arose. The man on Bill's right said, "Sounds guilty to me. He shore never claimed his innocence."

Bill's eyebrows drew together. Again and again, he had heard Sid declare his innocence of killing Ward and Meers. He wished Sid had been more forthcoming with declaring it now. Then again, he reasoned, Sid had killed Tom Paine. Perhaps that was why he did not declare his innocence more boldly. Whatever the case, the preacher had been right in his prayer when he had said, "God, and God alone, is the final judge of every man." Bill grimaced as a black hood was placed over Sid's head.

Just then Sid cried out, *"Lord, remember me, in thy Kingdom!"* Bill knew enough scripture to know those were the last words of another dying man, the thief hanging on the cross next to Christ.

Throughout Sid's speech and final declaration, Ruth Wallace had kept her eyes closed. Now she gave a low moan and sank against William. He held her up, never taking his eyes from the platform while the noose was adjusted.

Bill held his breath. The silence was palpable.

Suddenly, the drop fell.

A feeling of helpless rage coursed through Bill's veins. He had seen men die before, but it never got easy. And believing Sid was just a scapegoat made his death even harder. After a few spasmodic twitchings, a shudder passed over Sid's body. Then he went limp.

"Come on, Ma," said William, "Let's go home."

"Can I do anything to help?" Bill volunteered.

"Thanks, but no. Doc Connelly said they'd bring"— William's voice broke on the last words— "the body to the house."

Bill nodded and followed as they weaved their way through the crowd that appeared in no hurry to disperse. He couldn't wait to be gone, but he had to speak to Cravens first. He waited at the office for a while before the lawyer returned.

"I don't imagine they have any idea of keeping the boys locked up for long," assured Cravens. "I figure they'll be out in a few days, after this has had a chance to blow over. If they aren't back in a couple of weeks, I'll go see the sheriff and see what can be done."

Bill thanked him, exited the office, found the black, mounted, and left town as quickly as he could. The morning had taken a toll on his strength. By the time Hagarville drew into sight, he almost reeled in the saddle. He was anxious to get home but decided it would be best to stop at Quinton's and rest for a bit.

"Bill, you're white as a haint," said Quinton, who left off pounding a horseshoe to clear a pile of harnesses from the cluttered bench. "Sit down here quick before you fall. I reckon you felt you had to go to the hanging, but you ought not have pushed yourself so hard. You was at death's door yourself not long ago."

Bill sank onto the bench and gratefully took the mug of coffee Quinton poured.

"I reckon the deed is done?" Quinton asked.

"Yes."

"I was hoping the governor would intervene at the last minute." Quinton slowly shook his head. "Crying shame. I don't no more believe he done it than a goat. Didn't figure I could do him any good so I just stayed home. Did you get to talk to him today?"

"I did. Not sure I did him any good either, but I had to try."

Quinton nodded in sympathy. "Too bad you never found Harvey. I'd like a chance to put a hot poker to him myself to see what he'd say about Ward and Meers."

"If I catch him, I'll make him talk yet. It's too late to save Sid, but I'd like to clear his name."

"Most folks I know think he was innocent," avowed Quinton. "I heard hundreds signed that petition."

"Yes, but there's still plenty that think he's guilty." Bill let out a deep breath and then changed the subject. "By the way, I don't think I ever got a chance to thank you for saving my life. Toby said I'd have drowned if you hadn't risked your own neck to brave the current to pull me out."

Quinton pushed the words aside with a wave of his hand. "You'd have done the same for me. Have to say, I thought you were a goner by the time I dragged you to the bank."

"The last thing I remember is thinking the current was way swifter than I thought and then feeling the wagon tip when the wheel went into a hole. I reckon a log rolled off the load and knocked me out."

"Yep. We should never have tried crossing until the creek went down. But everything turned out all right. I even got a bonus for the load when I finally got it delivered. I figure Abigail gave you the money?"

"She did. Thank you."

"Oh hell," muttered Quinton, "here comes Zetta."

"Went to the hanging, did ya, Mr. Tanner?" she asked before clearing the doorway. Without waiting for a reply she asked, "Did they get his neck stretched?" Then she cackled at her own idea of humor.

"They hung him, Zetta," answered Quinton and followed the statement with a loud blow to the horseshoe on the anvil.

As soon as the ringing stopped, Zetta added, "Good. Now a decent woman might be able to walk down Main Street."

Bill glared and Quinton swore under his breath before saying, "Zetta, that is the stupidest thing you've ever said. No one on earth had ever suspected Sid Wallace of harming a woman. Far as I can tell, they hung a good man today, and some folks are going to have to answer for that on Judgment Day."

Zetta's lips curled. "I reckon yo're entitled to yore opinions, Quinton Rawlings, misguided as they may be." She heard a wagon pass and whirled to look out the door. "That looks like Hartsel Terry," she said with furrowed brow. "I wonder if he's stopping at Mildred's?"

"You better go see," said Quinton. His snide tone seemed lost as she quickly agreed and hurried from the building.

Bill let out a deep breath. "I'm almighty grateful she's not my neighbor," he said. "I'd have to strangle her and tell God she died."

Quinton chuckled in agreement. "Believe me, I've thought about it more than once."

Bill stood. "Well, I better get on home. I think I can make it, now. Thanks for the coffee." He started forward but weaved unsteadily on his feet.

Quinton frowned. "I have an idea," he said. "Why don't you sit back down for a few minutes and let me hitch up the wagon? David and Toby ought to about have another load of staves ready. I'll just ride over with you and see. You can ride in the wagon with me and tie the black on behind."

Bill gave in without argument. He could hardly believe how weak he felt as he climbed onto the wagon seat. He wondered if they would have to endure another inquisition from Zetta, but she was nowhere in sight as Quinton urged the mules forward. Sun had warmed the air just a bit but did little to warm the shiver deep inside of Bill. He supposed it was due to his weakened condition, or perhaps Sid's hanging had affected him more than he realized. He had seen plenty of death during the war and had done his share of killing. Death was never pleasant; however, witnessing the death of an enemy was a far cry from witnessing the death of a friend.

Quinton seemed to sense his mood, so they passed the time mostly in silence until he pulled into the yard. Then Quinton broke the silence. "Looks as if Abigail has put out a big washing—" His words abruptly halted. *"What the hell?"*

Bill had already sprung from the seat. He bent over the bloody remains of a body. Harvey's sightless eyes stared at the sky. Abigail's ax was buried deeply in his skull. In an instant Bill studied the signs. His blood turned to ice as he imagined what had happened. This had been no easy struggle. Harvey had been hacked in thigh and arm, and even a good distance away there was more blood on the ground. A wooden whistle lay near one puddle of blood. Jacob had such a whistle. Bill had seen it the last time he visited Abigail on the mountain. With a pounding heart, he wondered how much of the blood might be hers.

"Abigail!" he shouted as he ran toward the porch.

"Bill," yelled Quinton, "yonder she is, coming out of the barn."

Bill wheeled, heading for the barn where she exited leading one of his mules. The animal was saddled and bridled. She struggled to mount, hardly giving him a look when he arrived. Her hair was disheveled, and blood streaked her dress and had soaked through a rag tied around her hand.

Bill put a hand on the bridle. "What happened?"

"Oh Bill," she cried, "he took Jacob and tied him up in an old deserted cabin near Ned's. He said he didn't hurt him, but"—her voice broke in a sob— "what if he did! He'll die if I don't find him! Let go of the bridle. I have to hurry!" she cried, wild-eyed.

"Abigail, stop." he ordered sharply. "You can't just head off without a coat or hat or any supplies. It'll be dark and cold tonight by the time you get to Ned's." He halted her interruption, "Now, listen to me, and don't argue—if Jacob is missing, Ned will know it by now and he and Elijah will already be looking. They're both good at tracking. We need to get supplies loaded, and then we'll go together in the wagon. I'm the best tracker in the country. I figure Harvey was lying about taking him in the first place, but even if he wasn't, we'll find Jacob."

With a hand still on the saddle horn, she looked toward the mountains, and then her shoulders sagged as she slowly nodded. She took her foot from the stirrup. "All right. But please, hurry."

Quinton now stood close by. "I'll hitch your team," he said, "while you get supplies together."

Bill turned. "Abigail, get your stuff, warm clothes, and a little food and fill a couple of canteens. I'll be there in just a minute."

They waited until she was out of earshot.

"What do you aim to do with the body?" asked Quinton. "Do you want me to bring the sheriff out here or just take the body into town?"

Bill looked at Harvey's prone form and for an instant saw an image of Abigail dangling from a noose as Sid had done. He would do anything on earth to prevent that. But he was so weak right now he could hardly stand. He looked back at Quinton. "If I wasn't so weak I'd bury him and hide the grave. I won't ask you to be involved in that. But I don't trust the law now, Quinton, not one damn bit. Harvey was one of that nest of vipers. They know Abigail is my woman. I don't figure she'd get a fair shake, not any more than Sid did. You know none of us Confederates are getting a fair shake now."

"Then what are you aiming to do?"

"Find the boy. After that we're leaving and never coming back. I'll ask you to help me get Harvey's body into the barn for now. And then hold off until tomorrow before you accidentally find it. That will give us long enough to get a head start. You can tell the sheriff you have no idea which direction we headed."

"Now, hold on, Bill," he urged. "You're too weak to go traveling across the country. Look at you—you can hardly stand now. You're not thinking clear. It's plain as the nose on your face she was just defending herself. The public won't stand by and see a woman hung for defending herself."

Bill's eyebrows quirked. "I'm not too trusting of the public after what I've seen today. Besides, you know the sheriff is already watching us. This might open a whole new can of worms."

Quinton quickly put in, "Be that as it may, let me talk to Pa. He's the constable at Hagarville, and he has some sway around here. He'll know what to do—who to talk to. Besides, you've worked too hard to just walk off and leave everything."

"Do whatever you think is best," said Bill, "but I'm taking no chances with Abigail. I'm throwing a few things into the wagon and then we're heading out. When we get settled I'll get word to you somehow. Tell David and Toby the place is theirs as long as they want it. You fellows can keep running the sawmill. Tell them I said to share the profits until I get in touch."

"Of course I'll do whatever you want," said Quinton. "I still say there's no need to run. I don't figure Harvey was too well liked, even by his cronies. And no one will tolerate a kidnapper."

"He may have been lying about taking Jacob. Even so, they're birds of a feather, and that doesn't brood well for someone who kills one of 'em. Like I said, I won't risk Abigail."

Quinton sighed. "All right. I reckon I understand. You go on and do what you need to do. I'll tote his body into the barn and explain to David and Toby and wait till tomorrow to tell Pa."

Bill thanked him and then hurried to the chicken house. He went inside, grasped the roost pole, lifted it from the notch that held it to the wall, and then shoved a board aside and reached deeply into the space between the rough board and the outside wall. He drew out the leather pouch that had cost Harvey his life. Bill slung it across his shoulder and hurried to the bunkhouse. Mind spinning, he made and then discarded first one plan and then another. He got his rifle, drew blankets from his bunk, and made a bundle of his clothes before going to the house.

Abigail was not in the kitchen when he arrived, although a small pile of food and the canteens sat on the table. He heard her in her bedroom and went through the door.

"Abigail, take all of your clothes. And if you have anything else you don't want to part with, grab it too. I'll have Quinton tote it all to the wagon."

"Why on earth—"

"We're not coming back," he said. "We're going to get Jacob and Talbert and then head up through Newton County and on to Missouri."

Her mouth dropped open. She looked totally confused. "Not coming back," she echoed in amazement. "Why?"

"I'll explain later. For now just hurry," he said before heading back out the door.

Quinton had moved the body. A large pool of blood remained. Bill bent down, picked up the whistle, and pushed it into his pocket. He prayed the boy was all right. He had grown very fond of him, more so than he had realized until this very minute.

✸ Chapter 13

Abigail sat on the wagon seat, staring with unseeing eyes at a wooded landscape still stark with winter bareness, although already holding the first greening tinge of spring. She felt numb, and yet her thoughts jumped erratically from topic to topic, like a hunted squirrel jumping from limb to limb, running for its life. Mostly she feared for Jacob, her heart going out to him across the miles, willing him safe and free. If anything happened to him, she didn't think she could bear it, especially if she was partly to blame by murdering Harvey.

The idea that she had murdered Harvey—for murder is all it could be called since he had been helpless by the time she sank the ax into his skull—made her palms sweat and her stomach queasy. Bill had said they were never going back. She must be in mortal danger for him to consider such a thing.

She looked over. He held the reins, guiding the mules at a fast pace. His face was gray with fatigue, and from the looks of him, he might collapse soon. She feared this was a crazy plan. She wished she had insisted on riding ahead. Every minute put Jacob in more danger.

"Bill, let me take the black and ride on ahead."

"I don't think that's a good idea," he reasoned. "Night will catch you. You wouldn't be able to search for him in the dark anyway. We'll get there soon enough."

She felt impotent knowing he was right. And yet she must do something besides sit idly on the wagon seat. It was driving her crazy.

"Then let me drive the team. You need to lie down."

"Maybe later," he said. After a while, he said, "You've had quite a day yourself."

She let out a deep breath. "I certainly have," she agreed.

"Need to talk about it?" he asked. "In the war after a horrible battle, some men got real quiet, but others needed to talk, to get off their chests the things they'd seen—and done," he added softly.

She dropped her eyes and twisted her hands together nervously. "While I was doing the wash, he came up behind me before I knew he was around. I could see he had a pistol and a knife, but he didn't pull either—at least not then." She had told Bill almost everything before she had to stop, lean over the side of the wagon, and vomit. He handed her a handkerchief and a canteen. After she had wiped her face and rinsed her mouth she sat silent.

Finally he spoke. "You had no choice."

She whirled. "You need to know something, Bill. I did have a choice. He was down and helpless and begging me to stop. I knew he couldn't get at me. He was too crippled. In spite of that, I just kept thinking how he had threatened Jacob, so I raised the ax..." A shudder passed over her entire frame. "I can still see his wild, panicked eyes. I'll see those eyes until the day I die."

"Yes," he agreed, "you probably will. I still see plenty of them. But one thing I want you to put out of your mind right now—you had no choice. When someone threatens your family you can't just let 'em walk away."

Her voice filled with tears. "But I never thought I'd be a murderer."

He was quiet for a moment and then said, "You

remember me telling you that my real pa, Jared Rawlings, burned Elijah's house and caused Cindy to lose her baby?"

Abigail nodded. Now that she knew Elijah and Cindy it seemed even more tragic.

"Remember how I told you about Elijah tracking Jared into town that day? David Hadley was only a pup when it happened. He saw it all, and years later, he told me about it. Elijah found Jared inside the mercantile and without warning blew him away with a shotgun. It was a horrible sight, and yet it was the best thing Elijah could have done. And you did the best thing too. Harvey was as dangerous as a rabid animal. You can't just wound a rabid animal, let it run off, and hope it never returns. It could be waiting for you the next time you step out the door. Harvey was like that. Neither you nor Jacob would have been truly safe until Harvey was dead. If you hadn't killed him, Abigail, I would have. I wish it had been me. I'd give anything to spare you this, but what's happened can't be undone. You need to accept it and move on and trust that the Good Lord is merciful, even to murderers if they ask for mercy. As Granny was fond of saying, 'There's not a sin Jesus ain't already paid for,' and I believe that."

"I believe that, too," she said. "Thank you. That helps. If only Jacob is safe, I think I can bear anything."

Bill squeezed her hand. "We'll find him. And then we'll make a fresh start in Missouri, or if we don't like it there, we'll find someplace. I've always hankered to see the West. I'll bet Jacob would like that," he said with an encouraging smile.

When they finally turned north, Abigail could see the mountains in the distance, and yet they still seemed so far away. She noticed Bill turn to look behind. She looked back too. So far the trail was empty. She prayed it stayed that way.

He waited until they had gone a good way before finally saying, "If you're sure you're up to it, I will let you drive. Think I will lie down for a while. I'm feeling sort of woozy."

She took the reins while he climbed over the seat and into the wagon bed and lay down on the pile of blankets. She had driven a mule and even a team of horses, but never a team of mules. However, the animals kept going at a steady, brisk pace, not seeming aware that different hands held the reins. Soon Bill's deep breathing signaled he was asleep.

Now that she was finally doing something, Abigail calmed a bit. Everything Bill had said seemed more reasonable now. Harvey had no reason to harm Jacob. He would want him alive for a bargaining chip. And it was possible that Harvey could have taken the whistle without even taking Jacob. She hoped that was the case. She drew a deep breath, let it out slowly, and whispered another prayer, the same plea she had uttered a hundred times already. *"Oh Lord, please protect Jacob!"*

She wondered if perhaps she must ask forgiveness for doing murder before God would hear her. There was scripture about that. She had to admit she wasn't sorry Harvey was dead. However, she did want God's blessing, so she compromised by asking for mercy. She would sort out repentance later.

Bill groaned. She looked back. He was restless, but still asleep.

She could hardly take in the idea that he was willing to walk away from the land he loved because of her. It seemed unthinkable and yet it must be so. His belongings were stowed in the wagon along with hers. Her eyes widened with that thought. *Bill Tanner loved her. Truly loved her. Not Cindy. Her.* He loved her enough to walk away from everything he had slaved for and everything he had dreamed of achieving here. Right in the midst of her terror and anxiety a soft glow grew in the center of her heart. She contemplated this as miles passed beneath the plodding hooves.

Finally Bill roused, stretched, and soon joined her again on the wagon seat. He took the reins from her hands.

"Looks like you handled them fine," he said.

"Do you feel better?" she asked. Even though he answered in the affirmative, he still looked ashen. She slipped an arm into his, leaned on his shoulder, and said, "I love you, Bill Tanner."

He kissed the top of her head. "Love you back, Abigail Anderson."

She smiled softly, knowing he could have said it a thousand times without making her truly believe it, but his actions today left no doubt. If only Jacob was safe and if only they could get safely away to Missouri, everything might work out just fine.

Nevertheless, as darkness fell over the rough wagon road, her throat tightened and her pulse raced. Poor Jacob would be cold, hungry, and exhausted by now. The tall pines, casting black shadows in the moonlight, striped the trail like prison bars. Abigail supposed that fanciful idea was triggered by her sense of guilt. Bill felt her shiver and handed her a blanket.

"Wrap up. We still have a ways to go. I don't reckon you'd consider getting a nap?" he asked.

"I couldn't. How long before we get there?"

"A few more hours, but this bright moonlight helps. We're making good time."

"I suppose we'll go straight to Ned's?" she asked.

"Actually, I plan to check a couple of deserted cabins that will be right on the way."

"Good," she said and grew quiet. It did no good to fret aloud. Besides, she was too weary to talk.

Hours dragged. Owls hooted and night creatures scurried away in the darkness as the wagon creaked past. Abigail must have dozed in spite of herself. She jerked awake as Bill pulled the team to a stop. The dark outline of a large log cabin shown black against the gray night sky.

"Where are we?" she asked, heart pounding.

"We're not far from Ned's. This is the Matthers' place. It's been deserted for a couple of years."

Abigail started to jump down.

"No!" he ordered sharply. "I'll go check."

Then she knew, with pounding heart, he was afraid of what he might find. As if reading her thoughts he spoke again, this time more gently.

"There's no need for both of us to go stumbling around in the dark. I'll bring him right out if he's here."

She sat, hardly breathing, ears straining for every whisper of sound. In a few minutes Bill called out, "No one's here." He soon climbed back into the wagon. "No one's been here in a long while. But there's another cabin just off the trail up here a ways. We'll check there and then go on to Ned's."

When he drove off the main trail and onto a deeply washed-out path, Abigail strained forward, trying to see through the thick, dark woods. The wagon lurched in and out of deep ruts. Bill had to slow the mules to keep from breaking a wheel or axle. Soon a tumbledown shack loomed ahead. Abigail's heart quickened. It seemed a likely place to keep a captive. Surely Jacob was here!

Bill was back too quickly. "No sign of him," he said.

A sob tore from her throat.

"Abigail, like I said, more than likely he's in bed sound

asleep at Ned's. We'll be there in no time."

However, even Bill stiffened as Ned's cabin came into sight with all the lamps blazing. Several horses were tied to the hitching rail.

"Something is wrong," cried Abigail. She was on the ground and running even before the wagon stopped. She pushed open the door and then stood frozen. A dozen men were in the room, some seated at the table, others in chairs and more hunkered near the fireplace that held a blazing fire. Talbert sat near the fire, his face drawn with worry.

Becky quickly set the pot of stew she dipped from onto the table, crossed the floor, and gathered Abigail close.

"They'll find him, Abigail. Many's the time both men and boys have gone hunting and gotten lost in these woods. Not one has ever come to harm. The men are going back out again just as soon as it's light and they'll find him. Why, Jacob will be back here in no time, hungry as a wolf and raring to go hunting again."

"No!" Abigail cried. "He's not lost! Harvey took him and tied him up somewhere!"

"Agh!" cried Talbert and slumped back as if he had been struck.

Every man in the room grew taut and still. Bill stepped inside. His eyes sought and found Ned.

"It's true. Harvey kidnapped Jacob to force Abigail to give him money. He said he tied him up in a deserted cabin near here. I already looked at Matthers' and Heavy's old places."

A wave of talk swept the room. Elijah stood. "I think I know where he is. I cut a fresh horse trail today, over close to the Millsap's place. I never followed it because we were looking for a boy on foot. No one's lived there since Cora moved out three years ago."

Ned grabbed his coat, and Bill turned on his heel to follow Elijah from the cabin. Abigail followed.

"Abigail, please stay here," called Becky.

Abigail kept walking. She was going. No matter what anyone said.

Several men riding horses joined the cavalcade. Bill didn't argue as she climbed onto the wagon seat. She stared at the night sky and prayed while a cloud drifted over the moon and then slowly drifted on. If Jacob was there, they would find him soon. If not...she could not face that possibility.

The horses ahead soon turned from the main trail onto a narrow, rough path obviously not much used. Bill turned the mules and followed.

"How far?"

"About a half mile," he said.

Abigail steeled herself to wait a while longer. No one rode fast in the dim light, but as the horses drew ahead the wagon had to slow even more to avoid chug holes in the trail. Before long she heard shouting. She strained forward but still could not make out the words.

"They found him," exclaimed Bill, "and he's safe!"

"Thank God!" Abigail sagged back against the seat, covered her face with her hands, and sobbed. In a few minutes horses appeared. On the first one, Jacob rode perched in the saddle in front of Elijah.

"Jacob!" cried Abigail. She sprang from the seat and rushed to gather him into her arms before his feet had even touched the ground. She held his face in her hands, trying to see his features in the dimness. "Are you all right?"

"Yes'm," he said, raising his hand to quickly dash away unwanted tears. "I sure am glad y'all found me."

She laughed and cried at the same time and gathered

him close again. "I sure am too," she said and kissed the top of his head.

Elijah dismounted. "Let's get you home," he said and lifted Jacob into the wagon and then helped Abigail onto the seat. "Ma has hot food and a bed waiting."

Abigail wanted to take Jacob onto her lap and hold him tightly; however, she contented herself by snuggling him close on the wagon seat.

"Bill, you gonna make it?" asked Elijah quietly. "You look like you're on your last leg."

"I am about done in," he admitted.

"Scoot over and I'll drive." Elijah tied his horse on behind, and after turning the mules, he drove back to the lighted cabin.

✕✕✕

Abigail hovered near while Becky served enough stew to finally fill Jacob's empty stomach. He did seem—as Ned gladly declared—no worse for wear. And while Jacob related the details of all that had happened, from the moment Harvey had come upon him in the woods until Elijah had burst into the dark room to set him free, Abigail's throat tightened with thankful tears, knowing it could have ended tragically. Finally the neighbors who had helped in the search drifted away, and Talbert had been persuaded to stop holding onto Jacob and go to bed.

"Jacob, you need to go to bed too," said Becky as she gave him a loving pat on the shoulder. "And I won't even make you wash up first. Plenty of time for that in the morning."

Abigail didn't want to let him out of her sight, but Becky was right. He was exhausted. When Abigail returned from tucking him in, Becky was reaching a hand to touch Bill's forehead. "Bill, you need to lie down," she observed. "You're feverish. You can use the spare bed there in the corner."

Abigail was chagrined. In her anxiety over Jacob, all concern for Bill had fled. Becky was right. He looked awful.

"Thanks, Becky, but not just now. Ned, Elijah, can I talk to you outside for a minute?"

As the men headed out the door, Abigail faced Becky. "He plans for us to leave in the morning, heading for Missouri."

"*What?*" exclaimed Becky, dropping into a chair at the table. "Why on earth?"

Standing across the table, Abigail gripped a chair back and drew a deep breath, hardly knowing where to begin. "I've killed Harvey—with an ax. And after what happened to Sid Wallace, Bill doesn't think I could get a fair trial."

Becky's face had a blank stare. Her eyes blinked rapidly. "Upon my word," she finally said. Then her eyes went to the door. "He's in no shape to travel. Did you see how flushed his face is?"

"*I know,*" said Abigail in distress. "It's a crazy plan but he's determined. He told me to get all of Jacob's and Mr. Anderson's things from you. He plans to leave at first light."

Instead of asking for details, Becky stood and began dipping another bowl of stew. "Well, Ned will talk him out of it. There's no way that man is going anywhere tomorrow unless he wants to end up in the cemetery. And you're about to drop yourself." She set the bowl in front of Abigail. "You haven't eaten a thing all day, have you? Eat this, and then we'll get you to bed too."

Abigail tried to swallow. The food lodged in her throat. She was too upset to eat. Bill should not have made this wild ride. All her life she had heard that a backset from pneumonia was worse than the original, and he had barely survived the first time. *After all of this would she lose him?*

When Bill finished talking, Elijah let out a long, low whistle. Ned just stared at the ground for a while before saying, "Since you asked, I think Quinton is right. Running ain't necessary. Harvey kidnapped the boy and threatened the woman. I don't care who his cronies are—this isn't like Sid where they needed a scapegoat. Not a man in town will come down against Abigail on this. Billy, you got a good head on your shoulders, but you're sick and right now your thinking is foggy. Go back inside. Let Becky put you to bed. Sleep on it and you'll see more clear in the morning."

Bill brushed a hand over his face. "I have been thinking that the kidnapping puts a new slant on things."

Ned was right about another thing. He was sick. His head felt about to split wide open, and his heart raced as if he were running. Just then his knees buckled, and Elijah caught him and helped him inside.

When he awoke, late afternoon sun came in at the cabin window. He heard deep voices on the porch outside. Abigail sat in a chair at the table. She saw him stir and hurried to the bedside.

"How do you feel? You certainly look better than last night, and your fever is gone."

"I feel worlds better." He nodded toward the closed front door. "Who's out there?"

"Quinton and the sheriff. Elijah went to see them last night to tell them about Jacob being kidnapped. They're talking to Ned now."

As he started to rise, she quickly pushed back on his chest.

"Lie still." Tears sprang into her eyes. "It's all right. Everything is all right. He's not going to arrest me. He just came to ask some questions. I'll have to appear at a coroner's inquest, but he said it's just a formality and I have nothing to worry about. He's bending over backwards to be nice. Oh, Bill, I think this nightmare is finally about to end!" She smiled through her tears. "Jacob is fine. You're getting better. And soon we can go home!"

"I ought to get up and go speak to Quinton and the sheriff," he said.

"No," declared Talbert suddenly, stepping near the bed with the help of a walking cane. "You l..lay still," he stammered, "and get yore st..strength back. Qui.. Quinton and Ned can handle the sh..sheriff."

Bill and Abigail exchanged surprised smiles. Talbert was right. Besides, it felt good just lying there holding Abigail's hand.

✖✖✖

It was a week before Bill was back on his feet and ready to make the trip home. Abigail, Jacob, and Talbert Anderson were all waiting in the wagon while he lingered in the yard, shaking Ned's hand and thanking Becky one more time for all she had done.

She gave him a big hug. "Why, Billy Tanner, that's what families are for—to help in times of need. You'd do the same for us."

He wasn't the crying sort, but there was a lump in his throat as he kissed her cheek. He climbed onto the seat alongside Abigail, gathered the reins, and after starting the mules, he reached to take her hand. It felt soft and warm against his rough skin. He knew the horror of what she had done would torment her for a long while to come, but he would be there with her every step of the way. For the rest of their lives, together, they would face whatever came.

The sun shone. It seemed that every bird in the mountains competed to announce the arrival of spring as they drove along the trail where green grass now edged the worn ruts.

"What a pretty cemetery," said Abigail. "Just look at all those giant oak trees."

As the wagon rolled slowly past the plot that held Viola Tanner's remains, Bill nodded. "I reckon it is a nice cemetery," he said.

Still holding hands, they rode on in silence. "What are you thinking?" she finally asked.

"Oh, I was just thinking what a difference a good woman can make in a fellow's life."

More on Sidney Wallace

When I read the actual transcript of Sid's murder trial, I was appalled. I have no way of knowing if Sid murdered Judge Meers and Doc Ward, the town constable. Of one thing I am positive—his trial was a farce of the worst kind. And at the time, the political climate of Johnson County was much the same as that of Pope County, where carpetbag officials were being murdered at an alarming rate. There was great indignation and a public outcry over the 1872 election in Arkansas between Democrat Thomas Gunter and Republican William Wilshire. This resulted in a congressional investigation and eventually in the overturning of the bogus election of Wilshire. I found it an odd coincidence that Meers and Ward were both called to testify in this investigation only a few weeks before their deaths. By the way, so far as I could ascertain, Sid Wallace had no interest in politics. In this novel the testimony in Sid's trial, as well as the testimony in the Congressional hearings, is verbatim, with the exception of what my fictional characters say.

Made in the USA
San Bernardino, CA
15 September 2014